SOMEONE LIKE YOU 1

Special Edition

ALEXANDRA SILVA

Someone
LIKE YOU

USA TODAY BESTSELLING AUTHOR
ALEXANDRA SILVA

Cover Design: LJ Designs
Editor: Readers Together
Formatting: LJ Designs

DEDICATION

For my boys—Jasper, Mylo, and Lucas.
Always remember that...
Wishes come true. Magic is real.
Love will always win.
All you have to do is believe.

EPIGRAPH

"Meeting you was fate,
becoming your friend was a choice,
but falling in love with you
was totally beyond my control."
— UNKNOWN

CHAPTER 1

Jake

"**O**ne more, Uncle Jake!" Molly sang before she gave my phone camera her best pout. I held her stiffly posed body closer to my chest and grinned as we both garbled out another, "Cheese!"

I couldn't believe how quickly time had flown, how was she six already? It seemed like just yesterday she'd given me her first ever tiny smile.

Wind or not, it had been mine.

"That one good?" I asked as she scrutinised my screen. "Molls, we can't spend the rest of the party taking selfies, your mum will get cross and I'll get it in the neck...*again!*"

She laughed loudly at the funny face I'd pulled, her eyes

rolling as if she were the grown-up and I were the child. Her giggles died down in a flurry of expelled breath.

"But I like selfie time with you," she whined as she looked up at me, her face contorted with exasperation. Boy, right then, she looked so much like her dad. Her dark hair fell in mussed ringlets and her blue eyes shone from under her dainty scrunched eyebrows.

"I know, but we've already taken so many, plus, don't you want to open your presents?" I asked as I carefully put her down on her feet. I'd always been so careful with her, I didn't know why considering she was such a rambunctious child. I had this thing that made me all too aware of how small she was. Sometimes I looked at her and I couldn't help but ask myself how on earth Jamie thought that making me her godfather was a good idea.

Most parents would probably want their kids to have someone a little more poised to look up to, but not Jamie.

"Come on, Molls," I cooed at her as she continued giving me her puppy dog eyed pout. "I reckon there's some pretty amazing stuff in that pile."

"I guess." She sighed deeply, like she hadn't been begging to open her presents a couple of minutes ago. She grabbed my hand and started walking us toward the gift table. She stopped here and there to chat to some of her friends that were running around, taking full advantage of the indoor play space.

"You know, you probably need to spend some time with your friends." I told her as she grasped my hand tighter when I tried to take it from her. "They've come to see you and have fun with you, Robin."

"Why can't I be Batman, again? I'm always Robin!" she

grumbled as she waved to one of the boys I assumed was a friend from school or one of her extracurricular clubs. "You can't be Batman all the time, Jake."

"Why not?"

"Because…"

"That's not an answer, plus, I'm bigger and I can throw you around."

"So?" She looked up at me, her eyebrow quirked in challenge.

"Trouble in paradise?" We both looked up, my hand was dropped quickly and without a second thought as Molly launched herself at Dorian.

"Auntie Dorian!" she screamed as she deftly climbed up her aunt's body.

"Hey, princess." Dorian cupped her face and brushed her messy waves back before kissing the tip of Molly's nose. She pulled back slightly, her smile soft as she said, "Hey, Jake."

For a moment I was too lost in the slightly husky sound of her voice. The way one side of her smile always quirked a little higher, making the dimple on the right side of her face a little more pronounced. Her cheeks were slightly blushed and her eyes…her stunning eyes were so bright.

Dorian had always been beautiful. Her hair was thick and long. It fell short of the curve of her peachy arse and it wasn't straight or wavy, it was something of a wild mess between the two. The milk chocolate brown colour that lightened to a mousy chestnut at the ends made the green in her hazel eyes pop. She had cheekbones that other women would empty their bank accounts for and her nose had an upturn that made her look regal almost. Not to mention her willowy height and limbs.

Looking at her was enough to make my mind wander…

She's your friend. She's Jamie's sister. Do not touch. Do not smell. Do not imagine naked.

Off-limits.

"It's rude not to say hello back, Jake." Molly said as she stabbed her finger into my shoulder. "Mummy says that you should always smile and say hello when someone says it to you, unless it's a stranger."

Dorian laughed, her lips rubbing together as her shoulders shook with mirth.

"Hey, Dor."

"Okay, can we go open my presents now?" Molly jumped down from her aunt's arms and looked around before asking, "Where's Daniel?"

"He ran off with Pippa, I think they went toward the big climbing frame at the back." She pointed at the floor to ceiling apparatus, "You want to go find them?"

"In a bit, I think we should take a photo first. Right, Jake?"

"Another?"

"With Auntie Dory."

Dorian shuffled slightly, her hands running through the shorter lengths framing her face. Her teeth sunk into her peachy, glossy lips as her eyes rounded. She wasn't one for photos, I'd learned this a long time ago.

"How about we take it later?"

"Why?"

"Because we should let your aunt get comfortable before we spring the camera on her."

"It's only a photo." She looked between us both, her Puss in Boots eyes making me feel rotten for even suggesting we do it later. "Please?" Her eyes trained on Dorian's, "Pretty please?"

"You see what you started with this selfie thing?" Dorian said as she pursed her lips, a smile trying to breakthrough. "This world does not need another tiny narcissist."

I doubt she even knew what *narcissist* meant, but as always, Molly was very quick to defend our photo tradition. "They're memories, Auntie Dory."

"Exactly." I smiled as I pulled my phone out again.

Since Molly had been a baby, I'd taken a photo of her or with her and sent it to an email I'd set up for her. There must've been hundreds of photos in there from over the years, and hopefully when she was old enough, I'd give it to her and she would be able to look through our memories. She'd be able to see herself grow up, like I was watching her blossom into a pretty wonderful human.

"Come on then, you two." Dorian crouched next to Molly, her arm wrapping around her small waist.

I followed suit and held the phone as far as I could to make sure I got all three of us in the shot. "You ready? Three, two, one…"

"Wait!" she yelled, my phone slipping from my hand as I jumped at her outburst. "One second, please."

Dorian looked over at me, her brows furrowed in confusion. Even with her face screwed up like that, she was pretty.

"Pippa! Daniel!" Molly shouted, her voice cracking with the shrill volume. "Hey! Guys!"

Pippa and Daniel stopped in their tracks, their heads turning our way before their bodies followed. Before we had a chance to prepare ourselves, it got very loud and excitable very quickly. Pippa wrapped her arms around Molly and they both started jumping up and down on the spot like they hadn't seen each other in years. I could imagine Dorian and Quincy, Pippa's mother, doing the same thing at their age. Their laughter infectious.

Daniel stood beside me, quietly watching his younger cousins with a smile on his face.

"You alright, buddy?" I asked.

"Yup." He grinned at me, his light brown eyes glowing with elation. "Mum, have you asked him yet?"

"No." Dorian enunciated clearly as I asked, "Asked me what?"

"Nothing." She replied as he whined, "Pleeeeeease, Mum."

I looked between them, his eyes were wide and hers narrowed at him, "One of you needs to come out with it."

"Don't encourage him." She turned her narrowed gaze on me, like she did when she wanted me to drop the line of conversation.

"You promised."

"Daniel, I said maybe. I said I'd think about it. I didn't promise anything. Uncle Jamie already said he'd look at his diary."

"But he just said he can't."

"What if Jake can't either?"

Okay. "Well, Jake is right here."

"I said, *no.*"

"Why? *Please*, everyone else is going. It's not fair."

"Okay, well, maybe we should just take the photo?" I said as I grabbed both of the girls and pulled them to us. "Come on, Danny, why don't you squeeze in?"

"I don't think so." He murmured, his voice sounding a little wet like he was about to cry. He looked at his cousins and then his mother, and before I had a chance to convince him to get into the photo, he wandered off. His shaking head lowered and his shoulders hunched with his balled fists clenching at his sides.

"Right, let's take this photo, then." Dorian chirped a little too gruffly as she went down onto her knees. She pulled Pippa towards her as Molly settled between me and Pippa. "Ready? Say cheeeeeese…"

I took the photo, quickly locking my phone and slipping it back into my pocket before Molly had a chance to ask for another.

The girls scurried away towards the climbing frames and an awkward silence fell between me and Dorian.

Her eyes looked everywhere except at me as she stood. She opened her mouth to say something, but she shook her head like she'd thought better of it and walked away. I didn't even get a chance to ask her what that whole conversation had been about.

I watched her wander off into the maze of kid friendly scaffolding and primary coloured netting. She paused at the edge of one of the large ball pits and looked back at me lost in thought as she sat with her twin sister and their best friend.

My heart raced as she continued looking at me through her long fringe, even when Willow and Quincy started throwing balls at her. It wasn't until the girls joined in that she turned and sunk into the midst of them.

Still, I took her in. I could hear her soft laughter in my head as she spoke to the other two women. Her shoulders shook as the three of them playfully threw balls back at Molly and Pippa.

"Everything okay?" Jamie asked as he gave me a friendly slap on the shoulder.

"Yeah, same old." I replied a little too stiffly, I could feel him looking at me.

Stupidly, I couldn't turn away. I couldn't look away. I never could. Not when it came to her.

* * *

The party was wrapping up. The kids were off making the most of the time they had left here. I wandered over to where Dorian was tackling the presents into large bags, ready to take to the car. She stiffened slightly, almost unnoticeably as I approached, yet she didn't acknowledge my presence.

I watched her while she carried on with her task, sighing once in a while. I let her go on, hoping that she'd get fed up of the awkwardness and say something. She didn't.

"Dor…"

"Don't, Jake."

"Don't what?" I asked as I took the bag from her and held it open so she could put the larger present in.

"Don't start with the *Dor* crap."

"You can ask me anything, we're friends, aren't we?"

She paused in her tracks, her chest expanding as she took in a long exhale. I could almost hear her plead for more patience. Something she did quite a bit whenever I pushed something that she clearly didn't want pushed.

She exhaled again as her eyes narrowed on mine and without saying a word she went back to packing up the presents.

"Come on."

"Please don't make this harder." Her voice broke slightly, like her throat was dry. "And yes, we are friends, but this is hard enough without—"

"I know it's not easy, nothing about the last eight years has been easy for you. But you could've asked me."

"Do you even know what it was he wanted me to ask you?" Her gaze set on mine, and from the look she gave me I could tell that she knew that I'd been digging. "Seriously, you and Willow are impossible meddlers."

She looked behind me to the chairs where Willow was still sat and rolled her eyes.

"It's a football match, Dorian."

"It's not though, is it? I can't keep asking you, Jamie and Dad to stand in. I mean, why do they do these stupid events with these ridiculous ideas? They know the situation, but sometimes it feels like they go out of their way to make it obvious. To rub it in." Her voice was terse and every one of her words seemed to jamb into each other. "You and Willow need to let me handle this my way."

She picked up a couple of the bags and started for the exit, I quickly followed with the bag I was holding.

It looked like it was about to rain, the sky was an unsettled grey with heavy clouds. I hated it. I hated the way it made me feel. I hated the way it reminded me of things I didn't wish to be reminded of.

There's something about a grey sky that is incumbent of bad news.

She made quick work of getting the bags in the boot of Jamie's Range, and once I'd done the same she slammed the boot down with a little too much force considering all she had to do was press a button and it would shut on its own.

"I get that it isn't ideal, but I like Daniel. I've seen that child grow from a tiny little thing into an awesome kid, he was almost born on my lap for fuck's sake. Do you really think I'd be put out by a silly football game? Come on, you know me better than that."

"That's not the point." She closed her eyes as she took in another deep breath, her arms crossed over her chest making her oversized fluffy jumper bunch up under her chin. The shorter tendrils of hair around her face tucked into the wide high neck.

"It is, though. I know you don't like imposing on people. I know that you don't need anyone to step in and parent him, you do a great job at that as it is, but it's okay to let others give you a hand with these things. He's a child, Dor, he doesn't deserve to feel left out because his dad isn't around."

"Phillip's dead. His dad is dead. It's not simply that he's not around."

"You know what I mean."

"Jacob, I said no. I meant no." She sucked her bottom lip into her mouth, the light in her eyes completely dimmed. "Just drop it now."

"Fine." I blew out before I turned and started walking away.

"Fine?" she asked from behind me, the soles of her flats grinding the gritty tarmac under her feet.

"Daniel's your son, you know best." I said without looking back. "You're the one that's going to have to live with knowing that he's missed out because of your pride. You don't even have to ask, Dorian, you only have to tell me the date, time and place."

It was a little harsh, something I didn't intend it to be, but sometimes the only way to get through to her was by getting to her.

"Fine." She grumbled from behind me, my feet halting at her words. "Six weeks today, at the Chelsea grounds…all day. Oh, you also have practice every Thursday evening and Saturday morning at the school fields until then. Happy?"

"I will be once you tell Daniel."

"You're impossible." She muttered.

"Doesn't it feel good to know you've just made Danny's day...possibly his week?" I chuckled as she walked past me toward the building.

"His name is Daniel." She called behind her, her head shaking even as her voice had an upbeat trill to it. "You should know, after all, he was almost born on your lap."

We barely ever referred back to her labour with Daniel. She always got a little too embarrassed about the whole thing. I sort of got it, it must've been weird having your brother's friend carry you around one of London's most popular parks as you're about to drop a kid.

Honestly, I wasn't fazed by it. At the time I was too worried about her to care that she was leaking amniotic fluid all down me. I was more concerned about her wellbeing, than I was about getting wet, and since I'd started my medical career, I'd been covered in a lot worse.

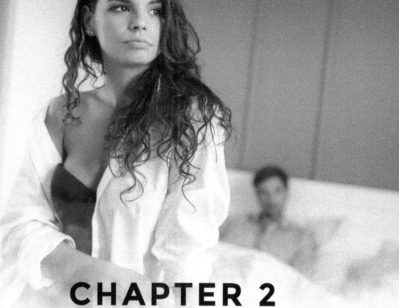

CHAPTER 2

Dorian

I was lagging, and there wasn't enough coffee in the world to perk me up. It was a bloody nightmare considering Mrs Fletcher's medical negligence case I'd taken on last month was taking up a lot more of my time than I thought it would.

Every day had stretched from super early mornings to late evenings, and like the last few weeks, today was no different.

The Chambers were already quiet, the cleaner patiently waited for me to gather my things so she could do her job.

"Sorry," I smiled at the older woman as I slipped my files into my large tote with my laptop. "I lost track of time, again."

I took another look around my office, making sure everything was as it should be.

"It's okay, Miss." She smiled in return, her voice hushed. "I'm early today."

"Well, it's all yours." I said as I made my way out, checking my phone for a text from Daniel or Jake to let me know that training was over. "Have a good evening."

I sent a quick message to both of their phones to let them know I was leaving work and that I'd meet them at the school's playing fields. Something I'd done every single Thursday evening for the last month.

A couple of times I'd managed to get to the playing fields before training had finished, and it had been nice to see Daniel so happy. In general, he was such a content boy, but he had his father's temper. If you got on the wrong side of him, God help you.

By the time I'd hailed a cab and gotten to the sports field it was dark, the floodlights the only thing brightening the evening. It was damp and cloudy, the moon barely visible through the rain filled clouds. I could already imagine the state Daniel's kit was going to be in—grass stained, muddy and smelly. Almost as bad as a wet dog.

I sat on one of the benches by the changing rooms, waiting for Daniel and Jake to come out as I read through a couple of emails on my phone. There was nothing new.

Digging dirt on the surgeon I was meant to be suing for negligence was proving almost impossible. All his previous clients we'd managed to get to talk to us did nothing but sing his praises. His office was organised and compliant. The guy was a clean, open book. Which meant that he was either very good at concealing his failures, or there weren't any.

Everyone has failures. Everyone.

It didn't make sense that someone with a career as long as his, had never put a foot wrong. Through fault of his own or not.

There's got to be something. Somewhere there has to be something I'm missing.

"Hi, Mum!" Daniel chirped excitedly before dropping his kit bag next to me.

Jake looked between us both with his brow quirked in a way that told me he wasn't altogether impressed with Daniel's greeting.

"I hope you don't expect your mum to carry that for you, bud." He picked the bag up and handed it back to Daniel before he turned to me with one of his soft smiles. "Hey, Dor."

My chest warmed as it always did whenever he used his nickname for me. My thoughts slowed and stumbled like always.

Jake had always had a way of distracting me, of numbing my thoughts and pulling me out of my head.

Every time we were together it felt like we'd always been this way. Like we'd always had our own little bubble where it was safe to just be and I didn't have to feel lost or sad.

Maybe that was what friendship was—a safe bubble where the outside had no bearing on what you felt or thought on the inside. It was a safe zone from all the crap. A reprieve.

I don't know, there was something about him that made me feel at ease and excited all at the same time.

He made me feel things that I shouldn't, because he was my friend, and I'd never been abundant in those. I'd always been nonchalant about friendships, until Jake. He made me curious to know all there was about him.

Stop it!

"How was practice?" I asked, slipping my phone back into

my bag. I followed them towards the car park as I tried to clear my head.

"It was good." Jake replied.

"It was amazing, Mum. Jake was better than almost all the other grown-ups. I think we've got this bad boy in the bag!"

I couldn't help but chuckle at his enthusiasm. "Bad boy, huh?"

"We wiped the floor with the other team."

"Competitive little sod, isn't he? He forgets that today he was playing against his own team." Jake laughed as he opened the boot to his fancy, black Mercedes GLE and threw his gym bag in before taking Daniel's. "I'll drive you guys home."

"You don't have to, you've done enough." There was something about the way that he was always ready to do another little thing for us. "We can get a cab."

"Don't be silly." He stated as he shut the boot and opened the back door on his side for Daniel. "Come on, Dorian, get in."

"Fine. If you're taking us home, you have to let us do dinner." I said as I rounded the other side and got in. The plush dark leather interior was immaculately clean and smelled very much of him. Citrusy and peppery. It was a scent that had become somewhat comforting and almost homey.

He started the engine, the almost silent rumble blending into his muted voice. "You don't have to do that. I was going to grab something on the way home."

"I want to," I said quickly, before adding, "to say thank you."

"Can't we get a Chinese instead?" Daniel asked from behind.

"No, you had a burger for dinner last night with Uncle

Jamie." Every Wednesday Daniel and I would meet with my brother for dinner.

"How's he doing?" Jake asked whilst watching the road.

Since Jamie's split from his wife, I liked to keep a close eye on him. My brother wasn't great at dealing with big things—like an unfaithful wife, a crappy friend and not seeing his daughter every day. He was soft and because of it, people didn't often see how much he was struggling. "Okay. I just want him to find his footing again, now that his divorce is finally settled, you know?"

"I get that. I also think that it's something that he needs to do for himself. You can't force it on him." His voice took on a sad, wistful edge.

I looked up at him as he focused on the road ahead, and sure enough, the sadness in his voice was right there, glittering in his eyes. It always caught me by surprise. It was something that to me had become so very Jake, but at the same time it was so unlike him.

He was always the one to make light of things. Always the one to crack a joke. That wistful weariness always seemed a little unfitting for him.

However, the more time we spent together over the years the more I saw it. The darkness in his eyes that beckoned to me. It called to all the broken pieces of me like a magnetic force. It was like it drew out all my pain and fed on it, and as messed up as it was, I liked it. I liked not being alone in my own bleakness and obscurity.

What I liked even more was that he never tried to fix it. He let it be like he too enjoyed the way we were connected. It didn't make sense because that's what people did. That's what I liked to do. Fix.

Except when it came to him. To me Jacob Roth was just right the way he was.

That thought was something that always made me feel too aware of him. Too knowing of him, even though he was a master at hiding.

The only thing I wished I could do when it came to Jake, was let him know that it was okay for him to have pain. That it was alright to let me see it. To let me know what caused it.

"I wish I could." I sighed as I looked away from him and took in the busy lit up London roads.

* * *

Jake was the kind of person that took everything in his stride. He was so laid back, he was horizontal, and when things started to get a little much…he found a way of making light. However, there were times, times like these when we were together, alone, that I wondered what it would take to fluster him. To ruffle his feathers.

Everyone was so quick to assume that he was your average happy-go-lucky bachelor. That, his career and parents aside, the most important thing in his life was who he'd bed next.

Don't get me wrong, I knew that he wasn't the sort of guy that you got attached to beyond friendship, but sometimes, the way his jaw tightened and his throat bobbed as he looked at me with his deep, rich milk chocolate eyes, it made me wonder what it would be like to be the most important thing to him.

It was a silly thought to have but I knew that beneath the shallows, there was a depth he wasn't comfortable allowing anyone to dive into. Not even me, and it made me all the more curious to figure him out.

Jake was a master at controlling how much you saw into

him. However, once in a while he'd say something or do something so left field that, *God*, you were incapable of unseeing or unfeeling it.

"Dor?"

"Yeah?" I fumbled with my rushed reply. "Sorry...I..." My words trailed off at the feel of his hand on my arm as we stood in my kitchen.

Jake wasn't a tactile person, he very rarely touched anyone. But every time he laid a finger on me, it was like the ground beneath me and the air around me shifted in two completely different directions. Leaving me caught in the static between them. Even my pores stung with the current that raced through me.

I'd like to say that I was comfortable with it. I'd like to say that it didn't make me feel like I was wrong for feeling it like that, so deep and breath stealing, but I couldn't.

"You?" He beamed down at me, gently. "You, what?"

His deep, smoky quartz eyes skittered down to where his hand still grasped my arm lightly. His tongue dipped out of his mouth as it licked the seam of his lips. His soft, evenly plump lips that seemed to have been expertly moulded with his cupid bow dipping perfectly where his bottom lip was fullest.

Looking at his lips somehow always made me want to touch my own. I told myself it was a normal thing to do. However, I knew that imagining the heat of my fingertips was that of his lips wasn't.

Jake is your friend, Dorian.

"Coffee?" I blurted as I took my arm back. "I was thinking about making coffee, I have a tonne of paperwork to go through and I need the boost."

"I'm okay, I have surgery first thing." I couldn't help but follow him with my eyes as he rounded the breakfast bar and leaned on it. "It's getting late, and if you have work to do, I don't want to get under your feet."

There was a stretch of silence, as we sort of just looked at one another like two pleasantly struck strangers. His crinkled eyes searched my face as I took in the way his nails scratched the short, dark scruff along his jaw.

I didn't want him to leave. I never wanted him to leave. Another thing I knew that I shouldn't feel or want, but couldn't help.

"Can I ask you something?" I smiled, hoping that it would buy me a little more time with him.

His eyes focused on mine again, wide and expecting. "Shoot."

"Would you ever perform surgery on a relative? A friend?" I grabbed the kettle from the side, filled it with water and put it on before I grabbed a mug from the cabinet.

I could feel his gaze following me, boring into my back as I prepared the instant coffee.

"Dorian, I..." He paused for a beat before carrying on, "You—"

I spun quickly toward him, "It's not for me. I'm not asking for me."

"Good."

"It's a general musing. Research, you could say."

"No, I wouldn't ever perform surgery on family or any of my close friends."

"It's not illegal." I said as I turned back to the freshly boiled kettle and finished making my coffee.

"I know, obviously, but it's asking for trouble. There's always risk with any surgery, and honestly? I'd hate to be put in a position where something goes wrong or the person isn't happy in the end and then things become complicated. I'd refer them to another surgeon, one I trust."

"So, you'd never be tempted? Not even if that person was adamant they only wanted you?" I leaned on the counter, opposite him, cradling my steaming coffee.

"Nope." He replied, popping the P. His eyes narrowed on mine as he leaned forward, closer to me, he searched my face for a moment before he asked, "Why are you asking? If it's Willow, you can tell her no way, and that she should've asked me herself."

I rolled my eyes at his chuckle. "It's not. It's work, a case I'm working on."

"Is that why you brought me here? You thought you'd feed me and then pick my brain?"

"I didn't bring you here, you wanted to come and I'm not picking your brain. I asked you a personal career question." I dropped my eyes to my steaming mug as I brought it to my lips and took a tentative sip. I regretted it instantly as it cremated my taste buds. "Fuck!"

His eyes widened at my outburst, a heated smirk bracketing his lips as he chuckled, "That's still picking my brain, Dor." He grabbed his keys from the counter, straightened and pocketed them along with his wallet. "I'm going to get going, before you make me spill all my secrets."

"Really? That was not a secret!" I followed him towards the front door of my flat.

"Where are you going?"

"I'm seeing you out."

"You don't need to do that." He murmured as he put his trainers on.

"I know." My voice cracked a little too huskily as I took in his jean clad butt.

He opened the door, turning towards me before he walked out, "I'll see you Saturday."

My breath snagged at his soft grin, his eyes intent on mine, and all I could manage was a slight nod. My heart raced at the measured step he took toward me and my eyes zeroed in on his lips as he gnawed on them.

One of his hand's cupped the back of his neck and squeezed so hard his fingertips dipped into his flesh, blanching it. For a split second all I could imagine was what it'd feel like for him to touch me like that. With the intensity that always brimmed in his eyes as he looked at me and the marking force with which he touched himself.

"Don't work too hard, pretty girl." He breathed as he dropped his hand from his neck and then brushed a tendril of hair from my face.

My mouth felt dry and my chest tight as I tried so hard to say something other than the squealy "mmmhmmm," that I manged to croak out.

I wanted to reach out and smooth the lines from his drawn brows and searching pout. I wished I could brush back that one curl that always fell across his forehead when his hair was getting a little too long in between trims.

The way he stood so still in front of me, just inside my door, with his hands tucked into his jean's pockets was like he was waiting for me to do it.

To touch him.

I couldn't do it, though. I couldn't touch him. If I did, every vestige of control I'd held on to around him all this time would break. I couldn't let that happen, not when he was the only person who didn't look at me with pity and remorse for something that they hadn't done. I needed that more than I wanted to touch him, I think.

"Goodnight, Dor." He finally said with a deep sigh as he turned and walked out of my home.

"Night, Jacob."

CHAPTER 3

With the exception of training days, Dorian and I hadn't seen each other until today. Game day. She was working late most nights so she could have the weekends mostly free. I was busy with work. I always got busier in the lead up to Christmas. It was like people wanted to go out of their way to catch Santa's eye...or whatever. Although I mostly did onco-plastic breast surgeries, basically reconstructing breasts after mastectomies, I also did some aesthetic work in between.

So, yeah, I hadn't spent as much time with her as I normally would, and I knew it wasn't wise on my part to feel this way, but I missed her. So very much.

I'd known Dorian for over thirteen years, but it wasn't until the last nine years that we became friends. It felt strange being friends with a woman. Especially because I'd kept my distance at first, only really interacting with her when we were around each other socially. When Daniel's dad went to Africa, little by little we formed a friendship. Then he died and our friendship grew deeper roots.

I'd always found her pretty. The funny thing was that she had no idea how stunning she was. And beyond that, she was smart and tenacious. But what made it impossible for me to stay away from her was her heart.

Dorian was one of those people that cared, sometimes I thought she cared too much, but that was the beauty of her. She had a face that could steal your breath, a brain that could challenge any scholar and a heart of a Saint.

That was the reason we had to remain just friends, she deserved more than me and my complicated life. She deserved someone that could give her more than a good time, who could let her in completely. Unfortunately, for me, I wasn't him.

However, that didn't stop me from spending as much time with her and Daniel as I could. Which meant that I was pretty switched on to his moods, and I could tell that he was anxious.

The kid was more competitive than I had thought, and because of his anxiety his attitude was a little on the rough side today. Dorian had spent the duration of our journey to the football grounds trying to get him to calm down. She wasn't getting anywhere and if anything, he was getting even more aggravated. If he got any more worked up he'd give himself an asthma attack.

"You don't get it, Mum." He grumbled after she threatened to pull him out of the game completely. "Thomas' dad is a pro.

We're screwed."

"Excuse me?" She turned so fast in her seat that I was astonished her neck didn't get a crook. "Say that again. I dare you."

"What? I didn't say anything wrong."

"I'm warning you now, Daniel, you either adjust your attitude or…or so help me God…"

"I didn't say anything bad." He gritted.

"How many times do I have to tell you to mind. Your. Language? Do you think your coach is going to let you play if you carry on like this? Not to mention that sort of language is grounds for exclusion. Do you want to be thrown out of St. Joseph's?"

"No."

"Enough with the language and attitude, then." She turned back to the front, her cheeks a blazing red, and took a deep breath before she mumbled, "Sorry."

Why she was apologising I had no idea. If it were me, I would've ignored the whole screwed comment. I'd heard a lot worse, but then again Daniel was eight years old, and I understood why she was upset about it.

"Okay, so Thomas' dad, who is he? Who does he play for? And why are you getting so bothered by it?" I asked him as our eyes met in the rear-view mirror.

"It doesn't matter."

"If it doesn't matter, why were you getting worked up about it?"

"Jake." Dorian sighed in a way that told me she wanted me to drop it. She shook her head as I looked over at her.

"It's not fair." Daniel sighed, his tone a lot cooler than

before. "How is our team meant to stand a chance at winning?"

Well, fuck me sideways, the kid is more switched on than a bright light bulb.

"Even if we don't win, won't it be cool to play against a pro footballer? It'll be like a real life FIFA game."

"I'm not a loser."

"Neither am I."

"I hate Thomas." He stated as he looked out of the window. The tops of his cheeks reddening as he swallowed. He looked genuinely upset. Like he was about to burst into tears.

"Why?"

"Why what?" he asked, his voice a little husked and wet.

"Jake, leave it, please." Dorian urged, her voice taking on a similar edge to his, as her hand paused in the air, just above my thigh. She quickly took it back and ran it through her hair, again and again, before she laid her arm back on the arm rest of the centre console. Her breathing did the thing where it sounded like she was about to either fall apart or have a full blown panic attack as silently as possible. And I wanted to reach out and comfort her whilst I made her tell me why they were both getting so upset over this Thomas kid.

"He told everyone that I'm a loser." His lip wobbled a little as he spoke. "He said I'm a loser because I don't have a dad. He says that everyone has a dad, so I'm a weirdo."

Not many things got to me. I'd learned to take life with a pinch of salt, to focus on the bright side of things. I'd learned the hard way that if you focused on shit, you'd end up sinking into the pile. I'd taught myself to keep going and do what I could. But right then, the look on his face, it made my blood boil. It was as if my intestines were strangling my heart.

"Danny, you have a dad."

"Not like them."

"It doesn't matter if he's like theirs or not, you don't want yours to be like theirs. Your dad was far cooler."

He rolled his eyes, a whatever grunt leaving his lips.

"Doctors are definitely niftier than someone who kicks a ball around. We get to cut people open and rummage around inside them. We fix them and make them better. Come on, that's definitely a lot better than playing around with a ball."

"I know what doctors do, I'm not a kid, you don't have to explain it to me."

"Well then, Mr. not a kid, we better get our heads in the game and show them who's best." I caught his gaze in the mirror. "I don't care who his dad is, I can promise you, we aren't losing to their team."

"You can't promise him that, the kid's dad plays in the Premier League."

"And?" I turned to her as we stopped at a traffic light, "We have moves, you know? We've got skills, right Danny boy?"

Daniel snickered behind me, a smile slowly spreading across his face as I watched him in the rear-view mirror. "Right."

Dorian sighed a silent chuckle as she shook her head, when she looked up at me she mouthed, "On your head be it."

I'd had a lot worse problems on my head, although, looking at the way her brows were raised and her eyes were wide, I was beginning to get a little worried what would happen if we didn't win this school football match. They only got bragging rights, surely, the blowback couldn't be that bad?

Still, ice cream and chocolate existed for a reason. I opened the centre console and pulled out the share bag of Magic Stars I kept stashed in there. I took a small handful and threw them into my mouth before I passed Daniel the bag.

"Here, we need all the magic we can get. Make sure you get the ones that have the extra happy faces, they might help with your lack of smile situation."

"I'm not a baby anymore, I know that they're just star shaped chocolate buttons. They're not actually magic." He rolled his eyes as he looked into the packet and rummaged around before he took a handful for himself.

"Of course they are, can you not read the packet? Magic. Stars. They have to be magic, otherwise it's false advertising and your mum needs to sue them."

"You've got more chance of finding a unicorn grazing in the park." Dorian laughed as she took the packet and resealed it before putting it away again. "I bet you think you're some sort of Peter Pan."

"Depends, are you Wendy or Tinkerbell?" I murmured to the road ahead, not realising I'd said it louder than I meant to.

I could feel her staring at me, and as much as I knew I should look at her and smile like it was another joke. I couldn't. I didn't want to.

* * *

Dorian. Dorian Anson was a bad decision waiting to happen. I knew it. Every fibre of my being knew it. I think even she knew it. However, it didn't stop me from taking every opportunity I came across to spend time with her, or Daniel.

Our little post-match celebration had only served to prove that I was fucked when it came to her. I kept listing all the reasons why she was a bad idea in my head, but considering how smart I prided myself on being, she had a way of making me pretty fucking stupid.

She rounded my car slowly, like she was dragging her feet. Her teeth worrying her smiling bottom lip as she fussed with her hair. Her fingers running through it in that way she always did when her brain was going over something she didn't want it to. Or when she was nervously trying to hide something from you.

She laughed a little tersely at Daniel. He was still so excited about being on the winning side that he was buzzing with energy. He hopped from foot to foot at the top of the shallow steps that led up to the front door of their building.

"Daniel, you're going to wake the neighbours. It's late, sweetheart, you need to calm down." Her voice was soft and giggly even as she tried to rein him in.

It was already way past his bedtime, normally, Dorian was a stickler for his routine. Especially given that when he got that little bit run down, his asthma got exacerbated.

We both couldn't help but laugh at his high-pitched squeal as he swung his kitbag around.

"Aren't you going to say thank you and bye to Jake?" she asked him like he had an option not to, but her raised brows stated otherwise.

"You've both done a lot of thanking already." I told her as she stood in front of me, her head tilted to the side as her smile softened ever so slightly. "Plus, I had fun too."

"Thanks, Jake." He called to me as he caught the keys Dorian threw up at him. "I thought you were coming up?"

"Not tonight, buddy, but I'll see you soon." His shoulders slumped at that, a pouty frown furrowing his brow.

"Anyone would think that he barely sees you." She shook her head and continued, "Anyway, thank you again for taking part in the football match. I know you're busy and you really didn't have to do it, so…"

I'd enjoyed every minute of it. Spending time with her and Daniel. He was a great kid.

"Anytime, Dor." I told her as she turned back to me, Daniel had opened the door and gone in already.

"Okay, well," she murmured, her breath drawing out the Ls. "I'll let you go. Thank you."

"You're welcome." I could barely keep my hands tucked into the back pockets of my jeans as she stood there looking at me with her mesmerising eyes and the pretty, almost shy, happy slant to her mouth.

"Alright, bye, Jacob." My heart paused for a moment as she took a step toward me and then stopped. Her smile straightening as she leaned her face close to mine. She pressed her lips to my cheek quickly and drew back a tad.

We both stayed quiet for a moment, neither one of us moving. I could hear her deep, wistful breaths and it made me miss her already. I hadn't even left her yet and my chest already felt heavy.

"Bye, Dorian." I breathed as our eyes met and my chest filled with warmth. My heart was racing so fast that it felt like it would be impossible to slow down ever again. "Dor?"

"Mmmm?"

I had the words right at the tip of my tongue— *Would you like to maybe go for dinner or drinks, or both?* —but as much as I wanted to ask her, for years I'd wanted to ask her, I couldn't. I couldn't do it because if it went wrong, things would get complicated. And I had enough complications.

I didn't want to compromise our friendship. I didn't want to risk my friendship with her brother, either. He'd been more of a brother to me than my own.

"You should get inside." I laughed as I settled on keeping things easy.

"Oh, yes," she fumbled with her words, something that always made me smile considering how brilliant she ordinarily was with them. "Good night."

"Night." I blew out as I stepped back and watched her ascend the steps and disappear behind the shiny black door to her building. Her teeth gnawing on her lip again as she fussed with her hair whilst she closed the door.

I hated the resentment that flooded my thoughts as I wondered why it was so easy with other women, but when it came to her, everything felt so much more perplexing and knotty. I continued to mull it over as I got back in my car and drove home.

CHAPTER 4

Dorian

Over the years our girls' nights had become more of a child friendly affair. Gone were the cocktails and in was the tea. Willow and one of our friends, Beth, had stumbled on this gem of a tearoom a while back and we'd made it a point to hold our monthly catch-up sessions here. It was a small little teashop in a quiet little residential backstreet close to Willow's flat in Kensington.

Molly and Pippa enjoyed the vintage dress up box and us older girls liked the natter. Quincy, Willow and I were childhood friends.

Quincy was probably the strongest person I knew. We'd lost Phillip, her brother, and on top of that she'd suffered a stillbirth and divorced her cheating, scumbag of a husband after finding out she was pregnant with Pippa.

I thought that I'd die when I'd found out that Phillip was gone, I couldn't remember anything but the sheer pain. There were times that it still hurt as much now as it did then. Especially when Phillip's absence, his death, impacted our son. Losing the man you thought you'd love for the rest of your life was a bitch, but merely thinking of the possibility of losing Daniel, that was enough to truly kill me.

My sweet boy.

"Oh god, this has got to be the best brownie I've ever had." Quincy moaned as she shoved the rest of the small square in her mouth. "If we come here more often, I'll have to join a gym."

"I think it might be worth it though." I giggled, as I watched Molly and Pippa wrap white feather boas around Beth's and Willow's shoulders.

"What're you giggling about over there?" Willow looked between me and Quincy, her eyes narrowed at us like she suspected we were keeping something from her.

"Nothing."

"The cake."

"You say nothing," she gestured toward me and then over at Quincy, "she says cake. Which is it?"

"Cake." Quincy and I both sighed. It was good cake, almost better than sex, or what I remembered of it.

"I can think of something better than cake..." Beth snickered, waggling her brows at Willow. Her Welsh twang was something that made me smile to this day, I swear she could make the Hail Mary sound dirty.

Molly looked between us, her face pinched in confusion as she said, "Uncle Jake says there's nothing better than cake and ice cream."

"Speaking of," Beth stood from her makeover chair and sat back at the table with us, "how did the football thing go?"

"Good."

"Just good?" Quincy asked as she examined one of the mini scones glistening with jam and clotted cream atop.

"Yes."

"Why're you being so evasive about it?" Willow gave me one of her curious looks.

"I'm not, the match went well, they won. It was nice of him." I glanced over at Pippa and Molly who were going through the dress up box again.

"Yeah, it was *really nice* of him." Beth sang a little too teasingly.

"Stop it."

"Come on, Dorian, you have to admit he's a little bit nice himself."

"Beth." I warned as she shrugged like I was the one being silly.

I didn't want to talk about him with them. I didn't want to think about him any more than I already did, especially about how pleasant he was to look at or spend time with.

"She's got a point, Dory, he's actually…you know…" Quincy smiled, her cheeks blushing like she was saying something inappropriate.

"Yeah, he's hot until he opens his mouth and then you want to slap him or snap his tongue off." Willow rolled her eyes as she poured herself another cup of tea. I internally chuckled at her indignation, she and Jake were very alike in the way they interacted with people. They didn't let many people in, but when they did, they were loyal to a fault. Not to mention that they were both great at pressing people's buttons.

"I love Uncle Jake, he's my goddaddy like you, Dory." Molly chimed as she and Pippa sat at the table with us.

"I'm your godmother, sweetie." I couldn't help but tap her little button nose with the tip of my finger, something she always pulled a sort of sour face about, but never complained.

God, I'm that aunt that pinches cheeks and coos like a bloody overbearing fool.

The thought alone made me cringe as I then started to imagine myself as the cat lady on the second floor of my building. Nice to everyone, but essentially invisible and alone. As unlikely as that would be with this lot around, it still struck a dissonant chord and it made me uneasy.

When did I become this person? I asked myself, the answer immediately flashing in my mind as a pair of distant, beautiful brown eyes and a soft cheeky smile. *Phillip.*

"I still struggle with that decision." Willow groaned.

"He's great with the kids," I sighed, trying to ignore the pang my thoughts had brought with them.

"Because he's a child himself."

"You know he's not that bad." I'd known Jake for over a decade. We'd spent a lot of time with one another. I'd learned that there was a lot more to him than what most people saw, and a part of me didn't know what to make of that.

I didn't understand why he'd allowed me to see him in all those lights, but it made me happy, even if that happiness brought a sting of guilt with it.

"But, he is hot, and he likes spending time with you." Beth smiled. "Anyone would think he might like you...*like you.*

Plus, you need to get back into the tango of things."

"I can barely balance Daniel and work, and thinking about people like that…well, I don't know, it seems wrong. Oh, and I have a child."

Thinking about Jake like that didn't feel wrong, what felt wrong was thinking about him in one breath and in the next thinking about Phillip. Sometimes I wondered if I would still think of Jake like that if Phillip were still here. If we'd even be friends like we are. The worst part of it was the panicked feeling at the possibility that we might not be the way we are if Phillip hadn't died.

It was a panic laced with guilt and self-loathing because what if I still felt all the same things toward Jake even if Phillip was here?

It doesn't mean you'd still be together.

The thought made me cringe. I couldn't imagine not being with him, not when we had Daniel.

"I have Daniel."

That was always my excuse. Anytime a man might get too close, or start sniffing around me, that was the first thing that popped into my head—*I have a child, I have Daniel.*

I'd tried to keep as much of Phillip as I could for Daniel. As silly as it may seem, I was scared that if I let myself get attached to another man, that all the memories I had of him would fade, that eventually I wouldn't be able to show or tell my son about his dad. And I wanted him to know all there was to know about Pip.

"You can't use the child excuse more than once, and so what?" Beth laughed in that knowing way she did. "Lots of other women have kids and date. You don't even have to date, just let him take care of—" She paused and cleared her throat as she eyed the girls. "Your needs. Being a mam doesn't mean you don't have them."

"True." Quincy blew out.

"True?" I asked her, "Do you date? Do you have someone taking care of your...ummm...*needs*?"

"Once. Only once, and it was nice, but the whole time I kept wondering when he was going to see my scar and put two-and-two together and run off."

"Why would he do that?" I took a quick sip of my Earl Grey.

I'd tried the whole sex thing a couple of times in the last few years and both times I was waiting for Phillip's ghost to appear and give me a tongue lashing. The tongue lashing never came, but the memories of how it felt to be with him, they were all there. I was thinking and imagining one man, whilst another took what had been his.

"And who is he?" Willow squealed, her face lighting up.

"I'm not talking about this in front of the girls. It was a one-time thing and like I said it was nice, but it was scary too. And, yes, he was alright, but the whole time I kept wondering why he was grunting like a hog searching for truffles." Her laugh set us all off.

"Was he at least better than *he-who-shall-not-be-named*?" Beth giggled as she referred to Quincy's ex-husband, Richard.

"Strangely, I couldn't say. It'd been a long time since, well, since Richard and I got personal." She blushed so deeply that her cheeks were only a few shades lighter than her red lipstick. "Honestly, it was just nice to have a man take care of things, rather than having to do it myself."

"The pair of you should've been nuns. I don't know how

you can go so long without it." Willow shook her head and grimaced like the thought alone was intolerable.

"It's different when you have a little person dependent on you. Plus, not all of us get around." I stuck my tongue out at her.

"I get that it makes it harder, but we're only young once, and it won't be long till things start heading south, so it's common sense to make the most out of it until it happens. Visit as many vineyards as you can before you settle on a vintage you love."

"Here, here." Beth high-fived her.

"We're in our thirties, we're not young anymore."

"We're thirty-three, we're not old. We've not even reached the mid-life point. Anyway, the point is, Dory, you need to get yourself back out there. You can't just become a born again V because you're too busy."

"Willow, it's easy for you. You don't have a child and you don't care about how many visitors sample your *wine*." I sighed, "Good on you for it, but that's not who I am and the thought alone is enough to make me sweat. I don't want a hog searching for my truffles, *God*, that's off putting."

"Hey, you're beautiful and you're smart. Guys would line up just to take you to dinner, or whatever it is people do when they're not *you-know-whating*." Quincy semi-whispered.

"Or maybe you only need a one-time fix to show you what you've been missing." Beth offered me the plate with the chocolate fondants. "If that's the case, why not let Jake take care of it? I've heard some pretty great things from a couple of nurses over at St. Thomas'. Apparently he's not just good with his hands."

Willow and Quincy laughed at her remark, "He's had enough practice."

"Jinx." Willow knocked her knuckles on the wooden table.

I took a bite of the moussey cake as I tried to find a way of telling them that although Jake was…handsome and I had no doubt that he was good, most likely great, in bed, that he was someone that I enjoyed talking to. We were friends and spent a lot of time together, he had a way of making me forget about all the serious stuff. He had a way of making me genuinely smile and laugh, and there was no way that I was going to spoil that because my lady garden needed tending to.

I swallowed down the chocolate mush that was clogging my mouth and making my stomach turn. It wasn't even the cake. The thing making the acid climb up my throat was Beth's comment about the nurses.

It didn't even make any sense for me to feel that way when he and I were just friends.

Just friends. Something I had to keep reminding myself of lately.

"Look, can you honestly say that the thought of his *you know what* doesn't make you a little curious of how good he is with it?" Beth said before she shoved a whole mini cream tart in her mouth.

"I haven't thought about his *you know what*." It was sort of true, I hadn't really. Well, not until I almost face planted on it that one time at Daniel's first birthday party, and then the thought had filled me with guilt.

I had enough guilt I didn't know how to deal with. I didn't need anymore.

Still, that didn't mean that I didn't notice certain physical things about Jake.

Things like how tall he was, or the way that he always wore

perfectly fitted clothes that although simple, made you look. The way his torso was lean and long, and tapered to his hips flawlessly. Or the way that it didn't matter if he wore jeans or suit trousers, they always just skimmed his legs and impeccably wrapped around his butt.

That image alone was enough to have my heart doing that stupid marathon pace thing it did whenever I thought about or noticed those things.

He was solid. His muscular arms made me feel safe even when they were barely touching me. His hands were soft and gentle, but so steady and sure.

"Come on, Dorian," Beth chided, "you can look and imagine, it's not wrong. I think we've all done it at some point. You have to appreciate certain things, and he is…"

"Okay, okay!" Willow slapped her hand across our friend's mouth, "We get it, you're creaming over him."

"Willow!" Quincy gritted as her eyes pointed to the girls sitting at the other end of the table, busy on their tablets.

"They're not listening." Willow said a little defensively and then continued, "Look, just try putting yourself out there."

"It's not like I haven't tried. I have. Twice. But it feels weird." I ran my hands through my hair as my chest constricted with the same niggling feeling I'd had both times I'd let a man *take care of my needs*. "As for Jake, he's Jamie's friend. I've been there, done it and had the cosy t-shirt ripped off me. No offence, Quincy," I smiled at her lightly. "Jake and I, we're friends and I don't want to go there."

"You don't want to?" Beth asked, her eyes a little wide with disbelief.

"Fine, I won't."

"Okay then, take Jake out of the equation." Quincy sighed, and in my head I could hear myself screaming at her—*No, don't!* "There's this one dad at the school that gives you the eye whenever he sees you…and he's single. I overheard two of the au-pairs say that his wife took ill and passed away suddenly a few years ago." She bit down on her lip as her face pinched slightly.

Yeah, the dead wife had made her think of Pip too. "Anyway, I think what Beth and Willow are trying to say is that maybe you need to stop dipping your toes in the ocean and jump in again."

"And you're jumping in, are you?" I directed my question at her. She gave me a wry smile, one that she always gave when she was trying to hold things back. "Oh, I see why you're being pushy now. Who's sniffing around your truffles then?"

"What are you on about?"

"That smile, it's your *I'm-a-little-too-happy-and-struggling-to-contain-it-all-inside* one." I took the small, pretty much empty china cup from her hand and put it back down on the saucer. There was no way I was letting her hide behind it.

"Why can't I be happy?" She shrugged as her smile pulled to the side.

"It's not a question of whether or not you can be happy, it's that we want to know what's making you so happy?"

"I've been waiting for this since Raj asked me what was going on with you and Jamie." Beth squealed as she fanned herself.

"Jesus, he's worse than you!" She rolled her eyes as she pointed at Willow.

"Hold on," I stopped Willow's comeback with my finger

on her lips, "there's something going on with you and Jamie?"

If there was, I'd be over the moon for them. It'd been a long time coming and it felt good to know that he was moving on from his disaster of a marriage.

"It's nothing." Quincy replied softly, trying a little too hard to be matter of fact. "He's got this really sick patient and it's been a little hard on him. This little boy is a toddler and he's got this brain tumour that's been silently, pretty much, killing him. Anyway, you know how your brother gets when he comes across a case like this."

"Okay, but what does that have to do with you? You're Cardio and he's Neuro, why would you two be working together on it?" I asked her as I topped up her tea, letting her pour the milk in herself.

"We're not, and it has nothing to do with me."

"So why does Raj think there's something going on? Something worth asking me about."

"Because it's Raj and he's a gossip."

"Why are you smiling like the cat that got the cream as you're saying there's nothing going on?" Willow shuffled her chair impossibly closer to the table.

"I'm not."

"You are." Beth interjected.

"Look, we're friends."

"You've been friends all your lives, so why is it that you're smiling like that as we're talking about him?"

"I don't know," she rolled her eyes, but the smile didn't waver. "Sometimes it feels like things are changing."

"Changing?"

"Yes."

"How?"

"I don't know, it's hard to explain. The way he looks at me, it's like he wants to touch me but he has no idea how. I don't know, it's probably nothing."

Her words nestled inside my ears, radiating heat down my body as I realised that I knew all too well what she meant.

"If it's making you smile like that, it has to be something." Willow said lightly, her voice almost wistful as she smiled.

"Maybe." Quincy sighed, her hands wrapped around her teacup on the table, as her eyes fell to her napkin covered lap. "Maybe I'm not jumping in, maybe it's more of a wade, but…I …I don't know, maybe it'll be worth it?"

We all fell quiet, pondering her words. I didn't know whether I had it in me to trust someone enough to allow them to love me, let alone for me to love them. I didn't want to depend on a man. I didn't want to invest myself in someone and then have it all unceremoniously snatched away from me. And yes, I knew that sex and feelings didn't have to be a combo deal like a large popcorn and Coke at the cinema, but that was how I worked. I didn't want to feel dirty or used. I didn't want to feel guilty, I wanted to be able to enjoy myself. I wanted more than a physical touch, because both times that I'd had a man touch me after Phillip, it didn't feel right. It didn't feel like it was enough.

Jake had barely ever touched me physically, but the way he would make a joke about something completely off-hand because he saw me get a little emotional. The way he sat for hours with Daniel playing silly computer games on his iPad. The way he listened when I did nothing but talk absolute nonsense. I couldn't jeopardise any of those things for sex.

I knew Jake was a one-night guy, and although one night

would be all I'd want from him, I couldn't imagine ever sitting down next to him on my sofa again. Doing nothing but watching a film, or eating a takeaway…or enjoying what silence sounded like with another person next to me.

I couldn't give all those things up. More importantly, I couldn't give up the friendship that we'd established over the last several years.

CHAPTER 5

I sat in the drawing room of my parents' large home. I took in the light wood half panelled walls as I listened to my dad tell me how disappointed he was that my sister had cancelled last minute. He was worried about her again, and from the way he was speaking I knew that his worry was something that I needed to look into.

"Your mother wanted to go and check on her, but I couldn't let her do it. The last thing she needs is to get stressed about her falling off the wagon again." He sighed, his fingers rubbing his eyes harshly before they pinched the bridge of his nose.

"Has Miles said anything?"

"No, but he's busy with the new club. It's not fair on him either, the boy needs to focus on his career and after what happened last time…" He topped up his Single Malt by another finger.

He had no idea what had happened last time. He knew a fraction of the full story. The parts that Jamie and I had told them when they'd met us at the hospital.

He took a sip of the fragrant, burnt sugar and spicy scotch before he concluded, "You know how it is this time of year, it's a race to get to the top of the league."

"I know, but he's been good at keeping an eye on her and keeping her stable." I took a sip of my water and followed it with a couple of the Magic Stars Mum had set out in a little ramekin for me. Something she'd always done.

When I was young and got home from school, she'd sit me at the dinner table to do my homework, she'd give me a small bowl of the chocolate stars and a glass of cold milk from the fridge. Then she'd sit next to me and watch me do my work as she kept up with her own. Sometimes she'd get the housekeeper to make shortbread cookies studded with chocolatey treats rather than ordinary chocolate chips. They were the best sugar fix ever, and to this day, there had never been anyone that made anything half as moreish.

"I keep wondering when she's going to relapse, she's been partying non-stop with some of the other footballers' girlfriends. Your mother is constantly checking up on her and I can't help but feel that it's not doing either of them any good."

"Do you want me to talk to her?"

"Which one?" he chuckled softly.

"Eleanor."

"I don't know, Jacob."

"Dad, if you think she's back on the pills…" I couldn't help but trail off as Dad stiffened in his seat. His eyes flashing to the door as he put his tumbler down on the small side table next to his armchair.

"Levi, you said you weren't going to say anything. You promised." Mum reprimanded him as she stood in the doorway.

"I know, but you're so worried and I don't like to see you stressed, Ruthie."

"I want to know, Mum."

"Oh, Jacob, you shouldn't be worrying about this." She breathed in exasperation before adding, "Dinner's ready."

"You shouldn't have to worry about this either, but it is what it is, right?" I stood from the sofa, wandered to where she was stood and gave her a quick squeeze. "If you'd told me about this before, I could've gone past their place and picked her up."

"I know." She smiled as her hand combed through my hair and then caressed my face. "I've never really had to worry about you, you were always so easy. Too easy sometimes, my boy. Bni." *My son.*

"Oh Mother, don't you start with all that." I laughed as I dropped a small kiss on her dark blonde hair and gave her a small push towards the dining room.

We sat in a loaded silence as we ate our food. Once in a while Dad would say something to lighten the mood, and eventually the two of them fell into an easy conversation. That was the thing about them, they always managed to find something good to focus on.

Something they'd taught me, too. Even when life wasn't perfect, there was always something to be happy about. Something to enjoy and relish.

I smiled and nodded at everything they said. Something I

very rarely did, my mother had a knack for weaselling things into the conversation when I wasn't exactly present. Normally it would be another one of her friends' daughters who happened to be close to my age and looking for a husband.

No, thank you.

"Are you listening to what your mother is saying?"

Not quite. "Sure."

"So, you don't mind and you'll come?" She smiled brightly up at me, she clearly knew I wasn't listening, thus the wide eyes and big smile.

Fuck, she was even doing the whole batting her eyelashes thing as she artfully poised her chin on her clasped hands. "It's one night. I feel so bad that we double booked it with your birthday and…"

Bullshit, the woman was more organised with her time than the Chancellor of the Exchequer with the national budget. She was plotting, and I could tell from the way she was using every single bit of her artillery to get at my heartstrings.

"You know, thirty-eight really isn't a big deal. Also, I'm pretty sure I'm a little too old for you to still be throwing me parties."

"You are never too old," she did that thing where she made her almost non-existent German twang a little more prominent. "You are still my boy."

Dad chuckled at the blatant emotional coercion, his brown eyes lighting up as he held her in his gaze.

"Oh, please, *Yacob*…" *Oh. Fuck. My. Life.*

"That's not my name, Mother."

"It's your Hebrew name." She said very matter of fact before she took a dainty sip of her wine.

"Whatever you say, Rooooot."

"Now you're just being mean." Dad laughed, his wide grin matching mine. "Ruth, if he doesn't want to go…"

"Nonsense, he loves the Royal Philharmonic. I still have your cello, you know."

"I'll make you a deal." I stretched my hand out to her over the dinner table.

"Okay?"

"I'll go to this concert, if, and only if, you promise this isn't a ploy to accidently bump into another of your friends that's brought their daughter along. Promise that this isn't you trying to set me up again."

Dad side eyed her like she'd just been rumbled. *I knew it.*

"She's a nice girl." She whined, her accent conveniently getting a little thicker again.

"Jewish, no doubt."

"And? She's beautiful, Jacob, nice long, fiery hair. Big, big blue eyes. She's a teacher, great with kids."

"So basically, let me get this right, you're trying to marry me off to a ginger that you assume will give you grandkids because she's a teacher, and so must want kids of her own?" She scowled at me. "Well?"

"I've seen some of the women you…" She grimaced as she gestured her hand toward me. "Look, I won't introduce you. I promise. Okay? Not unless we bump into her and her mother. She's smart, you know?"

Of course she was. I was sure she was beautiful too, but the last thing I wanted was a one-night stand that became stuck… thanks to Mother dearest, who'd probably help her and egg her on.

"Fine, you've got to shake on it though." I wriggled the fingers of my outstretched hand. "We never go back on a shake, do we?"

She placed her hand in mine, Dad's laughter earning him her stink-eye. "I don't know what you're laughing at, Levi, you know we have a few empty rooms."

I shook her stiff hand, and that was that.

* * *

I didn't stay late, I wasn't looking forward to the drive home and I wanted to try and get a hold of Eleanor. She hadn't picked up her phone the first couple of times I'd called, that in itself rang loud and clear alarm bells in my head. The third time I let it go to voicemail and left her a message.

"If you don't call me back in the next couple of hours, I'm coming to your place. Don't make me call Ryan. Love you, chipmunk." Eleanor was a pain in the arse to most people, but for some reason, she always seemed to respond to our older brother. He didn't live in the same continent, but fuck knows why, his words had more of an impact than anyone else's.

I was almost home when my phone started ringing, I checked the centre console screen and answered immediately. My finger pressed the little green phone on my steering wheel automatically and loud giggles filled my car.

"Dor?"

"Hi, Jake." Daniel sang before Dorian's screech came through the speakers. "I swear to God, Daniel, turn that damn thing off! It keeps shocking me every time I try and plug it into the TV!"

"Ummm, is everything okay?"

"No, Mum's trying to plug the PS4 into the telly, but she's

useless. She asked me to call Auntie Will, but she said she's not the IT department and Uncle Jamie didn't answer his phone. So I called you, because Mum's going to blow up the game before I even get a chance to play it."

I couldn't help but laugh at his surfeited tone, "Okay, where's your mum?"

"Lying on the floor…fried, I think."

"Have you turned the console off?"

"Yes, but I think she's doing something wrong because every time she touches the TV she keeps screaming."

"It's just static, mate."

"Whatever, she's annoying me. I've told her what goes where but she won't let me do it. She keeps saying it's dangerous. Even a dummy could do it."

"Put her on." The sound of Dorian growling at Daniel as he told her that he'd called me and that I wanted to speak to her made my laughter return.

"What're you laughing at, funny man?" she gritted. "I'm going to take that thing and shove it…" She growled again, I could imagine her hands balled like she was going to knock something out with her frustration.

"Calm down," I chuckled at her words, "If you tell me what's what, I can probably help you do it on the phone."

"I'm not touching that torture contraption again, he can wait until Jamie can come over and set it up."

I quickly deviated towards their flat. "Look, I'm in the car, I'll be at yours in twenty."

"No, don't. It's okay, he can wait till tomorrow."

"Dor, you can't buy it for him and then make him wait to play it. That really would make it a torture device."

Her laugh was cut off by the loud ringing of her house phone, she grumbled before she muttered, "I have to get this."

"I'll see you in a tick."

"See you soon." She said and before she hung up I heard her answer the house phone, "Hey, Willow."

My eavesdropping was brought to a halt as she ended our call, my previously not so great mood all of a sudden elevated by the prospect of seeing her and Daniel. Granted it'd only been a couple of weeks since I'd seen them, but still…

You are so fucked, dickhead.

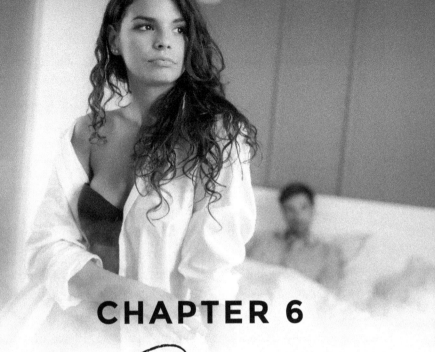

CHAPTER 6

Dorian

I'd sort of zoned out of the conversation a little while ago. Willow was still stuck on the whole Jamie and Quincy being together thing. It seemed that Quincy's wading was paying off, which then made me think of the conversation we'd had the other week at the teashop.

"Oi, you're not even listening to me!" Willow yelled from the other end of the line, I knew that she'd have a lot to say about Jamie and Quincy and the situation between Jenna and Richard, their exes.

"I am listening, but unless you're going to help me sort this stupid games console mess out, I need to go. I'm tired and grouchy and still a little shocked by the whole thing."

"I think we should call it baby gate. We could even hashtag

that shit, hashtag-baby-gate, hashtag-soap-opera, hashtag-I-can't-even…"

"Hashtag-will-you-stop-hashtagging-before-I-hashtag-gag-you?"

"Oh, hashtag-*kinky.*"

"I'm going now, do not text me any more hashtags, or I will post that video of you pole dancing drunk on your social media."

She gasped like she'd been winded by a knock to the gut. "You're fucking evil, mush."

"Aww, I know, but desperate times and all that." I jumped from the stool at the breakfast bar and almost knocked into Daniel who came bounding through the open plan living area, a wide grin on his face as he rushed to the door. "I have to go, bye, Willow."

"Who's ringing your doorbell at this time of night, whorebag?"

"Seriously? You're calling *me* a whorebag?" I had to chuckle. "Also it's not that late, it's still evening. Anyway, bye, chooch."

I ended the call and dropped my phone onto the polished concrete counter. Daniel's excited voice chimed from the hallway as he answered the intercom, confirming it was Jake, and then let him in.

He opened our front door and stood quite literally jumping from foot to foot. I could feel the excitement emanating off him, and I had to admit, that even I was a little on the chirpy side for seeing Jake tonight.

"You don't have to stand there and wait with me." He smiled at me as he glanced down the stairwell.

"Alright, but stay away from the railing, okay?"

"Yep."

"Okay, stay by the door."

As soon as he moved back to the threshold I wandered back into the flat, sticking the kettle on as I looked for something to do to get rid of the jittery energy coursing through me. I opened and closed the steaming dishwasher checking to see if it was ready to unload, even though its tell-tale loud beeps hadn't sounded the end of the programme yet.

I glanced down my body, pulling down at the hem of my black vest and then pulling the deep scoop neckline up to hide my braless cleavage. I tugged at my leggings, hoping that my knickers weren't showing. Stupidly I even checked my toenails for any chips...

What to do? What. To. Do?

I checked my emails on my phone and was about to reply to the most urgent one when Jake's deep laugh sounded through the hallway to the living area. Daniel's excited one-hundred miles an hour chatter chasing it up.

"What on earth?" He paused in the middle of the room, his gaze wide as he took in the mess I'd made of the TV unit.

"I told you!"

"She's really done a number here, huh?"

"Who's she? The cat's mother?" I said from where I was still leaning on the kitchen counter. "Hi."

"Did you want to pull every cable out?" he chuckled as he made his way to the kitchen.

"Don't." I rolled my eyes at his teasing. "I'm embarrassed enough as it is. You'd have thought that after eight years of doing this parent thing, I'd have it all sussed."

"You've got enough sussed, anymore and you'd really be a know it all, and no one likes a know it all." He took his keys and wallet out of his pocket and put them on the counter, in the same place he always did. It was like there was a marking for where his things belonged on my kitchen side. He followed it up with a small paper bag branded with my favourite patisserie's logo. "I thought you might need something to even out this disaster."

I tried so hard to bite down the smile that forced itself onto my face, "You didn't even know what you were walking into."

"No, but I figured you'd need something sweet to let go of the grudge you're holding against the console." He laughed.

"I don't think it likes me very much either."

"Well…" he chirped as he pulled out a small box from the bag and placed it in front of me and then took out a bag of Magic Stars and one of Daniel's favourite giant chocolate buttons.

"You bring me fancy confectionery and you only have baby chocolates?"

"Baby chocolates?" I couldn't help but giggle at the quirk of his brow. "I'll have you know that these are better than any macaroon you could put in front of me."

"If you say so, baby Jake." I teased as I turned to make myself a long, milky coffee and him his usual short espresso.

"You'd think that after all these years, you'd accept that I have a pretty loyal relationship with these."

"Oh, I accept it, but I still don't understand it. Even Daniel's grown out of those. You know they're eighty percent sugar, right?" I tempered my coffee with a generous drop of milk before I took his caffeine shot from the Nespresso machine I barely used with the exception of when he or Willow visited.

It was only then I noticed that he was unusually quiet. There was a cloudy, wistful look on his face which he tried to conceal with a shake of his head and a wide smile the moment he realised I was studying him.

"Thank you," he murmured as he took the tiny cup from my hand, his fingers brushing mine and even though he had it well in his grip, he lingered momentarily. His smile went a little lax and fell even from his eyes as they wandered down my body, blinked rapidly and then flitted back to mine. His tongue did that thing where it wet his plush lip before he sucked it between his teeth. His nose flared as he took in a long breath…

Oh man, I could feel my cheeks heat as I struggled to look away from him.

"Yes!" I pulled my hand back a little too quickly as Daniel perched himself up on the kitchen counter and made for the packet of buttons. "Are you going to stay for a little bit after we've connected the PlayStation? We could play Sonic again. I think I can beat you now."

"One game and then it's bedtime, buddy."

"One game? That's nothing, one tournament, please, Mum? It's the weekend."

"We could be here a long time with a tournament," Jake said as he threw a few chocolate stars in his mouth and followed them up with his shot of coffee. "How about we do one of those six game matches. You win and I'll get you the game on your iPad, but you can only play when your mum says it's okay."

"Deal." Daniel jumped down from the counter and raced to the sitting area, "Come on then, we don't have time to lose here!"

"Slave driver." Jake muttered with a grin as he tipped a few more chocolate bits into his mouth and then sauntered off towards Daniel and the mess that was my TV unit.

"You started his obsession with that game." I took one of the small macaroons and took a slow, delicious bite. My eyes closed as the rich nutty, chocolate goodness made me sigh, "Mmmm, these are the best I've ever had."

I opened my eyes, still enjoying the lingering pleasure on my taste buds, to find Jake ogling me. His jaw a little too tense and his fledgling smile completely gone.

"What?"

He shook his head as he took a deep breath, his hands running through his hair as he muttered something to himself and spun back towards the sofa.

* * *

"I can't believe you let him win." I sighed as we pushed the TV unit back to its spot. "I should've known that's what you were going to do when you said you'd get him the game."

He smiled as he wrapped a few spare cables that had come with the console. "He's a good kid, Dor."

"I know. I'm lucky." I took the cables from him, our hands brushing again and in the dim lit space it felt like that one little touch was magnified. It felt like somehow he was touching so much more than just my hand.

"He's lucky," he murmured as his gaze studied the contact of our skin. He laughed huskily and let go of the cables before he added, "You know, we're getting closer to Christmas and you've pretty much shot yourself in the foot in terms of presents."

"I know, but I promised that I'd buy it for him as soon as he got into all the top classes. I thought they'd wait till the end of the autumn term to tell him if he'd been moved up or not, and I figured it'd be a kill two birds with one stone sort of thing." I tucked the cables into one of the drawers of the unit and stood to face him. "I'm sure he'll want something else as much by then."

I'd finished getting everything back to normal when I turned to find him stuffing his wallet in his pocket. Disappointment flooded me as I realised that he was leaving now that Daniel was asleep and order was restored. A feeling that had been becoming more prevalent over the years.

At first I used to think it was the loneliness, the dread of not having someone there. But then I'd started to notice little things like that he'd always linger a little before he left. Or how he'd always look back after he walked out of my door, and he'd always give me that soft and genuine smile that made me feel almost too warm inside.

I stood in the middle of my lounge, watching as he studied his keys in his hands. Procrastinating as usual.

With the kitchen strip lighting glowing around him it was impossible not to admit that there was something about him that made me want more time with him. Like it didn't matter how often we saw each other, I'd always want to see him again the minute he descended my stairs and I shut the door of my home.

Jake was tall, he was lean, but he was also very well built at the same time. He made tall, dark and handsome seem bland with his shining chocolatey eyes and his almost too perfectly symmetrical lips that were a little too plump for a man.

Not to mention his imposing demeanour. Considering how buoyant he was, or could be, he never sought out to be the centre of attention. It was never something he worked for, you just couldn't help but be drawn to him and his better the devil you know charm.

"You okay?" I could hear him ask as I continued to take

him in. The way his long sleeved, white t-shirt fit perfectly snug to his arms and his torso. The way it stretched lightly across his chest and loosened to a just fitted fit as it tapered down his stomach to his hips. And even though I could hear myself respond something along the lines of "just thinking," the only things running around in my head were Beth's words—

Can you honestly say that the thought of his you-know-what doesn't make you a little curious of how good he is with it?

I could feel my breathing speed up as my heartrate picked up in my chest.

Thump-thumpthump-thu-thump...

My mouth was watering and I had no idea why, because seriously, how did that even happen only looking at a person? And as I thought that things couldn't get any more dangerous in my head, my eyes fell on the buckle of his belt and I couldn't help but study how his t-shirt was slightly tucked in behind it. Just. So. And as my eyes continued heading south I could picture the way his tight jeans always left little of what was underneath to the imagination.

Fuuuuuuck.

I swallowed down the pool of saliva that had collected in my mouth as my legs crossed and heated chills coursed through me.

Why not let Jake take care of it?

I shuddered as goose bumps broke out from my head to my toes. Everywhere. And I had to admit that right there and then, I couldn't remember why exactly I'd thought liking Jake more than a friend should was a bad idea.

"Dor?" his low hoarse call had my focus drawing back to him, and I couldn't believe how far gone into my thoughts I'd been. So far gone that my feet had voluntarily carried me to him. "I don't know what you were thinking about, but I think it's my cue to head out."

"Why?" I cringed at the panic in my voice as I slowly ambled closer to him. "I mean, you don't have to. For once I'm caught up with work and I'm waiting for people to get back to me. I was going to stick Downton on and have some wine."

"I can't believe you've started it without me." His chuckle had me relaxing into the still pulsing warmth from my thoughts. "I'm hurt, Dor."

"I think your Magic Stars have gone to your head." I teased him as I tapped my index finger lightly to his temple.

God, why did you touch him? I asked myself as the contact sparked something in me that I thought I'd lost a long time ago. A deep simmering need that had me curious of what it would feel like to touch him in other places. A lust that I was finding impossible to step away from.

"I don't think so," his murmur was so gravelly that I had to swallow back the sigh that bubbled up my throat as his raspy words worked their way down my body. He was so close. I could feel the heat from his breath spread across my cheeks. "I think those macaroons have gone to yours."

"Maybe, it was a lot of chocolate..." I hardly recognised my wispy voice as I mused his words. I couldn't tell if it was my breaths that were so loud and fast, or his. I couldn't tell if it was my own body heat that was making those breaths almost impossible to draw in, or if it was the heat radiating from him, from our closeness.

"Not to mention all those nuts." He murmured on a muted chuckle as he pulled his wallet back out of his pocket and threw it on the counter behind him. Right back onto that place that it always seemed to find on my kitchen side. "Nut allergies can do that to a person…make them a little doo-la-ly."

I watched the way his Adam's apple bobbed as his hands touched my hips and for a moment that small contact was enough to set off these incredibly big winged butterflies that didn't seem to have enough room to flutter in my stomach, so they had no choice but to travel up my chest and throat.

"It's the peanuts that do it." My voice shook as I brushed my hot cheeks.

All I had to do was reach out. All I had to do was roll onto the tips of my toes and turn my head a tiny fraction to the side…

He cleared his throat as his hands gently squeezed my flesh and before I could make sense of it I was watching him saunter to the sofa.

The way his tight, dark jeans skimmed his backside and his thighs…

Damn the sex talk.

I hadn't been able to stop thinking about our girls' chat the last couple of weeks. And now I couldn't seem to ignore it or push it to the back of my mind. It was like some switch had flipped and I was completely and utterly screwed. My brain clouded and impaired. Unable to shut down all thoughts and imaginings of what Jake's bare skin would feel like under my hands. What his lips would feel like pressed to mine. What his breaths would taste like as they coated my mouth…

"So, where are you up to?" he asked drawing me out of my thoughts. The way he spoke so nonchalantly was like he hadn't just had his hands on me and like I hadn't been about to do something that could've possibly ruined us.

"Pamuk has popped his clogs in Lady Mary's bed," I tried to level my eager and shaky voice as I followed him to the sofa and sat next to him. "It's quite the scandal, and now she's noticing Matthew."

A bit like I'm noticing you. My throat constricted at my admission to myself.

"Episode five, then?" he asked even though it was more of a statement. He adjusted himself slightly into my deep yellow sofa as he reached for the remote and found the boxset quickly. He was even quicker to put the episode on and pause it until I'd settled next to him. "She's a right floozy, Mary, I think I'd like her."

"Of course you would, although, she's got a little too much class for you."

"I like classy women, they always turn out to be not so classy behind closed doors."

"Whatever," I couldn't help the sting in my voice as I sat a little straighter next to him and shuffled closer to the other end of the sofa. A bucket of metaphorical iced water drenching my overactive libido as Quincy's and Willow's words echoed in my head.

He's had enough practice.

"I thought you said you wanted wine?" his voice sounded a little confused as he paused the TV again. He looked at me and then the space I'd put between us. His brows pinching as his gaze travelled up my body to my face.

Crap, every one of my pores zinged as they acknowledged his gaze. Even my nipples decided to get on board the traitor train as they hardened and ached under my thin cotton vest.

As much as I wanted that wine, I had to keep my wits about

me around Jake. He was a wonderful person, an irreplaceable friend even, but when it came to women…I knew that he wasn't constant. He took fun to a whole different level, he was a pro and I wasn't even in the amateur league.

I tucked my knees up to my chest and wrapped my arms around my legs, hoping that it would be enough to stop me from inching closer to him. From allowing our bodies to touch, even a little. Even though I wanted to more than anything. I wanted to feel his warmth.

I wanted him to do that thing he did where he put his arm across the back of the sofa as we watched the telly, like he was putting it around me without even touching me. I needed that, but more than that, I need to remind myself that he was my friend.

Friends do not need or crave one another's touch. Friends do not cross lines. Consider yourself reminded, it's a disaster waiting to happen.

"I think I'm okay. You can press play now."

CHAPTER 7

T wo weeks. That's how long it'd been since the last time I'd seen Dorian or Daniel. We'd spoken on the phone a couple of times briefly, but she was all awkward and odd. Even when we were talking about the episode of Downton we were meant to be watching together down the phone to each other. Awkward was something we'd never been around one another, and for the life of me, I had no idea why.

I always held myself in check with her. Always. Which wasn't easy when we were so comfortable around each other. There were times when I found my control lapsing and myself saying things that I shouldn't because it allowed her to get deeper under my skin than she already was.

That's the thing, I'd never had a problem separating myself from other people. The only person who knew all the ins and outs outside of my family was Jamie, and I knew for a fact that he kept it all quiet. But with Dorian, there were times when I wanted to vomit everything, but then I was too scared that somehow she would completely shut me out. No one in their right mind would want to expose themselves, let alone their child, to all the ugly parts of my life.

I didn't want to expose Dorian or Daniel to it. She'd been through enough, and he…deserved better.

"You need to eat your food, Eleanor." I said, rather hypocritically as I pushed my lunch around my plate.

She sighed, her sullen face a little too pale for my liking. She squashed her salad with the bottom of her fork, her eyebrows drawing with quiet irritation.

"If you don't like the salad, we can order you something else." I knew it wasn't the salad, it was her favourite.

"I know what you're doing."

"What's that?"

"What she's been doing every fucking day. Checking up on me again, and again. Hovering from a distance." She grumbled as she pointed to the chair Mum had vacated to visit the ladies room. "I'm fine."

"Are you?" I asked as I dropped my cutlery on my food and wiped my mouth with the linen napkin from my lap. I folded it a couple of times to try and ease the trembling of my hands, before I dropped it onto my plate. "What do you expect us to do?"

"Trust me." She replied pointedly as her muddy green eyes snapped to mine.

I wanted to. More than anything, I wanted to trust that she'd stay clean. She'd realise that she was better than all the shit she put herself through.

"Trust is earned, Eleanor. It's built over time, but you make it so hard."

"I'm trying." The grit and grind of her words were like a knife to the heart. It hurt, because I knew she meant it. I knew she was trying, but she'd tried before and it hadn't lasted. Her efforts had snapped and she'd fallen down the slippery slope all over again. "It's so hard, Jake."

Her hands shook as a tear rolled down her face. For a moment, I felt sorry for her. My heart squeezed with the apparent pain that hung on her words and that dulled her eyes. I took her cutlery from her hands and put it down on the table, she looked at me confused as I grasped her hands in mine.

"It's not meant to be easy, that's why you stay away from it in the first place."

She shook her head as she took her hands back and said, "It's always so easy for you, though. Everything has always been so easy, Ryan gets it. He understands me. You're so perfect, so clean…so pristine with your career and…and…"

Anger simmered inside me at her words. Easy? She thought this was easy for me? Watching her destroy herself?

"This isn't about me." I growled. I took a deep stabling breath before I continued, "Make me understand, Eleanor, because you're right, I don't. You've had every privilege, every opportunity…you've had everything you could possibly need. *Everything*…Mum and Dad have bent over backwards for you."

"Actually, Mum and Dad are dead, they gave me nothing. Absolutely nothing." She snapped, the lines of her face dark and cold.

"Don't start this, you didn't know them. The only parents you've ever known, you've ever had, are Levi and Ruth. You don't get to blame your problems on the dead. You don't get to feel sorry for yourself over this." My throat clogged like it did every time we had this conversation. "You have parents that love you, that have done and will continue to do everything they can for you. I get that you feel like you missed out on knowing Isobel and David, in some ways you did. I know Ryan's told you a lot of things, but he's only told you the good stuff."

The begrudging look on her face shifted and gradually morphed into a tell me more expression.

"You don't need to know everything, you only need to realise that although they were our mother and father, Ruth and Levi are our mum and dad." It was the truth, she didn't need to know that our father wasn't a great dad, that he wasn't a good husband, and she didn't need to know that our mother enabled him.

David was a selfish drunk. I could still remember all the times he'd get home late from work, clambering loudly up the stairs and through the hallway until all I could hear in the stark silence of our house was her tears. Her cries, because all she wanted was for him to be there, to care. He wasn't violent, but he was volatile with his indifference.

"Is everything okay?" Mum asked as she sat back into her chair, she carefully spread the napkin over her lap again before she looked between me and Eleanor.

"Yes." I smiled a little too forcibly.

"Yeah." Eleanor sighed like she had been exhausted by our conversation.

"So, I was thinking," Mum announced a little too gingerly. "Actually, it was more of a hope, that maybe we could all go to the concert at the Royal Albert together. It'd be nice to go as a family, maybe you could bring Miles, Eleanor."

"I don't know, he's on a tight curfew now that he's playing for a big team." She replied slightly brusquely.

I caught our server's eye as he walked past and signalled to him for the bill with my card in my hand.

"It's for your brother's birthday, maybe you can come, even if he can't?"

"Maybe."

"You don't have to, if you don't want to." I volunteered, she looked like she was still a little on the defensive about us wanting to spend time with her. "It's not a big deal, Mum." I added before she pushed.

The waiter came back with the card machine. As usual Mum tried to argue that it was her that should be paying for her children's meals, where she got that logic I had no idea. It didn't stick with me, she'd done enough for us, this was the least I could do.

"I have to get back to work," I said as I finished paying and put my card back in my wallet.

"Let me know about the concert." Mum told Eleanor as we made our way out of the restaurant.

"I'll think about it, and I'll check with Miles." She smiled tersely as she hoisted her raspberry pink, cushioned designer bag on her shoulder and then covered most of her face with some over the top bug eye sunglasses even though there was no sunshine.

She wrapped her coat tighter around her body and then

tightened the belt to the point that it looked like there was nothing of her.

"Alright. Well, I'll see you soon, darling." Mum stroked her face before she pulled her into an awkwardly tense hug. She gave her a quick flash of a smile as she let her go and turned to me, "I'll see you this weekend?"

"Of course." I gave her a quick squeeze and murmured in her ear, "Stop worrying, you'll end up driving yourself and her insane. Okay?"

She pulled away slightly as she cupped my face and nodded before she kissed each of my cheeks and cooed, "Bni." *My son.*

I hailed her a passing black cab and it wasn't until she'd gone that Eleanor said, "She loves you more than anyone else, you know that?"

"Don't. Don't go there, she loves you. She drives herself crazy with worry for you." I told her as she hailed herself another passing taxi.

"Maybe." She shrugged as she turned towards me again removing her sunglasses. Her sheepish gaze looked up at me through her long, dark lashes. "But you're her favourite, bni." She said the last word a little bitterly, like she was mocking our mother's words.

"I am pretty fucking awesome." I chuckled trying to lighten the mood before she left. She shook her head as she rolled her eyes, resisting as I tugged her in for a quick hug. "On a serious note," I said as she leaned her head onto my shoulder, "stop thinking about all the shit you don't need to think about. You confuse yourself, with all that stuff. They love you, I love you, we all love you, chipmunk. We worry about you because we only want what's best for you."

She nodded slowly before she huffed, "Stop calling me chipmunk."

"Do you still sound like one when you get all excited?" I chortled into her ear, sounding more like a banshee than a chipmunk.

"Dick." She pushed off me.

I grasped her hand as she turned towards the cab again and opened the door. "Listen, keep trying, okay? And if you need anything, I'm always here."

Her eyes rounded as her gaze met mine, and for a split second, she looked like my baby sister again. Not the girl who lost her way and made some shitty decisions.

I helped her into the cab, kissing the top of her head before I closed the door and watched her go.

I hoped that she'd keep what I told her in mind. I'd rather get a call from her, asking for help, than a call from my mother telling me she needed help.

I must've stood there for a little too long, because by the time my haze had cleared, the cab was gone from sight.

"She was a little young for you?" A familiar teasing voice sounded from behind me.

"Are you stalking me now?" I turned to find two shining hazel eyes scowling at me. Willow.

"You wish, I had an audition at the theatre down the road. I'm meeting my sister for a late lunch here, some guy is meeting her after."

I widened my grin as my insides churned. My hands fisted in my coat pockets. Dorian was going on a date? I hadn't seen her for the last couple of weeks, and even though I'd told myself that she was busy and she had better things to do, I couldn't deny the truth anymore. She was avoiding me. I had no idea why, but there was this desperate need inside me to know and fix whatever it was that I'd done to result in her evasion of me.

"So, the teenager…" Willow scoffed.

"Before you say something offensive, she's twenty-nine and my sister."

"That's your sister?" she asked, sounding amazed and perplexed at the same time.

"Yeah."

"God, you must've kept your parents' hands full for them to wait that long." I chuckled a little tensely at her remark, and before I had to think of something to say she asked, "What?"

"Nothing. I need to get back to the clinic, I have an appointment in a couple of hours." I sighed.

"She's pretty." She smiled at me, almost too softly for her. "I've seen her at a couple of parties and she was meant to be in the murder mystery production I was in at the beginning of the year, but they said she pulled out last minute."

My stomach dropped to my feet, panic flooding me as I tried to figure out what to say. "Ummm…"

"I was surprised because she was better than some of the older, more experienced cast."

"She's definitely got great acting skills." Pity she only put them to good use when she was trying to hide her problem from us.

"She does. You want to know what's funny? I thought she looked familiar, I wracked my brain trying to figure out where I'd seen her before. I guess now I know."

I smiled at her, I wasn't quite sure what else to say. I didn't want to talk about Eleanor, and my stomach was still in knots thinking of Dorian meeting with some guy, as Willow had put it.

"Are you okay?" she asked, her face pinched with concern. "You're not being a dick."

"I'm not always a dick."

"Oh, I know it's not always…just ninety-nine percent of the time." She chuckled. "Seriously, though?"

"I'm good. But I really do need to go, catch up soon?"

"Gin Palace?"

"Sure."

"Saturday evening?"

"That works."

"Good. Mum has Daniel, so maybe Dory can come too. We're trying to get her back out there."

"Out there?"

"Yep, you know…having fun, meeting people, having sex…she needs to have a life outside of work and motherhood."

"Oh. Great."

"Don't sound too excited."

I'm not. "Yay. Happy?"

"It's a start, maybe we can get you laid too and they might be able to yank whatever stick has gotten lodged up your arse out." She chimed.

"Whatever." I groaned as I looked at my watch. "I'll see you then."

"Okay." She waved as she turned for the restaurant and I started towards the clinic. "Oh, and Jake?"

I turned to find her standing by the door, "Yeah?"

"Cheer up."

I couldn't help but laugh as I crossed the road. Willow was abso-fucking-lutely nuts, but she was great at disarming you with her brand of crazy.

CHAPTER 8

Dorian

I handed Mum Daniel's weekend bag, my heart always doing that apprehensive squeeze it did when I said goodbye to him. It's not that I didn't trust him with his grandparents, it was just that he was my companion. I knew that it wasn't the normal way to feel about your child, but it had been only me and him for so long. Since the beginning.

He was the be all and end all of my world. And I struggled with letting go when it came to him.

"Will you stop looking at him like you're never going to see him again?" Mum muttered as she took his coat from my hand and flung it over her forearm much like she had thrown his backpack over her shoulder.

"That's not funny." I rasped in return, my thoughts

immediately going down a dark road.

She pulled him back to the front door from where he stood behind her, "Give your mama a cuddle, Daniel."

He hitched his brow at her even as his arms wrapped around my waist. He did that sigh that he always did when he was happy and relaxed.

"I love you, baby." I whispered into his ear as I crouched in front of him.

"I love you more, mama hen." He murmured in return with a soft giggle.

"I've put his spare inhaler and his menthol plug-in in his bag." I said as I looked up at my mother, my arms tightening around my boy a little more. "He's been a little stuffy today, so keep an eye, and if you think he's getting worse give me a call."

"Dory, he's eight years old, he'll be fine. I've got an inhaler for him at home and a menthol plug-in in his room."

"Don't argue with me, okay?" I snapped at her defensively. "Not about this."

"I'm not, I'm only trying to point out that you're stressing for nothing. Stop worrying and go have fun. Live a little, please, and don't worry about us. Your father and I have him covered."

"She's right, Mum, you should go wash your hair out." Daniel smirked up at me. "We're going to be good, Nanny and I are going to teach Grandad how to play Mario."

"It's let your hair down, not wash your hair out." I sighed as he gave me one last squeeze and let go. "Good luck with Grandad."

"Luck? Please, Mum, I don't need luck. I have skills." He laughed as he regurgitated something that no doubt Jake had taught him.

Jake. I'd been avoiding him like the plague for the last couple of weeks. There was this tectonic shift between us that was shaking things up inside me. It was making me feel things that were impossible to ignore and forget.

"Right, we better go before you start tearing up. I have his spare uniform, so if you don't feel up to picking him up tomorrow, I'll take him to school on Monday. Okay?"

"I don't know what you think's going to happen tonight, but we're not going crazy."

"When was the last time you went crazy, or simply had fun?" She marked me with one of her wide eyed *I dare you to lie to me* stares.

"Don't you start with your *you only live once* preaching, I'm well aware, which is why I focus on my baby."

"I'm not a baby!" Daniel growled from the stairs.

"He's not a baby, he's a gorgeous, smart and joy of a boy, and you need to keep that in mind when you incessantly worry. We'll be fine."

"Okay, okay…I get it, I'm a worrier. That's what I do, I worry about my son."

"Well, for once, worry about yourself and having some well earned fun. Act your age, not mine." She smiled her crooked, tilted head smile that she reserved for when she felt a little emotional. Which she did often when we spoke of my little letting go predicament. "You look lovely by the way."

"You think?" I looked down my black jeans on black cold shoulder blouse attire. "Not too much black?"

"Well, I mean…it could do with some colour." She mused as she looked behind me into the airing cupboard that had become my shoe store. "Those patent yellow Louboutin's are nice, especially with the Mulberry your sister and I got you last Christmas."

"A little bright for winter, no?"

"I think you'd get away with it, we're on the cusp of the season change."

"I suppose." I murmured as I watched Daniel sitting on the bottom step of our flight of stairs, his shoulders hunched as he concentrated on the game on his iPad.

"We better go before Willow gets here and starts whinging about how late you are."

"Don't, she'll find something to moan about, she always does."

"She takes after your grandmother," she rolled her eyes dramatically, something she and Willow had down to a T. "Wear a coat, it's cold out there and I can feel the rain in the air. Those clouds are bearing down."

I watched as she made her way down the stairs, Daniel getting up to follow her. "I checked the weather app, it's a crisp, dry night with mild gusts of wind."

"It's lying to you, I promise, I can feel the moisture in the air." She looked up as she got to the top of the next set of steps and smiled wide.

"Bye, Mum." Daniel waved.

"Bye, sweetie. Make sure you do four puffs before bed, okay?"

"I know." I knew he knew, but I needed another thing to say, to have him look at me. His light brown eyes crinkling at the edges as he gave me his wide closed lip grin. "Have fun."

I couldn't help but laugh at his command, his voice echoing up the stairwell as he disappeared from view. I continued listening for a bit, until even the sound of their footsteps had disappeared. My heart beating a little too fast as it repeatedly echoed my love for him.

* * *

Willow ordered her usual Rum Collins, the cocktail waiter giving her a weird look as she gave him specific instructions on how the rum was to replace the gin in a Tom Collins and instead of a cherry and lemon twist garnish she asked for mint and a lime wedge.

She was very particular about her drinks. Me, not so much. I was happy to go with the sweetest, easiest to drink concoction… normally they were also the deadliest. But I had been nagged to have fun and let my hair down, and for once, I needed to do it.

Work was insane, I was regretting taking on the woman suing her ex-husband for her boob-job going wrong. It was all a bloody mess, and honestly, it was pointless. She was going to win, because precedent in that particular scenario was sketchy.

It should've been easy, but their divorce was still being finalised, and she kept bringing things up that quite frankly were irrelevant to my case. The meeting I'd had earlier in the week with her divorce solicitor, had been pointless considering all he'd conveyed was what I already knew. The whole thing was litigation hell, and if it wouldn't affect my record, I would've dropped it already.

As we waited for our drinks Willow offhandedly said, "Jake should be here soon, he was dropping his sister home and then heading here." She smiled down at her phone. "She's really pretty."

My heart sped in my chest, pretty much clanging my ribcage like a gong. "You didn't say he was coming." I tried to comment coolly.

"Yeah, sorry, I must've forgotten. I saw him before we met for lunch the other day."

"Oh."

"Oh? What's *oh* about it?" she asked, her brows scrunching as she looked me over quizzically. "I think he had lunch with his sister, I only saw him sticking her in a cab, but he seemed off."

"You saw him sticking her in a cab. How'd you know it was his sister?" I asked as the waiter put our drinks on the table. For all she knew it could've been one of his classy women that wasn't so classy behind closed doors.

So bitter.

I'm not bitter.

Fine, jealous then.

I'm not!

Are.

Not.

So are.

Shut up!

I gritted my teeth as I put an end to the fight with myself…in my head, as any normal person would do, right? Another reason why this whole Jake thing was a bloody stupid idea. He was driving me insane, even though I'd put space between us.

The waiter smiled at me as he put our drinks down in front of us. His smile lingering a little too long in my direction. "Thank you."

Willow narrowed her eyes on me and then diverted her attention to the waiter, "Can I order a Dirty Martini, please?"

"Of course." He nodded at her.

"No gin, tequila. Oh, and make it extra strong…ah, and

not too much olive brine. Thanks." She watched as he walked away, and then turned back to me. "I thought she was a date or something, she looked too young, but…"

"Why are you ordering him a drink?"

"How'd you know it's for him?"

"Tequila." Jake didn't drink often, but when he did, tequila was his drink of choice. I don't think I'd ever seen him drink any alcohol other than tequila or wine.

"Anyway, his sister is stunning."

"You keep saying." I quipped.

"Sorry, it's just that I was thinking about it and it hit me, we've never met any of his family. He doesn't talk about them… and get this, you remember the Agatha Christie production I was in last year?" She took a sip of her cocktail and hummed her pleasure. "Well, she was meant to be a part of it, but from one day to the next she quit."

"And?"

"It's strange, don't you think?"

"Willow, people quit jobs all the time." I sighed.

"Yeah, but I saw her out at a party the weekend before and she was a hot mess."

I took a long gulp of my lychee and hibiscus martini, "You're a hot mess at the best of times."

"I know, but it's weird, I've never quit a job like that…and her hot mess makes my hot mess look rather well put together."

"You're prying, and you're prying with the wrong person because I've never even laid eyes on her." I said a little too gruffly.

I was a little jealous that she'd met his sister, that she knew something about Jake that I didn't.

Maybe if you stopped ignoring him…

"Seriously, why are you so grouchy?"

"I'm not." I snapped, completely disproving my reply.

"You are. You're the kind of grouchy I get when I'm horny and can't get any…maybe you two should help each other out if he's still acting weird."

"I don't think so," I rasped a little too quickly, "if I ever went there, I'd expect you to talk sense into me."

"Probably for the best, wouldn't want to ruin your friendship if things went wrong…or if he didn't live up to his reputation. Although, I have to admit that I am a little curious."

"Really?"

"Yeah, although, I'd probably kill him before we got anywhere and it's nice having one straight guy that I'm friends with. You know?" Her laughter turned into a snort as her eyes became stuck behind me, and I felt him.

I felt him even before I heard him or even saw him.

I felt his eyes on me and I felt it when his gaze left me.

The way my heart swelled in my chest like it was being pumped full of warm air when I could feel his eyes on me and the way it deflated when I couldn't.

Traitor! I accused it as it raced the minute our eyes met. God, he looked good with his stubble and his black t-shirt and black snug jeans.

"Did you two co-ordinate your outfits?" Willow chuckled as he sat beside her in our corner booth and she put his drink in front of him.

A feeling of complete disappointment settled in my stomach and tightened my chest.

Why didn't he sit next to me?

His eyes met mine for a moment and I looked for his smile. I looked for the soft and warm gaze he always gave me with his deep and drawn out hi or hey. It wasn't there, he didn't even greet me.

To be fair he didn't greet Willow either, but that didn't mean that I wasn't feeling the loss of his words.

"Drink it!"

"What the fuck is it?" He grimaced at the murky concoction as he held it up in front of him.

"That is *you* in a drink." She laughed and encouraged him to taste it with her hand.

He sniffed it again before he took a sip, his grimace deepening as he shuddered. "The only thing this shit is, is vile. It fucking stinks and it tastes like fucking piss…that is not me in a drink."

"I meant the name, Dirty Hornitini, not the taste. It was bound to be a disappointment with the lack of rum."

He pushed it away from him and signalled over the waiter.

"Sir?"

"Sorry mate, can I get a water to wash that monstrosity off my taste buds, and a tequila on ice. Make it a double. Dorian?" his lips quirked as he said my name and it felt like an answered prayer.

"I'll have the same again, please."

"I'll have the same again too." Willow chimed from the corner of the booth. "In fact bring two of each, that'll save you having to come back and forth. Just the one water though, in case you were wondering."

The waiter laughed at her as he collected our empty glasses and Jake's unfinished drink, shaking his head as he headed back to the bar with our order.

"I'm going to empty my bladder now, getting up in these heels will be a bitch after a few." Jake stood to let her past and then sat back down. She took a couple of steps toward the loos and then turned around, hands on her hips as she urged, "When I come back, at least try to look like you want to have fun."

The silence that fell between us was awkward to say the least. There was this current that had so much to say, yet, it felt like all words had been robbed from our vocabulary.

I looked around the deep mahogany table top for something to invest my attention on, and when that failed they moved to the deep emerald green velvet seats.

"Don't pick your nail polish." His rumbly voice cut through our background music deafened silence as his hand landed on top of both of mine.

I relished the warmth that blanketed my skin. The feel of his skin on mine, and the weight of his hand. It stupidly made me want to cry with relief.

Who fucking cries because someone touches their hand? Seriously?

"I can't help it." I croaked out, answering myself at the same time as I reminded him of my nervous habit.

"Why're you nervous?" He squeezed my hand gently before he took his back.

My eyes rushed to meet his like they had to make sure that we maintained some sort of contact. Eye, physical…it didn't matter. It never mattered with him. It was the fact that he was there, and that he saw me. That he wanted to be there with me. And as I'd started relaxing, the thought made my insides clench all over again.

What if he doesn't want to be anywhere near you?

It didn't even make sense to ask myself that. I'd put space between us because I didn't want to complicate things. Because, if I was honest with myself, I'd been jealous of his off-handed comment about women.

A generalised comment.

God, you're fucking idiotic sometimes.

"Dor?" he rasped my name, and my stupid insides felt like they were floating.

"Yeah?"

"You didn't answer my question."

"Oh, I'm not…it's just…" Just what?

His dark eyes searched my face, there was this uncharacteristic uncertainty clouding them. "Just?"

"You didn't say hello." *Oh, Jesus, sweet child of Mary and Joseph.*

Face planting the table, that would've probably been more dignified.

Blood rushed to my face as he looked at me quizzically. Like I'd said something completely nonsensical. Which I had. Which was also not like me. And to make matters worse, in case he didn't hear me, I had to go repeat and clarify my ridiculous statement. "When you got here, you didn't say hi and you sat over there."

Do yourself a favour and shut up, Dorian!

He barked out a laugh, his eyes regaining some of their shine even as I felt my insides wilt with embarrassment.

Great, laugh at me why don't you?

What was wrong with me? Why couldn't I have kept my mouth shut? My eyes stung with hot, foolish, angry tears.

My teeth mercilessly cut into my lip as every cell in my body became very aware of the way he was looking at me. The stupid grin on his face and the shameless laughter.

I don't even know what possessed me to do it, but every one of my instincts beckoned me to run. To spare myself even the tiniest drop of dignity. So I did, I ran. For the first time in my life, I ran from something, and it just so happened to be Jake.

CHAPTER 9

Jake

I was still a little awestruck by her statement. It took me a moment to get up and go after her. I wasn't prepared for her to say something like that to me, and with the surprise all I could do was laugh.

Arsehole!

I couldn't help it though. I had to, it was my go-to thing. Some people bite their nails, others develop an awkward and unrelenting itch…I laugh. It was my shock response.

I followed her out of the side entrance, glad she hadn't chosen to go through the busy hotel lobby in which the bar was situated.

"What were you even thinking? I mean seriously? You didn…" I could hear her rambling to herself loudly as I chased her up the steep side street.

"Dorian?" I called as I grasped her wildly swinging arm. "Will you stop, please?"

"You laughed at me." She spat as she spun towards me in her rich yellow sky-high heels. The grit in her tone made her already smoky voice huskier and sultry, even with the bashfulness that softened it.

The way she looked at me, the hurt in her eyes, it was staggering. I had no idea what was happening, but the first thing to pop into my head was, "Hi."

"That's not even funny!" she hissed as she tried to yank her wrist out of my hand.

"I was…you said…" I tried to explain that I was only giving her what she wanted. I was saying hello.

I hadn't quite realised how much strength was inside her slender frame, until I was having to hold on tighter than I ever had to a woman. Not that I'd done much holding onto a woman outside the bedroom, but…

Probably not the right time to be thinking about holding on to other women, bellend.

A lot of things seemed to be happening, it was a snowball effect. One minute we were standing in the middle of an abandoned side street that was barely lit up by the here and there lamp posts in one of the busiest cities in the world. The next minute we were tucked into a darkened emergency exit alcove, that probably stank of piss, and yet all I could see, smell and hear was her.

"Jake." Her rasp had her voice and breath catching as she drew out the A in my name. And all the other times she'd uttered my name, all hundreds and maybe thousands of other times that my name had left her lips seemed insignificant. "Jacob."

Her hand grasped my t-shirt and twisted in it as the other clung to my shoulder. Her eyes looked between mine and as her breaths quickened and splayed on my jaw they rendered me breathless.

She was so fucking pretty. She made my hands ache to touch her, any part of her in anyway.

"God, Dor." I was so, so thirsty for her lips. Her glossy, peachy lips that always looked so sweet and plump.

You're not even making sense dickhead!

Her shoulders hit the granite slab wall behind her and a whoosh of fruity, florally breath warmed the skin on my neck. The skin on her bare shoulders prickling as the nippy, fresh winter bluster swept our little alcove.

I couldn't help but watch, mesmerised, as she licked her lips and when I cupped her jaw she gasped. It was breathy and soft and I could taste the yearning in her exhale and I could feel it in the way her eyes were fixed on mine.

I tried so hard to bite back the need, the greed for her that was boiling over inside of me. Burning each and every one of my organs, making my veins engorge with my thick, bubbling blood.

She smiled as I tipped her chin up, holding her face to mine.

"Pretty girl, you should tell me to stop." I breathed as I kissed the tip of her nose lightly. She hummed as she leaned her face closer to mine and rested her hands flat on my stomach.

It felt like no touch I'd ever felt before. It was soft, tentative and warm. It was gentle. I couldn't think of a woman ever touching me like that, like they wanted to feel me and not what I could do for them. And for the first time ever, I wanted to be gentle too. Not just because I wanted to savour the moment or even her, I wanted to give her some of what she was giving me.

Her eyes closed as her tongue licked across her lips, her wet breath coating my mouth as I cupped her face and brought her closer to me. Her nails dug lightly into my torso as I kissed the flushed apple of one cheek and then the other. The heels of her shoes scrapped along the ground as she brought herself impossibly closer to me. Our belt buckles knocked as one of her legs tucked between mine and she straddled one of my thighs.

"Jake, please…" She whispered as our noses touched, our breaths mingled and our body heat permeated between us.

I kissed the corner of her mouth as I inhaled the scent of her florally shampoo and her fruity perfume. It was so overwhelming and encompassing together with the feel of her hands reaching up between us and her fingers hooking into the rounded collar of my t-shirt.

Her breath hitched when I ran my lips faintly over her plump cupid's bow to the other corner of her lips.

"Kiss me." She murmured.

I planted a slow, languorous kiss where her laugh line crossed through the faintest of beauty freckles. Something you had to look for in order to even know it was there. She tilted her face, her fingertips caressing the hollow of my throat and then sliding over my shoulders until they hooked around my neck.

My mouth watered and if it was at all possible, my heart rammed into my ribs even harder and faster than it already was and…

"Shit." She pulled away from me far too quickly.

"Huh?" I watched as she pulled her buzzing and flashing phone from her back pocket and held it between us. "Typical!"

"Willow?" she answered.

I was about to kiss her and she answered her fucking phone. It was probably the most insulting thing a woman had ever done to me. Especially after she'd asked me to do it.

"We're coming back in now." Her tone was curt as she huffed down the phone to Willow. She ended the call as she clasped her phone tightly in her hands. "I left my bag, our bags...she's pissed."

That's all she's going to say?

"Dor..."

"I know," she rasped before she cleared her throat. "It's probably for the best, especially with your taste for classy women." She started back towards the bar. Her heels clacking with her every step as I followed her.

Yeah, no. It wasn't for the best and there was no fucking way I was letting anything go.

"I suppose since you're having midweek dates..."

"What?" She stopped dead in her tracks and turned to me. "Excuse me?"

"Nothing." I shook my head as I walked around her.

"Wait!" she growled as she grabbed me by the crook of my elbow. "You can't just walk away from me."

"You walked away first." I blurted before I could think better of it, and the hurt on her face was gutting.

"I-I...I'm sorry." She whispered sheepishly. "We're friends and..."

"Dorian, people can be friends as well as other things." I caressed the bridge of her nose before I ushered her the rest of the way back to the bar.

My chest still felt achy with the regret of what I'd said to her. I knew how hurt she'd been all the times Phillip had walked away from her. Physically, emotionally, even metaphorically, he'd managed to leave her time and again. I knew that it was a sensitive spot for her, but stupidly I'd still said the words.

"So, we're friends?" she asked with a hopeful trill to her words as she walked beside me.

"We are."

We walked back into the hotel through the side entrance, she took a few silent steps beside me towards the bar.

"Do you still want to kiss me?" her breathless question caught me off-guard as we stepped back into the bar.

It took me a little longer than usual to get my words together as I watched her watch me with uncertainty blanketing her face.

"I don't know, you'll have to see." I chuckled, my breath pushed out of me as she slapped my stomach.

"That's not funny."

"Oh, I know."

CHAPTER 10

Dorian

The crazy thing about being a single mother is that even when I got that odd night off, in the back of my mind, I was still parenting. I watched as Willow went through drink after drink, and all the while I was nursing mine because I couldn't bring myself to get into a state where I was helpless. The thought alone was enough to make me shudder. I wasn't a control freak, but my responsibilities were impossible to forget.

What if something happened to Daniel? I'd need to be fully cognizant and able to act. It was something that had been triggered the moment I'd found out about him.

It had taken me a while to grapple with that overwhelming feeling of needing to protect him. At the time it'd felt crazy.

It'd felt like all of a sudden I wasn't just me anymore. And then Phillip left and that feeling completely took over me, and it never waned. I think that's why I struggled with letting others step in. I struggled with letting go.

So it didn't make much sense to me why I'd let the whole thing with Jake escalate.

Sure, I could be big enough and admit that I might like him a little more than I should.

Honestly? I liked him a lot more than I should, he was a distraction and he had this way of making me forget about everything except for the moment we were in.

It's not that it was a bad thing, it was just that living in the present moment when you have someone's future in your hands, it felt reckless. And that wasn't me anymore.

I used to think that I had forever. I thought forever was a thing, but life had set me right on that one.

Forever was an optimistic word that people used to fool themselves into thinking that they had all the time in the world. But actually, you don't.

Time is limited. It's a circle that pulls you in and turns and turns about you until it decides to stop. And then you stop. Then you cease to exist and all that's left of you are the people you chose to love.

I had been one of those people to someone.

To Pip.

I think that I'd let him become my time circle. I'd let him become the thing that turned and spun around me. My future. And then he stopped and it was only me and our unborn son. Then I'd ceased to be me, and I'd become someone that wasn't really anyone.

That's what'd happened when I had let someone become my whole life.

Now I had my son, and yes, he was my whole life, but the love I felt for him was different. It was different to anything I'd ever felt. It was incomparable to any other longing that had ever inflated my chest. It was something that made me...me.

Yet, as I sat thinking over my past, there was this completely different longing simmering deep in my belly and shaking up my chest, and it was all for someone that had a way of making me feel like that silly, naïve girl all over again. And as much as I wanted to ignore it, I couldn't.

Jake saw me. He saw me far too clearly, and it scared the living daylights out of me.

It was shocking and something about it left me disconcerted. He could see through me so easily, like the walls that I'd built around me were nothing. Like for him, they were non-existent.

"You should probably take the ring off, you know. You're not exactly approachable with an engagement rock on your finger." Willow gestured toward my hand with her cocktail highball.

I slipped my hand under the table, onto my lap, my other hand covering it like it was protecting the thing from her words. She'd been nagging me about it on and off for the last few years. It's not that I'd never taken it off, it was that every time I did I felt this odd sense of guilt.

That ring had meant something, and meaningful things didn't deserve to get discarded, or abandoned...forgotten about.

"I hardly think it matters." Jake sighed, as he signalled for the waiter again, before saying, "We both know that it's not her hands guys will be looking at."

"I meant decent guys, dickwaffle." She retorted with a snide grin. "That's what she needs, a decent guy."

"And you know about decent guys how?" he teased her. "Decent guys like decent women, and we both know you don't fit that category."

"You mean that because I'm a woman who happens to enjoy herself, like you do, that I'm not decent?"

"Don't play the down beaten sex card on me."

"You're a fucktard."

"Who's being derogatory now?"

"I never said—" She started to retaliate before he cut her off, "You implied it."

"I don't get why you're even butting into our conversation." She rolled her eyes and I couldn't help the laugh that escaped me. That was Willow down to the marrow, she'd rampage around and when she didn't get the last word she'd throw a strop or make some childish comment about the state of conversation.

Growing up it'd been so annoying and more often than not, things would get heated between us. Sometimes, if she was being particularly exasperating, I'd have to get physical. Although, most of the time she'd play dirty and I'd be the one with the nasty graze or scratch.

As we grew older I began to appreciate her foot-in-mouth disorder. The more aware I became of people, the more I liked that she didn't give a shit. Well, she acted like she didn't, but the reality was that she was a bit like a Gobstopper. Her outer layers were hard and took time to get through, but at her core she was soft and she cared more than she would ever admit.

The waiter approached our table already with another full round of drinks. I'd noticed how since coming back in Jake had swapped the hard-core stuff for a soft drink. I'd only ever seen him drunk once in my life—at Jamie's wedding. That'd been such a long time ago. When things with Phillip had slowly started unravelling without my knowledge.

"Thank you." I said as he put another Lychee and Hibiscus martini in front of me.

He smiled at me softly, almost tentatively like he was trying to read me. "I thought you might want this too." He lowered his voice as he came a little closer. He took a bottle of Perrier from his tray and bent over me to put it in front of me with a glass of ice.

His stark blue eyes met mine with an impish grin and it was only then I realised that he was flirting with me. Badly.

Flirting had never been something I was very good at. I always felt too stupidly self-conscious to actually enjoy it. But even in my inexpertise I knew that his flirting game was quite simply atrocious.

"How thoughtful of you…"

"P-Paul?" His voice shook as he questioned his own name and I had to shove the giggle that was trying to bubble its way up my throat all the way back down.

"Thank you, Paul." I murmured as I watched his gaze drop from my eyes to the rosary type beaded necklace that was wound around my neck and fell into the lace neckline of my cold shoulder blouse. I watched the way his throat bobbed as his eyes dropped lower…

"We'll take the bill." Jake hissed. "We've got somewhere to be."

"Do we?" Willow quipped as she took a long pull of her fresh drink. Her eyes were glowing as she watched the waiter almost fall over himself as he straightened.

"Yep, we do." He replied as he took his card out and slapped it on the dark table top. "Can we make this quick, please?"

"Of course." The kid blustered as he picked up Jake's card from the table and started towards the bar only to return and put the card back, "I don't need that, I'll bring the machine over. Sorry."

Willow's cackle burst through the blistering quiet between me and Jake. I could feel his hard assessing gaze on me as I pulled on the beaded cord around my neck.

"Oh my life, we have to get you out more often." She wheezed through her uncontainable laughter. "Did you see his face? Bless, I bet he wouldn't even know what to do with a pair of tits."

Jake gave her a glowering side eye and then narrowed his eyes on mine. I thought he'd say something, but he just looked at me and he seemed more pissed off than annoyed.

"I'm going to the loo, all this laughing is going to make me pee my pants." Willow chuckled as she pulled a few twenties from her purse and dropped them next to Jake's card.

She stumbled slightly as she got up from her seat, but quickly righted herself even before Jake managed to offer her some steadying support. "Good thing we're moving on!"

"Maybe we should call you a cab instead."

"Don't be so fucking stupid." She retorted hastily and clearly at me before she sauntered off to the toilet.

Her hands pulled at the short hem of her tight, black dress and I had to chuckle at the way guys followed her path with their eager eyes.

"Oh boy, she's on one tonight." I sighed as Jake grabbed the money she'd left on the table and stuffed it back in her bag. And I suddenly felt very conscious of the fact that it was just the two of us again. "So, where to next?"

"Where'd you want to go, Dorian?" He looked at me pensively. His voice was all rumbly and gruff. It made my stomach flip and my heart squeeze.

Was that what he sounded like first thing in the morning? When he woke up, before he cleared his vocal chords?

"I don't know, where do you want to go?"

"A friend of a friend's playing a gig, I said I might meet them for a drink later."

"I should probably get Willow home, I don't fancy going out on the razzmatazz with her when she's already half giddy. I could do with the early night anyway."

"You can come with me, you both can." He smiled as he sighed and just as quickly a scowl marred his expression as he gritted, "Here comes your new fanboy."

"Stop it."

"Thank you, Paul." He crooned sarcastically sweet. "He's barely legal."

"I thought you said that legal is legal, barely or not."

He gave me a pouty glare, and I knew that it wasn't meant to be, but it was cute on him. His full lips jutting out in a pout and his soft, warm eyes contradicting the unimpressed look he was giving me.

I shuffled along the curved booth seat until I was sat next to him. I watched as he took the card reader from a very silent and sheepish looking waiter, I knew better than to argue about splitting the tab. He would only get antsy about it.

He stabbed his pin into the machine, all the while his eyes

kept flitting to the kid who'd been serving us.

I inched a little closer and whispered, "If it makes you feel better, he's not my type."

My cheeks heated the minute the words were out and my heart might have cracked a few ribs with how violently it thrummed in my chest.

What the hell, Dorian?

My vision went a little blurry as embarrassment made me cringe from head to toe. I couldn't even blame alcohol for my loose tongue and my even looser actions.

Jesus twatting Christ.

I scooted away from him, but before I could put any real distance between us, his hand fell on my thigh. The heat from his skin permeating my black jeans and setting off tingles in the pit of my stomach.

My toes curled in my heels as he squeezed and pulled me close to him again. My hand fell on his and man, my breath jolted out between my lips.

He dropped his card onto the table as he turned his face to mine, his cheeks sucked in as he studied me.

He took a deep breath, his hand slid up my thigh to my hip as he turned his body into mine. "You don't say shit like that and then make a run for it."

Ironic because in my head there was a very loud alarm that screamed at me to leg it. That warned me about how much of a bad idea this closeness between us was.

"What's your type, pretty girl?" he rasped into the confined space between us.

My throat swelled with the choking beat of my erratic heart. "I don't...I...I..."

My tongue curled around the words pulsing behind my lips. *Someone like you.*

Him. I didn't have a type, but if I did, it would be him. I was so sure of it. Sure enough that not a single brain cell managed to muster the courage to question it.

His dark eyes meandered over my face, coming back to my lips again and again.

"Let me know when you decide." He rasped as his hand dropped from my hip and onto the seat before he turned away and went about putting his card back into his wallet.

He stood and grabbed my coat, holding it up for me. I scooted to the end of the bench seat and got up, I threaded one arm into my coat and before I could move my hair, his hand was curling around it. He twisted it firmly at the nape of my neck and pulled it to the side, and as I pushed my other arm into my coat sleeve he said, "You're playing a dangerous game, Dor. Don't mistake my niceties for compunction. I don't chase, but if I did, it wouldn't take me long to catch you."

His fingers trailed along the collar of my coat, the tips of his fingers lightly scraping along my neck. My whole body felt ready to collapse into itself with all the shuddering sparks rioting through me.

He dipped his face into my neck as his fingers combed through the tousled lengths of my hair, pulling here and there and making the aching roots zing with electricity.

His breath was so hot on my neck and so bloody wonderful. Just as I thought I couldn't take anymore, he took in a deep breath, groaning as he breathed all the heated air between us into his lungs.

My skin pulled tight all around my bones and had I not been

sandwiched between him and the table, I would've collapsed into one big boneless mess at his feet.

I shuddered as he took a sudden step back. My body wincing at the loss of his warmth on me.

I had to take a couple of seconds to find my very wobbly feet again. Maybe wearing one of the highest pair of heels I had wasn't the best idea.

I'd forgotten how giddy it felt to be the epicentre of someone's attention. How thrilling it was to feel someone else's need for you.

* * *

The plan had been to go home. Go home, have a cup of tea and possibly do a couple of episodes of Downton. I hadn't gone near it the last couple of weeks, it felt wrong watching it without Jake. Especially when I was avoiding him.

All the good that did me because now that I was sat in a cab with him, having dropped Willow at some grungy stables that had been converted into a club in the middle of Camden Town, every single cell in my body was buzzing for me to get a little closer.

The silence between us was heavy and my mind kept whirring over his murmured words.

You're playing a dangerous game. It wouldn't take me long to catch you.

The thing was that I felt well and truly caught up in him already. I just didn't know how to go about the saying and doing part of all this.

All this what?

I didn't even know what *this* was. All I knew was that things had been bobbing along and now it felt like they were racing.

Zipping and zapping between us, and I had no idea how to make heads or tails of it because he'd quite literally breathed me in.

I could still feel the weight of his hand on my thigh and the heat of his lips on the tip of my nose and my cheeks. Now that I knew what all those things felt like, I wanted more.

I didn't want him to chase me, because up until tonight I'd never ran from him. I'd kept a measured distance. A careful space that we both were good at manoeuvring around. But that space had shrunk, and now it was gone and the only thing in its place was a loud, blaring warning...

Don't take what you can't keep.

He wasn't a keeper, and I didn't want to be kept. I didn't want to be someone's something. I'd been that before and when it broke, when he died, I had no idea how to be me again. Sometimes I still had no idea how to be just me. Sometimes it felt like I was still someone's, even though he wasn't here anymore. Technically, I was free to do and feel and want as I liked.

I felt the cab jolt to a stop and as I looked out of the rain stained window, I realised that we were outside his house.

Another thing I never quite understood about him. He had a house, a big house that you'd expect to belong to a big family. A nice family, not a single guy that wasn't even interested in having a relationship.

"You want to come in for a drink?" he asked as I looked up to find him hunched by the taxi door, his hand on the pull, ready to open it. His too tall frame looking a little too squished for comfort.

"Sure." I didn't know if I wanted a drink, but I knew I wanted more time with him.

I watched as he barely managed to move to the door on my side of the cab. He took my handbag from where it was on the bench beside me and opened the door. He stepped out, stretching to his full height, before he took my hand in his and helped me out.

His hand felt so warm compared to my clammy one. It was so much bigger than mine that it completely engulfed it. And all of a sudden every part of me felt so small next to him. Even my feet felt lost in my fashionably tight shoes.

The taxi drove off and in the quiet of the grey night sky, all I could hear was our breaths mixed in with the come and go bluster of the coming winter wind.

My blood rushed a little louder as he led me towards his orange brick home. He opened the short black gate and walked me up the short black and white chequered path that ran parallel to the drive leading to his garage.

My chest felt a little tight as I watched him open his perfectly red front door, and as he took a step back to let me in, something went off inside me. I didn't know what, just that it was because of the way he was looking at me. The way his eyes seemed to become glued to mine and how even in the dark they had this beautiful lustre. This pull, like something inside him wanted more of *me*.

It was the way his gaze flitted back and forth with mine. It was as though he were measuring the distance between us and the backward steps I was taking through his threshold.

It was like a silent calm before a frenzied storm.

I could feel it brewing. I could feel it coming in the way he licked his lips and clenched his fists around the strap of my bag and his keys. In the way his steps got wider until he was so close that his breaths fluttered my lashes.

He threw my bag onto the tiled floor of his hallway, his keys onto the narrow sideboard by the door. And before I could step into the house, he took hold of my arm, his eyes dropping to where he held me.

"Just a moment," he murmured as he ran his hand to my elbow. His eyes fluttered up to my lips as he licked across his own.

My lungs burned with the need to breathe and as he trailed his hands up my coat sleeves to my jaw, I couldn't quite manage to.

His fingers pressed to the column of my neck as his thumbs tugged at my chin. Pulling at the soft skin as his breath bathed my thirsty lips.

I wanted to scream at him. I wanted to yell at him to kiss me. To kiss me unlike I'd ever been kissed before.

Instead I moaned. A soft guttural rumble that vibrated all the way from the pit of my stomach, up my sternum...my throat and fizzed on his lips. His soft, almost inaudible gasp pushed a heat unlike anything I'd ever felt all the way down my body.

It seeped its way from the inside out, warming my skin so blissfully that even in the dark, cold night it felt like I was laying in the most beautiful, exotic sunshine.

There was a nagging feeling in the back of my mind that told me I should stop. That I should push Jacob Roth away and run. Run for my life, my sanity, for all that was good in my world. I should've fought this, but fuck it if I did. If I could.

I had tried for so long and I succeeded for a while, until that moment.

I wasn't running.

I wasn't fighting.
I was surrendering.
I was putting my hands up and letting it all be.
And boy, it felt so fucking good.

CHAPTER 11

Jake

I t was all too much…just for a second. And fuck me if it wasn't one of the most ironic things that had ever happened to me. I'd imagined how this would go, this kiss. I could fucking picture it, but the moment my lips even slightly brushed hers and her mouth opened. The moment her tongue eagerly licked my top lip even before I had a chance of feeling the full cushion of my lips on hers, it was game over.

Her fingers wound into my hair as I sucked her tongue and lower lip into my mouth. Her sighs were so breathy as they vibrated down my throat. It was delicious, and it was like nothing I'd ever tasted before.

I hadn't realised how hungry I'd been for her until right then.

I'd wanted this for so long, that now that I finally got it, I was having trouble computing how to go about it. I wanted to do everything at once. I wanted to devour and savour. I wanted to go fast and go slow. It was all opposites and pushing and pulling.

When I bit into her lip, I wanted to lick it better and at the same time I wanted the sting to remain for days. When I tugged on her hair, I wanted to rub my fingertips right where her roots stung to make it all better.

With Dorian all bets were off. It didn't matter how many women I'd kissed before, or how I'd kissed them, because they hadn't been her. She was different. I knew her past. I'd seen her pain. I'd fucking felt it.

And yes, I wanted to fuck her. Hard, deep, fast and slow. I was ready. My dick was aching as it pressed to my fly. I wanted to fuck her in every possible way. But there was this niggling little bastard of a murmur inside my chest that was begging me to fix her.

The reality, however, was that she didn't need to be fixed. Despite what she thought, she wasn't broken or damaged.

I'd seen broken. I'd touched damaged. And Dorian Anson, was neither of those things.

"Jake?" her voice echoed across my jaw and into my ear. "You stopped. Why? Am I that bad?"

Her hands dropped down to my chest and as she pushed herself a little from me, my ribs tightened around my lungs and my heart. The feeling far too piercing to allow me to catch my breath.

"No." I managed to rasp as her eyes rounded on mine. "You're definitely not bad, Dor."

Her breath hitched and her mouth fell open as I swept my thumb across her wet lips. Her chest was heaving so fast that the collar of her jacket kept brushing the side of my hand.

Before I could even make sense of what was happening my lips were smashing down on hers, our teeth were scraping together and our tongues were duelling. It was a fucking terribly messy kiss, I'd done better, but with her?

It was fucking perfect.

She sighed into me while her fingers worked the buttons on my coat. Her whimpers as I bit and sucked on her lip made me want to push her up against the wall of my porch and rip her clothes off so I could taste every single inch of her skin right there and then.

Her hands pushed open my coat before she grabbed my belt. A low moan leaving her lips as I kissed the curve of her neck.

"Are you taking me inside yet?" she breathed into the air above our heads.

I couldn't help but chuckle as I licked up her neck and sucked her lobe into my mouth. Her earrings scraped along my tongue and my lips. Her hands clenched and I couldn't stop the shudder that ran through me at the feel of her fingertips so close to my erection.

Her breaths became louder and faster as I kissed along her jaw. Her hands slipped into the top of my jeans as I licked into her mouth and then sucked her lip between mine.

A bright satisfaction settled deep in my belly as her body completely sagged into mine. "You know what's going to happen when we go inside?"

She nodded and pulled me flush to her body, her face burrowing into the crook of my neck. And then she did something that I'd never expect of her. Her nose traced my skin on a deep inhale as her warm hands flattened on my belly. She hummed as she licked up my neck to my ear, leaving a wet, cooling trail behind.

She sighed as she puckered her lips right by my ear, a silent and soft whisper of a kiss that had every single one of my cells on high alert.

I was trying so hard to rein in every single instinct that told me to wrap her around me and lose myself in her, but then she murmured, "Are you going to fuck me, Jacob?"

There was a slight teasing and almost daring lilt to her words. My whooshing blood rushed in my veins and my already tense muscles steeled.

She would regret asking me that.

I wasn't just going to fuck her.

I was going to fuck her better than anyone before me.

Yes, it was an arrogant and possibly naïve notion with her past and all. But I was as serious as all the years of pent up frustrations screaming around inside me, like the criminals in Arkham Asylum—heckling and wailing to be set free. To be given autonomy to take every single possible liberty. On her. In her. With her.

My hands slid down her waist to her hips in a torrid rush before they cupped her arse and hitched her up my body.

Her long, slender legs wrapped tightly around my waist, over my coat. A husky whimper scrambling between her lips and straight into my ear as her arms wound around my shoulders.

"Shit, my shoe." She giggled as the *thunk* of it hitting the floor registered over our breaths. "Fuck it, leave it."

No fucking way. I loved those shoes, I could still remember

the first time I'd seen them on her at Daniel's christening. Her lemon yellow lace dress paired with those shoes had me clenching my hands in my pockets and my eyes constantly roving up and down her legs imagining what they would feel like wrapped around me.

I was pretty sure you weren't meant to think those things in a church and the whole time I was waiting for lightning to strike me.

I kept asking, *how are you not smiting me right now, oh Lord?*

"The shoe comes with."

"Fine, kick it in." She huffed, her fingers winding into the longer hair at my crown as she pulled tautly.

"Really?"

"Right now, I couldn't give two shits about the shoe," she gritted.

I turned in a circle trying to find the bright shoe in the dark. I needed to get the porch light fixed, we wouldn't be having this fucking problem otherwise. I impatiently bent forward to pick it up the moment my eyes landed on it.

"If you drop me, I still expect you to fuck me." She yelped as her legs tightened further around me. Her thighs widening and her crotch rubbing on mine.

Fuck me, "I'll fuck you, concussion and all." I tightened my arm around her. I had no intention of dropping her.

"You should get to it then."

Little Miss Bossy. I couldn't help but smile.

I remembered slamming the front door shut. I remembered the feel of her body pushing up and down on mine as I took the steps a little too hurriedly. The sting of her teeth as she bit down on my lip and the balm of her slick tongue as she licked it away.

I remembered all those things like I'd seen them in my peripheral vision. Like I'd been watching two other people wrestle each other with kisses and looks and needy touches.

But the moment we were in my bedroom, something changed. It was a seismic shift. Something that creates continents and breaks them apart.

I threw her shoe on the cushioned bench at the foot of my bed. The bright yellow standing out in stark contrast to the white material.

As I sat her on the edge of the bed her eyes met mine in the dim light. They were round and wide whilst her hands slipped down my chest as I stood. Her breath hitched, the tip of her nose raising slightly as she breathed in deep. Her inhale catching and snaring with the jolting rise of her chest.

"You're so fucking pretty, Dorian." I couldn't help but tell her as I stroked my fingertips down the side of her face.

Fingertips that I couldn't help but kiss before they touched her beautiful skin.

The feel of the tips of her fingers tracing the ridges and grooves of my stomach had me bunching the muscles in my arms and legs to stop myself from shuddering.

"How do you want to do this?"

She looked a little panicked at my question, "I-I don't...I don't know."

"You don't know?"

"I haven't-I-I'm rusty at this." Her eyes dropped to her lap with her hands as she sighed.

I crouched in front of her, my hands taking her fidgeting ones and stilling them. "It's like riding a bike. Easy. Your body never forgets."

"Not for me and not mine."

Right. "Get up," I said as I took her other shoe off and threw it next to the other. I pulled her up with me and took a step back from the bed before I pushed her coat over her shoulders and down her arms until it was off her. I threw that too, somewhere near the shoes.

Her breathing picked up, her breasts strained against the lace tipped neckline of her top. Her beaded chain brushing up and down the creamy valley of her tits.

I had to shake the clenching heaviness from my hands. I'd done so many risky things with these hands and never once had they felt so tight with trepidation for their task.

Her eyes fell to where I scrunched the black, cool fabric in my hands and tugged it from her jeans. She gasped as I pulled a little harder when it became stuck in her belt.

"Lift your arms." She did as I asked without a second thought.

I tugged the blouse over her head, gritting my teeth in frustration as the off the shoulder sleeves became stuck on her bangles.

"Sorry." She whispered at my low growl at the same time she untangled herself from the top.

The perky swell of her velvety breasts adorned with the delicate lace of her strapless bra had my mouth watering and every one of my taste buds coming to attention.

I took one of her hands and slipped the gold bangle off before doing the same with the other two on her left arm. I chucked them with a loud clatter onto the bedside table. "You don't need those right now."

She said nothing, just eyed me as I continued to undress her. I unbuckled her belt and popped the button of her jeans and then pulled the zip down.

My heart faltered in its rambunctious rhythm at the sight of the pretty black lace along the smooth skin at the base of her tummy. Buttery, luscious skin that had me using all my strength to control my too eager to taste it tongue.

I shimmied her snug jeans down her legs as I crouched in front of her. I worked them down her lush pins even as my face came to a stop at her lace covered pussy. Her thighs clenched as my breaths splayed on her goose pimpled skin. Her hands fell to my shoulders.

"Jake." She rasped languidly, her nails digging into my cotton t-shirt covered skin.

"Feet." I demanded a little too brusque. I could smell how wet she was and I was struggling to keep this easy for her. I wanted to selfishly rip everything from her body and feast on her hot flesh. I wanted to lap at her cream. I wanted to have her arousal coat every inch of my mouth, face, hands, and fingers.

She's going to think you're a fucking nymphomaniac, bellend.

I discarded her jeans somewhere behind me. My nose rubbing along the edge of teasing lace. Her legs and stomach quivered as I drew in a deep, delicious lungful of her. Her sweet, flowery and turned on scent.

It was suffocating me in the best possible way. It was setting fire to my insides and fucking with my senses.

It was impossible not to taste her. It was impossible to be this close and not put myself out of my misery.

She rolled onto her toes with a sigh as I dragged my fingertips over the backs of her legs. Her peachy cheeks clenching as I cupped them in my hands and squeezed. Her heels dropping to the ancient rug on the wooden floor.

"Jacob…" She whimpered at the feel of my tongue licking up her wet satin covered slit all the way to the bottom of her belly. I couldn't help but close my eyes, relishing the feel of the lace covering her soft skin on my tongue.

Her hushed whimpers and rapid breaths wracking through her body while I sucked and nipped my way up her stomach, trying to keep her steady as I went.

I got rid of her bra when I reached her breasts. My tongue revelling in the taste of her skin as my hands ran back down and took her knickers with them.

I licked the underside of her breast and the tremble that wracked through her body was like oxygen breathing life into the flame inside me. Her hands squeezed around my shoulders as I sucked her hardened nipple into my mouth. My eyes straining to make out the way her lips puckered with her long blown out breaths.

It felt like a sin to feel and taste her and not see her properly.

I pushed up on my feet, my teeth snagging the turgid point of her boob and she flinched, a long breathy sigh escaping her lips. Her fingers curled into my flesh as I turned to the bedside table and tapped the base of the lamp for light.

She tensed as the room brightened around us. Her arms wrapped around her torso as she huddled in on herself.

"What are you doing?"

Her eyes lifted slightly from the floor, her lips pressed into a nervous line and her nails dug into her sides.

"Wh-Why did you do that?" she asked as her gaze dropped

to the dark oak floor.

"Look at me."

"Jake..." she rasped, her eyes searching my face but never meeting my eyes.

She took in an unsteady breath when I stepped back toward her, her arms tightening around her so taut that her shoulders looked like they were going to pop from their sockets.

"What?"

She shook her head at her feet. Her ankles crossed like she was trying to close in on herself.

Gone was the confident and strong woman and in her place stood a stranger that oozed doubt and uncertainty. It was fucking criminal. I had no idea why she felt like that. I had no idea what had made her feel that way. But, I sure as fuck wasn't going to allow whatever it was to settle between us.

I paused for a moment as her eyes looked up at me through her long, dark lashes. I took a step back, closer to the bed. The distance I'd put between us too much.

"Come here."

She sighed as she tentatively met me at the edge of the bed. Her eyes widened when I pulled my t-shirt off. Her breathing shallowed when I slowly unbuttoned my jeans, the zip whirring down on its own with the press of my hard cock.

She blinked, her eyes focusing on my body.

Shit, don't fuck this up. Don't. Fuck. It. Up.

I removed my wallet from my back pocket and threw it onto the bedside table. Her bangles clattering again as they skittered along the dark wooden top.

Her rough intake of breath as she perused my torso sounded more like a low gasp. Her pupils magnified to the point the muddy green of her irises was the tiniest ring.

"Like what you see?"

She swallowed.

"Good, I love what I see."

Her eyes flashed to mine for the first time since I'd turned on the light. I held her wrists and gently pried her arms back to her sides. I took my time appreciating every one of her soft, fluid curves. The few faint silvery lines at the base of her tummy.

"Jake..." Her voice was almost broken with how low and rusted it sounded.

"You keep saying my name and I'm not even inside you yet."

Her gaze flashed down between us. Her tongue licking across her lips whilst her fingertips grazed the opened top of my dark jeans. They rose slowly, barely skimming the top of my boxers. Her eyes blinking as my dick throbbed at the closeness of her touch.

Her slim fingertips traced up the light trail of hair to my belly button. My vision blurred slightly with how fast my heart was thrumming when she splayed her hands on my stomach. Her long, elegant fingers stroked across one of the muscle grooves.

She looked so mesmerised, so enthralled. The whole time I let her take me in, my hands were burning to touch her again.

Her eyes narrowed as they roved up my body and a small smile painted her lips. "I know what all the fuss is about now," she shrugged.

"You haven't seen anything yet, pretty girl." I chuckled as I anchored her hips with my hands and pulled her to me. "The main attraction is still under wraps, and I've been told it's... ummm...impressive."

"I'll bet." Her hands skittered back down my torso and her fingers started working my jeans and underwear over my arse.

"No need, I'll show you mine since you've shown me yours." I pushed my bottoms down the rest of the way. I pulled each leg off quickly and my socks with them.

I straightened myself, my lips finding hers as her hands bracketed my hips. Her hair tickled my hands on her waist.

Her rapid breaths hitched as I lowered her to the bed, my hands sliding over the slender curve of her hips, to her quivering thighs. I slid down her body while she laid back on the bed, her arousal slicking a wet trail up my body.

I could smell her all around me, her skin was a little moist with sweat. I could hear her heart thumping wildly in her chest as I tongued my way down her body. I palmed her firm tits and she squirmed beneath me. The harder I squeezed the more frantic her gasps became.

I was so fucking desperate to taste her, to bury my face in her pussy. The moment my knees hit the floor, I hitched her legs up on the bed and swiped my tongue up her middle. From her opening to her clit.

The way her hands clasped the duvet on either side of her body made me smile. I'd licked her pussy once, and her back was arching off the bed. Her moans as I flicked her clit with the tip of my tongue were so fucking breathy and beautiful, and as I licked down and into her tight cunt, she groaned.

She fucking groaned so fucking loud that I swear my dick jumped.

Her nails clawed at my arms as I pulled her further to the edge, spreading her legs with my shoulders.

"Oh fuck," she breathed as I licked her clit again, pushing a finger into her hot pussy.

The way she squeezed and kneaded her breasts made my cock ache with the yearning to spill all over them. Her gorgeous, supple tits.

"Fuck me, Jake." She gasped as our eyes met across the length of her body.

Her cheeks were a beautiful ruddy rose, her lips were a gnawed rosy pink. She looked so fucking beautiful, even with her eyes all unfocused and ready to roll to the back of her head.

"Please," she begged.

"You want me to fuck your cunt with my cock that badly, then you better come on my tongue, pretty girl."

Her pussy clenched tightly around my finger as I pulled it out and thrust my tongue back inside her. I strummed her clit with my thumb as she undulated under my mouth. Her breaths so hoarse that it sounded like she'd been screaming for hours.

Fuck, there was nothing quite as sexy as feeling such a put together woman fall apart beneath you. I was almost tempted to give her what she wanted so I could watch her lose herself as she creamed on my dick.

I hummed at the feel of her pussy squeezing my tongue. Her hands fell to my head and grasped my hair tightly pushing my face completely flush to her. I could hear the blood rushing inside of me as I struggled to breath around her.

Death by pussy.

There were a lot worse ways to go.

My ears rang with her moans, her hands pulled at my hair, her body thrashed beneath me. Her sweet smelling cum gushed onto my tongue, its slightly salty essence making my body heat. And fuck, my cock was so hard that even its begging pulse hurt.

I was so fucking turned on that my dick was weeping for her.

I released her hands from my hair as I straightened on my knees. I pulled her arse right to the edge as I sat her up and wrapped her legs around my waist. Her still shaking legs fell to the sides as my cock bobbed at her entrance.

"Now, I'm going to fuck you, Dor. I'm going to fuck your pretty little pussy, pretty girl." Her eyes rounded on mine as I reached for my wallet and took a condom out.

"Bite," I said as I pushed the tip of the foiled packet between her teeth. The minute she bit down on it I twisted it, ripping it open and taking the condom out before she spat the packet over my shoulder.

She fucking surprised me at every fucking turn. I'd expected her to use her hand, not her tongue, to discard the wrapper.

Dorian was so different to all the other women I'd ever had. She was like a fireworks display. It started off a little tame and quiet, but as it went on it got louder and better and colourful. It became unpredictable and exciting. It mesmerised you. Completely captivated you. That was her—mesmerising and captivating.

She excited me.

I finished rolling the condom on and checked it to make sure it was good. Her wet pussy at the edge of the bed lined up perfectly with my cock. As I swiped my crown over her glistening lips she sighed so breathily and longingly. Like she'd imagined this so many times before, like I had. Like she'd been hungry, starving even, for me.

Her warm hand cupped my face, and that little gesture was enough to make me want to fuck her forever. Again and again.

Then she kissed me with her eyes wide open and stuck on mine, and all I wanted was to ram into her. I wanted to tear her apart and discard all the shit that she should never have accumulated on her beautiful bones. And after I wanted to put her back together with a perfect space right at the core of who she was, a space that was just mine.

Her gasp as I slowly pushed into her mingled with mine. Her eyes widened as the arm she was leaning on for support trembled.

Her tongue licked into my mouth as she echoed my name again and again. My hands fisted on the bed on either side of her, bracing myself.

Her pussy was so fucking tight it fucking hurt as I pressed into her. Her walls clenching around the intrusion and quite literally choking the tip of my cock.

She closed her eyes as her lips rubbed softly on mine.

"You feel so good, so tight it hurts, pretty, pretty girl."

She stiffened as her eyes flashed open. They were a little red and watery with dark smudges lining her tear lines, and fuck me if I didn't want to fuck all the tears out of her.

"S-stop. Stop calling me pretty." She gritted as the hand that cupped my face slipped down to my shoulder and clawed as she added, "I hate pretty."

Before she had the chance to distance herself from me I thrust into her completely. My whole body shuddered as my dick bottomed out in her pussy. I'm pretty sure her nails broke my skin as she yelped out an almost tortured moan.

"You're fucking pretty, Dor." I managed to rumble into her gaping mouth. "And you've never been fucking prettier than you are right now with my cock throbbing in your clenching cunt."

Her heels pressed into my glutes as her flat stomach pressed to mine. Our pleasure quite literally dripping down my balls.

She buried her face in my neck as she urged me to go faster, her arms tightened around my shoulders and her fingertips pressed into the sweat moistened flesh of my back.

Her hoarse muted cries vibrating down my spine as I gave her everything she asked for, how she asked for it. That's all I wanted to do, give her everything and anything she wanted and needed.

It was a fucking stupid thought to have, I knew it, but it was unstoppable. It was something that happened, naturally.

I could feel her thighs stiffen and shake. Her pussy squelched as it greedily sucked at my cock.

"God. Shit. God…Jacob. Oh my, fuck," she muttered huskily as her whole body shook and vibrated flush to mine. Her skin tinged pink as her rushing blood rose to the surface with her orgasm.

Her heat radiated through me and all I could think was, "holy shit," as I came inside the condom. My heart pounding so hard and furiously that I thought it might break out of my chest as I collapsed with her back onto the bed. My face buried in the shallow valley of her breasts as her pussy continued squeezing my still spurting dick.

Yep, you are definitely fucked now, my friend.

I don't know how long we were like that for, but my knees were aching and burning as the rug weave stamped my skin. I pushed up onto my feet, legs still shaky. She whimpered as my dick slipped out of her pussy.

"It's cold," she breathed.

It really was. My skin was covered in goose bumps as I wandered to the bathroom. I took care of the condom, all the while debating whether to clean her up or let her settle. I liked the idea of her smell on my sheets, on me, and my scent covering her. I wanted her to wake up in the morning and feel, taste and smell tonight.

She grumbled as I picked her up off the bed and peeled the duvet back before I laid her back down and scooted in behind her. A deep contented sigh escaped her as I draped myself around her and pulled the duvet over us both. She wriggled her back flush to my front and then unexpectedly she asked, "Why the big house, Jacob?"

Her question blindsided me. It made my insides twist and my chest ache. Something I didn't want to feel right there and then.

"Go to sleep, Dor."

She turned towards me. Her eyes squinting with the light from the lamp behind me.

"You want me to go to sleep? In your bed? With you?" Her brows drew in as she raked her nails up and down the light smattering of hair on my chest.

"Yes."

"I thought you didn't sleep with the women you fuck." Her murmur made my chest burn.

"I don't, but there's always a first."

"Never?" Her eyes widened a tad as she pulled her face back to look at me before she whispered, "Why not?"

"It's not my thing." She narrowed her eyes, pensively. "I don't like strangers in my space."

"But you sleep with them."

"Means to an end."

"Why, though? You could get to know someone and maybe—"

"Are you really going to Willow over this?" I asked pointedly, trying to shut off the line of conversation.

"I don't Willow." She murmured softly, her body rocking slightly away from me.

"Then go to sleep, pretty girl." I reached behind me, tapped the light off and pulled her back to me, snugly.

"Stop calling me pretty, Jacob."

"You are pretty, Dor, and you've never been prettier than you are right now smelling of great sex and you and me."

CHAPTER 12

Dorian

The Uber driver was clearly enjoying my state of embarrassment as I clambered into the back of his car and sat there with my cheeks blazing and my mind screaming the whole drive to mine.

Leave it to you to do your first walk of shame at thirty-three.

I kept thinking of how stupid I'd been. How reckless it'd been to let things go so far with Jake. I could still feel him inside of me like a ghost reminding me of what I'd done. I'd complicated our friendship. And as I took each step up to my flat, I could still smell him on me. His warm peppery and lemony scent that seemed to be coating my body and filling my lungs to the point that they were so tight and ready to pop like an overfilled balloon.

I dumped my shoes by the door and went straight to my bathroom.

My body was sore, and my skin still felt like it sizzled to the touch as I stood in front of the mirror.

My hair was a knotted mess and my jeans felt sticky as they rubbed on my skin and my sore pussy. It'd been impossible to find my underwear in the dark.

I think at some point Jake must've drawn his curtains during the night.

It'd been impossible to find most of my clothes. But I figured that my jeans, his t-shirt and my coat were sufficient enough. Except now I had to find a way of giving him back his t-shirt without being awkward about it.

Well done, Dorian, way to make life easier.

I had to find a way of not making things awkward between us full stop.

I stripped out of the clothes and went straight for the shower, the first cold stream of water making me wince.

I felt so fucking stupid.

I let it happen and I enjoyed every bit of it until he started with the whole pretty girl thing. It wasn't his fault. He wasn't to blame that such an inconsequential word could carry so much shit with it. He didn't know what it meant. How it had been the start of something so beautiful that had ended so bloody ugly.

"Phillip Christopher Cavendish, I should cut off your ears and your hands for bastardising my babies!" Gwen gritted as she took the fluffy flower from my hand and snipped the stem diagonally with the scissors she'd been using to cut herbs for dinner, before returning it to me.

"They're so pretty," I whispered as I brushed my fingertips lightly over the slender golden petals. "I've never seen anything like them."

"They're called Teddy Bears. They're not your usual Sunflower," she smiled.

"I think I love them."

"See, Mum? It was for a good cause." Pip grinned up at her as he wrapped his arm around my shoulders. "Dory's smiling again, so it counts as my good deed for the day."

"Tell that to the poor flower," she huffed slightly as her smile spread across her face. She ruffled his hair at the same time as he tried to smack her hands away, eventually she gave up with him and just combed my fringe away from my face with her fingers.

"What am I going to do with the lot of you?" she laughed as she shook her head and wandered back towards the house.

"You didn't have to do that," I smiled up at him.

"I thought it might cheer you up," he shrugged.

This had always been a memory that made me smile. It had always served as a reminder of when things between Phillip and I had been easy. Before we were an us and were only friends. Too young children with a long and carefree future ahead of them, or so we thought.

I shuddered as the rest of it played out in my head, like some ultra HD home video. I swear I could hear every little wobble of his adolescent voice and feel the warmth of the warm breeze that smelt like all the flowers in his mother's garden.

He picked up the Sunflower and brought it close to his face, twirling it like he was studying it. "You're right, it is pretty, like you."

I hated that word. I hated that word so much, and yet whenever Jake used it, it made me want to smile. It made me want to ask him to only ever call me *pretty girl*.

Somehow it made my heart warm, and that was the problem, it shouldn't. It shouldn't make me feel good because it wasn't his word to use on me. Like I wasn't his to fuck.

Yet, he knew exactly how to do it so perfectly that I could still feel him pulsing inside me. I could still feel the way his skin felt as it slapped and rubbed on mine. And I hated myself for it because I couldn't remember how it had felt with the one person I thought I'd love forever. I thought all those moments would be singed in my brain, but they weren't.

What kind of person does that make you?

Love wasn't meant to wither and fade. But then, I'd let him go when he was so quick to leave me. Sometimes I wondered if he ever really loved me, or if I was just me—his friend. His friend's sister. Someone he'd grown used to more than liking.

I wasn't sure whether it was hot water or tears streaming down my face. I think maybe it was both even though it felt mostly like the latter.

This was why I didn't sleep around. This was why I didn't let myself get involved with men. This was why fucking Jacob Roth was a bad idea. It had been a terrible mistake, no matter how good he made me feel.

As if to make the point stick further Phillip's ring glinted in the light, casting off rainbow filled beams onto the walls and glass…onto my body that was still aching and yearning for another man.

I would've ripped it off my finger and never looked at it again, except even if I did it, the tiny sunflower tattooed underneath would still be there to remind me. The pale lines would still mark its place and even if they disappeared the callous on the padding of my palm, right beneath where it sat, would never soften again.

That reminder that my forever was gone was suffocating. It had died and now all I had was half faded memories of something that I wasn't even sure was real. The only real thing to come out of it was Daniel.

He was the only one who had a right to me. To my affection. To my love.

Him and no one else, and I'd do well to remember that.

* * *

The rest of the day was sort of a blur. I picked up Daniel from my parents' and took him out for dinner. He kept going on about how he had to tell Jake that he'd almost completed all the levels in the game he'd bought him. And the whole time I was dying a little inside.

It only got worse when he called and I blatantly sent it to voicemail. What could I possibly say to him?

I had fun, but when I woke up and all I could feel was your body on mine, well, I panicked and legged it.

Somehow I don't think that was something he wanted to hear. Except then my phone vibrated across the table at the restaurant and I knew that I was in trouble, because I'd never been so quick to check a text before.

JAKE

Rule one of sneaking out: Don't leave half of your outfit behind. Unless you plan to go back and collect it.

My cheeks flamed, and if I'd been eating my food rather than playing around with it, I probably would've choked. I took a large gulp of my water as I read his message again, and before I could stop myself I'd spat it all over the table the second his next message came through.

JAKE

Your expensive underwear still smells of you. In case you're wondering.

I'd never seen Daniel look so affronted and disgusted in my life as he wiped my spewed water from his face.

ME

Stop it.

I replied quickly and dropped my phone on the table like it was burning my hand. My whole body felt like it was on fire. My insides were fluttering to the point that I felt a little nauseous, and to make it worse, my phone was vibrating again.

I'm not going to look.

Not going to look.

Not going to look.

Do.

Not.

Look.

Fuck it.

JAKE

For a moment there I thought you were ignoring me.

I wasn't sure what to reply to that. Did I straight up lie and tell him that I'd been busy all day? Well, it was sort of true I guess, I'd been busy going over all the reasons why me and him were a bad idea. Why I shouldn't want to repeat last night.

What did it say about me that the only reason I could think of was another man? A dead one at that.

"Mum? Mum!" Daniel waved his hand in front of my face in annoyance.

"Yes?"

"It's for you," he sighed as he held his phone up to me. "It's Jake."

Fuck my life.

I covered the phone with the palm of my hand and whispered, "Tell him I'm not here. I've gone to the loo."

"He can hear you, the microphone's on the bottom not on the screen." He looked at me like I was the biggest idiot. "He said it's important."

Seriously? I didn't know whether to be angry or impressed that he'd been that resourceful to get to me. I mean, it was sort of sweet that he'd thought of Daniel's phone. I was guessing most men wouldn't think to go down that route. So yeah, it was a little endearing.

But then at the same time, it was frustrating. He'd actually gone through my child to get to me.

Clever.

Not clever, Dorian. Stu-pid.

I took the phone from Daniel and held it to my ear, "Really? You called my son's phone to talk to me?"

"Needs must." I expected his tone to be a little humoured, but it was deep and serious and it had my throat swelling. "We need to talk, Dorian."

"I know."

"Do you?"

"Yes, but not now," I sighed.

He cleared his throat, the rumble working its way through me, adding oxygen to the furnace inside. I could still hear the way he moaned as he fucked me with his tongue, and that rumble, that depth in his voice was only making it louder.

"Fine, but we're talking about this even if I have to tie you down. Last night was pretty fucking incredible, Dor. I liked it. A lot."

My heart did that weird gong thing where it made my chest vibrate.

"So did I," I said before I could think better of it.

"Good, then we can do it again."

"Jake."

"You're saying my name again." There was a humoured wistfulness to his voice that made me want to ask him where and when and how.

"I'll send you a message in a bit."

"Okay, but I'm going to warn you now, if you conveniently forget, I'm going to be knocking on your door. I know where you live, in case you've forgotten."

"I haven't." He was pretty bloody impossible to forget. There were times I found myself thinking of him without any reason, just little memories. Little things that made me smile. Little remarks that made me chuckle.

"Good."

"Okay."

"Message me."

"I will."

"How sore are you?" he murmured, his voice sounded so

breathy, like it had when he'd pushed into me and told me I was pretty.

"Jake."

"Tell me."

"Maybe I'm not."

"We both know you are, I can still feel you and I can smell you every-fucking-where." I heard him swallow.

His words and his voice were making my thighs press together and as I squirmed it felt like I was still full, tight and in need of him.

"You should shower."

"I have."

"Again, make it a cold one."

"I don't think so, I like the way you smell, pretty girl."

"I need to go, Daniel and I are having dinner."

"Okay."

"Bye, Jacob."

"Bye, Dorian."

Daniel whined as I ended the call, it took a very large gingerbread sundae to get me back in his good graces and an extra twenty minutes of game time when we got home.

I'd finished showering and gotten myself into bed when my phone buzzed. I knew exactly who it was before I even checked it. I wasn't entirely sure how it was possible for my body to be excited all on its own just knowing it was him that was messaging me.

JAKE

I'm still waiting for your message. I've got my keys in my hand and I will come knocking.

I had no idea why I was smiling. It was silly, but I was really smiling. Still, there was a part of me that felt like I shouldn't be.

For one, he was being obnoxious, and he knew it too. Then there was also the same niggling feeling that kept telling me to watch out. Telling me that I had no business getting into anything with Jake.

The problem with the latter was that although it had only been one night. One time. It felt like I'd already gotten into something. Something that felt a little out of my depth.

It made no sense feeling that way. Not when I knew that Jake was more of a fun sort of guy. Not when I was still feeling guilty for feeling like last night had been one of the best nights I'd ever had.

But the thing was that I liked it. For a fraction of time I felt like me again, and not because I'd forgotten my responsibilities or the pain that I still carried around with me. The reason was quite simple—I'd felt seen. I hadn't felt like just another of the seven-point-four-four-two billion people on this earth.

I don't know what it was about Jake, but it felt like he'd awakened a part of me that I'd forgotten existed. I liked that he wasn't trying to put on graces for me. Merely thinking of his crass words, his desperate touches and reverent looks was making me crave more of them. More of him. More of the way he made me feel like me. Not even the old me, a new me or one that I didn't know existed.

I was still trying to understand how his gruff rawness could make me feel this good. How it could make me feel so free.

My bones felt lighter. My smiles felt easier.

I couldn't remember the last time I felt that way. Happy.

It had been fun, even when it'd felt intense and consuming.

So maybe, I could have more fun. Fun without consequences.

Fun without responsibility.

Just fun.

ME

> You know, needy sort of looks good on you.

Flirting had never been my game.

Willow would probably send something sexy. Knowing her, she'd probably send a nude with her address and some dirty thing she'd do.

Not me, though. No. I had to message something that didn't even make sense.

Needy sort of looks good on you? Seriously? WTF?

To be fair though, Jake already knew my address by heart. And although he'd seemed rather happy with my body, I wasn't going to pretend that stretch marks were sexy. As faint and small as they were, I'd rather not draw attention to them.

JAKE

> Are you ready to talk?

My heart dropped to the pit of my stomach as I read his reply. I hadn't expected him to be so direct. I expected some dirty come back, I would've settled for funny.

He clearly meant business, and after the way I'd left, I felt like I owed it to him to be straight. Even if it was retching up my nerves and making me a little anxious. I was so used to him being playful, that I didn't know how to take his serious side.

ME

> Friday?

JAKE

> FRIDAY?

Oh, shouty caps. I don't think he'd ever sent me a text with shouty caps. It felt strange, not in a bad way. It was different to our usual messages. Obviously, we'd never messaged each other about sex or the need to talk about it.

ME
Friday.

I watched as three little dots wiggled around at the bottom of my screen. They showed up and stopped. Showed up and stopped, until eventually one simple word lit up my phone.

JAKE
Fine.

I could picture him furrowing his brows as he pouted at his phone. And even that little image was bringing my smile back.

ME
Daniel has a birthday party on Saturday morning close to Mum's. He's staying the night on Friday.

JAKE
Okay.

ME
Goodnight, Jacob.

I couldn't help but sigh as I whispered his name at the same time as I tapped it out.

JAKE
Keep saying my name, pretty girl. X

I managed to take a deep breath with those words. My smile widened, my chest felt fuller and my skin tighter.

ME
Stop with the pretty.

JAKE
No.

JAKE
Go to sleep.

ME
Why?

JAKE
You are fucking pretty, Dorian. Never prettier than you are right now, smiling at your phone. I know you're smiling. I can feel it.

He was right. I was smiling. I may have been beaming, and it was all because of him. It should've surprised me that he had those lines in him, but for some reason they felt so worn in and homey. It was like he'd said them to me a world of times.

JAKE
Goodnight, Dor. X

ME
Goodnight, Jake. X

CHAPTER 13

I managed to make it to Monday afternoon before I messaged
her again. I'd never felt this want to communicate with
someone so much. It was a completely foreign sense to
me. I found myself looking at my phone and thinking
about what I could message her. What I could tell her to make
her smile, even when I couldn't see it.

By Tuesday I was beginning to regret changing my sheets.
Even though it felt like her scent was embedded in the walls and
on my skin. It felt wrong waking up to the smell of clean sheets
rather than hers.

This alone should've been a warning sign. This should've
been enough to have me put space between us. A boundary that
would keep her away from all my shit.

The problem was that there was this twist in my gut that kept urging me to tell her about everything. I wanted to warn her about all the things that should keep her away from me. All the things that made the lines of my face mismatch my smiles, like she'd told me so many times.

You like to laugh and smile a lot. Why don't the lines of your face reflect that?

I don't get how you have frown lines when all you do is smile and laugh.

There were things she didn't know. Things I wanted to protect her and Daniel from.

By Wednesday I was going stir crazy. Rebecca, my assistant, had been teasing me the last couple of days about my aloofness. I was not aloof, not in the slightest. I was preoccupied about how I was going to make whatever was happening between Dorian and I work without having all the crap outside of it interfere.

Thursday came and quite frankly, beating one out over her, wasn't enough anymore. I stared at her folded clothes in my wardrobe. Francesca, my housekeeper, had left me a note on the bed next to them telling me she didn't know what to do with them. Where she should put them. I'd left them on the chest of drawers for the first couple of days, but then I couldn't stop looking at them and thinking of her. Thinking about how she'd felt wrapped around me. How she sounded as her pussy clenched around my tongue.

So I put them away, where I could only see them when I needed to get my own clothes out. They were just fucking clothes, but them being there was a reminder that she'd been there. She'd been in my room, in my bed…and then she'd left without so much as a whisper of a goodbye.

Sure, I'd seen the funny irony at first, but then this panic set in that I'd fucked up. I'd taken things too far and our friendship would change. It would become something awkward and strained. I couldn't fathom that possibility.

I looked around my desk again, I was meant to be catching up on my notes. Instead I was ruminating over Dorian and scoffing Magic Stars. She was stealing every one of my thoughts to the point that I was struggling to switch off and focus on my job. On my patients. It was frustrating.

I checked the time again, I had lunch planned with Eleanor today. I hadn't heard a peep from her the last week with the exception of actually arranging it. I hoped she'd show up. I was trying to give her the benefit of the doubt. I was trying to give her the trust she'd asked for.

Trying being the operative word.

As if on cue the reminder to leave blared on my phone. I was so tempted to send her a message to remind her too, but I didn't want to get her back up. She was so sensitive about us checking up on her, that I didn't want to ruffle her feathers before we'd even met up.

It took me a little longer than I'd anticipated to get my shit together and leave. The traffic was a bit of a killer, nothing out of the ordinary for a Thursday. By the time I got to the restaurant I'd agreed to meet her at, it was packed. The lunchtime crowd noisy. It took me a moment to spot her, but the moment I did, it felt like a weight had been lifted off my shoulders.

She'd remembered and she'd been on time.

There was a bit of a smile on her face as she waved at me from our table. She looked well. Radiant even, as I made my way to her. The tightness in my chest easing up as I took her in.

Her make-up was light, her hair was shiny and even her clothes seemed softer on her.

"Hey, chipmunk." I ruffled her hair lightly as she rolled her eyes.

"Stop calling me that." She laughed a little, her voice doing that excited squeaky thing. "It's annoying."

I sat next to her feeling relieved. She was here and she was okay. She looked more than okay.

"Miles went to the loo. Training was cancelled today, so I thought I'd bring him along." She gave me the puppy dog eyes she always did when she thought I might be upset. "I hope it's okay."

"It is. You look good."

She sighed happily, "I feel good. Better."

I felt my chest warm and my eyes tingle.

I loved Eleanor more than anything in the world. From the moment Ruth had brought her home from the hospital and fawned over her like she'd given birth to her...I had loved her more than I cared to admit. Even with the situation with our parents, she made me smile.

I think that she'd been a kind of silver lining in a moment where I felt lost and uncertain about a lot of things. About where I would fit in. Who would keep me after Mum and Dad had died.

But then she was there and she had the same dark blonde hair and muddy green eyes and even her skin was so milky like our mother's. In a way it felt like a part of her was still there, and I clung to it so desperately.

I wouldn't leave her side for the first few weeks, even when I was at school I'd be counting down the hours and minutes to when Ruth would come through the gates with her massive navy chariot of a pram.

I used to hate it when all the mothers gathered around, taking up all the space, as they cooed over her. I wasn't jealous. Not at all. I only wanted her to myself.

It was so silly, but in my head she was mine.

She was a reminder that I'd had a mother. That I'd had a family.

I was nine years old and terrified of being alone.

I remembered Ryan being angry. At everything. Everyone. He was so mean to Ruth and Levi, and I used to think that they would get upset and leave us because of him. I was so scared that I tried not to say anything more than I had to. I thought that if I didn't make a peep that they wouldn't mind all his noise. That maybe they'd forget I was there and that even if they didn't want to keep me, they'd forget to get rid of me.

"You're doing your broody thing." She shouldered my arm lightly.

"My broody thing?"

"You know, you look like you're reliving all the wonders of the world at a distance."

"Maybe I was." I shrugged because quite clearly I was struggling to keep myself in check with her. I'd grown so used to being the person that tried to sort her shit out. I think somewhere along the way I'd become used to being stern with her rather than being her brother.

"So, your birthday."

"What about it?"

"Miles can't go, curfew and all that jazz." She huffed as she rolled her eyes. She looked so young when she did that. "But I'll come. It's not every day you turn thirty-eight and I'd like to try and make amends for…ummm…just…everything, I guess."

"You don't have to do that. You only have to keep on trying. That's enough."

"I really am, Jake. I'm trying…" Her eyes fell to her lap as she picked at her mustardy yellow nails.

The yellow colour had me thinking of Dorian, it was her favourite. It made me smile. It made my heart squeeze and my blood warm.

I thought that she and Dorian might like one another. Or at least, Dorian might like this version of Eleanor. The sober one.

Her eyes met mine, a little duller than before.

"I'm trying really hard, but trying is so difficult," she rasped, continuing to pick at her fingertips. "It's like I have a sensor and I can find it everywhere I look and go. I keep telling myself I don't need it, that I'm okay, that I can go one more day without taking anything."

"Eleanor…"

"I see other people take this little pill and everything slows down for them. And I can't help but think how good it would feel to slow down too. Everything is so fast and quick all the time." She looked at me warily. The weary look on her face making her look older than her twenty-nine years.

"You don't need a pill to do that, to slow things down, Eleanor. You can do that for yourself, if you step outside of the circus."

"I want to, but—" She cut off suddenly, and quickly plastered a smile on her face.

"Hey, Jake." Miles greeted me with a pat on the shoulder before he sat opposite me, on Eleanor's other side. "Sorry, one of the guys from the team is sat back there with his agent. We got talking and I lost track of time."

"I thought you might have fallen in." She quipped lightly.

"Maybe I should have."

"Everything okay?"

I couldn't help but watch her interactions with him. They were a little off and forced. It didn't make much sense.

"Yeah, dandy," he replied as he picked up his menu and perused it.

She looked up at me, a silent sigh swelling in her chest before she let it out, and then she smiled again. It wasn't as radiant as when I'd come in, but the fact that she was still trying made me swell with pride for her.

* * *

Finally, Friday was here and thankfully my one surgery had been first thing in the morning. I'd spent most of the day catching up with the paperwork I'd been procrastinating over. By the time I was ready to leave it was all done.

Of course, Dorian's text telling me that she would come and meet me at the clinic had put a rocket up my arse. Last thing I wanted was to be stressing over my notes when I wanted to be focused on our conversation.

It was just getting dark outside when Rebecca knocked on my door. She'd been my assistant for years, she was my life saver when it came to keeping shit together around here. She made sure I knew what I needed to know, and she kept my Magic Star supply bountiful.

We'd started off a little shaky, but we'd sort of warmed to one another and now, I couldn't imagine not having her around. She called me Jake, I called her Becca. She brought me lunch when I couldn't make it out, I brought her coffee and shortbread every morning.

She smiled at me a little too enthusiastically as she popped her head into my office. Her silvery grey curls falling around her face as she trilled, "There's someone for you."

"Is there?" I smiled back at her.

She opened the door a little wider, stepping into the gap. "Lovely looking she is."

"Why are you talking like a squeaky Yoda?" I asked trying to maintain a straight face even though every one of my cells was urging me to smile. "It's a bit late for a consultation."

"She's not a patient," she deadpanned knowingly, "she asked for Jacob Roth, not Doctor Roth."

"Do people actually call me Doctor Roth? It sounds so old."

"Do you think you're getting younger? And yes, people ask for Doctor Roth, I correct them all the time, Mr. Roth."

"That doesn't sound much better, Becca, you need to sort that out." I chuckled at her.

"She's waiting for you by my desk. Very proper, even with her blushing smile."

"She's blushing? She's pretty when she blushes."

"I think she likes you, my boy." Oh dear, she was on the grandmother path.

"I hope so, it'd be awkward if she didn't and I'm taking her home for dinner."

"Why're you keeping her waiting, then?" She gave me a bit of a scowl.

"She's made me wait, I think it's only fair." I shrugged as I stood from my desk chair. "You should probably let her in before she runs away though. I'd have to sack you for that."

"Oh, yes," she laughed as she opened the door wider and

started for her desk.

"Becca?"

She turned, as I called to her, and asked me, "Cab?"

"Please." I responded as I took my coat from the rack by the window and started putting it on.

I knew the minute Dorian walked into the room, and not because of the sound of her heels on the floor. I felt it. I felt this compulsion to turn around.

"I've never been here before," she crooned from behind me. "I thought it'd be different to St. Ermin's, but it's pretty much the same."

She blinked a smile as I turned toward her, her cheeks were flushed and her lips looked like she'd scraped the gloss off them with her teeth.

"It's still a hospital," I said, trying to keep my voice steady as I took her in.

She had her grey coat folded over one arm and her large bag hanging at the crook of her other elbow. Her light mink oversized jumper was tucked just so into her matching mink and black chequered pencil skirt that made her legs look like they went on for miles in her skin-coloured pointed heels. Her hair was partially pulled back from her face as it fell in thick waves around her shoulders.

Man, she was pretty. That's all I could think when it came to describing her.

I'd seen so many beautiful women, but there was always something a little try hard about them, with her it just was. She was genuinely pretty. It was effortless and natural.

"I know it's a hospital, Einstein, I just expected it to be more glamorous. When the taxi pulled up outside I thought they were dropping me off at a hotel, not a hospital."

"It's part of what people pay for, I guess. That and the no expenses spared technology." I told her as I grabbed my satchel and went to her.

She looked up at me with a soft, shy smile as I stopped in front of her and she murmured, "Hi."

"Hi." I murmured back reining in my yearning to kiss her.

"So, what's the plan?"

"You hungry?"

"A bit."

"Let's feed you then, shall we?"

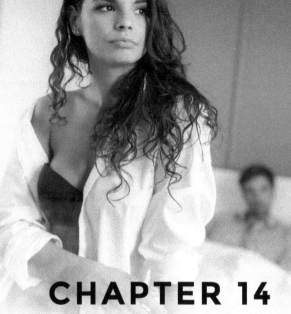

CHAPTER 14
Dorian

It felt a little discombobulating sitting at Jake's kitchen table as I watched him cook. I didn't even know he could cook. Obviously, I knew he had to feed himself, but I guess I'd never pictured him moving around a kitchen knowing exactly what he was doing. It was bewildering and at the same time it was sexy.

My cheeks heated at the thought. I don't think my body temperature had ever risen this much only thinking of someone as sexy. I think I now understood what it was like to be in heat. The constant summersaults in my stomach, the rushing waves of warmth all over my body, the goose bumps, dry lips, racing heart…

How do people live like this?

I couldn't remember ever feeling this way. Like I was one heartbeat, one breath, away from combusting.

"Do you want some wine?" he asked, as he stood in front of his double fronted fridge. It always made me smile how organised everything was inside. "I know you like water, but you can have something else."

"Are you trying to get me drunk?"

"Will it make the talking easier for you?" He turned to me as he took a bottle of white wine from the fridge and pushed the door shut behind him.

"Probably, but I'd rather do it with a clear head. I like going in with all my rationale intact."

"Lawyers." He muttered with a scornfully mocking roll of his eyes as he opened the bottle.

"Barrister, actually."

"Ohooo, fancy." He teased as he sat opposite me and poured two glasses.

It smelt sweet and fruity as he pushed it under my nose. It had a lovely earthy sharpness to it, and my mouth was watering for a small, cool mouthful.

"I know how much you like Riesling."

"I do." I sighed, a grin forming on my lips as I took a sniff of the good stuff. I held the scent in my lungs for a moment, hoping that it was enough to give me the Dutch courage I needed to start the conversation. "I'm sorry I left without waking you."

I looked up at him from where my hands were splayed on the black granite table top.

He looked so serious as he trailed my face quietly with his studious eyes.

"Why did you?" He looked genuinely baffled. "We're

friends before any of this." He gestured between us.

I took a sip of wine, hoping it would ease my nerves. I hadn't intended on giving him the whole soliloquy of whys. I hadn't intended on saying much on the matter except that I liked what had happened and that I wanted it to happen again, so long as it wasn't all serious and filled with expectations. I wasn't good with expectations, it seemed that my whole life had been filled with them and I didn't want more.

"Dor?"

"Give me a sec, I'm trying to think of how to say what I need to say without sounding like a complete moron." I flinched at the coarse way I'd replied.

"Here's the thing, we can sit here all night and wait for you to figure out how to say what you need to say. We can waste as much time as you like searching for nicer ways of saying something that essentially will still be said using the words you already have in your head." He thrummed his fingers on the table top. "It's only me, Dorian, you don't have to use fancy words. Just say what you need to."

He didn't get that that was the problem. It was him, my friend, and I didn't want to hurt him or our friendship.

But he wanted the unpolished truth, and in a way I felt like I owed it to him.

"I panicked," I breathed out a little too quickly. "I woke up and I panicked because you were too warm on me. I know it's ludicrous, but my head started working overtime and then I felt guilty because I liked it. I really liked it. It's just that when I've…after…well, it didn't feel like that, Jake. Not that I sleep around, I don't."

"I know," he rasped, his voice catching in his throat.

"I've had sex twice since Phillip. And both times it felt like whatever. I didn't not enjoy it, but it wasn't amazing either, it was …mediocre, I suppose."

"Explains a lot," he mused.

I shook my head at his remark, "Don't go getting a bigger head, yours is big enough as it is."

He pursed his lips as a laugh filled his mouth, his eyes welling with mirth.

"Really, Jacob? I thought we were having a serious conversation."

"We are, but you can't say something like that and not expect me to at least laugh."

"Whatever," I mumbled before I took a long sip of my wine.

He got up and wandered back to the cooker and took the steaming pot from the heat before straining the contents into a colander.

"What are you making?"

"I told you to wait and see." He chirped as he drizzled some olive oil over whatever he'd strained into the sink. He shook it around as he said, "Carry on."

"Carry on?"

"I'm listening." I watched as he poured the contents of the colander into another pot.

My stomach moaned at the strings of pasta slipping into the pot. I loved pasta, I could live on it forever. It was my go to comfort food.

"Keep talking, Dorian." He poured some kind of sauce into the pan and stirred it quickly.

"Oh, right. Okay, well, what I'm trying to say is that I was overwhelmed with a lot of things. Mostly a lot of things in my head, and I thought that if I left that maybe…I don't know, maybe I wouldn't feel guilty for…liking it too much?"

God, that sounds so fucking pathetic.

"We're being honest, right?" He sprinkled some herbs over the food and tossed before he turned to me and continued, "Did you feel guilty because it was me, or because it wasn't him?"

I almost choked on my tongue at his words. I should've expected it really. Jake was very switched on, he noticed a lot of things that most people didn't care to. He and Willow shared that trait. People often thought they let things go over their head, unnoticed, but they didn't.

"Neither," I murmured. My chest was burning with how tight it felt.

When I chanced a look at his face again, I could've cried. He was looking at me with a sort of serious smile that wasn't simply wonderful it was kind and precious and winsome.

"You're probably going to think I'm fickle after this, but the truth is that it scared me that I can't quite remember what it felt like with Phillip. I know it was good, really good, but I can't remember how it felt.

"I could feel you all over me, like it was there and then, but I couldn't even remember how it felt with him. I thought I'd remember all those things forever. I thought they were etched into my brain. Into me."

He walked over to me slowly, his head bobbing from side to side like he was having a conversation with himself. The closer he got the faster my heart raced, waiting for some accusatory slew of words that would devastate me.

I wished I'd kept my mouth shut. I wished that I'd held something back from him.

I had no idea what possessed me to think that it was a good idea to talk to Jake about Phillip. It was stupid. Selfish. Hurtful. I knew I shouldn't have done it.

He crouched in front of me and took the wineglass from my hands. There was a look of lament on his face that made my heart hurt as he twined his fingers with mine.

"Here's what I think about this. Bear in mind that maybe I'm wrong, maybe I have no clue what you're feeling." He shrugged. A contemplative sadness shadowing his face. "But I understand where you're coming from."

He searched my face in the silence between us. His thumbs caressing mine as he held onto my hands tighter.

"At one point or another everyone loses someone they care about, Dor. People die, that's just life. Good people, shit people, nice people…arseholes and even middling, ordinary, so-so folk. People you care about." He paused for a moment, a sorrowful and breath-taking pause that made the air thick and my eyes water.

I watched as his eyes shimmered and reddened as he looked at our hands. He turned them over again and again as he took in deep breath after deep breath.

"You don't forget them, but as time goes by certain things become a little murky. You can't quite remember what they sounded like. You can't remember what they smelt like.

"Touch and feel are the hardest ones to remember. Something so simple as touch. You think it's simple and every day, but touch is probably the most unique thing about a person. The texture of their skin. The warmth of their blood. The density of their muscles. Even the weight of their bones. All of those things factor into the feel of someone's touch."

His hold loosened on one of my hands and slowly he caressed my face with his knuckles. His thumb trailed the bridge of my nose and a gasp pressed out of me as my eyes closed.

"You can clone smell and you can replicate sound, but you can never simulate an individual's touch. Once they're gone, it's gone with them and eventually it's forgotten. You're left with a makeshift memory that never lives up to the real thing." He dropped my other hand into my lap and cupped my face, and the feel of his hands on me, the way they trembled as they touched me…my heart couldn't take it.

The enormity of his words and the follow up of his touch, it was heavy. And in my head all I could wonder was how he knew this.

How did he get so wise and experienced on the loss of someone's touch?

"Jake…" I whispered as he kissed the tip of my nose lightly and then my forehead. "Jacob…"

"You're not fickle, Dorian. You are perfectly human," he breathed as his forehead touched mine. "And it's okay to panic. But you need to know that it's okay to move on too."

"I know that, but I also want to keep him alive for Daniel. He deserves to know his dad, even if it is through my faulty memories. That's my priority. He's my priority. Daniel."

"I know that," he murmured lightly.

"I can't promise you anything, Jacob. I'm lucky that I've had two nights off in the last week, I never get that."

"I know that too."

"I don't want any more expectations thrust on me, or commitments. I want to enjoy myself. I want fun, I never got to have fun."

He chuckled as he stood, his eyes perusing me from head to toe. "Fun is definitely something I can do. But, you need to know that repetitive fun has consequences."

"I don't want things to be awkward between us. Daniel likes you, and I like you…"

He shook his head as he laughed, "I should hope you like me, otherwise this would definitely be awkward."

"I don't want that."

"So we're clear, if things were going to get weird because we're having sex, we wouldn't be having this conversation. As long as we're honest with one another, we'll be okay." He grinned at me as he wandered back to the pot he'd left on the stove. "We should probably eat before the food gets cold. I'm not even sure if it's nice, I sort of worked with what I know you like."

"It smells good," I said as he started dishing up. "What is it?"

"Carbonara. Well, kind of."

"That's my favourite," I smiled. My hands and feet clenched and curled with excitement.

"I know," he grinned smugly as he put a plate down in front of me and then sat opposite me with his own. "I hope it's nice, I've never made it before."

"I thought you didn't eat bacon?"

"I don't, I used turkey bacon. That's why I said it's sort of Carbonara."

I took a forkful into my mouth and chewed it for a moment. It tasted like it. Eggy, smoky…kind of bacony and earthy from the herbs.

"It's nice, tastes so good. I've never made it myself, I order it in when I fancy it."

"I've never had it before, it's really good though."

"I know this is going to sound stupid, but I never pictured you as a cooking kind of man."

"I do have to feed myself on a daily basis. I couldn't live off of takeaways and junk. Growing up we never really ate anything other than home cooked meals." He paused for a moment, a faraway longing look rippling across his face as he ate a bit more of his pasta. "The only time we'd eat out was when we went to events and functions or when we went out for special meals. Mum was funny about what we ate."

"Feeding kids is a job all of its own, Daniel would have junk over anything I cook."

"I think it's a kid thing. My dad used to sneak me a McDonalds once in a while when Mum left us with him. He loves bacon. He's not your typical Jewish bloke. He goes to the Shabbat service every Saturday morning with my mum, but apart from that they're pretty lenient with their practice."

"Oh," I whispered as my mind instantly went on a tangent of its own trying to piece together his words from earlier and the long story that he wasn't telling me. "Can I ask you something?"

He looked up at me with his soft, brown eyes half lidded like he was trying to gauge what my question was and if he should give me the okay to press on. His chest rose and fell on a long exhale before he said, "Sure."

"Those things you said before?" I breathed in deeply as I tried to steady my voice, merely thinking about his words was making my eyes tingle and burn.

"Mmmm…" he rasped, the lines of his face setting into a soft frown.

"How do you know them?" My voice cracked a little.

He wet his lip with the tip of his tongue before he ran it across his teeth. His deep inhale snagging as his chest trembled almost unperceptively.

"It's a long story." He repeated on a sigh.

"Won't you tell me?" I asked softly. "I'd like to know. I feel like I should."

"Maybe," he smiled pensively.

"Okay."

I watched him finish the rest of his food in silence as I sipped at my wine and wondered about the story that he would maybe tell me. I hoped he would.

We knew so many little things about each other. Little things that amounted to so much. Yet, with the knowledge that there was something that he wasn't telling me, I felt like there was so much I wasn't aware of. So much I wanted to learn. There was this need inside me that yearned to know all there was to know about him.

I'd never given it too much thought, but Jake was a big part of my life. Daniel adored him, and I'd be lying if I said that it wasn't a mutual adoration. Jacob had been there from day one. From the silly and inappropriate slogan bibs and bodies to the little christening bangle he'd gifted him. To all the football games he'd taken him to with Jamie and all the hours he'd sat in my lounge playing on Daniel's consoles.

"What are you smiling about?" he asked as he stood from the table and took our plates.

"Do you remember that body you got Daniel with the fox?"

"I should get him the t-shirt," he laughed.

"I don't know how I feel about him going around with a

t-shirt that says *zero fox given* on it at his age. It was cute and witty when he was a baby and didn't understand."

"Do you know what I remember about that thing?" he cringed. "That day he was sat on my lap, wearing it, and he quite literally shit the place out. I've never seen so much crap in my life."

"It was everywhere."

"Everywhere?"

"It took me days of scrubbing the chair you were sat in to get the stain out completely. I almost gave up and threw it out." I laughed as I got up to help him clear up.

"My clothes went in the bin. I couldn't look at them again after that…shit-a-geddon."

"I had to bleach the body, and even then I couldn't get the stain out."

"His poos were lethal for a while. There was this one time when Jamie was looking after him and he came over. We were on the sofa watching Nemo for the umpteenth time and out of nowhere he shoved his fingers in his nappy and then up my nose. It was fucking gross, I could've bleached my face."

"Oh god, I'm sorry." I cringed whilst he sat me up on the counter by the dishwasher. His laughter rumbling through me. "I didn't know about that one."

"Jamie still has a right laugh at that little memory once in a while." He brushed the loose tendrils of hair from my face with both of his hands.

His lips whispered across one of my cheeks, a warm silence settling between us. His big hands cupped my face as his thumbs stroked across my lips.

"I've been counting down the days to seeing you all week.

It feels like forever since I kissed you." His murmur was soft and sweet as I wrapped my legs around him. My skirt hitched up my thighs, the short split pulling open as he settled between my shaking legs.

"I think you should kiss me now," I breathed into his parted lips.

He gazed pensively into my lust hazed eyes. "You do?"

"Yes."

He smiled as his thumbs pulled at my lips, tracing down to my chin. The tip of his nose brushing mine as he tilted his face and slowly closed the miniscule distance between our mouths.

The raspy groan as our skin touched and our breaths mingled had my hands slipping off the counter and up to his waist. He felt so tall as he leaned over me with his breaths melting into my heated skin. His teeth gently nipping at my bottom lip before he sucked it into his mouth pulling a lust filled moan from me.

I could feel his smile as he pulled at my lip and it slipped out of his mouth with an inaudible pop. His hands slid down my jaw to my throat, rumpling the wide high neck of my jumper.

"Are you going to stay?" he asked, as he kissed the edges of my mouth, his thumb lightly pressing to the hollow of my throat.

"Do you want me to?" I moaned as one of his hands inched down between us as he lightly cupped one of my breasts over the soft knit.

He licked up to my ear, dropping small, quiet kisses and said, "That's a pointless question."

My insides fluttered as he tilted my head to the side gently and kissed down my neck, the hand cupping my boob trailing down before he pulled my jumper free of my skirt. He hummed as his hand inched up over my stomach, beneath my jumper.

God, his touch felt so good. It felt like it was melting with my skin and caressing my muscles and bones.

My head fell back as he kissed up the column of my throat, nipping the fiery skin all the way to my lips and before I could even moan, his tongue was licking into my mouth, so softly at first. And as it explored, it got more urgent and needy. His touch got deeper and rougher.

My bones felt like they were vibrating inside me with how fast my blood rushed through me. My entire being was begging for more of his. It was a sort of desperation I'd never felt before. It was exuberant and encompassing. It was delightful and pained.

I thought I knew how deep someone could touch you, but this felt new. It felt raw and resplendent. Maybe he was right, maybe I did know. Maybe I did recall, but like he'd said, the memory was inadequate.

Whatever it was, it wasn't this.

It wasn't here.

It wasn't now.

And I wanted here and now. I craved it. I craved him. Whether it was wrong or right, I was hungry for Jacob and his touch. His sound. His smell. His taste. It was a blistering and maddening hunger that had my hands pulling at his shirt tails and my nails clawing into the skin of his back.

His hands fell to the counter on either side of me as his tongue swirled with mine and as my legs and arms tightened around him, he scooped me up from the counter. He pushed me further up his body so I was leaning down on him. His face tilted all the way up to mine and my hands simply had to cup his lightly stubbled chin. I kissed him with every bit of want and need that he was rousing in me with his touch and his gasping breaths. He took a few steps to his kitchen island and sat me down on the edge.

His hands twisted into the hem of my jumper and yanked it over my head. My arms instinctively lifting to allow him to strip it off me. He dropped it on the island top somewhere behind me and without hesitation his hands were splayed across my back. His fingers pinched the clasp of my bra loose and the straps fell to the crooks of my elbows.

My pussy clenched as he licked out of my mouth and down my neck. His hands tangled into my hair as he bit down on the lace of my bra and dragged it down with his teeth before he nipped his way back up to my breasts.

The way he groaned as he tasted more and more of my skin was the best kind of turn on. My pussy was pulsing with need for him. My toes were curling as heat rolled through my body.

"Shit," he cursed as his hands loosened from my hair. He pulled away hesitantly. "I need to get that."

"What?" I breathed, a little confused.

"My phone, it's…ummm…" He grumbled with frustration coating his words. "I need to get it, it's important."

He reached behind me, my face burying into his racing chest. His citrus and pepper smell clinging to every one of my senses as I breathed him in through his fitted white shirt. My tongue dipping out and twirling around one of the pearlescent buttons because I couldn't keep it in my mouth. I was so desperate to have more of him, that I didn't care how I got it.

He gave me an apologetic smile as he straightened in front of me and answered, "Hey."

There was a long moment of silence as I watched his eyes close and his head fall with a silent sigh.

"I'll be right there," he said as he stepped further away from me.

I pulled my bra into place and started doing it up again as he ended the call.

"I'm sorry, Dor. I have to go deal with this."

"It's alright," I smiled at him, hoping that maybe he'd smile back.

I studied his sorrowful face, my mind was racing as fast as my heart.

I wanted to ask him if he was okay, but something told me to leave it.

I slipped off the counter and grabbed my jumper, putting it back on quickly. I watched as he tucked his shirt back in, and before I could say anything he pulled me into a hug.

It was hard and crushing. It was the kind of hug you gave someone when you needed them to return it as much as you needed to give it.

"Stay," he murmured into my hair. "I'll be back in an hour or so. It won't take me long to get this sorted."

I'd never been in his house without him.

"Please?" he asked, as he pulled back to look at me.

"Okay," I said before I could stop myself.

"Thank you." He gave me his sad, apologetic smile again before he dropped a quick chaste kiss on my lips.

I watched him grab his keys and wallet as he rushed out of his door. And as I stood there, the lights of his car shining in through the coloured glass panes of his door, I couldn't help but feel like maybe I should've gone with him. That maybe he needed someone with him.

CHAPTER 15

I was driving like an arsehole. I knew it was a reckless thing to do, especially when the streets were packed with people that had more alcohol than sense in their body. However, Eleanor's phone call had left me panicked.

She'd never called me before. It was usually one of our parents asking me to find her, or to help her. So this was something completely new. A part of me was relieved that she sounded okay even in her rushed flurry of frenzied words.

After our conversation yesterday, the last thing I wanted was for her to backpedal. I knew too well how quickly she could fall off the wagon again. How much worse it got every time she relapsed.

My heart felt like it was hammering its way out of my chest.

My hands were clammy around the leather steering wheel, and the traffic was making me feel like I was miles away from her, rather than the twenty minutes it should've taken me to get to the bar she'd told me she was at.

A part of me was angry that she would constantly put herself in an environment that she knew wasn't good for her. The other part wanted to get her the fuck out of there.

My stomach was still churning with the look of confusion on Dorian's face as I rushed out of the house. She looked like she had a thousand and one questions, and after tonight, I knew I was going to have to tell her about Eleanor.

I shuddered as bile rose up my throat. The thought of telling her and having to watch her run a mile was adding to my panic. My muscles were protesting and aching with how tense I was.

She didn't want expectations and commitments, but I was laden with those. And although I didn't want to put any of them on her. I knew that the moment I told her about the shit storm that was my life at times, she wouldn't see the fun in me. She'd see warning lights and blaring sirens. That's what I saw as an outsider looking in.

She's not an outsider.

Maybe she wasn't, but there wasn't anything fun about dropping everything to make sure that Eleanor would stay sober for one more day. There was nothing fun about all the times that I'd driven in circles around London looking for her. Hoping that she was okay. Hoping that it wouldn't be the time that I'd find her or get a call telling us it was too late.

I knew she would see this as a bad idea. She would close up and push me away if not because of her, it would be because she wanted to protect Daniel. I couldn't blame her for that. If anything, I felt like a bastard for not telling her and giving her the opportunity to cut and run earlier.

I needed to tell her. I needed to let her do what was right for her and Daniel, because I wasn't it. I couldn't give her the fun she wanted when I was having to drop her for my sister.

I parked the car in one of the backstreets, slamming my door carelessly as I made a run for the club Eleanor was at.

Did I lock the car? My mind was a fucking jumbled mess. I couldn't even remember what I'd done not even a minute ago.

I stopped outside the place she said she'd be. She told me she was waiting outside. She wasn't. And that panic that I'd been feeling, that I thought was tearing me apart? It was nothing compared to the dread stampeding through me. It was choking me. Like pressure plates crushing my chest.

I spun around, twisted and turned trying to spot her. Hoping that I had somehow missed her amongst the other people walking by or standing around smoking and chatting.

She's not here. She's not here. Think, Jake. Think!

It was like my common sense had taken a hike. Waved goodbye and waltzed off into the night for a jolly.

I'd just managed to talk myself down and turned to go into the place when Eleanor pushed out of the doors. Her hair was in a state. Her dress was barely covering her dignity. She looked a fucking mess.

Shit.

My heart dropped to the pit of my stomach as she stumbled toward me. She looked so thin now that she wasn't all covered up. I didn't even know how she could stand in the cold in that dress.

I should've gone to her. I should've helped her. But I was

glued to the spot. My feet felt set into the concrete beneath them.

The closer she got the worse I felt. Her eyes were red and there were black tracks down her cheeks. Her red lipstick looked smeared all around her lips.

Her legs buckled in her heels and it wasn't until her hands grasped my shirt that I managed to move and hoist her up.

Her eyes met mine, her lips trembling as her chest heaved. "Please take me home," she whispered as heavy tears sluiced down her pale cheeks.

I thought I was going to burst with anger. I thought I was going to shake her until she spewed whatever she'd taken. But as she wrapped her arms around me, I couldn't help but do the same to her. She felt so small. So fragile as the sobs racked out of her.

"I don't want to be here anymore, Jake," she whimpered into my chest, her arms squeezing a little harder around me.

It was only when the force of her hug registered that I realised that she was okay. She would never be able to hold on to me like that if she'd taken something. She wouldn't even be able to talk properly. And she was talking. She was sobbing and whimpering, but she wasn't slurring.

She looked up at me, her nose red and her face blotchy. Her eyelashes were clumped together with black tinted droplets hanging on the tips.

"I'm so cold," she whispered into the crook of my neck. She leaned her head on my shoulder, huddling into me for warmth.

"Where's your coat?" I asked as I tried to comb through her knotted hair with my fingers. I gave up with her hair and stroked the side of her face instead.

"I don't know. I think I left it on the sofa I was sitting on."

"I'll go get it for you, okay?"

She looked up at me panicked. "No! I want you to take me home, please? I want to go home with you, I don't want to go in there again."

I took a step back from her and held her up in front of me. "What's happened?"

"It doesn't matter. Everyone's drunk and it's so loud. People keep touching me and talking at me…" She shook her head manically as she looked around, her nails digging into her jaw and her neck as she cried.

I was back to square one. The way she was clawing at herself and looking around like she was being followed. She looked like she was on the verge of a breakdown.

"Eleanor?" I called her attention back to me. "What did you take?"

She shook her head again.

"I need to know what you've taken, I can't help you if you don't tell me."

She stilled and took in a deep breath. Her eyes meeting mine again. They looked normal, red and swollen from her crying, but normal.

"I didn't. I didn't do anything," she suspired.

"Okay." I wrapped my arm around her and started to walk her to my car. "Let's get you home then."

We'd barely made it a few feet down the road when someone started calling her from behind us.

"Don't stop. Don't stop. Please. I'm trying. I'm trying. Don't stop." She chanted between sobs.

I paused as her phone started ringing in her bag. She looked back as she took it out. Her hands shaking so badly I had to take it from her and answer the damn thing before I handed it back to her.

She looked at me like she didn't know what to do with it. She passed it from hand to hand as I continued holding her up. It wasn't until I turned around that I realised it had been Miles calling her.

"What's wrong, Eleanor?" I asked her as that same off feeling I'd felt when he'd sat at the table with us yesterday tightened around my stomach.

She looked down at her phone again before she put it to her ear and said, "I hate you."

Her tone was harsh and indignant. Condemnatory. It was hateful. I'd seen many things from her. I'd heard her say hurtful and spiteful things, but the venom in her voice, it was cold and sharp.

I hate you. That was all she said before she turned off her phone and slipped it back into her bag. She clung onto me as she turned back towards my car. She said nothing else, she just cried. Heavy, woeful tears that drowned her breaths.

She huddled into the front passenger seat of my car, and the minute I turned my engine on she cranked up the hot air and the seat heater. She slipped off her heels and brought her legs up to her chest, bunching herself into a tiny ball of silent sobs and clawing fingers.

I knew how dangerous it was for her to sit like that. I knew that if anything happened and my airbag activated, that her legs would crush her chest. The thing was, she didn't look like she could be crushed and broken any further. And I didn't care how slow I had to drive back home. How many quiet backstreets I had to drive through to stay out of any reckless traffic. I'd do it if it meant that she hung on for what was left of today, so she could keep trying tomorrow.

* * *

It took just under an hour for her to calm down and relax. I'd driven down every possible back road from Mayfair to Hampstead Heath. My eyes were blurring with how exhausted I was from listening to Eleanor's sobs.

The only thing that was keeping me awake was my mind whirring on, trying to find a way of explaining everything to Dorian without making a scene in front of Eleanor. I could imagine the way her face would fall as I walked in with Eleanor in tow. The way she was out, I'd probably be carrying her in.

I thought that maybe I should call her. Pre-warn her about the state Eleanor was in, but then I'd be giving her a chance to skedaddle before I got there.

This whole mess was blowing my mind and all I wanted was to walk into my house, sort Eleanor out and fuck everything else away. I wanted to close my bedroom door, strip Dorian naked and lose myself in her.

That sounded like a plan.

Maybe I could hope that she wouldn't see the shit side of everything, that maybe she'd see that I was still me, even with all my fucked up baggage. I hoped that she understood that I didn't expect her to take any of this on. No expectations or commitments on my part.

The only expectation I had of her, was that she would come as much as I made her.

I parked the car in front of my garage and took a moment to get my head straight. I was still fretting about what had happened between Eleanor and Miles tonight. I was fretting about everything.

I was still asking myself why I hadn't gone back and demanded he tell me exactly how he'd let her get into that state. Why she was that angry with him. Why he hadn't been looking after her. How he could leave her like that.

"I've always wondered what it's like for you to live in this house." I heard her hoarse whisper as I rested my chin on the steering wheel. "How can you wake up every day in their house?"

"It's like living in any other house. There are stories in every wall. Memories in every corner. I just happen to know what they are, the ones I can remember."

"Sounds like a mindfuck."

"It's not," I sighed as I sat back in my seat. "What happened tonight, Eleanor? Why didn't Miles take you home earlier? Why were you even there?"

"I don't want to talk about it right now." She shook her head as her fingers wiped at her eyes again. "Your lights are on. You shouldn't leave your lights on, it wastes energy."

I couldn't help but smile, knowing that Dorian was still there. Hoping that maybe she'd still want to stay.

"I know you don't want to talk about it, but I need to know that you're okay. Here's the thing, Eleanor, there's someone in there—"

"I don't have to stay with you," she said quickly.

"That's not what I was trying to say."

"I don't want to get in the way."

"Dorian doesn't know about…your problem."

"Right." She looked at me like she knew what I was about to say, her eyes rounded as she swivelled towards me. "You're going to tell her."

"I have to, chipmunk."

"Why?"

"Because…" *I can't have you in the same house as her, and not tell her.*

"Is she your girlfriend?"

"No." I swallowed the sigh that pushed up my chest.

"So why does it matter if she knows?"

"Because she matters," I said a little short and surly. "She's a friend…"

"You're fucking."

"Hey, you may have had a rough night, but you don't get to comment on our friendship. You don't get to say anything mean about her. She's a good person, Eleanor."

"I'm not being mean. She's a stranger to me." She glanced at the house and then looked toward me again. Her chin resting on her knees as she continued hugging her legs to her chest.

"She's Jamie's sister."

She smiled at me with the googly eyes she reserved for my friend. "Mmmm…Jamie."

"Don't start."

"You're the one fucking his sister."

"Stay on track, Eleanor," I breathed as I rubbed my face with my hands. We were both quiet for a moment. "I need to tell her because she has a child, and she deserves the option to decide if she's okay with this."

"Why does it matter? You're the one she's sleeping with, not me."

"What do you think will happen if I keep ditching her for you?"

She nodded as she realised what I was trying to tell her. "I'm sorry I ruined your night."

"You didn't ruin my night, but I do need to explain to her why I was so quick to leave earlier."

"Okay," she conceded a little and, I suppose, understandably grudgingly. "I'm tired."

"You feeling warmer now?"

"Yeah."

"That dress is obscene, by the way," I told her as I got out of the car and went round to her side. "I should burn that shit," I continued grumbling to myself as I opened her door, she got out slowly, her feet unsteady in her heels.

She didn't say anything more as we continued to the front door, I rubbed my hands over her arms whilst she walked slowly in front of me. The cold blustering through the cotton of my shirt and chilling my skin.

She took a deep breath as I opened the front door and held it open for her. Her hand shading her eyes from the light coming down the hallway from the kitchen.

Her shoulders hunched as she turned away and faced me and I couldn't help but pull her in for a hug. Even with the trepidation over the conversation I was about to have pulling and squeezing my insides, I still felt relieved that she was okay.

I only hoped that I'd be okay too at the end of the night.

CHAPTER 16

Dorian

T he moment I heard the lock of Jake's front door click my tummy twisted. The worry I'd been feeling for the last two hours dulled. In its place a sort of heart pumping relief had me taking my first full breath since he'd walked out.

I took another look around his kitchen to make sure that I hadn't forgotten to put anything away. Between our conversation, heavy petting and his phone call, the dishes had been forgotten. It wasn't till I dragged my feet back into the room that I realised that we'd completely gotten side-tracked from the cleaning up.

He was so good at making me forget things, our surroundings…everything really.

I'd spent the first few minutes pondering any excuse to

leave, anything that wouldn't scream—*this is fucking insane and I have to get out of here before I lose my mind over you anymore than I already have.*

Of course, I didn't. And the reason I didn't was because I was too caught up in my worry over him.

That was crazy too. It wasn't the first time I'd seen that frustrating sadness on his countenance, but after our talk and everything he'd said I knew there was more. I knew he had a story I wanted to unravel from him. I just wasn't sure how to do it.

Maybe it was the barrister in me that was trying to piece everything I already knew of him together. Maybe it was that drive that had me desperate to fix whatever it was that had him so melancholy.

Whatever it was, it had me unable to leave. Unable to walk out of his house even though I could feel this insidious morbidity settling in the pit of my stomach. Almost like it was readying me for whatever it was he wasn't telling me.

The clattering of heels in the hallway had my body tensing and the hoarse, broken whispers that followed had me questioning whether I should have stayed.

I scrolled through the document I'd been working on blindly. My vision lending its sharpness to my hearing as I tried to pointlessly make out what was being said.

All I could tell was that he was talking to a woman.

I leaned back in my chair and glanced down the hallway, straight at the front door, my heart lurched when I saw them.

His arms wrapped tight around her and her face buried in his neck as her long hair spilled over his shoulder and down his back.

Her dress was more of a long top that banded around her tall frame. It stopped at the top of her thighs, leaving her long legs out for yonks.

Even in the dim porch light that spilled in from the glass panes of the door and collided around them with the light from the kitchen, I could tell that she was skinny.

People called me skinny, but I was sure that next to her, I'd look like I had a lot more meat on my bones.

I turned back to my Mac, debating whether or not to close it and pack all my things away so I could leave. I was beginning to feel like I was intruding. Like I should be anywhere but here.

I saved my work. I must've done it at least twice in my distracted state. My fingers lightly tapping the keyboard in a weary Mexican wave of sorts.

What am I doing here?

I kept asking myself the same thing. Even as I heard their footsteps up the first flight of stairs. My instincts were telling me to leave, but there was this voice that kept reminding me that I said I'd stay.

My head was all a messy mishmash of his downcast eyes as he asked me to stay, my assent and the echoing question of why I was still there.

It's a long story.
Won't you tell me?
Maybe.
Maybe.
May—be.
May. Be.

My heart raced as I twisted and turned that word in my head. I broke it down and said it a hundred different ways to try and figure out what he meant by it.

Maybe he'd tell me?

Maybe later?

Maybe one day?

Maybe was such a perfidious word. It wasn't yes and it wasn't no. It wasn't anything concrete. It was the answer I gave Daniel whenever he wanted something and I didn't want to tell him no. Maybe if you're good—because I know you're going to do something that will give me reasoning to say no. Maybe if the weather doesn't change—because the weather was always bound to change. Maybe next week—because by next week you won't even remember this conversation.

Maybe. What a faithless, unreliable word.

His presence had me out of my head the minute I felt it. I closed my laptop and slid it into my bag on the chair next to mine. His soft approaching steps paused by the cupboard next to the fridge. He took out two tumblers and filled them with ice from the fridge dispenser and then pulled out the rolling larder and took a fancy conical bottle out.

Whatever it was the stopper looked heavy and the bottle itself old and expensive.

It was one of those moments where I knew that he was about to tell me something I didn't want to hear.

Careful what you wish for, Dorian.

He put the bottle down with the glasses in front of me. My eyes instantly focusing on the gold gilded font. Tequila. Very expensive tequila.

"Everything okay?" I asked as I splayed my left hand on the cold, dark granite in front of me. I pressed it to the warm patch where my Mac had been, hoping that it would soothe the cold that was running through me.

He took a deep breath as he moved my bag to another chair and sat down next to me. He reached for the bottle and poured us both a good measure.

I didn't mind tequila, but it wasn't something I drank back like that. Wine was the drink I ordinarily went for. I'd never enjoyed the burn of strong liquor down my throat. But then, I'd never been one to drink my feelings or problems. I was more of a distract myself with work kind of person.

I pulled and twisted at the ring on my finger. His eyes narrowed on it and his jaw clenched as he breathed out through his nose.

"I'm sorry I took so long," he sighed. "She was in a bit of a state and I needed to make sure she was okay."

"She?" I asked as he took a long sip of his drink.

"Eleanor," he breathed. "My sister."

Oh. "You know, I can leave. I don't have to stay tonight; I wouldn't want to impose…"

One of his hands paused over mine, the tips of his fingers rubbing my almost black purplish polished nails. He swirled the tumbler in his other hand, the ice knocking together as he turned it so that the deep amber liquor licked at the rim of the glass.

"You asked me how I knew all those things earlier."

"You said it was a long story." My voice was breathy as my violently beating heart stole all the power from it.

"It is," he retorted distantly.

His hair looked messy like he'd been pulling at it. His lips looked a little too raw like he'd been worrying them. His eyes though, his eyes were what made me ache. The pain in them was so vivid with the way it swirled around the dark depths, framed by his thick lashes.

I grabbed the bottle from the table and stood. I turned my palm up and threaded my fingers through his as I gave him a tug.

"I've got all night to listen to you, but we need to move somewhere a little less formal. We're friends talking, not people doing business." I smiled as he finished the drink in his glass and got up.

I took in his wry closed lipped smile for a moment. I wish I hadn't, because all it did was ramp up the worry that was clawing at my insides.

"Come on, Doctor Roth." I gave him another playful tug, my heart wincing slightly at the narrow eyed look he gave me. "What? Would you prefer Mr. Roth? They both sound equally as aged."

"You heard that, did you?" he asked as he followed quietly behind to his lounge.

"I guess fancy hospitals are a little quieter. Sound travels a lot better." I shrugged as I put the bottle of tequila down on the coffee table.

He sat on the long sectional, his head shaking in his hands on a low chuckle.

I sunk down on the edge of the chaise end trying to calm my racing heart and all the thoughts that were running around in my head.

His sofa was big, the chaise corner almost the size of a single bed. Much like the house, it was what you'd expect of a family home.

"Do you remember when you sat next to me on the bench at the memorial? I didn't want to talk to anyone, I didn't want people trying to understand what I was feeling. I didn't want their pity. But then you sat next to me and you didn't even say anything, you simply sat there and I remember feeling a little less alone. You made me feel a little less lost in the chaos of it all."

I reached for the bottle on the coffee table and shuffled back into the sofa. I took a quick swig from it and shuddered as the liquid burned down my throat. My stomach lurched as the tequila warmed it a little too much.

Christ, definitely won't be doing that again.

"For a moment you made me think of something else other than how I was going to make it through losing Phillip and how I was going to be able to be a good mother to Daniel without him there to help me do it." I offered him the bottle, feeling relieved when he dragged himself closer to me to take it.

I rested my hand on his as he grasped the bottle, his eyes meeting mine in the dim yellow light streaming in from the window. "I couldn't stop wondering why you had these deep frown lines when all I'd ever seen you do was smile and laugh, tell jokes and tease people. I tried to think of all the possible reasons why your face was set that way, and for a moment it was a reprieve from all the hurt I was feeling."

He nodded another tight-lipped smile at me. His eyes focusing on our hands around the bottle.

"You don't have to tell me anything you're not ready to. I want you to, but I can wait."

He sighed a dry chuckle as he took a drink, his tongue licked at his lips before he said, "There are certain things you can never be ready to talk about, Dor."

I took the bottle back from him and tapped my thighs. I think it was a mum thing to do because it was something I always did when Daniel was upset and he didn't particularly want to talk.

Much like Daniel he quietly laid on his side and rested his head on my lap. A long tired sigh escaping him as I rubbed his head, my nails lightly raking through it.

"She's like our father," he said after a long moment of silence. "She's intelligent, but she's got an addictive personality. She's always been like that. When she was little it was harmless things like a certain meal, drink, sweet. She'd obsess over something to the point that she couldn't think of anything else. She's always had this inexplicable longing for more."

He paused, his eyes drawing in like he was mulling over his thoughts as he raked his teeth over his lip.

"There was this one time where my dad bought her a Kinder egg and she got this doll thing inside it, anyway she got so worked up about having to have the rest of the dolls that my dad went out and bought her all these eggs. She ate one after the other, my brother laughed as she almost pulled her hair out every time she got a doll she already had. She was so wired and frantic, we thought she was going crazy on the sugar, now I sort of feel like I should've done something about it other than watch her lose her shit." His voice was unbearably taut and sorrowful as he breathed each word.

His jaw was clenched so tight as he lost himself in his memory for a moment. I could feel his teeth grinding together as I stroked along it. My nails catching a little in his stubble.

"She ate herself sick. She spent hours in the toilet throwing up. My mum was so angry that she and my dad had this massive argument about it. He ended up in the spare room for days, she was so upset with him." He shuddered, taking a deep breath. "Eleanor was so sick that she couldn't eat dinner and my mum had to shake all the fizz from a whole bottle of lemonade to make it flat, so she could settle her stomach. It was so bad, but the next day, she took the pocket money my parents used to give her and she went and bought a whole load more. She didn't get as sick that time, or if she did, none of us knew about it. She kept doing the same thing until she got all the dolls. When she did, she didn't even play with them. She didn't keep them long."

I stroked his cheek as he screwed his eyes shut. His fingers toyed with the hem of my skirt as we settled back into a sort of expecting silence.

"As she got older we grew used to her obsessive episodes. They were a part of who she was." He cleared his throat as he ran a hand down his face. "It wasn't until I got back from the States and I moved back in with my parents for a while that I started noticing certain habits. She'd get home from college and not leave her room until Mum had to force her to come down for dinner. She would always complain of some sort of ache and pain, and she'd do it until Mum would give her a painkiller. I'd never known someone to have so many ailments in my life. My mum used to take her to the doctor and they'd be flummoxed as to what was wrong, but she'd cry and they'd prescribe her something a little stronger than the last."

He swallowed thickly as his lips trembled. His chest heaved as he rubbed at it with his fist.

Realisation can be a cruel thing. It washed over me as his words settled and the look on his face grew more pained and angry. My chest felt like it was about to split with how brittle my bones felt taking the hammering from my pounding heart.

"That's how it started. Painkillers. It wasn't until she had to have her appendix out that it got worse. She'd been whingeing for days about how she couldn't take the pain, but it was nothing out of the ordinary for her. She was always in some sort of pain, and she didn't look like she was sick. Mum thought it was something to do with her period. Dad gave her a once over, I did too and she seemed fine. We thought it was stress from her A-Levels, you know? I was in my first year of core training and I knew how badly stress and lack of sleep could fuck your body over. I assumed that's all it was, as did everyone else, but the next day my parents got a call from her college saying that she'd been taken into hospital. She'd collapsed during one of her exams."

"What happened?" I asked as he turned in my lap, his eyes darting to the ceiling.

"Her appendix ruptured, she was rushed to theatre. Mum and Dad were a mess, and all I could think was not her too. She was the last thing I had of our parents. Ryan had left and we'd grown apart. She was the last thing that I had that reminded me of my mother."

"I don't-I don't understand." I was trying so hard to make everything he was saying fit. But the pieces didn't meld together.

The last thing he had of his parents? The last reminder of his mother?

"What? Jake, I don't…"

"Jamie sat with us the whole time. He would go and try and get news on how she was doing, but it wasn't until she came out and we were told that she was okay that I could breathe again." He took a deep breath before he carried on. "They dosed her up on morphine and, I think, that's what broke the camel's back. She became dependant on it and when they sent her home a couple of weeks later with a prescription for Sevredol, it was the worst thing that could've happened to her."

"I don't know what that is." I murmured as I stroked down the bridge of his nose with the tip of my finger.

"It's an opioid painkiller. It's used to help with severe pain after major surgery or trauma. It's morphine in a tablet."

"Why would they give her something like that to take at home?" The strongest painkiller I'd ever taken was after I'd had Daniel and it'd been something I could get over the counter.

"The procedure they had to do after the rupture wasn't exactly small. They ended up having to remove contaminated tissue to reduce the chances of her developing sepsis and when you start removing tissue it's hard to know what the recovery of a person is going to be like. You start touching other organs and that in itself can lead to a more painful recovery.

"It's a bit like when you have a baby, your organs have to readjust and settle back into their places. For some people it's something they don't even blink at, for others it's as bad as having the baby itself." He smiled weakly back at me like he was happy with the analogy he'd given me to help me understand.

"Okay," I mused.

I went over what he'd told me so far in my head and made notes on things to ask once he was done.

"She was slowly weaned off the morphine. They downed the dosage and then replaced it with codeine. She was given a string of addictive drugs and I wish to god that I'd been better at noticing that she wasn't using them to manage her pain. I wish I'd realised how reliant she'd become on them. I didn't and as a result when she went to Uni her dependency got out of control. She used it as a way to cope with stress and the hype of the party scene.

"The night before the memorial, it was bad. She'd taken so much codeine she couldn't even breathe for herself. Breathing is first nature, it's instinctual, and she was so out of it she couldn't do it."

The only times I'd seen Jacob Roth shed a tear had been when he was laughing his arse off at some stupid joke or funny situation. I never in a million years thought I'd see him shed a sad tear, and I definitely never thought I'd be doing it with him.

All of a sudden all those times that I wished I knew what clouded his smiles. All those times I couldn't stop thinking about it, I wished that I'd known so I could maybe have given him something else to cling on to. Something to really make him smile, even for one quick second. For a heartbeat.

"The paramedics took almost twenty minutes to get to us. I spent all that time giving her rescue breaths, you'd think that as a fucking doctor I'd be a marvel at it. Turns out that keeping a stranger alive was a lot fucking easier than my high as a kite baby sister."

I couldn't stop the tears from running down my face. Or the sobs from wracking my chest as I traced the solitary tracks of his tears with my fingertips. Acid burned in my gut and my throat throbbed as I tried so hard to swallow my tears down. I could feel my heart tearing and bleeding in my chest. A continuous bludgeoning of my insides that made it impossible for me to catch my breath.

I wanted to wrap my arms so tightly around him that somehow I'd absorb all his pain. Somehow I'd lighten his load.

"They got to my parents' house and gave her an antidote injection. By the time we got to the hospital she was breathing on her own. She was hazy and confused, but she was breathing.

They kept her for observation, for one whole hour before they discharged her. One hour. She could've lost her life, and that's how long they kept her in. One whole fucking hour of leaving her in a room with a respiratory monitor."

"But you sat with me, you smiled and made stupid conversation." How selfish it seemed of me. How unfeeling to be sat next to someone and not know the pain they were in. The turmoil that must've been twisting him up inside. And all the while, he was comforting me.

This man, my friend. How could I never have felt the extent of his hurt?

"Do you know what I realised when I sat next to you that day?"

I shook my head as I swiped at the tears rolling down my cheeks.

"It could've been a lot worse." He chuckled scornfully like he was taunting himself. "You made me feel like all I had to do was push, smile, joke, push and eventually the anger and disappointment would fade."

"Did it?" I asked as I stroked his cheek with one hand and wound my fingers into his hair with the other.

"It did right up until the next time I found her off her face, and every single time since. She goes through phases. Patterns. She gets clean and feels good, she's happy. So happy she thinks she can take on the world. Then she starts to party too hard and starts to wear herself down, so then she can't cope with it and that's when she starts taking a little something to allow her to relax. So she can pick herself up, but then the little pick me up wears off and she needs a little more, and then that's not enough so she has to go for the stronger stuff. Eventually she has another incident where she overdoes it and we start all over again. It's never ending, Dorian."

"Why are you telling me all this now? Why didn't you tell me before?" An irrational anger clawed at my chest. How could he not tell me? How could he not let me in when I'd let him see everything?

"Because I…" He shook his head on a deep exasperated sigh. "We…umm…"

"You weren't fucking me?" I asked, sharply. Too sharp even for my own ears.

"Something like that," he replied his head lifting off my lap.

He fell back as I pressed my hand on his chest. "We're not finished."

"That's all there is, a never ending circle of hoping this time she's clean for good. That it sticks. And then when it doesn't, of hoping that this won't be the time she overdoes it and ends it all."

"What about help?"

He laughed bitterly. It was a vacant laugh, nothing like what I was so used to hearing from him.

"Do you know how hard it is to keep someone in rehab? Getting them there without their consent is pretty much impossible, even when they are a danger to themselves. I've tried it all, Dor, I've pulled favour after favour. But it never sticks. So, all we do is try. She tries to make it one more day without using, and I try to make it one more day without losing my sister."

That was the killer. That was the breaking point. Up until that moment in time, despite losing Phillip, I'd never imagined what it would be like to lose one of my siblings. But the moment the words left his mouth, the chill that shuddered through me was nothing short of paralysing. Devastating.

"You asked me for fun, today hasn't been anywhere near fun." He sighed as he cupped my face. His eyes lingered on mine for a moment before they fell to my lips as his thumb stroked along their seam.

His soft touch and his tear blotched face had my anger fading into the background of every other emotion and feeling coursing through my body. At that moment, all I wanted to do was give him a reason to smile.

I didn't even care which smile it was, as long as it was a smile. I'd take what I could get.

"I don't know about that, I quite enjoyed watching you cook. You should definitely do that again." I grinned as he tucked some tendrils behind my ears. "The night's still young."

"I'm not dragging you into this mess. But, I wanted you to know because you're a good mum and Daniel is a great kid and I don't want to expose him to any of this."

Of course, his worry would be with my son. Forget everything else we talked about, Daniel was clearly the worry here.

"I'm sorry I didn't tell you sooner, I know I should have and I get it if you're upset."

"I'm not upset, I'm more cheesed off that you didn't tell me because we're friends before anything else." I watched as his eyes narrowed on mine in confusion. "You've been there for me and Daniel since before he was born. You let my brother drag you into decorating his nursery. The pair of you turned your football games into a kid friendly affair for him. You do a lot for us, Jacob."

I had to take a moment to catalogue all my thoughts and feelings as my mind raced through every single memory of how he'd been there. It was impossible to do it. It was impossible to go through everything. Big thing, little thing, odd thing, special thing, everyday thing…so many things he'd done with us and for us. "You even got into Downton because Willow isn't a fan and Quincy doesn't really watch TV."

"Let's not be hasty about this, Lady Mary is a permanent fixture of my wet dreams." He chuckled, his smile reaching his puffy eyes.

Finally, a smile.

"Don't ruin it. I was on a roll." I laughed as he shuffled up my lap, laying his head on my forearm as I cradled his stubbled jaw. "So yeah, you got into Downton for me, and you bring me macaroons from a fancy patisserie even when you only get yourself Magic Stars from the corner shop."

"Magic Stars are…magic!" He gave me his *I dare you to contradict* me look.

"Whatever," I rolled my eyes at his almost Jake grin. "You also cooked me my favourite meal, when I don't know how to do it for myself. I have to say, that I really liked it, even without the bacon."

"Bacon's overrated."

"Somewhere there's a swine god that's just added you to his shit list." I cautioned him jokingly, enjoying the small respite from our serious conversation before I continued. "I wished you'd told me sooner because it would've saved me a lot of time trying to understand those lines on your face when I could've been imagining what you would feel like inside me."

His jaw dropped at my words, his breath leaving him in a

rush as his eyes widened on mine.

"What am I going to do with you, pretty girl?"

"I don't know, like I said, the night is still young and I think we could both do with some folly."

He grinned up at me as his hand cupped the nape of my neck. His face inched closer before he touched his lips to mine and whispered, "Thank you."

"For what?"

"Staying." He rasped as his tongue licked into my mouth. His kiss was so soft even with the simmering need behind it.

He hummed huskily as I kissed him back, and for that moment it was enough to just taste him. To touch him. To feel him.

I still had a hundred and one questions to ask him, things that he probably didn't even realise I'd picked up on. Probably things he didn't realise he'd said. But right now, all I wanted was to give him a little bit of the reprieve he'd given me all those years ago when we'd sat on a stone bench together.

CHAPTER 17

Jake

My body ached as I stretched. Yet I couldn't help but smile as I breathed in her scent. I couldn't even remember drawing the curtains, but the room was still dark with a glint of light coming from the bathroom. I turned over slowly as my hands searched the other side of the bed for her.

I was still taken aback by her reaction to our talk from last night. I'd expected her to bolt, but she hadn't. Instead we'd laid in bed with a bowl of ice cream, Magic Stars, Jammy Dodgers and Downton on the telly whilst she cuddled into me.

It wasn't exactly the night we'd had planned, but it was nice to simply have her there. It was strangely calming and soothing after Eleanor's episode and our talk.

I was surprised she wasn't bombarding me with questions, especially since I could see them churning around in her head every time I looked at her or she smiled at me. I was even more surprised that she initiated sex with me.

There I was trying to give her a bit of time to digest things, to mull over everything I'd told her, and she went and practically jumped my bones. I liked that she took what she wanted without waiting on me. I liked that even with her abashment and reservation, that she climbed on top and took control.

I ran my hand through the sheets, shuffling a little closer to the other side of the bed. Disappointment flooded me as I opened my eyes again to find her gone. My morning wood losing all its glory as I took in the empty space she'd left.

Seriously? I thought as I pushed the pillow she'd put in her place off the bed. For a moment my heart lurched in my chest, but then this frustrated anger reared its ugly head. I thought she'd been okay. I thought that we'd been okay.

I sat up a little too quickly, my head doing that pulsing thing it did when I'd had one drink too many. Not enough for a hangover, but enough to dry my mouth and earn a headache. I pushed back the duvet, wafting her perfume around me, as my phone glowed up at me from the sheet.

I was so tempted to ignore it, but the bright green notification had me thumbing it open quickly.

DORIAN

> I couldn't sleep and you were out like a light. You probably didn't hear it, but I did say see you later. X

I read her message again and again. I never thought that she was that slippery. I wasn't exactly a heavy sleeper, but the way she managed to sneak off—because she had, regardless of her unheard *see you later*—was unnerving.

ME

It doesn't count.

I replied to her message as I got out of bed. My good mood dwindling quicker than sand in a holey bucket. I showered quickly, there was no point in even trying to go back to sleep. It was almost midday anyway and I wanted to make sure that both women in my house wouldn't give me the slip.

I didn't get it. She couldn't sleep. So what? I thought we'd ascertained that beds weren't just made for sleeping.

I pulled on a pair of jeans and as I opened the other side of my wardrobe to grab a t-shirt, her clothes caught my attention. Again.

I stood there smoothing over the lace of her bra with my fingers. Wondering why I was so upset. I guess her message was something. Last time she'd left and ignored me. At least she'd sent me a message this time. Which was sort of funny because I could picture her trying to figure out how she'd leave me a note when there wasn't a pen and paper lying around.

Still, note or not, she'd scrammed before I even had a chance to see what she looked like first thing in the morning. It was a bit of a silly thought, but I'd watched her sleep for a while the first time we'd fucked. Not in a creepy way or anything. It was just that her eyelashes fluttered with every one of her sleepy breaths. The pout of her bottom lip as she rested was adorable as fuck. But what intrigued me was the way one hand cradled the swell of her breasts, like she was holding her heart in place or something.

Maybe I should too, because I'd only fucked her twice and I was already having trouble trying to remember what it was like to fuck anyone else. Even worse, I couldn't imagine fucking another woman. There was no back-up for when she decided she'd had enough fun with me.

Is this what women feel when they wake up and I'm gone?

Nope. It couldn't be because they knew going in that it was a one-time thing. Like I knew Dorian and I were a fun thing. Right?

Just fun.

Or maybe, it could be more than fun. Kind of like long-lasting fun?

Long-lasting fun? You don't do lasting fun, arsehole. Quick, easy, simple…get in, get out and find another.

But Dorian wasn't just another. And long-lasting fun meant commitment. She didn't want any more commitments. Plus, that meant opening myself up to the possibility of disappointment. One day she could be gone and then what?

Coffee. I needed coffee to clear my head and think logically. This whole heart doing the thinking thing was making my pulsing head a lot worse. It was also allowing the frustration of her leaving to sink a lot deeper into my bones.

Pull yourself together, man.

I shook my head, trying to clear it or at least compartmentalise all the shit going around in it. Well, not quite shit, but thinking about all this was pointless, especially when I had Eleanor to deal with.

I opened my t-shirt drawer and took the first one that came to hand. I pulled it on before I rummaged through my gym gear drawer trying to find the ridiculous leggings Willow had bought me last Christmas. They were right at the bottom with the equally ridiculous vest that was two sizes too small to actually allow for any movement, let alone exercise.

They'd have to do. I had nothing else that could potentially fit Eleanor. There was literally nothing that would stay on her.

Something else that we really needed to talk about. Not from an aesthetics point of view, but from a she needed to strengthen her body realisation. Watching her walk in her heels had been painful. Every step had me wincing and hoping that she wouldn't snap an ankle.

I grabbed my phone from the rumpled, unmade bed and headed toward what used to be my childhood bedroom. The house was so quiet that my light rap on the door echoed through the hallway.

"Eleanor?" I called softly through the door before she opened it. Her hair was even more of a mess, but at least the make-up was gone. The robe I'd given her last night swallowed her up. She looked down at my hands as I held out the clothes for her. "This is all I could find that might be okay on you."

"Athleisure. Wonderful." She gave me a grimacing smile.

"Beggars can't be choosers, chipmunk." I teasingly patted her hair. "We can get something whilst we're out."

"Out?"

"Yes, we need to talk and eat. Francesca is re-stocking later today, so we have to go out."

"I don't want to go out." She sighed, her fingers twisting into the clothes. "Can't you order something?"

"I can, but I'm not going to because fresh air is good. Getting out and about is good."

"Can't we have a lounge day?"

"No, Eleanor. We're going to go out, get you some new clothes and then we're going to Mum's for dinner." Her sallow face fell and her dark green eyes shuttered at my words.

"No."

"We don't have to tell her about last night, that stays between us, but I'm not cancelling on her and I'm not leaving you today."

"I'm fine."

"Good." I smiled at her as I tugged the strand of hair she was sucking on out of her mouth. "Let's keep it that way, okay?"

She sighed and burrowed her face into my hand as I cupped her cheek. "Okay."

* * *

I sat waiting for Eleanor to change into her new clothes. She'd been tugging and pulling at the clothes I'd given her earlier every step she took. It'd been irritating as fuck to watch. To make it worse I could tell she was freezing, which made me feel like a right dick for making her leave the house in nothing but the leggings, vest and one of my heavy hoodies…and her heels.

I hadn't thought things through. People were staring at us like we were some kind of spectacle, and all I wanted to do was yell at them to mind their own fucking business.

At one point I thought the security guards were keeping a close eye on us, trailing us around the large department store like we were about to make off with something.

I was an idiot. But all I wanted to do was get her out of the house and maybe get the whole story from yesterday. Not that she was talking to me, she definitely had the hump and I couldn't blame her because, well, I'd unwittingly made a show of us in public.

I gave a pregnant woman my seat as she stood waiting in the queue to get to the fitting rooms. I checked my pocket again for the receipt, last thing I wanted was security making an even bigger palaver. I paced up and down and around the racks of clothing. In my head nodding at the pieces that I knew Dorian would wear.

Eleanor was coming out of the dressing rooms when my phone started going off. I would've ignored it, but with my head being on who it was, I couldn't. It was like somehow I'd conjured her call with my thoughts.

"It counts." She said as soon as I put my phone to my ear.

"Hello to you, too."

"Oh, hi," she crooned. "It counts."

"You still left." I stated as I smiled at Eleanor and mouthed, "All good?"

She nodded.

"I did, but it wasn't because of last night or because I wanted to. I thought that you could do with some space to talk to your sister."

Eleanor paused in front of me as we walked to the escalator. Her eyes narrowing like she'd heard what Dorian had said.

"If I was her I wouldn't want to talk with a stranger around the place."

"I told her I was telling you."

There was a moment of pause before she said, "Still, knowing that someone knows your story, doesn't make it comfortable to talk about it in front of them."

"Maybe."

"Not maybe, Jacob," she retorted soothingly. "I did the right thing, even if you don't believe I did."

I couldn't even argue back, because the way she'd put it, she was right. Annoyingly so.

"I was going to ask if you wanted to come over for dinner. I've picked Daniel up from his friend's house and we're going to pop to the shop to pick up a few things. Apparently he's in the mood for fajitas. I've never made them from scratch before, but Gwen's sent me the recipe he likes."

"I can't," I sighed as I followed Eleanor down the escalator. "I'm spending the day with Eleanor, otherwise I'd love to."

"Is she okay?" she asked, her voice so soft.

"Yeah, we've picked up some clothes. I didn't have anything for her to wear at mine."

"I wasn't only asking about last night. Is she okay?" she repeated her question, the emphasis on the word okay making it clear what she was asking.

"For now. One more day." I replied as I smiled at Eleanor. She reached into my coat pocket and took out the folded receipt and held it up to the security guard at the door with her purchase bag.

"Okay, well, if you want…" She trailed off as Daniel said something to her. "Daniel says he needs to show you something or other on the game. Anyway, if you do want to come and have dinner with us, you can bring her along. We can even go out, rather than me ruining a perfectly good recipe."

"I can't do that, not with Daniel." I said as I followed Eleanor back to my car.

"Okay, but Jake?"

"Yeah?"

"Don't forget she's a person. Underneath it all, the good

and the bad, she's a person. I know you're trying to do the right thing, but sometimes, the right thing isn't the best thing."

"I know that."

"Well, the offer is there, if you want it. If she's herself, then it's okay."

I stopped a few strides away from my car. Eleanor was already standing by the boot, waiting for me. I unlocked it for her and watched as she threw her bags in and got into the passenger side quickly.

She looked a lot better than she had last night. Her colour was coming back and now that her hair was knotted on top of her head, she looked like herself again.

"Rain-check?"

"Absolutely," she chuckled. "If I'm still alive after making these fajitas."

"Maybe it'd be safer if you ordered them in?"

"Maybe," she mused and then her voice soured, "I've got a call coming through. Call me later?"

"Definitely," I smiled at her request. She had a way of making me see through the crap, of making me look forward to the simplest things.

I knew it shouldn't make me feel this good to know she wanted me to call her later, but it did. It really fucking did.

"Oh, before I go…" She had that I'm going to have the last word lull to her voice. I paused by my door, my hand ready to pull on the handle. "It counts."

"I thought you had another call?"

"I'll call them back." She giggled and it made my face ache with how big it made me smile. "But yeah, it so counts."

"Whatever," I laughed.

"Goodbye, Jacob." She sang as I got into the car.

"Bye, Dor." I ended the call as I turned the engine on.

I could feel Eleanor's eyes on me as we drove towards our parents' house. She was watching me quietly, like she was assessing me. Her manicured nails rapping on the leather armrest between us.

I knew what she was doing. She was prying without actually asking anything, and it was making me uncomfortable. Being under her scrutiny was making me feel awkward and self-conscious.

"So…" She crooned, it was the first time since last night that she'd spoken without sounding like she'd had the life sucked out of her. "Jamie's sister, huh?"

"Her name's Dorian."

"Yeah, I got that." She looked down at her lap and smiled so lightly that it made me wonder if she was trying to hide it from me. "She's really pretty."

Her emphasis on the pretty made me look away from the road and straight at her. Her eyes were narrowed like she was gauging my reaction.

"She is."

"Yeah, I assume that's why you call her pretty girl?" she chuckled like there was something terribly funny about me calling my…

I tripped over my thoughts.

My what?

Friend.

Dorian is your friend, dickhead.

There was nothing funny about calling *my friend* pretty.

Yes, she is a pretty girl. That's your friend. Don't go getting

ahead of yourself.

"Don't make that face, it's so cute," she cooed at me. "How much do you like her? Like? Love? How long?"

"Considering you still haven't told me what happened yesterday, you're asking me a lot of questions." I snarked at her.

Her face fell, all the happy brightness that had been there evaporated and was replaced with sadness. Frustration. Pain.

"What happened, Eleanor?"

"Life. Life happened, Jake. I got overwhelmed and I panicked. I needed to get out of there."

She wasn't lying, but she wasn't telling me the whole truth either. I could tell from the way she looked in my direction, but not at me. Even when my eyes were on the road.

"What about Miles?"

"Like I said, life happened." Her hands scrubbed down her face roughly, and from the way the tops of her ears were reddening, I could tell she was upset. It was one of her tell-tale signs that she was about to either burst out in tears or lose her fucking cool.

"That's not an answer, chipmunk."

"You didn't answer my question either, *Doctor Roth.*" She looked at me wide eyed and with a smirk on her face. "Oh, that's right I heard a lot of things last night."

I felt my face heat as I cringed at the fact that my little sister had gotten an earful of our shenanigans. "We should've bought you some earplugs too."

"Oh, it's alright, maybe try not to be so loud next time." Her quip was dulled by the way her smile thinned out to a serious pout. "On a serious note, it wasn't that bad. I couldn't sleep, and even if it was, it's your house."

"And yours."

"Fine, it's your home."

"Eleanor?" I called her softly as she focused on the dark weave of her new jeans. "It's your home too, whenever you need it to be."

She looked at me and her lips quirked a tiny bit in acknowledgement of what I'd said. We didn't talk much after that. She put the radio on and hummed along to the soft classical music playing on her favourite radio station.

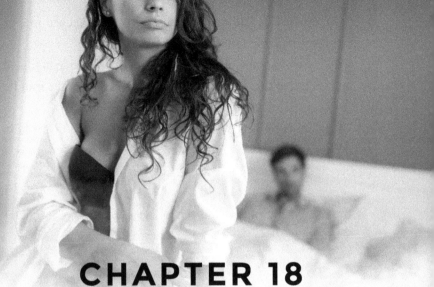

CHAPTER 18

Dorian

I sat in my car, waiting outside the capoeira club Daniel should be coming out of soon. I checked the time again, I still had another twenty minutes till kick out, I wanted to chance it and go grab a coffee to perk me up, but I knew that the moment I moved my parking spot would be gone and I'd have to drive around the block until Daniel came out.

Not worth it.

I contemplated going through my emails, but my head wasn't in the right space. All I could think about was how much I missed Jake. I wanted him so badly that it made my body ache.

I missed being with him. So, much that it was absurd. I liked my space. But it seemed that I liked having him around more. It wasn't even the sex, although that was a big bonus. It was like all my Christmases had come at once when he touched me, or even when I imagined him touching me.

My eyes wandered over to my phone. The voice in my head telling me not to do it. Not to invite him over. It was the middle of the week. A school night.

But then there was another voice that reminded me of how tired Daniel always was after capoeira. He always went to bed earlier, and conked out like a log.

Fuck it.

I grabbed my phone and typed out a quick text as I sang along to the song on the radio.

ME

Want to come over tonight? X

I kept reading it again and again until the three little dots blinked at me.

JAKE

Sure. What about Daniel?

I smiled at his reply, my body heating from the thrill of knowing I was going to see him tonight.

ME

It's a school night. I'm picking him up from the afterschool club now, he'll be out like a light early. X

JAKE

See you later, pretty girl. X

I beamed at the kiss he tacked on to the end of the message. My bottom lip protesting at how hard I bit down on it.

I had no idea how long I'd been ogling his message but the minute light flooded the interior of my car from the opening door of the studio I dropped my phone into my bag on the passenger seat.

I got out of the car as the instructor approached. He looked at me a little disgruntled and from the way Daniel was trailing sheepishly behind him I knew something had happened.

Great, my day was going so well...

* * *

Daniel was flat out ignoring me. It was infuriating, to the point that my blood was still boiling. I was upset with him. I was angry at the child that clearly had it in for my son. But more so, I was angry with myself for not doing something about it sooner.

I knew what life at St. Joseph's was like. I had first-hand experience on how spiteful and entitled some of the kids could be. Especially when they were aware of how liked their parents were by the staff.

Not that it was any excuse for the way he'd lashed out at the other child. Violence wasn't something I'd ever encouraged, but I'd be lying if I said that I wasn't a little bit proud that he'd stood up for himself.

The problem was that his capoeira instructor was also one of the P.E. teachers at the school. He said he wouldn't bring it up as it was an external incident, but he also said that the other boy's mother had mentioned going to the headmaster.

I took another sip of my coffee as I stood in his doorway and watched him sleep. He'd barely touched his dinner, and gone straight to bed like I'd told him to. I could feel his anger still roiling inside, and when I heard him cry himself to sleep I just wanted to cuddle him. My heart was breaking for him, but as much as I wanted to comfort him, I also wanted him to understand that physical retaliation wasn't okay.

This was one of those times where I had to be the bad guy,

the strict parent and not his friend. And it killed me. I hated the way it made me feel.

I wiped the tears that rolled down my face as the sound of my phone ringing came from the kitchen. I was so tired that I wanted to ignore it, but I couldn't.

I'd been waiting on tenterhooks for Jake. My heart sped up as my quick glance confirmed it was him, and then a stab of disappointment hit me right in the gut. I hoped he wasn't calling to cancel, I needed the distraction he provided.

"Hello?"

"Hey, pretty girl." I could hear his smile in his voice. "Everything okay?"

"Yeah," I sighed, trying to keep the nasal, teary edge off my voice.

"Really?"

"No." I breathed.

I checked the time on the oven clock. It was only seven.

"Shit day?"

"Something like that."

"Want me to make it better?" he chuckled softly.

"Please."

"Want to buzz me up?"

"You're *here* here?" My heart squeezed at the same time that my eyes stung.

"You did ask me to come over, didn't you?"

"Yes."

"Good, I wasn't imagining things then."

I buzzed him in as he hung up, my thoughts racing at the same speed as my manic heart.

He's here.

A happy voice sounded in my head, an unexpected sort of relief coming over me. I wasn't alone.

I wiped my hands down my face and brushed my fingers through my hair quickly. Last thing I wanted was to look a mess. I looked down my blouse to make sure it was still clean and smoothed my skirt.

My heart paused, skipping a beat as he rapped lightly on my door.

I took a deep breath before I opened it and tried to settle my feelings from the whole fiasco this afternoon.

When I pulled the door open though, I don't know what happened. I got overwhelmed all of a sudden and everything came barrelling down with the small glimpse of his soft smile and warm eyes.

Before I could stop, I was flinging myself at him, my arms wrapped around his neck and my face buried itself perfectly into the top of his chest and those fucking stupid tears I'd tried to wipe away decided to pour with a vengeance.

Fuckers.

He didn't say a single thing, he dropped whatever he had in his hands and wrapped his warm arms around me. And for that one little moment it didn't matter that I was the bad guy. That I had to parent my son by myself. Nothing else mattered because I wasn't alone.

That should've been a sobering thought. It should've rang all the alarm bells, but right then I didn't care. I knew it was selfish. I knew that maybe I'd come to regret it. But fuck it.

Fuck. It.

Jake was here and everything felt better, bearable. I didn't care whether or not I was setting myself up in the long run. Right then, I simply wanted to feel a little less desolate and forsaken.

That's exactly what Jacob did for me.

With his strong arms and his big hands. With the way he swayed me ever so slightly from side to side in a comforting rock.

Even when he dropped one arm and bent over awkwardly to pick up whatever he'd dropped to catch me, he never let go of me.

Not when he walked us clumsily through my flat. Or even when we gracelessly collapsed onto my bed. All arms and legs and elbows and knees. And the whole time my face stayed perfectly tucked to his warm chest.

I dragged his balmy scent into my lungs. It heated my insides like freshly cracked pepper flecks. It burned my lungs with its sweet lemony bite and all I could think was how much I wanted more.

I wanted more of him.

I wanted more of the me he brought out.

I wanted more.

I just had no idea what that meant, because I wanted the fun too.

I was also well aware that this was Jake. He already had so much on his plate, he didn't need all my baggage too.

He might like me, and he might like my son, but that didn't mean that he was ready for us. That didn't mean that he'd want to have us.

What person in their right mind would want to take us on?

"Dor?" he whispered into my ear as he brushed the hair off my face. "What's wrong?"

I shook my head slightly.

"Are you okay? Is Daniel?" he asked as he tipped my face up to his with the tips of his fingers. His lips puckered softly on the tip of my nose. "Talk to me, pretty girl."

"I'm trying, Jacob. I'm trying so hard to be a good mum, but it's so hard." I rasped as my tears prickled again.

"You're an amazing mother, Dorian." He said it so matter of factly, like it was something that just was.

"Why don't I feel like it?"

"I don't know, but whatever made you feel like crap, it's wrong." His thumb stroked the length of my jaw soothingly.

"Daniel got into a fight today."

"He's a boy, he's going to."

"No, Jake. He told another child that he was going to 'fuck him up' and then proceeded to punch him."

"What did the other kid do?" He pulled away from me slightly, his face was drawn and serious. "He'd never randomly go at someone, there has to be a reason."

"He was teasing him and calling him a bastard, apparently."

"Well then, the little shit got what he deserved."

I pushed away from him and sat up. He didn't understand the seriousness of the situation. How could he? He wasn't a parent. He had no idea what being a parent entailed.

"You don't understand, he already got a warning a few weeks back because the boy's sister was picking on Molly and Pippa and he took matters into his own hands." I sighed as he sat up straight, his face contorting with a mean grimace.

"What have you done about it?"

"I don't know what to do, I spoke to the headmaster, but he won't do anything about it. Those kids have wealthy parents. Wealthy, married, catholic parents."

"That's bullshit. They're kids like Daniel and the girls, it shouldn't matter if their parents are fucking saints, you all pay the same fees and did all the same shit to get your kids into the school."

"It's not about fair, it's playground politics. We were lucky that our older siblings were popular, but even then Willow was the only one who never got any shit."

"Then move him." His eyes rounded on mine and his hands grasped my crossed legs.

"It's one of the best schools in London, in the country even. It's not that simple."

"Yes. Yes, it is because it's not the best if he's being bullied and nothing is being done about it. He's eight years old, Dorian, he should be enjoying himself and not worrying about some dipshit, spoilt brat."

His words stung, and the way he spoke them made them hurt even more. There was some truth to them though, and the problem with there being truth behind them was that it made me feel even worse about not comforting my boy earlier.

"You're not a bad mother, so don't even think it." He murmured as he tucked my hair behind my ear and then wiped my tears away. "And Daniel's a great kid. Maybe he has a temper, but so do lots of other kids. You shouldn't be crying over this, you're smart and you could argue the tail off a donkey. Go in and put your foot down, it doesn't matter whether or not you're married, and anyway, you probably make more money than some of the families put together." He grinned at me and I couldn't help but chuckle.

"He's not even talking to me."

"He'll come around, he's a mummy's boy." He leaned

forward and kissed the top of my head. "You ready to be cheered up now?"

He reached over the side of the bed and put a familiar bag in front of me. He brushed my hair back again and pushed it behind my shoulders before he said, "It's all yours."

I peered inside and I couldn't contain the smile that forced itself on my lips. "You brought me fancy macaroons."

"I did." He smiled smugly as I took the small box from my favourite patisserie out and put it on the bed next to us.

"Magic Stars, obviously…"

"Downton?"

"Matthew Crawley won't cut it today." I replied as I moved the treats to the side and clambered a little too clumsily onto his lap. My skirt rode up to where his hands held my waist as my arms and legs wrapped around him.

His chest pressed to mine as he kissed my lips. Slowly at first, it was always slowly and savoured at first, but then his tongue licked into my mouth and it was like opening Pandora's Box.

Our moans mingled in perfect harmony as our tongues twirled around one another. Our breaths caught in each other's mouths as our hands worked frantically to undress one another.

It was glorious, fumbling bliss. And again, I wanted more.

CHAPTER 19

Jake

It'd been a little over a week since we'd seen each other. We'd planned lunch on the Thursday, but she'd had some sort of urgent meeting. On the Friday she'd text me about lunch, but I was in surgery. It was like we kept walking towards each other but instead of meeting in the middle, we completely missed one another.

I was getting more frustrated than a teased bull in a ring. I didn't think I'd ever been this agitated in my life. It was like my body was fighting me. I needed to focus, but my brain was busy either thinking about fucking or trying to find time to fuck.

She was all I wanted. All. The. Fucking. Time.

See? Fucked, buddy.

I looked from the TV to my phone on the bedside table. It

was already late, but I knew how she stayed up working most nights.

I picked up my phone and before I could talk myself out of it I messaged her.

ME

Want to come over tonight? X

I hoped she was awake, I'd had a shitter of a day and quite frankly I just wanted to hear her voice.

Earlier today the daughter of one of my patients from a few years ago came to see me. Like her mother, she wanted a single mastectomy. She didn't want to try all the other therapies and treatments, she wanted the problem eradicated.

As a surgeon, I was with her. Getting rid of the problem was a lot better than treating it, but she was in her mid-twenties. She still had her whole life ahead of her. We spent a good hour discussing all the other options, but she was set on the procedure. When I'd asked her why, her answer brought tears to my eyes.

"I don't want to be too late. I don't want to give it a chance to spread. I don't want to die like my mum."

I didn't know her mother had died. I'd had no idea, that the woman I'd gotten to know had lost her battle. It was sad. I hadn't thought about her in years.

My phone lit up and rang from my lap as I sat on the bed. Her name flashing on my screen like a beacon.

"Hi," I answered, my heart clenching with the anticipation of hearing her voice.

"Doctor Roth."

"Stop with the Doctor shit," I chuckled lightly.

"I see, so it's okay for you to call me pretty girl, but I can't call you Doctor Roth?"

"You are pretty."

"You are a doctor." She snickered and my ears perked up at the sound of sloshing water.

"What're you doing? It sounds wet?"

"I'm having a bath. I needed something to help me relax after spending my evening arguing with Willow over which acts to book for the New Year's fundraiser. She and Amelie are draining my patience with their too cool for school choices. Anyway, what are you up to? You sound how I feel."

"One of my patients died, and I didn't find out about it till today when her daughter came to see me about herself." I sighed.

"I'm sorry," she murmured. "What can I do to help take your mind off it?" her breathy tone made me smile.

"What did you have in mind?"

"I'm naked, Jake. I'm naked and I'm wet, and I can't stop thinking about when I'll see you again."

Oh fuck, my dick immediately called to attention at her words. Heat radiating all over me.

"Close your eyes, pretty girl." Her sharp intake of breath had my cock pulsing. The temperature in my room rising to a blistering heat. "My hands want to touch you so badly. It's like my fingers have a permanent itch to feel your skin."

"Jake..." Her husky voice rumbled over the line and it was like she was right there, next to me, her shallow breaths whispering over my face.

"Use your hands, Dor, touch yourself like I want to. Feel your skin like I need to. Trail your fingers down your soft skin, all the way down, baby." I murmured as I followed my own directions, imagining it was her touch. My heart was racing, beating faster and faster the further south my hands travelled. "Can you feel me, pretty girl?"

"Mmmm…"

"Does it feel good?"

"Mmmhmm…"

"Part your legs, spread them for me, let me see that pretty pussy." My balls tightened as I pictured her spreading herself open for me. Her tits shaking with her desperate breaths. Her stomach clenching as I licked her once…twice. "You taste so good, I could spend hours feasting on you. Fucking you with my fingers as you tighten around me. How many do you want? One finger? Two?"

Her languid breaths bathed my senses. My hand grasping my cock tightly, tugging again and again before it rounded my weeping crown, the pre-cum lubricating my strokes.

"Slip your fingers in, slowly, do you feel the way your pussy clenches so greedily. How it gushes for me?"

"Jake…" She murmured, a hint of embarrassment and shyness tinging her words.

"It's just you and me, Dor. You and me. My dick is throbbing in my hand, and it's only for you." I rasped, my words hitching unevenly with my long, rough strokes. "Touch yourself, pretty girl. Fuck your pussy like I'm dying to."

I knew the minute she pushed her fingers inside, her groan was long and shaky.

"That's it, good girl." I managed to murmur as my strokes became faster, my cock hardening further at her breathy sighs and short, gasping breaths. "Faster, baby."

"Ohmygod…" She gasped, the high-pitched grit in her desperate words letting me know she was close. So close, and like it didn't want to be behind my dick swelled in my hand. "Oh god, Jake."

I could hear the water sloshing around her as her gasps became hoarse and choppy.

My balls ached as they tightened. "Fuck. Fuck, pretty girl."

I could almost feel her nails sinking into my shoulders, as she moaned louder, her words garbled. My muscles tensed and tightened until all I could hear was her calling my name, again and again with every hot string of cum spurting onto my stomach, dribbling down my fist.

Fuck. Fuck, fuck. Fuuuuuuuck.

"Jesus, we need to do this again." She chuckled breathlessly.

"Dor, if I keep knocking one out over you like this, my hand and my dick are going to have matching chafe marks. As good as this was, and it was fucking glorious, I still want to fuck you myself."

"I want you to fuck me too." She yawned. "I'd say I'm thoroughly relaxed."

"Good."

"You know, you could always come over again...if you want?" she murmured, her voice tinged with a shy softness. "I mean, you come over all the time anyway, you could stay a lot longer and *not* watch the telly."

"Isn't it risky with Daniel there?"

"He sleeps like a log." Her chuckle made my chest fill with a buzzing excitement.

I wanted to say I was on my way. I wanted to go to her and get lost in the soft, slender curves of her mouth-watering body. I wanted to hold her and know that there was one thing in my life that was untainted and untouched by all the other shit.

"Don't think too hard, Jacob, or you'll start greying." She teased as she broke the silence. "Although, I bet you'd look just as good."

I couldn't help the grin her words brought to my face. The way she found something to say to bring light to a situation or conversation made my heart swell. Made me feel things I knew I shouldn't feel, because that's not what she wanted.

I took a deep breath as I tried to steady my thoughts. "I've got a late surgery tomorrow, let me see how it goes?"

"You know where I am." I could hear the soft smile in her voice and it made me fill up with warmth. It made my entire being sigh with contentment. "Good night, Doctor Roth."

"Na-night, pretty girl."

* * *

I was still grouchy and grumpy. All because I was missing Dorian. The other night had been great, but as good as it felt imagining her touch and feel and hearing her over the phone, it was no replacement for the real thing.

I still hadn't made use of her open invitation to call on her. I desperately wanted to, but with work running late the last few nights, I hadn't been able to. I also didn't want her to think I only wanted to use her for the sex. I knew that we were meant to be fun, but she was still my friend and I wanted to spend time with her.

I wanted to talk to her. I wanted to listen to her ramble about everything and nothing in particular. I wanted to savour her voice, her touch, her feel. I wanted to laugh with her because she was good at making me forget all the reasons why I shouldn't.

It was a Friday night and I couldn't face going back to an empty house. Ordinarily this would be when I'd go out for a drink with one of the guys, it had been mostly Jamie before he and Quincy became a proper thing. Once in a while, Willow and I would meet for drinks too, but the lead up to Christmas was ridiculous for her. She always managed to get into some sort of seasonal show.

After having Eleanor at the house, it felt weird being there alone. It felt lonely, and I was not good with loneliness. Loneliness was another one of those things that led to a lot of unnecessary thinking.

I grabbed my coat from the rack in the corner opposite my office door. Becca had left over an hour ago, leaving me with the last bits of paperwork she needed me to sign off for the week.

The hospital was so still as I walked out, my phone in hand as I debated calling Dorian.

Just do it.

I called her before I sent myself crazy. What was the worst that could happen?

She picked up on the first ring. Her voice was hoarse and tired. She sounded like she was about ready to either throw something at someone's head or make a run for it.

"You alright, pretty girl?"

She sighed with frustration and I could imagine her pulling at the shorter strands that normally framed her face. Combing them back like it was them that were irritating the shit out of her.

"That bad, huh?" I smiled into my phone.

"Don't, we've had a 'mare of it today. One of our court dates was moved forward and we've literally been pulling everything together like maniacs. My brain is fried. I want to go home, down a couple glasses of wine and forget that today ever happened."

"Want company?" I asked, my heart picking up the pace as I waited for her reply.

"I still need to pick Daniel up from Gwen and Liam at Quincy's. I was meant to pick him up from school and take him to football, but I didn't even have time for lunch and—" She stopped abruptly, took a deep breath and then continued, "Christ, I can't even answer a damn question without blathering on like an idiot."

I knew from the way she was going on that she was sending herself doolaly.

"Dor?"

"Yeah?" she replied raggedly.

"Do you need alone time?" Disappointment filled my chest at the possibility that I might not see her again.

"No." She rushed to reply. "I need to take my mind off today."

"I'll come meet you now." I signalled a black taxi down, got in quickly and told the driver where to go. "Inner Temple, please."

"Okay, see you in a tick," she said before hanging up.

I couldn't stop smiling the entire drive to meet her. By the time I got there she was already waiting outside.

Her eyes met mine through the glass and as she stepped toward the cab I opened the door for her to get in. Her pretty face was flushed from the cold. I helped her in and took her bag as she settled in the seat next to me. Her head rested lightly on my shoulder as her arms wrapped around mine whilst I gave the cab driver Quincy's address.

Considering how busy the roads were it didn't take us long to get to Daniel, I sat in the cab, waiting as Dorian went in and

I don't know how she managed it, but she was out pretty quick.

Daniel was a non-stop talking ball of excitement the whole way home. He kept going on about some project he had to work on over the weekend for school. It had something to do with the Christmas play and him getting an actual talking part.

It made me laugh as he ran to his room and got his bible. He sat on the sofa with me and proceeded to tell me all about his role as the Angel Gabriel.

"So, I have to get Mum to go through this bit," he handed me a paper with his messy scrawl noting the book, chapter and verse, "and we have to write the lines the angel says and then I have to remember them."

"Sounds like you're looking forward to your part." I chuckled as he put the bible on my leg and gave me the look he always did when he wanted me to get into something with him.

"I beat Thomas to it. He always gets this part, but I got it this year!" He punched the air right in front of my face. "I think that my teacher is scared of my mum, now. She was really cross when she talked to her the other day."

Pride filled my chest as I realised that she'd gone in and dealt with the situation she'd been crying over the last time I'd been here.

"I have to dress up too, and Mum has to make my costume."

"What do I have to make?" Dorian chimed as she walked down the hall from her bedroom. She'd cleaned her make-up off and put some leggings and a vest on.

She always looked so fucking good in those clothes. Her legs looked fucking lethal, like they went on for days and her arse...I loved her arse. It was so fucking tight and pert, and the way it clenched when she was about to come on my—

"Dinner?" she asked as she sat on the armchair closest to me. "I'm so hungry, I could eat a flaming cow."

"I ate with Pippa and Nanny and Grandad." Daniel said as he picked up the book on my leg and went over to his mum. He squeezed in on her chair with his legs over her lap as he handed her the note he'd shown me and then told her everything he'd told me.

"Why don't we look at this tomorrow morning?" she cooed as she swept his messy curled fringe from his eyes and kissed his cheek. Her sigh as he melted into her made my heart want to burst with the warmth that filled it.

Seeing them like that always reminded me of how my mother used to hold me the same way. How she used to kiss me every chance she got and the way her kisses always lingered with her soft perfume. A part of me felt like I should be sad that I lost that, but the simmering warmth and buzz inside me always overrode it. Seeing them like that, it made me happy.

It was silly. It wasn't a moment or gesture I was a part of, but watching them…it was as good as. Maybe better. I loved seeing her face light up and her eyes soften like she was putty in his hands.

"Tomorrow morning, we'll sit and work on this, okay?" She wrapped her arms around him and buried her face in his hair, breathing him in. "It's getting late already, way past your bedtime."

"Can't I stay up a little bit longer? Just while you have dinner?"

"And then you promise you'll go straight to bed?"

"I'll need to brush my teeth first, but after I promise, I'll go straight to sleep."

"It's a deal then." She kissed his cheek again as she squeezed him in her arms.

"Thanks, Mama." He smiled brightly at her and kissed her cheek in a flash.

Seriously, the kid was a testament to her. For an eight-year-old he was switched on and so caring that it put some grown-ups to shame.

"So, dinner?" I managed to ask without sounding like all my insides were mush.

"Pasta? We can order from the place down the road, it won't take them long." She got up with Daniel wrapped around her. "You're getting far too big for me to carry you, baby."

She plonked herself next to me as I opened one of the takeaway apps and ordered our usual from the Italian she liked.

"Can you do me a favour?" Her eyes settled on Daniel's, "Go put your PJs on for me?"

He jumped up without protest and ran to his room, taking his bible and note with him.

As soon as he was out of sight she pressed a quick, warm kiss to my lips and brushed my hair back. It was such a small and mundane gesture, but from her, it felt like the deepest caress I'd ever had.

"What was that for?"

She shrugged with a lopsided grin stretching her lips. "I need a reason?"

"I'm not complaining, just surprised. Daniel's right there…"

"It takes him a while to choose what PJs to wear." Her eyes sparkled as she did this cute head bob from side to side, like she was an excited child. "How's Eleanor?"

Her question threw me through a bit of a loop. Not that she

was asking, but that she'd remembered to ask in that moment. She'd asked about Eleanor in the same breath as she'd spoken about Daniel.

She cares.

I felt my heart go soft all over again. It was beating, skipping and summersaulting in my chest.

"She's okay. I think her and Miles have made up, she's gone back to their place. The house feels stupidly empty, like everything is rattling around in it."

"It's a big house."

"It didn't feel that big before. I never noticed how quiet it was, even after Jamie found his place."

She smiled at me knowingly. "You don't love my brother like you love Eleanor. That house could be tiny, and it would still feel massive now."

"That makes no sense." I chuckled at her goofy grin.

God, she's so fucking pretty it hurts.

"It's like when Daniel isn't here, everything sort of feels empty and lonely. It's an emotional thing. I miss him and because I miss him I notice the silence and the way his things aren't all over the place. I miss it. The mess. The weird shows on the telly. The way he leaves his cups half-filled on every possible surface."

Her eyes zeroed in on the photo on the coffee table and she shifted closer to me. So close that her thigh was pressing into mine firmly. Her head rested on my shoulder and she sighed.

"I'm going to see her tomorrow." A soft murmuring buzz lit up my chest at the thought of seeing Eleanor. I hadn't felt that in so long. I remember feeling it all the time, especially when we were little and I knew school was almost over and I was going to see my baby sister again. "I'm taking her out for dinner, it's my way of checking on her without being overbearing about it."

"It's good that she knows you're there for her. Maybe that's all she needs to keep her going."

"Maybe." I sighed as I felt her hand rest on my stomach and then travel all the way up till she cupped my cheek. Her head tilted back at an angle as she looked up at me.

"You're a good man." She whispered, her thumb trailing over my cheekbone and her eyes looking between mine. "You should always know that."

I don't think anyone had ever said that to me quite like that. With the exception of my mother, I don't think anyone had ever called me a good man. I'd been called many things, but that wasn't one of them.

She laid her head back on my shoulder and turned the television on. We settled back into silence as we listened to the almost muted TV and Daniel fumbling about in his room.

"I'm at home all day tomorrow, if you wanted to, you could bring her here for dinner?" she said it a little too nonchalantly for me to process what she'd said at first. It took my brain a few runs over her suggestion for me to make sure that I hadn't made it up in my head.

No! Don't do it. It's a bad idea.

I ran through all the reasons why bringing Eleanor here was a bad idea, and still, there was nothing I wanted more than to give Dorian the opportunity to get to know her. To get to know the brilliant side to my little sister, but I also wanted to protect her and Daniel.

"I'll bring her to dinner, but I don't want her near here. I'm not bringing trouble to your doorstep, got it?" I hoped this wouldn't backfire. I hoped that I would never regret this decision.

"I got it. Loud and clear, Doctor Roth." She sang, her voice light and smiley as she looked up at me with victory shining in her eyes.

"Where do you want to go?"

Her eyes, shoulders and lips hitched at the same time as she said, "Pick a place she likes. Give her a reason for one more day, Jacob."

It was at that precise point in time that my heart decided it was never letting her go.

A simple, selfless act on her part that I knew I'd never be able to go back from.

I'd never be able to forget the moment a strong, gorgeous woman put a stranger before herself.

I wasn't stupid or gullible enough to think that it was something more than an act of kindness.

I also wasn't naïve and senseless enough to believe that it was a plain graceful gesture towards me.

She'd listened to every word I'd told her. She'd kept them inside her, and she'd clearly thought about them.

CHAPTER 20

Dorian

I'd spent most of my afternoon *umming* and *aahing* over what to wear tonight, and then after trying on more outfits than I cared to recall, I went with the first. Grey jumper, light semi-fitted jeans and the black Loubies. Basically, what Willow would call standard Dorian.

I considered something a little sexier. But we were under six weeks away from Christmas, it was colder than a nitrogen chamber and I didn't quite fancy freezing my tits off, not completely anyway. It also seemed a little silly to do sexy when it was another low key, friendly dinner.

Who are you trying to kid?

Or so I kept telling myself. I still couldn't stop thinking of everything Jake had told me. I didn't want to pry, so I didn't ask him for any more than what he'd shared with me. But there was one particular thing that kept revolving around in my head. Round and round like a repetitive advert that draws you in but gives nothing away. So you keep watching it every time it comes on the telly and every time you're left frustrated because you're left knowing as much as the last time you watched it.

She was the last thing I had of our parents.

She was the last thing that I had that reminded me of my mother.

I'd never met his parents. But Jamie had and he liked them. He spoke of them fondly and he always asked after them. So, Jake's words didn't make sense.

I replayed them again and again, trying to make sense of them. But I couldn't and I was getting restless with the need to know. Up until the morning after his revelations I'd never actually seen his sister. The hallway had been too dark the night before, and all I could make out was her long hair and her almost gangly limbs. It wasn't until I'd been leaving and she'd been in the kitchen, that I managed to really take her in. Her face was a mess of smudged mascara and blotchy foundation. Her eyes were puffy and red.

She said nothing. I said nothing. We both sort of tried to look the other way, except that something had made me look at her. I think it was the sadness in her eyes and her quietly laboured breaths. I could feel it in my bones, much like her brother's. I'd seen that sadness in my own eyes, and on bad days, I still did.

I didn't say anything, but I did what I thought any good person would do. I acknowledged her. I took out the baby wipes from my bag and put them down in front of her as she sipped her coffee. All she did was smile. Nothing else. But it was enough.

It was enough to make me want to know more about her. I'd never known anyone with a problem like hers, I didn't know all the ins and outs of it. I was sure that Jake had softened it all for me. Sugar coated it enough to keep himself together. I could feel the anger and turmoil simmering under his skin as he'd told me about Eleanor's addiction. I could see it in the shadows in his eyes.

I think it should've made me want to run away. Run as far from it as possible, but it didn't.

It made me want to take it on. I wanted to pull it out of him and set it on fire until there was nothing but ashes left. The wind could take those. I could blow them as far from him as possible, and I'd keep blowing whenever they blustered our way again.

That's all I could think about as I drove Daniel and I to the place Jake had messaged me. I'd never heard of it before; I'd been to the hotel it was in though. Which made me wonder what possessed me to drive there in the first place.

God only knows.

We ended up parking a ten-minute walk from the restaurant. Daniel was so excited I practically had to run in my heels to keep up with him. The whole time he kept stopping and looking back at me like I wasn't walking as fast as I could. Maybe I should've worn flats. But with the rest of my outfit I needed something to make it suitable for dinner at one of the nicest hotels in London.

By the time we actually got to the restaurant, I was ready to plop my backside down and chug a pint of water. However, the moment I laid eyes on him, my tired feet were a distant thought as I tried to figure out how to greet Jake.

I could've jumped him all over again. I could've kissed every square inch of his stubbly jaw.

I don't know how he did it, but even in jeans and a t-shirt he looked so…yummy.

I smiled as Daniel ran ahead of the host waiter that led us to the table. He talked a thousand words a second as he did his usual fist bump, handshake thing with Jake. It was like they hadn't seen each other in ages.

"Thank you." I said to the waiter as he pulled out my chair and then helped me take off my coat.

"My colleague will come by to get your drink order." He chuckled as he watched Daniel's enthusiasm.

Eleanor was sat in the chair opposite mine. She smiled and waved quietly at me as I sat down, a little disappointed that I didn't get a chance to greet Jake.

"Coat, Daniel." I reminded him as he sat in his chair, his iPad already out on the table as he showed Jake something to do with his game. "Have you said hi to everyone?"

"Oh, yeah. Hi," he said as he grinned at Eleanor. For a minute he narrowed his eyes at her like he was trying to make out whether he should know who she was or not. "I'm Daniel."

Eleanor laughed at his outstretched hand and as she gently shook it she replied, "I'm Eleanor. You can call me Ellie, though."

"Hi, Ellie." He smiled as he stood and took his coat off, hanging it on the back of his chair.

He looked at me a little confused.

"Eleanor's Jake's sister," I told him.

"Cool." He retorted as he looked between them. "I didn't know you had a sister."

"I have a brother too." Jake said with the usual soft smile he reserved for the kids.

"Molly and Pippa are going to have a baby brother too, or sister."

"I know." Jake said as I felt his hand squeeze my thigh before he murmured quietly at me, "Hi."

"Hi." I squeezed my thighs together at the feel of his hand on me.

Jake had smiled at me many a time. It was something that kind of just was, his smiles. Sometimes they were big, others they were tentative, but the smile he gave me right then was completely different to any other he had ever given me.

It was breath-taking and beaming. It was so bloody beautiful that it made everything else around us fade. It made me want to reach out and stamp it on my lips and my face. All over my body.

"Jake!" Daniel called a little too loudly. "You're not listening."

"Sorry, mate." He laughed as he looked at the tablet thrust in his face. "Tell me again."

I expected him to take his hand away, but if anything he squeezed a little harder. His fingers slipping between my thighs as he relaxed his hand on me. I could almost picture how blushed my cheeks were, maybe I should've left the blusher off, because I clearly didn't need it with the heat that glowed on my face.

I ordered mine and Daniel's drinks as the waiter laid the informal place setting menus in front of us. It was all very straight forward and casual.

Salads, bagels, burgers, mains...caviar? Really?

It made me giggle the way they'd plonked one of the most expensive delicacies in the world right next to the burgers and bagels.

"I know, it always makes me do a double take whenever we come here." I looked up to find Eleanor leaning towards me, chuckling.

"It has tickled me. Although, it hasn't helped with what to order."

"Well, I always start with the Matzo ball soup. I could eat it till it comes out of my ears, even if it's not as good as Ima makes it."

"I think you lost me at the ball. Who's Ima?"

"It's the Hebrew equivalent of Mummy." Jake explained as Daniel looked between him and Eleanor curiously.

"Ima." He repeated softly.

"Almost." Eleanor bent a little closer to him and then said, "Ee-mah. Mama, not Mummy. It's a very old word."

"She's right, the soup is good." Jake murmured as I continued watching the way Eleanor explained the Aramaic origins of the word to Daniel. "It's a bit like chicken noodle, only with a matzo meal ball rather than pasta. You'll like it."

"It's not a ball, it's a dumpling made from finely ground Passover crackers." Eleanor explained animatedly with her hands. Every once in a while she'd look over at her brother and smile wistfully. "When I was little my mum used to put the crackers in a bag and let me bash the life out of them with a rolling pin. Jake used to love it, his were always a little too fine, but with mine they worked."

"My nanny lets me do it to her digestives when we make cheesecake." Daniel said as he took a sip of his drink.

"And isn't it fun?"

"She says it's satisfying, especially if I imagine the things that make me angry and sad."

"And you know what? She's absolutely right." She cooed at him, slapping her small hand lightly on the table.

"What do you think I should get for my dinner?"

"I think the schnitzel is the best, and if you want, Jake can always ask them to make you some buttery pasta with it. That's how he likes his."

"I do, it's like heaven on a plate."

"Can I have that?" he asked, looking up at me from the menu.

"If that's what you want."

"What are you having?"

"I think I'm sold on the soup."

"You know it's a starter, though, right?" Jake asked as he slid his hand off my thigh and then rested his arm on the back of my chair.

"I like to have the pierogi with mine. It's not too heavy that way."

"Isn't that the point of this food? To leave you stuffed for days?"

"No, that's what eating at Mum's is like." She rolled her eyes at him.

"She's got all her recipes out and ready for this year."

"Oh, god. She always cooks way more than we eat. No wonder she has to put Dad on a diet after Hanukkah is over."

"What's that?" Daniel asked them.

"Umm, it's a celebration..." She started explaining to him.

It was nice listening to their conversation. It was even nicer that she went out of her way to include Daniel in it. Even throughout our meal, they talked and talked. About the food, the language and even some of their childhood memories.

I watched Jake watch her with the same adoration that he looked at Molly or Daniel.

The conversation wasn't anything over the top or too intimate, but it was the fact that she was trying.

I didn't quite understand what Jake had meant about her trying and making it one more day. I didn't get it, until then. I could see why it was so important to him, I could see the way he loved her.

Not your ordinary sibling love, it was more. It reminded me of how I loved my son.

It was obvious from the way he smiled at her and teased her with a little more finesse and softness than I'd seen or heard him tease anyone else.

I could feel him relax the deeper into the evening we got. I didn't think I'd ever seen that side of him before, the one where he wasn't smiling because he felt he had to. He wasn't joking because it was a way of focusing on something else.

I liked it.

I liked it so much that I would do whatever it took to always see him that way, regardless of what happened between us outside of our friendship.

"What're you thinking about?" he murmured in my ear whilst he put his arm back around me.

He rubbed his belly with his other hand like he was so stuffed he was about to pop.

"Nothing. I'm enjoying this." My hands were itching to run through his hair and stroke his face. It was like they missed the feel of his skin and his warmth on them. "She's not what I expected."

He looked at Eleanor's empty chair with a fondness that

was so precious and enthralling, I almost couldn't help but sigh.

"What did you expect?"

"She looked so glum the last time I saw her." She'd looked like she bore the brunt of the world's hurt in her soul.

"You saw her?" He turned to me with a curious look on his face.

"When I was leaving, she was having a coffee…she looked how I felt all those years ago. A little bit heartsick, a little disappointed, like she'd had enough."

"Is that why you invited her to dinner?"

"No. I wanted to see you again." I felt my face heat with my admission.

A wide smile cut across his face as he said, "You wanted to see me? You saw me yesterday."

"I know, but work was stupid silly yesterday and I was tired. My head wouldn't switch off and it was making me restless. Plus, every time I throw you out I wake up feeling all guilty and like I'm missing out."

He marked me with a wry grin. "You are, I'm ready to go before I even open my eyes."

"Stop," I sighed, my stomach was flipping and turning like a tumble drier on shrink mode.

My cheeks were blazing as I turned toward him and leaned my cheek on my hand. My elbow precariously close to the edge of the table.

I growled softly with frustration at his impish smirk. "I know I'm missing out, so please, don't do this to me."

"Me?" he murmured into my hair. "I'm not doing anything, pretty girl."

Every part of me clenched as his fingers traced up from

my knee stopping at the very top of my thigh. His other arm crossing my shoulder as it stayed on the back of my chair.

"You know exactly what you're doing."

"I'm just enjoying the way your nipples are getting all hard under your jumper. I have to say that braless really works for you." He breathed almost too quietly into my ear. "It'll work later when I'm thinking about you too."

"Good for you."

"It will be. I'll think about the way they pebble under my tongue. The way you gasp as I roll them between my fingers."

"Jake." My hushed whine heated up the close space between us.

"It's your moan that gets me really hard. The way it catches in your throat like it's strangling your breath. The way it draws out as I suck harder."

Swallow. For fuck's sake, woman. Swal-low!

"And then the way you dig your nails into my shoulders… exactly like you do before I make you come. I can almost feel it. I think I could make your pretty pussy gush for me by simply sucking on your tits."

Holy fucking cumballs! If he didn't stop, I was going to come from his words alone.

"This is torture."

"I know." He chuckled, his fingers curling into the inside of my thigh as he leaned back into his chair, readjusting himself.

"I fucking hate you right now." I gritted quietly as he reached over and took the iPad away from Daniel. "Mate, you're going to get cross-eyed if you don't give this thing a rest."

"That's not true, and you were talking to Mum." He shrugged with a toothy grin on his face. "It's so rude to whisper.

Nanny says that it makes your ears fall off."

"Only if you're being nasty," I winked at him.

"That's not what Nanny Gwen said."

"I guess she forgot to mention that part."

"What were you whispering about, then?" My heart stuttered at his question.

"I'd tell you, but then it wouldn't be a secret." Jake ruffled his hair.

I listened to their back and forth until Eleanor got back from the loo. She sat back down looking at ease and smiley.

She wasn't what I expected at all. She was like her brother, she smiled but the smile never quite made it to her eyes. Even when she made light of something she always had a faraway look on her face. It was like she hadn't mastered the hiding behind a façade trick, not like Jake had anyway.

We didn't stay much longer after she returned. It was getting past Daniel's bedtime. My brain was caught somewhere between not being able to stop replaying Jake's dirty words and still trying to put two and two together about the conversation we'd had the night he brought his sister home.

It was a mental tug-of-war between sex and curiosity...and sex curiosity because I was definitely curious about what else Jacob could do to my body. To me.

There were times when he touched me that it felt like I had never been touched before. Times where he made me feel things that I didn't know I was capable of feeling again.

It was terrifying sometimes the way his touch reminded me of Phillip. It made me feel ashamed. But then, it would be so quickly overshadowed by him, that the shame morphed into guilt.

I didn't think I could live with guilt, but when it came to Jake, I was finding that I could do a lot of things I didn't think I could.

CHAPTER 21

I needed to figure out a way of seeing Dorian soon. The longer I went without seeing her, the crankier I got. We were halfway through the week. I hadn't seen her since the dinner on Saturday.

I was such an idiot riling her up the way I had. It'd done me no favours in the downstairs department. I'd fucking blue balled myself.

Fucking, dipshit!

My birthday had been on Sunday, and it was a long day. I was horny, tired and crabby. Eleanor wasn't in the best mood either even though she and Miles had made up, I could tell he wasn't in her good graces. I still had no idea what their lovers' quarrel had been about, but I'd be lying if I said that it wasn't putting me on edge with the way she still felt unsettled with it.

The whole day was so fucking awkward with Mum fawning over us and Dad trying to get her to relent and be easy about things.

The best part of the day was the video from Molly and Daniel singing a very out of tune, slightly screechy rendition of the birthday song. The text from Dorian was pretty fucking nice too.

Happy Birthday, Doctor Roth. I need to book an appointment.
X

But even that message hadn't been enough to pull me out of my Dorian deprivation funk.

Becca had already threatened me with cutting off my Magic Stars supply, and I could tell that she meant it. The only reason she didn't do it was because she knew it'd only make me worse.

I chucked a few more chocolatey stars into my mouth. Enjoying as they melted on my tongue like sweet velvet.

I made it a couple more lines down my notes before Becca rapped on my door with her usual three soft knocks and a fourth louder one before she opened the door and peered in.

"I need the notes for Mrs. Ellis so I can get the discharge papers in order and you have a visitor." Her eyebrows quirked at the last part.

"What happened to me being busy and indisposed?"

"You happened." She approached my desk, leaving the door a tiniest bit cracked. "I don't get paid enough to cope with your petulance, you know?"

"I'm not petulant."

"Tell that to everyone you've managed to irk the last week. The cleaner threatened to wrap the waste bin around your head if you told her to make sure she emptied it, again."

"Whose side are you on?" I asked as I held the notes up to her. "Has that prick, Woodford, been bringing you coffee and shortbread again?"

"No, you ruined that for me with your passive-aggressive bribery jab. And let me deal with the cleaner, she's new, she doesn't understand that you're funny about having an empty bin every morning." She sighed and gave me the stink eye. "Anyway, you want to see this *visitor*."

"Who is it?"

"Just stick a smile on your face and try to cheer up. You're much nicer when you're being an irritating clown. You also don't forget to add milk to my coffee in the morning."

"I didn—" She cut me off with a glare.

"I like the extra shortbread though, you can keep that going." She started for the door and then stopped abruptly before she said, "Keep it PG, keep it clean. No funny business."

"What?"

"Just keep that in mind." The look she gave me was like she was talking to a child as she stepped out of my office and I heard her say, "He's all yours, good luck."

What the actual fuck?

"Thanks." My heart skipped a beat at the sound of Dorian's voice and even my dick felt the need to register her being so close. She walked in, her face bearing a wide, amused grin. "Hey."

"Hi," I replied quickly, my fingers tapping on the wooden top of my desk in a happy crab dance. "You're here."

"I had to go see a client down the road and I thought that I'd pop in seeing as it's almost lunch time." She dropped her handbag and coat in one of the chairs in the seating area.

She looked lovely and bright in her mustard skirt and simple white blouse that skimmed the top of her breasts.

My mouth was watering just looking at her. Salivating like she was a Michelin starred meal.

I could've made a meal out of her. I could've feasted on every fucking square inch of her pert and slender body.

"I know you're getting close to forty and all, but it's still a little too early to start drooling all over yourself." She perched herself on the back of one of the armchairs and teased.

"Did you come here to tease me about my age? If you did, it's the wrong thing to tease me about." I pushed away from my desk and leaned back in my chair.

Her eyes trailed down the front of my shirt to my lap. Her teeth sunk into her lip before she sucked it into her mouth and her fingers combed her glossy waves back from her face.

"I have something for you, a birthday present of sorts..." I could tell she was up to something from the glint in her eyes.

She reached back into the seat and pulled out a small white paper bag. Her cheeks were blushed a deep rose and her hands were shaking a little.

"What is it?" I asked, scrutinising the bag with the chemist's logo on it.

My heart started doing that racing thing that made me feel all funny inside. Even my skin felt prickly to the touch.

"Becca said you're being grouchy, so I don't know whether this will help. I had to pick up Daniel's inhaler and...it was there." She held the bag up in front of her. "After your little gripe last week..."

"My gripe?"

She shrugged as I stood and wandered toward her. Her smile stretching the closer I got. She kept dangling it, pulling it closer to her the nearer I got. She crossed her ankles as I stood in front of her. The bag held up right next to her face and when I tried to take it from her she reached up and planted her lips on mine.

Man, I could listen to her moans all day long on repeat.

Her hand clutched around the bag tightly as I tried to make for it. Her other hand fell to my belt and she tugged, pulling me closer to her. I could feel her smile broaden as her teeth sunk into my lip and gnawed languidly.

It felt so good to feel her warmth again as I grasped her small waist with one hand and tried to pry the bag from her with the other.

"If you don't kiss me properly, I'm not giving it to you." She gritted playfully against my lips.

"Give it to me and I'll kiss you anyway you want me to." I replied, my tongue dipping out of my mouth a little. Enough to tease the tip of hers.

"This isn't a negotiation," she sighed breathily. "I'm out of office."

Her hand slid along the top of my trousers to my back and then inched down to the top of my arse.

"It always looks so biteable, but I think I could break a nail digging in." She tipped her head back as she squeezed.

"Give me the bag."

"Kiss me like you want it, badly." She licked the underside of my lip.

"Tell me what's in it."

"Kiss me like you really want to know."

She sighed as I licked into her open mouth. Her back arched, pushing her chest to mine and all I could picture was her perfect, perky tits rubbing on my chest as I fucked her. The drawn out moans vibrated down my throat and swelled my dick as the base of her belly rubbed along it.

My hand dropped from the bag and cupped her face, the other trailing up her body to meet it. The way she craned her neck up to give me full access to every bit of her countenance was making me want to devour her.

Fuck it, I already wanted to devour her. It was a permanent state of want for me. No off button, no pause, no fast forward. A constant urge that was wildly exacerbated when she was right there with me.

I had no idea when she'd gone from being perched to being sat on the back of the heavy chair, but the feel of her legs hooked over either side of my waist...

I needed to get inside her so bad. My dick was aching. My bollocks were pulsing. Every bit of me was go, go, go. Fuck, fuck, fuck.

I swear I could feel how wet and hot she was through her underwear and tights, and my clothes. I could fucking smell the way her pussy was begging me to fill her.

Fuck, I needed this. I needed it more than I needed anything else.

I needed to hear the sounds of her dripping cunt milking my cock. I needed to feel her body shaking beneath me. Above me. I wasn't fussy. I just fucking needed in.

Problem was, this wasn't the place for it. And yes, I'd had fantasies about this. I was having them on a daily basis. I'd imagined licking her pussy on my desk. I'd imagined her on her knees beneath it, gagging on my cock. On the coffee table.

Against the wall. In my chair…the possibilities were endless.

They really were, but I was very aware of how thin the walls of a hospital are. The last thing I wanted was for rumours to spread about us. I was also pretty certain it was a sackable offence. I'd heard of people who'd done it and everything was dandy, but I wasn't about to shit where I ate. Not even with her.

"Don't stop," she whined into the crook of my neck as I pulled away a little.

"I don't want to, but this isn't the right place to fuck you."

"They do it all the time on the telly, it's all the rage."

"Yeah, on the TV. No one actually…" I stopped at the wide-eyed look she gave me.

"He's a dick and she's not you." I kissed the tip of her nose. "You don't want to be anything like Sam and I'm certainly not taking a leaf out of Richard's book. It didn't end well for him."

"Dick."

"Exactly, see? We agree."

"Fine," she groaned and then a mischievous look lit her face, "Daniel has capoeira today, he'll be tired and zonked out."

"I'm meeting Jamie for a drink. We've had this planned for ages, I can't cancel on him."

She scowled at me, "You're picking drinks with my brother over sex with me?"

"No, I'm going to have drinks with my mate whilst I'm regretting not having sex with you." I brushed my fingers through her soft, brown hair.

"Good answer." She smiled as she stroked the side of my face.

Man, this was so fucking confusing. Her words and her actions were complete opposites. She told me she wanted fun, but then she touched me like it was more. She looked at me like it was more.

Not that I was complaining. I wasn't. It just made it so fucking difficult for me to rein myself in. To gauge where I stood.

"He sleeps the whole night through," she murmured.

"What?"

"Daniel, he sleeps the whole night through. If you wanted to, you can come over after your drinks." Her eyes were wide and asking.

"Let me see what time we finish. He wanted to talk to me about a patient and a couple of other things."

"Other things?"

"Don't you worry about it."

"Now, I am worried."

"You shouldn't be. He's asked me to find this book for him, my uncle's looking into it."

Her eyes narrowed on mine. "A book?"

"An old book."

"How old?"

"I'm not saying anything else, also, I want that bag now. I believe I kissed you thoroughly."

"You did. I should've raised the ante." She chuckled as she reached down and picked the bag up from where it'd fallen onto the chair.

She handed it over to me with a smirk. Her lips pursing like she was trying not to laugh.

I kept my eyes on her as I opened it and then I looked in, "Lube? You got me lube?"

She burst out laughing. Her eyes watering. "You were

complaining about how your dick was getting friction burn from your hand, so…"

"So…you got me lube?"

She took the bottle from my hand and inspected it before she said in a soft and sultry tone, "It's not just any lube. It lasts longer, making a little go a looooong way. Oh, and apparently it tingles in all the right places."

"You got me tingly, long-lasting lube. Exactly what every guy wants for his birthday."

"I got you something else too." She reached into her bag and took out a small cardboard box with a little blue bow stuck on top.

"Oh wow, is this a cock ring to go with the lube?" I asked teasingly as I took the box from her. "You shouldn't have."

"Shut up and open it, Becca was right, you're testy."

"Stop calling her Becca, she's not your friend. She's my assistant."

"Open the damn box before I take that one back." She poked my shoulder.

After the lube, what else could she possibly get to top it? I sighed as I lifted the top of the box and then I was actually speechless.

"Well? Is that better? Is sir happy now?" She smiled at me as I looked at her a little confused as to what this meant.

"Where did you get it?" I asked as I swiped my finger through the chocolatey cream, catching one of the Magic Stars that graced the top of the cupcake.

"Happy birthday, Doctor Roth."

Dorian had always remembered my birthday, for the past ten years I always got a text from her on the day. Then when

Daniel came along it was always a message from them both, until he started talking and then she'd send a video of him babbling away at first and as each year went by they got longer until he could sing the whole birthday song.

She had never bought me anything. Well, apart from a drink or a card, some years she got me a funny card. Another side of her people didn't see much of—she had good humour. She liked to laugh, trouble was, at some point I think she forgot how to. And it wasn't when Phillip died, she'd forgotten long before then, she simply hadn't realised it.

But I did.

I think everyone that knew her saw it happen. It didn't happen all at once. It was a gradual thing. It was like there'd been a woodpecker pecking away at her laughter. Little by little chipping at it. Until there wasn't any left. It was all gone.

I think it was Daniel who brought it back. Her smile. Her laughter. He gave it back to her. I think he gave her joy.

Beautiful, laughing, smiling joy.

Something there wasn't enough of in the world.

"Do you like it?" she asked, her thumb brushing along my bottom lip. "Lick it off."

"Are you trying to drive me insane?" I asked before I did as she requested.

She chuckled, "Do you like it?"

"The cake or you making me bonkers?"

"I meant the cake, but I guess it goes for both."

"The cake, I love. It's so good, sort of magic."

"Ha. Ha." She cupped my face and pushed the corners of my mouth together before she kissed me quickly. "Very funny."

"You making me crazy…that's a bit of a problem, but I've

had worse."

Her eyes searched my face for a minute, like she was trying to figure me out. To see something deeper. And for once, I wanted to show her. Problem was I knew she wasn't ready to see it and I wasn't ready for her to be done with me.

"You're going to get cake all over you. Brown on white always looks dodgy."

"Whatever, I'm not back at the office today." Her hands fell down to my shoulders and she wrapped her arms around them. Her fingers stroking the nape of my neck. "Your phone's going off."

"Surgery reminder, not that I'd forget, just Becca being Becca. She's a bit of a control freak." I put the remainder of the cupcake back in the box she'd put on the arm of the chair and silenced my phone.

"To be fair, she has to keep you in line." She stuck her tongue out at me. "Well, it's been fun. Thank you for seeing me, Doctor Roth."

"Are you really going to keep that up?"

"Becca reminds you of your surgeries, I remind you of your vocation…it means you get to focus on *other* things." She stood, making me take a step back.

"Believe me, I have no problem with the latter." I watched as she bent over the back of the chair, her arse purposefully touching my crotch whilst she got her bag and coat from the chair. "Dor, fair warning, I'm going to fucking destroy you next time I see you."

She stood and spun to face me, her teeth gnawing on that fucking glorious lip of hers again. Her hair cascaded down her arm as she tilted her head, watching me.

"Is that a threat, Jacob?" she tittered teasingly.

I took a step closer to her, my hands slipping into my pockets. Her face tilted up to mine as we stood flush to one another, an ill covered smirk lighting her features.

"No, it's a guarantee."

She licked her lips as her smirk broadened. "Good luck with the surgery, doctor."

"Luck? I don't need luck, I have skills, pretty girl."

"So you do," she murmured as the back of her hand brushed the front of my trousers. *Fucking hell.* She grabbed my belt with the other and pulled, before I could clock on to what she was doing, she slipped the lube bottle into the top of my trousers.

"In case you don't change your mind about tonight." She said as her hands splayed on my stomach, "Wouldn't want to damage the goods."

She dropped a quick kiss on my jaw and sauntered out of the office. Her arse sashaying as she put one sexily heeled foot in front of the other.

Fuck, if I wasn't careful I was going to develop a fetish for pointy, red soled, precariously high heels.

She opened the door and turned to look at me, "Cheerio, Doctor Roth," she sang with a wave of her fingers before she disappeared.

CHAPTER 22

I was walking around with a perma smile on my face. My head felt like it was back on straight, even with all the thoughts of Dorian in my head. The only problem was that now that I was sitting opposite Jamie, I was finding it hard to act like there was nothing going on between me and his sister.

I figured that if I let him lead the conversation then maybe it'd be okay, however, listening to him talk about him and Quincy was making me a little bit jealous that I couldn't do the same about me and Dorian.

I wasn't even sure if there was a me and Dorian. An us. She kept going on about us having fun, but the way things were going—it wasn't just fun anymore. At least not for me. If I was honest, it'd never been casual fun.

It was so confusing because she went out of her way to ask about Eleanor and even though we were careful around Daniel, she was still sneaking me in and out of her bed. It was more like we were sneaking around full stop than we were simply fucking.

That doesn't even make sense.

I couldn't make heads or tails of what was going on between us, and I wanted to talk about it with her, but I didn't want to scare her away.

Or maybe you're scared that she doesn't want you like that.

This was the reason I never got involved with women beyond sex. I hated feeling like I was one stone's throw away from being left high and dry. Of being lost.

I still remembered how it felt all too clearly, to feel unsure of what would happen. I still remembered the panic of feeling alone…abandoned.

"Do you think your uncle's going to be able to find it?" Jamie looked at me pointedly. I could tell he knew my thoughts had taken me somewhere else.

"I don't know, he said that if there's damage to it, there's a chance that it's not sought after. He thinks he knows who might've bought it, there's this woman that has a thing for first edition classics. He also said that she might straight up refuse to sell it or maybe ask for a lot more than what it's worth."

"I don't care what she wants for it. That book belongs to Quincy. She should have it back." He blustered as he took a sip of his beer. "Everything okay? You seem a little off."

"Fine. Same old." My stomach turned at the evasive answer I fed him. The acid in my belly burning my chest.

"By same old I assume you mean Eleanor?"

"She's doing okay, I think. She's trying and I think she's

realised she needs to get herself in order."

"Good. After what happened last time…" He sighed.

"I don't ever want to think about that again." A shudder ripped through me as the memories filled my head against my will all over again. Nightmares.

The music was so loud that the walls of the ransacked house pulsed around us. My eyes felt like they were about to pop out of my head as I looked around frantically. My skin felt like it was loose around my bones as the bass rattled my insides. The flashing lights making the nausea worse and my splitting headache scream.

"I'll take this side. You go that way. I'll meet you back here and then we'll do the upstairs. Alright?" Jamie yelled over the thumping and shrill noise.

"She won't be down here, it's too loud." I yelled back as I started for the bare and worn stairs.

How was this place still standing? The walls were papered with posters or covered with mildew. The air was stagnant with stale alcohol and dried piss. The wooden floors were sticky and soft with damp. The house was a death trap, and somewhere inside my sister was fucked out of her face.

I wished I'd picked up the phone earlier. I wish I hadn't been too busy fucking some random woman to answer my mother's call. Now it could be too late.

"Whatever you do, be careful of what you touch." Jamie said as he looked around at all the shit on the corridor floor.

I cringed at the way there were people passed out in corners on top of one another. My vision spotting as I swallowed down the vomit that burned up my throat.

She was meant to be okay. Clean. She'd even been cast in some play. She was doing well.

"Jake, mate, you okay?" he asked as he squeezed my shoulder. "You need to breathe."

I did, I tried to, but the air was so thick and hot and stale, dirty.

"Let's find her and get out of here, alright?" He urged me onwards, down the corridor.

Most of the doors were wide open, even with occupants. I'd been into some pretty diabolical places for her, but this? This was hell. I never thought that she could sink this low.

Jamie peered into the opened doorways, shaking his head as soon as he'd made sure she wasn't in one of them.

The panic inside me was taking over and I could feel my legs buckling as we took the stairs up to the next floor. And then for a tiny fraction of a second I froze.

The panic giving way to a red hot anger that had my limbs steeling and my hands grabbing hold of the cretin hovering over my half naked sister.

Everything drowned out to a blur as my hands closed around his throat and hung him up against the wall.

My raging blood coloured my vision red as he clawed at my hands. Gasping for air. Him, me...

I couldn't let go. Every voice in my head was yelling at me.

Hurt! Destroy! Kill!

But before I knew what was happening he was collapsing to the ground and Jamie was yelling. At me. In my face. I couldn't hear anything he was saying, only the voices. Just my blood furiously rushing in my ears and my hands.

Jake!

Mate!

Jacob!

He was pointing behind me. Trying to turn me around, but I couldn't. I was glued to the rotting floor, my eyes stuck on the devil in front of me as he clambered to his feet.

He hurt her.

He touched her.

Are you really going to let him get up? Walk away?

NO!

That was all I could think as my fists drove angrily at him. I didn't even care where they landed, so long as they caused hurt and damage and pain.

They went on and on and on until he was back where he belonged. On the ground. A slumped, bleeding mess.

"She's not breathing properly, Jake!"

Not breathing.

"We need to get her out of here!"

Not breathing.

Not breathing.

It felt like forever until it registered in my head and my body flung into action. But then it was like I had too many breaths inside me and I had to give them to her.

I had to save her.

Don't let her die, Jacob.

I turned quickly, my eyes finally leaving the mess on the floor. He could die. He should die. I hoped he did.

"Let's go." Jamie gritted as he carefully picked Eleanor up, his jacket wrapped around her dangling legs as he started for the stairs. "You need to go in front and clear the way. Got it?"

I nodded at him. My throat was still too swollen to respond.

"You're fucking dead, bruv." I turned back to look at the mess I'd left behind. Every cell in my body begging me to finish him off.

"He's not your fucking bruv." Jamie gritted from the step above me before he turned and said, "Move it, Jacob!"

I did. We did. It was like every fucker in the place had congregated in the trajectory of the exit. A sick sense of satisfaction blistered inside me as I swept and pushed people out of the way.

My hands were pulsing with hot, searing pain and as I tried to fist them my skin felt like it was ripping away from my knuckles.

"You drive, I've got her." Jamie said as he lowered himself into the backseat of my car, cradling her.

He held her the whole way to the hospital as I sped through some of the dingiest streets in London. The grimy ones that people liked to pretend didn't exist, or the super cool people liked to call up and coming.

He wrestled to keep her going, my mate, he fought for my baby sister like she was his own. And when I was still too messed up to comfort my mother, he did that too.

I never wanted to go through that nightmare again. Because the thing about nightmares was that they didn't only happen when you had your eyes closed. For me, they were living, breathing things.

"Are you sure you're okay?" He looked me over with concern in his eyes.

"Yeah, I really hope it sticks this time."

"Me too, if not for her, then for your sake." He smiled.

"I don't know if I could do it again, Jamie." I sighed as I drank what was left of my drink, the tequila warming my insides all the way down to my stomach. "Anyway, I'm glad that things are going well for you and blondie. Well…"

"Yeah, *well*." He rubbed his face with his hands. "It seems like there's a fucking surprise at every turn—baby, wedding abroad. Sometimes I ask myself if it's all worth it, all the shit with Jenna and Richard, and then I think of Quincy and I know it is. She's the light at the end of my really dark tunnel."

"And she likes me, so she won't give you shit for man time." I chuckled.

He shook his head as he laughed. "I guess even you get a benefit out of it, then. Which brings me to this—we're doing Christmas this year and I know how you always come over to see Molly. If you want to come and spend the day with us, you're more than welcome."

"Count me in!" I said quickly. There was no way I was going to miss it, not when it meant spending the day with my favourite people.

"It should be nice having everyone together for once."

It was great seeing him so happy. For a while he'd been all broody and angry, so it was nice having my friend back to his usual spirits.

"What's Santa getting Molly this year?" I asked as I signalled for the waiter to bring us a second round.

"I have no idea. The list is never ending."

"I saw. But so you know, I have the Batman Lego she asked for and the riding lessons. My mum has a friend that owns a school the other side of Richmond, she sorted me out with everything."

"Right, by everything I'm hoping you don't mean the horse too."

"Don't be stupid, I looked into a pony, but Mum said it was going too far."

"I'm glad one of you has sense."

"Whatever, Molly would've loved it." I grinned at the thought of her excited squeals.

"What you mean is that she would've loved you even more," he chuckled with an over the top eye roll.

"That too."

"I got her the ice skates and lessons. She's getting fed up of ballet and hopefully ice skating's girly enough that Jenna won't bite my head off for encouraging her interest. She's been going on about it since I took her last year."

"What about Pippa?" I asked as the waiter put our drinks on the table.

"Well, Quincy got her the eating, shitting and crying doll. Joy," he sighed. "I was going to get her the electric Mini she asked for, but Quincy gave me the stink eye."

"Aaaand?"

"And I would much rather be in her good graces with what I have planned."

"Fair play. Which Mini was it?"

"Don't do it."

"Why not? I'm not the one that has to live with her."

"Do you want to live past Christmas?"

"Please, Gwen always outdoes us all and she's still alive!"

"Gwen's her mum." He drank down some of his beer before he asked, "Are you going to the New Year's thing?"

"The fundraiser?"

"Yeah, I had to ask my sisters to help me out with a few things and they managed to rope me into it. From the sounds of it Dorian is about ready to throttle Willow and the other girl that's organising it."

"Yeah, I know." I said before I could think better of it. His eyes flashed to mine, narrow and searching. *Shit!* Before he asked anything that could possibly put me in an even more awkward situation I explained, "I saw her the other day."

I couldn't help but think about our exchange in my office earlier today. My girl was so full of surprises. *My girl. My. Girl.* Thinking about it only made me miss her more.

How the fuck do you even miss someone you saw not even twenty-four hours ago?

"Why do you look so happy with yourself?"

"The real question is, how're you going to feel if blondie says no?" It was a cheap shot, but I needed to deflect his unwanted attention, and seeing as I was pretty certain that Quincy would never say no to him…I figured it was okay. Plus, he was funny when he got flustered.

"You're a fucking twat." He responded in true Jamie fashion.

"Just considering all the possible outcomes."

"Fuck off." He rolled his eyes and took a look at his watch. "I have to go after this one. Dick and Jenna have the girls, so I'm going to make the most of it."

"Aww, anyone ever tell you you're cute when you're all loved up?"

"Are you trying to get uninvited?"

"I'd still show up, so…"

"I bet you would too, prick."

"Wow, I really touched a nerve." I laughed as I finished my

drink.

We both dropped a couple of tens to cover the drinks and tip, and headed out. The weather was absolute dog shite as we made our way to the taxi rank down the street.

"Should've Ubered it."

"Yeah." He replied as we reached the line of waiting transportation. "Give your mum my love, and if she gives you those Hanukkah donut things make sure you actually give them to me this year."

"No chance," I laughed. "Let me know if you need me to help with any of your Christmas stuff."

"Wrapping. I fucking hate the wrapping." He chuckled as we did our sort of hug/pat thing. "Thanks for looking into the book."

"I'll let you know how it goes, but fingers crossed."

"Thanks." He said again as he went for the first cab in the line, he looked over at me as I opened the door of the one behind it and smiled, "She's going to say yes, by the way."

"How much should I put on it?" I teased.

"All in." He grinned and got in the taxi and I followed suit.
All in.

I took my phone out of my pocket and called Dorian. Recalling her text earlier telling me Daniel had gone to stay with her parents for the night.

Maybe it was time that I showed her that *I* was all in. That I wanted more with her.

I had no idea how to go about it because I did not want to scare her away.

Dinner?

I hadn't had dinner yet and knowing her, she probably

hadn't had dinner either.

Maybe she wouldn't mind going for dinner together...on a date.

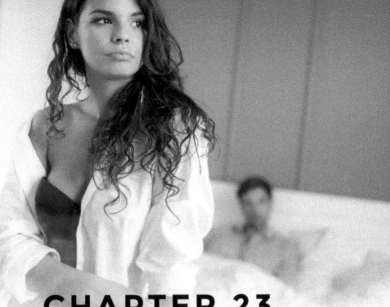

CHAPTER 23

Dorian

I had no idea where the last couple of months had gone, but they'd been good. More than good. Jake just seemed to be able to make up for all the shitty things. When I was grouchy and snappy he was capable of making me feel good, and it wasn't only the sex.

We'd gotten ourselves almost into a routine. There were a couple of times where he came over for dinner, as he sometimes did anyway, but instead of leaving once Daniel went to sleep he'd stay. Not the whole night, because try explaining that to an eight-year-old who happened to be good at talking to his aunts and grandmothers. But he'd stay late into the night.

At first I was always a little on edge just in case we'd be caught out. I also didn't want to be that person that pushed someone out of their bed the minute they were done. I didn't want that at all. I liked having him there, next to me, far more than I would ever admit. Even to myself.

I was having to remind myself that in spite of how it felt between us, we were two friends enjoying one another. But then we'd be together and it was all too easy to forget. It was all too easy to get sucked in when he called me pretty girl and baby. When he simply held me and we watched TV together.

The way he held my hand any chance he got. The way he took his time when he kissed me.

That was something that I never expected from Jake. He liked to kiss. Sometimes his kisses were sweet and soft, others they were hard and desperate—demanding even. But the ones I liked the most were the ones where he looked into my eyes and I could see the warm smile in them. I could feel his peace and contentment and it somehow made me feel the same. It was contagious.

Even thinking about it made my heart melt in my chest and my mouth stretch into a smile. The butterflies in my tummy fluttering around like it was the peak of summer.

I recalled the way he'd kissed me the other night after he'd taken me to dinner. Mum had taken Daniel Christmas shopping with Dad at the last minute and kept him at theirs for the night.

Jake called me after he'd met Jamie. I'd never heard Jacob Roth sound as flustered and unsure as I had then. He was always so confident…

"Well, would you like to…I don't know…have dinner with me?" The way he paused and hesitated followed by the slightly odd pitched uncertainty at the end made my heart stutter.

"What don't you know, Jacob? Whether you want to have dinner or have it with me?"

"Don't be facetious, Dorian." His voice lowered making my belly twist with how it reverberated in my ears and down my body. "I was asking you out."

"You were asking me out? Out where?" I tried to hold back the giggle that was bubbling in my throat at his heavy sigh.

"You're really going to make me spell it out, aren't you?"

"I wouldn't say spell it out, that would take a lot longer than it needs to. You could just ask me."

"Fuck me, well, here goes...and if you say no, I'm still taking it as a yes. After all this—"

"Can you ask me already? I could be getting ready right now."

"You even know you're going to say yes!"

"How'd you know I didn't mean ready for bed?" I teased, "I might be really tired."

"Too tired to fuck?"

"Is that all you think about?"

"No. I don't just think about sex," he paused for a second before carrying on, "I think about you too...naked and not."

I held in the laugh that bubbled up my throat and said, "Jake, fucking ask me already."

"Fine." He sighed with a chuckle. "Dor, would you like to, ummm, go out...on a date...with me?"

"A date? Jacob Roth is asking me out on a date." The smile that cut across my face hurt my cheeks. "Are dates part of the fun, Jake?"

"Yes, Dorian, they are."

"Well, I guess I can hardly say no then."

"Great, now you can go get ready." He crowed cheerfully. *"I'll pick you up at nine? That okay?"*

"An hour's good." Shit, an hour would have to do.

"Good."

"Good."

"Alright then."

"Fine."

"I'll see you in an hour."

"In an hour," I laughed. *"Bye, Jacob."*

"See you soon," he murmured. His voice was so low and husky that it was making me squirm. *"And Dorian?"*

"Yeah?"

I fully expected him to say something dirty and full of promise. I expected him to make me blush and heat with innuendo.

Instead he said, "I'm looking forward to seeing you tonight."

"Me too," I admitted.

"An hour, that's all you get."

"It's all I need," I replied, my voice breaking slightly as a thrill rushed through me with my heated blood. *"Don't be late."*

I'd almost been on time. I was going to make sure I definitely was tonight. I was looking forward to having him to myself. To not having to say goodbye.

I'd thought about what would happen when this thing between us came to an end. Or at least I'd tried to, but the truth was that I didn't want it to ever end.

However, that didn't mean that I wasn't constantly telling myself that it had to at some point. Getting attached to another person, needing them, the way I was beginning to need him. To the point that I constantly missed him when he wasn't there—I always wanted him to be there. Needing and wanting him that way was disconcerting.

I'd done this before, and it had ended badly. I'd lost Phillip and there was no way I could lose Jacob too.

Losing him was a perpetual state of fear that I was living in. The same state of fear that I had lived in before I lost Phillip. To live like that again wasn't something I could do.

So whatever it was Jake and I had, had to remain as nothing more than casual, no strings attached sex…between friends.

I needed him to remain my friend after this.

I took a deep breath trying to settle my thoughts. Trying not to let my feelings get the better of me as I sat at Gwen's kitchen table, listening to her make plans about when we should go visit her son's grave.

"Normally it's easier because Sue's there Boxing day morning to look after Daniel, but you could always bring him. He's old enough to understand now." She put the knife in her hand down and turned toward me. "What do you think, sweetheart?"

I took a moment to figure out the least hurtful way to tell her that I didn't want my son anywhere near a cemetery. I didn't want him anywhere near that morbid melancholy. "Gwen, I'm sorry but I can't do that. I know it means a lot to you, but he's only eight. He doesn't need to understand."

"Dory," she murmured, her voice fraying, "it's his dad's grave."

"I know, but I can't do it. I can't…I just can't, I'm sorry."

"Why? He deserves to know where his dad is."

"He's not there though, is he? It's a stone with his name on it and some nice words."

"It's a special place, regardless," she bit out as she continued chopping the carrots with a lot more gusto.

"I didn't say it's not a special place, just that my son isn't ready for it. Even when he is, I'll decide when I'm ready to take him."

"I thought we spoke about this last year?"

"He isn't ready, Gwen. I'm not ready to take what's left of his ignorance on this subject. Isn't it enough that we all tell him about his dad? Isn't it enough that he knows the good things? The ones that matter?"

I watched as she put the knife down and wandered out of the kitchen towards the toilet.

Great!

I took my mug to the sink and rinsed it out. For some stupid reason I carried on chopping the vegetables she had lined up for the dinner I wasn't even going to be eating. I felt bad that she was upset, I didn't want to upset her, but he was my son. My baby. I only wanted to protect him from the hurt and pain. I wanted to keep him innocent and ignorant to the feeling of loss.

Is that so terrible?

Once I finished with the vegetables I made myself another coffee and Gwen a fresh cup of tea. I used to love this house and its garden. I used to spend so much time here that it felt like a second home. But for some reason all of a sudden it felt less so. I felt like a real guest. It didn't matter that there were photos of my son on the sideboard by the table. Or that there were photos of me and Quincy and of Phillip and I on the dresser. None of that mattered. None of that made me feel like I belonged here anymore.

It hit me then with stark force—*I don't belong here.*

My son did. My memories did. But I didn't.

I took a sip of my coffee as I looked out of the window to the dimly lit garden. There were so many memories out there. Yet, the only one that I could remember clear as day was of a long, dark afternoon in which a friend had sat next to me and made me feel a little less alone.

My chest felt so tight at the thought. My eyes stung, and my lungs burned.

I knew I was in trouble.

I knew I should lock all these feelings away and never let them out again.

I knew that there would come a day I would rue the moment I decided to let Jacob Roth touch me. The moment I allowed myself to touch him.

But as I placed my coffee cup on the window ledge and removed the ring that had adorned my finger all these years, I knew that today was not that day.

I slipped the ring onto my right hand before I poured my coffee down the sink. I gathered my things whilst I waited for Gwen to come back. I thought she never would, but then she walked back in looking a little red eyed and apologetic.

"I know that Daniel is your son, but Phillip was mine and that little boy is all I have left of him. I didn't mean to push." She murmured.

"It's okay, I understand." I brushed my hair away from my face and pulled it up into a ponytail using the hairband on my wrist.

Her eyes paused on my hands, a long sigh leaving her lips as a pensive look crossed her face. She searched mine for a beat and then she smiled weakly at me.

"You know, I don't expect you to come with me every year. You're still young, Dory."

"I know," I said, stuffing my hands in the back pockets of my jeans. "I want to go with you. I loved him. I loved Phillip so much."

"You did." She reached out to me and cupped my face. The gesture warm and motherly, everything she had always been to me. Her smile widened a little as she stroked my cheek with her thumb before she dropped it again.

We didn't say much more. She continued with the dinner, and soon after I said my goodbyes to Daniel and left.

* * *

The drive from West to North London was frustrating, I was running late. And I didn't want to make Jake wait for me again. I had no intention of wasting a minute of our time alone.

God, where has it gone already?

It felt like it had been just yesterday that he'd kissed me on his porch and at the same time so much had happened between us that it felt like a lot longer. It seemed almost silly to feel some of the things I was, considering we'd only been sleeping together a little under two months. But the more time we spent together, the more time I wanted with him.

Not just time, I wanted moments. I wanted more memories like the bench. Memories that would make me smile and give me perspective.

I smiled in the mirror as I rubbed my lips together, spreading my light mauve gloss evenly on them.

I was getting better at this rushing around business, after he'd given me an hour last time I'd sworn I would never run around like a headless chicken again, but for him, I would.

I sprayed some perfume on whilst I gave myself a final glance in the mirror. I smoothed down my little black tea dress before I looked through my jewellery box in search of a simple gold thread and bracelet.

I needed something that would add a bit of intrigue to my otherwise very black attire. I knew exactly where the necklace I was looking for was, except that it wasn't there. I began taking the bigger pieces out of the bottom tray, and then I found it. The one necklace I did not want to find.

I pulled it out and smoothed my fingers over the sunflower and blackbird pendants. I still remembered the day Phillip had given it to me. It was our first Christmas as a couple. A couple of naïve and unexpecting youngsters who thought they had all the time in the world. Their whole lives ahead of them. We knew nothing of what life had in store for us.

Looking back now, I knew Phillip and I never really stood a chance because I had no idea what it was like to swim for our lives. To really kick my legs and scoop my arms.

Whenever things got tough he went his way and instead of me going mine, I stalled. I waited for him to come back. I waited for him to realise that I was there. When he did realise, it was too late. For me. For him. For us.

It was too late and he was gone.

I had been a gullible young girl with rose tinted glasses and too little experience to know that I was in over my head.

I dropped the necklace back inside the box carefully, and of course, I found the one I wanted right where I thought it was in the first place.

My chest felt like it was being squeezed to the point it was sore. My throat felt swollen and the air I was trying to suck in thick.

You're not doing anything wrong.

I kept repeating to myself as I put on the necklace and then the bracelet I'd settled on after realising that my bangles were still at Jake's. I should get them back with the rest of my clothes.

I grabbed my small Chanel bag and slipped my phone and purse in, followed by my keys, lipstick and mascara. My black strappy heels went on and as I was about to lock up, my phone started going off.

Jake: *I'm waiting for you downstairs. Don't forget clothes for tomorrow. X*

I hadn't even thought about where I'd spend tonight. I'd become so used to him staying here that I suppose I assumed that's what would happen after our date.

I rushed back inside and found my small Longchamp weekender bag. I threw in a pair of jeans, a nude jumper, underwear and my leopard print ballerina pumps. That would do.

When I got to my door again I slipped my red cashmere coat on and tied the belt at my back so that it would give it some shape even though I wasn't going to close it.

Seriously, it's a coat.

I was trying so hard to stay cool, to ignore the butterflies in my stomach.

We were just two friends sharing dinner.

Amongst other things.

I tried to get my thoughts in order as I reached the bottom step. I drew in a calming, steadying breath as I opened the door to the building…only to almost choke on it as I heard two very familiar voices.

"I'm so sorry." I looked straight at where Jake was handing my client her car keys as I took the steps down from my front door.

"It's alright, it happens." She chuckled as she took them from him.

"Mrs Fletcher? Heather?" Her eyes fixed on me as confusion filled me. "What are you doing here?"

"Oh, hi. I didn't realise you lived here. My flower shop is just down the road..." She smiled as she looked between me and Jake.

"Of course it is," I smiled back. "Is everything okay?"

I wasn't quite sure how to conduct myself. I'd never had a client this close to home.

"Arthur has the kids," she shrugged with defeat, "I found myself with not much else to do except work."

"Oh, I'm sorry." I genuinely pitied her as her shoulders slumped suddenly and tears brimmed in her eyes.

Her usually sleek ebony hair was frizzy and in disarray. Her face was shadowed with sadness.

Her eyes rounded on Jake as he wrapped his arm around my shoulders and took my overnight bag from me. Her gaze swept over him and then me. For some reason she smiled ever so softly at us both, her eyes were so wistful as she looked at him. It had me glancing between them.

"We should go, or else we'll be late." Jake said as he took a couple of steps back, taking me with him.

"Bye." She took a step back and raised her hand in a still wave.

"If you need anything, make sure you call Sophia. She'll be in the office the Wednesday after Boxing day." I told her before

I let Jake turn us both around and walk us to his car.

His arm tightened around me as I looked over my shoulder. I watched as she slipped into a Range Rover and drove off. The need to help fix things for her weighing on me.

"You alright?" Jake asked as he opened the passenger door of his car and helped me in.

"Yeah," I replied before he rounded the front of the car, still with my bag in his hand. He opened the back door, placed it behind his seat and then got in the car.

"Are you sure?" He started the car with a light push of a button.

"Yes." I slid my hand from the centre console onto his thigh and gave it a light squeeze.

"You can't keep your hands off me, can you?" He quirked his brow with a slight grin on his lips.

I shook my head at him as a laugh vibrated out of my mouth. "So, where are we going tonight?"

"Well…" He looked at me, chagrined, from the corner of his eyes. "I was going to take you to this little French place tucked behind St. Paul's. It's tucked right into one of the small, quiet backstreets."

"Buuuuut?" I sensed it from the way he dragged out the *well*.

"My mum called, normally I have dinner with her and Dad on Saturdays. But the last day of Hanukkah was on Wednesday and she did dinner then, turns out she did it today too. So we're going for dinner at my parents', if that's alright with you?"

I felt the blood drain from my face, my stomach turned and all of a sudden it felt very hot.

"You should have warned me. I should've worn something

different."

"I like that dress, it's easy access to my favourite parts of you." His hand slipped from the steering wheel and as if to prove his point he squeezed the top of my thigh.

"Seriously?" I sniped at him, smacking his hand off.

He looked at me with a sheepish quirk of his brow as we stopped at the red lights. "I am genuinely sorry, I didn't think. Do you want to go back and change?"

"It's fine, but you should've warned me. A girl needs warning for these things."

"Like I said, I didn't think. In hindsight it wasn't a good surprise, but my mum won't care what you wear. She's not like that, Dor."

"That's not the point, Jake, I'm freaking out enough as it is. Next time, warn me, okay?"

"Okay," he smiled softly and drove on as the lights turned green.

We both sat in silence for a bit. I could feel him look at me every now and then. Every time he did it made my heart skip a little bit faster than it already was.

I thought he was going to take me to another one of his favourite restaurants, like the Japanese we'd gone to the other night. I felt my aggravation cool off as I recalled the way the waiter had mentioned he'd called ahead to make sure they had a peanut free menu. I didn't typically eat Japanese because of all the nut oils they used, and it had taken me aback how he'd remembered and made sure that I would have enough choice.

I looked over at him, and as I studied his gorgeous side profile again he smiled at me.

"You look incredibly pretty," he said as his smile grew. "I

can't wait to strip that dress off you later."

"Really?"

"You're the one giving me the *fuck me* eyes!"

"You're a dick."

"You love my dick." He grinned.

I marked him with a scowl. "Don't be so full of yourself."

"You love being full of me."

"God, you're so big headed."

"Well, it hits all the right spots for you…" He laughed, his hand sliding up from my knee.

My skin heated at his touch even through my annoyance. "You're relentless."

"I am, but you beg me not to stop." His nails raked up the inside of my thigh, making goose bumps break out all over my skin.

"Arsehole." I sniped at him breathily as I smacked his hand.

He slipped his hand lower between my legs, his fingertips stroking the juncture of my thighs. "That can be arranged, we haven't used that lube yet."

CHAPTER 24

Jake

I had a contingency in place if Dorian had been adamant about not going to my parents'. At first, I thought she was going to dump her heels and leg it back to the safety of her flat. Not that I would've blamed her because I had been bricking it myself.

I'd never taken a woman to meet my parents. One, they never lasted that long and two, I had never wanted to before. And now I understood why—there was no other woman who could sit through hours of my mother's poking and prodding without breaking a sweat.

Dorian had been incredible, even when Mum had been forward with her questions about Daniel. She'd even showed her photos, which was something really surprising. She wasn't one of those parents who gushed about their child to anyone that would give them the airtime. As proud as she was of Daniel, she liked to keep him all to herself.

Unlike my mother who'd somehow managed to point out every single possible family photo she had in her sitting room, kitchen and dining room. Even the ones that crowded the top of the hallway side table. Everything had been going so well till she decided to point out the ones with Isobel and David.

I had no idea what had possessed her, maybe it was the wine. She'd been generous with it tonight. All I knew was that Dorian and I were now sitting in my car, in awkward silence.

I'd seen the dawning look on her face as realisation struck her whilst she looked between the photo of David holding me, and Levi. The way her eyes narrowed like she was trying to work it all out in her head. Unlike Eleanor, I looked like our father. Nothing like Levi or Ruth.

Maybe I should've let Ruth verify things for her, but I'd freaked out. Talking about Isobel and David wasn't something I enjoyed doing. It brought back all the feelings I'd had when they'd died.

She was so quiet. Her hands were clasped in her lap, her legs were crossed and her head was bowed as she stared into the kick well.

My chest felt so tight, it ached. My throat felt so thick that I felt like I was choking on air. I couldn't take it. I couldn't stand this distance between us. It hurt too much, more than I ever thought possible.

I cleared my throat as I focused on the road ahead. We were only twenty minutes from my house, and I knew that if I didn't try and fix this that she would leave the moment we got there.

"I've always said you can ask me anything," I said hoarsely. "What do you want to know, Dorian?"

She stayed so still. So very still that if I hadn't heard her sharp intake of breath, I would've thought she was asleep.

Her slight movement made me look at her, the way she uncrossed her legs and then tucked one behind the other as she adjusted the slit of her dress.

My gaze travelled up her body, to her eyes and it was the first time that seeing all her beautiful skin didn't make me think of all the things I wanted to do to her. Instead, it made me think of what it would feel like if she were to leave.

Her serious stare as I reached her eyes had my heart dropping even lower than I thought it already had.

"I can see all the questions in your eyes."

"Not all, Jacob. I'm smart enough to put two and two together. If it had been earlier, I probably would have a thousand and one things to ask you. Now, I only have one."

The way her eyes closed as she sighed, the way she kept playing with her ring…it had dread burning my stomach.

"Ask me," I murmured, my voice dry and cracking.

"Okay," she said quietly before she turned to properly look at me. I could feel her gaze boring into me even though I was intently focused on the road. "The only thing I want to know is why you find it impossible to talk to me? You can tell me anything, and I'll never judge you. You must know that, right?" Her low voice was like a knife to my already bleeding heart.

I took a deep breath before I told her, "It's not you—"

"Don't you dare give me that trite bullshit!" she spat at me, her jaw clenched as she scowled at me.

"I don't talk to anyone about it. It's not you, it's the topic, the subject of the conversation." I gritted out. "I hate talking about it."

"Why?"

"It's a pointless conversation. Nothing can come from it."

"How do you know?"

"Unless you can bring the dead back, it's a forgone fucking conclusion." My words dripped with bitterness. Bitterness I wasn't even aware was inside me.

I wanted to kick myself the moment I said those words. Whatever hell I thought I was in, I wanted to waft the flames and feed them till every part of me was scorched.

"I'm sorry, I didn't mean that."

"Don't lie to me."

"I...I'm..." I gripped the steering wheel harder, hoping that it would ground me as I spoke. "My parents died when I was nine years old. They went out one night and they never came back. Satisfied?"

"Your pain doesn't bring me satisfaction, Jacob."

"Why are you pushing then?"

"Because I want to make it better," her words faded as our eyes met. "I want to know you inside out and I have no idea why. I just need to, like you know me. Every bit of me. I want a level playing field. You know my pain and I want to know yours."

"My pain is nothing like yours." I said as I turned onto my street.

"Pain is pain. Whatever the cause, no matter how you dress it or express it...it's still pain. It still hurts." She murmured as I parked in front of my garage. We both sat there in the darkened silence for a moment or two until she said, "I don't want to leave, but I don't know if you want me to stay anymore."

It would've been so much easier, on me and on her, if I'd let her go. If I'd told her to leave, and the part of me that cowered away from this conversation was begging me to, but I couldn't. The thought of her getting into a taxi and me having to watch her being driven away from me was gutting.

"I've never asked you to leave before, and I'm definitely not asking it now."

I don't think she realised it, but her eyes said it before she did. They said a lot of things. Things that hurt. Things that gave me hope.

Without so much as a peep, they said more than a thousand words ever could.

"We weren't this before." She breathed, her eyes glittered as they looked between mine. "I don't even know what this is, all I know is that it feels like we're more."

That's all she said before she got out of the car and I followed suit. I got her bag out of the back and met her on my porch.

She looked the epitome of breath-taking grace with her long limbs and regal features. And although that dress would've probably looked indecent on another body, on hers it looked perfectly and subtly sexy.

It made me look and wonder what was underneath. It teased every one of my desires for her.

Once I opened the door, she waltzed right in ahead of me. She took her coat off and hung it on the post at the bottom of the stairs before she sat on the step and unbuckled her shoes. I watched as she left them neatly on the floor by it and then took the stairs slowly, one at a time, only looking back as she got to the first landing.

I followed behind her all the way to my bedroom where she went straight to the window seat and perched herself on it.

"Are we still just friends, Jacob?" she asked, so quietly that it was barely a whisper.

I dropped her overnight bag on the floor by the end of my bed and walked towards her. Her head tilted back farther and farther the closer I came until she was looking straight up at me. Her hands held onto the seat cushion on either side of her.

So fucking pretty.

That face.

Those eyes.

Those peachy lips.

I couldn't help but cup her face as I looked down at her. Her eyes searching. Her lips rolling between her teeth. Her deep breaths making her chest swell and her small, perky tits peek from the deep neckline of her dress.

Just friends? Please!

"No, Dor, we're more than friends." Her eyes widened and I had no idea if it was panic or something else. "We're more than friends who have fun. Who fuck. And if you want me to talk, then we're more than friends who talk, too."

She exhaled heavily and without taking her eyes from mine she pulled my white cotton shirt tails from my black jeans. Her hands traced up from my hips to my stomach and the pinch of her nails sinking into my skin had my breath rushing out of me.

"Right now, I want you to fuck me, Doctor Roth." She murmured huskily.

A deep blush coloured her high cheeks as lust hazed her light brown and green speckled eyes. She licked her bottom lip as she rose to her feet, and then onto the tips of her toes.

All I could do was hold onto her black velvet covered waist whilst a mischievous smile stretched her lips. One brow hitching as her hands traipsed up my chest and started working on the buttons of my shirt.

Her nose skimmed the underside of my jaw all the way to my ear as I walked her towards the bed, my heart beating wildly as goose bumps covered my electrified skin.

I couldn't help the gasp that escaped me as her teeth grazed my lobe before she murmured breathily into my ear, "I want you to fuck me now, and talk to me after."

CHAPTER 25

Dorian

Jake spun me around, his hand finding the zipper of my dress and working it off me without a second thought. He pushed my lacy thong down my legs and stood. Shivers wracked my body at the same time as his fingertips raked up my arms, so slowly that it felt like forever.

His touch felt so vital, so good. It was so soft even through his rough need. It made me feel so alive, and when his hand wrapped around my throat and his tongue licked inside my mouth forcefully, I couldn't help the needy, desperate gasp that whooshed out of me.

I'd tried so hard to suppress my feelings, to block them. I'd shoved them all in a box somewhere deep inside me and refused to ever look in it. The problem was that Jacob made me feel so much. He made me feel so many things that the box was overflowing. I had no choice but to revel in every single feeling—old and new.

I couldn't help but moan at the way my artery throbbed in pleasurable protest under his thumb. The way my blood was rushing and buzzing, fighting with itself to circulate around my body when all it wanted to do was rush down to my pussy.

Jake's answering growl deepened as his other hand kneaded my breast, his fingers occasionally pinching and rolling my nipple. And God, it felt like I was on fire.

My hands grasped at the fabric of his jeans pulling him closer to me, so close that the teeth of his zip bit into the skin of my arse cheek. I yanked down on his jeans, enjoying the scrape of the cold metal button and the buckle of his belt until all I could feel was his flesh on mine.

He pulled his lips brusquely away from mine, the grip of his hands tightening around my neck and on my boob. The feel of his nails grazing my skin making my pussy clench.

"Is this what you want, Dor?" he asked hoarsely, even as his eyes remained dark and focused.

He looked like the perfect predator, and I was more than willing to be his prey.

His hand slid down my torso, the other loosening and tightening around my throat as I moaned at the feel of his fingers on my hot skin. The feel of his hardened cock rubbing at the top of my arse, the leaking pre-cum leaving wet trails that pulled on my skin as they dried between us.

All I could think was *more. More. More. More.*

Jake bowed his head onto my shoulder, his tongue laved at my collarbone again and again as he worked his way up to where his hand was wrapped tight around me. He licked up to where his skin squeezed mine and the groan that left his lips had my knees ready to give.

"Do you know how incredible we taste together, Dorian?"

"Jacob..." I managed to rasp as his thumb caressed the side of my neck. It traced my artery before he pressed again.

Lightly he bit his way up my jaw to my lips and then he gently kissed them. My mind was reeling from the contrast and intensity of his every touch. He tilted my face up, his hand cupping my cheek to his shoulder as his fingers ran through my folds and pushed unceremoniously inside me.

God, the feel of his long, thick fingers filling me, curving and pushing into just the right place.

My legs shook and stomach muscles clenched as he held me tightly to him. Every cell of my skin was lit and burning as my orgasm rolled through my body and had me pulsing around his fingers and pulling them deeper into me.

His hand loosened around my throat and trailed to my shoulder before he pushed me onto the mattress, his fingers slipping from my pussy. My chest pushing into the soft bedding as his hand slid down my spine, trailing to my arse.

He aligned his crown with my still pulsing entrance and as he pushed in, his hand smacked down on my sensitive flesh.

The pain and spark clashed and buzzed inside and outside of me as a loud moan erupted from my lips.

"That's it, pretty girl, tell me how much you love my cock filling your pretty, little cunt." He grunted as our skin slapped together, his cock pummelling my pussy relentlessly. "Tell me, Dorian."

"Jake..." I whimpered as my insides started simmering once

again. That was all I could manage as the heat rushed to the surface of my skin. My hands clawed at the bedding beneath me, needing something, anything to grab hold of. To ground me as his punishing strokes bottomed out deep inside me.

"Your pussy is so greedy for my dick. So. Fucking. Greedy." He rumbled as his hands cupped my arse cheeks and squeezed them together.

His fingertips dug into my flesh with a pleasantly bruising force.

"Fuck. F-fuuuuck, Jake...I c-c-can't...please..." I didn't even know what I was begging him for.

My body felt so tightly wound, so highly strung that he either had to let me come or he had to let me be.

He bent over me, his chest sliding along my back with every thrust and his lips rested on my ear as he whispered, "What do you want, baby?"

I wanted to scream at him to make me come. I wanted to demand that he push me over the edge. That he give me relief.

"You feel so good, Dor. Your tight cunt feels so perfect around my cock."

Fuck, he was so deep that I couldn't tell where he ended and I began. His head hitting and rubbing as his hard, thick shaft pulsed and pushed at my walls.

My knees buckled as the waves of pleasure rolled through me.

"That's it, pretty girl, give me everything you've got." He growled as his hand slid down my thigh and pushed my knee up on the bed.

His dick pressed deeper and I couldn't help but scream at the way it hurt. And yet, it felt so fucking good that my toes were curling and my legs felt limp. My arms boneless and my neck unable to support my own head.

The reckless heat consumed me. My heart raced as my pussy clenched ravenously around him.

His grunts and hard, desperate thrusts refuelling my orgasm again and again until my body simply couldn't do it anymore and I was spent with him laying satiated on top of me. His chest to my back. His sweat rolling off his skin and onto mine. And all I could manage was a smile and a contented sigh.

Fuck me, he's good.

"I love that smile, pretty girl," Jake hummed as he kissed the tip of my nose. His cock softening slowly inside me.

My heart lurched as I opened my eyes to his, he looked so beautifully dishevelled as he pushed off me and I turned to see him standing over me.

His open shirt creased and rumpled with sweat patches, making the cotton a little gauzy. His trousers banded around the top of his knees with his boxers. That damn curl that never seemed to stay put teased his eyebrow.

"You need a haircut." I mused whilst I watched him pull his clothes off hastily.

"Yeah, I was meant to go today, but I wanted to see a patient and make sure she's alright. Her husband wants to take her away for New Year's and we wanted to be sure that she was up to it."

"Is she?" I asked at the soft look in his eyes.

"She isn't your typical cancer patient. She's one of the most incredible people I've ever known. You'd never know she was fighting for her life with the way she carries on. She's a terrible flirt." He smiled down at me and then started toward the bathroom.

I manged to push myself up and find my footing. "What happened to talking, Jacob?"

"I need a shower," his gravelly voice sounded from the bathroom as I approached.

I sat on the counter in his bathroom, it was such a sumptuous space with the dark marled granite walls and vanity. The black basalt walk-in shower encased in glass walls, and the bath. It was so freaking huge and thick. The rough stone exterior a complete contrast to the polished rim and smooth interior.

"That's a rather big bath for one person."

He looked at me with a confused look on his face. "My mother insisted on it, I don't think I've ever used it." He shrugged as he opened my legs and stood between them. His eyes trailed up my naked body as his hands grabbed onto my backside.

"Want to try it out with me?"

"Why not?" he murmured softly as he brushed my hair back and off my shoulders. He kissed my forehead lightly and then helped me off the counter.

I could feel his eyes on me as I sat on the wide edge of the bath and plugged it. I tempered the water and poured in some salts that were on the other edge. It was such a mundane and ordinary task, and yet, with him watching me so quietly it felt big and heavy.

"Dor?" I looked up at him. He was perched right where I'd been sat on the vanity, a look of trepidation colouring his face.

My heart froze and for a second everything felt so cold. "Yeah?"

"You're on some form of contraception, right?" his voice was cautious as his eyes fell to my lap.

"I am."

"Okay," he breathed out like he'd been holding his breath for an eternity.

"Okay." I repeated into the bath before I tested the water with a swirl of my hand. I swivelled my body and lifted my legs into the water.

"Are you coming in?" I asked as I lowered myself in and settled at one end.

"Where do you want me?" He smiled.

"Right here," I patted the space between my legs and then turned off the faucet whilst he got in. He lowered his back onto my chest slowly. His head resting on my shoulder.

"Are you sure this is comfortable for you?" He looked up at me.

"Yeah, this is perfect," I said, brushing his hair back. "Close your eyes and relax. Think of nothing…I always try and think of nothing but blackness to get me settled. Although it normally helps if the lights are dim."

"The buttons on the side of the bath are meant to control the lights and there's a sound system too, I think. I can't remember. I had to stop my mother somewhere, you know, draw the line." I giggled at the endearing way he rolled his eyes.

I could tell he loved her deeply, the admiration he had for Ruth was evident in the way he'd looked at her when she'd answered the door earlier. It was clear as day in the way he'd embraced her and kissed the top of her head like she was precious. Even when she'd put her foot in it with the photos, he was so caring and gentle with her. I could feel the tension rolling off him, but not once was he short or sour with her.

I played around with the buttons until I found the right one to dim the lights a little and then I settled back, my head resting on the rolled towel I'd placed on the lip of the bath.

We were both quiet for a moment, so quiet that I could hear the static of the air particles rushing around one another. The ripples in the water as he moved his legs and his arms.

I could feel his restlessness as I tried to relax and calm the thoughts that the mention of his mother had awakened. The truth was I couldn't. I couldn't ignore them any longer, and somehow, I was sure that he couldn't either.

"Why don't you like talking about your parents?" I asked in a hushed voice. I hoped that it wouldn't raise the argument from earlier. "I don't mean Ruth and Levi."

"I know, but you need to understand that they are my parents, Dorian."

"What about…"

"Isobel and David?"

"Your mum never mentioned their names."

"I know. We don't talk about them either. She never liked David, he was awful to her."

"Why?"

"He wasn't a very nice man. It's like Levi got all the good and he…" He took a deep breath. His fingers flicking the surface of the water. "I don't remember much of him, he worked a lot and spent a lot of time away from us. Most of my memories are of him drunk or drinking. He always had a drink in his hand when he was here."

"Here?" I asked quickly before he carried on. I wanted to ask every single question that came to me this time. I didn't want to give him the option of not telling me the full story.

"Yeah, here. This house. My mother loved it, she was so house proud. Even with the housekeeper she would still get on the chairs and dust the chandeliers. She used to clean and clean. Every day. Sometimes all day. Everything was always so clean, you could eat off any surface." He smiled fondly and as I wrapped one leg over his, he gave my knee a squeeze.

"She sounds like Gwen."

"Yeah," he sighed. "I used to think she was crazy for constantly cleaning what was already clean, now I know she was lonely. It's sad because she was an amazing person when she was happy. But the older I got the sadder she seemed. She cried a lot, mostly when she thought no one was looking or listening. She was so soft, too soft, nothing like David."

His words made me tense, my mind going straight to the worst case scenario. My fists balled across his chest and I swear I was more than ready to hurt anyone that hurt him.

"He used to shout at her a lot. It was worse when he was drunk because he couldn't rein himself in. He never laid a finger on her, at least not that I know of, but his words were cruel. He called her lazy and spoilt, she was anything but."

"Why was she with him, then?"

"She was from a strict Jewish family. I'm guessing she didn't want to disappoint them…bring shame on their name."

"But she wasn't happy."

"Sometimes she was. When she found out she was pregnant with Eleanor things changed for a while. She smiled a lot more and she sang all the time. It was new to me, and I loved seeing her like that. She used to sit at her piano for hours, and she used to teach us. Ryan wasn't much for it, he was fourteen at the time and he used to go out to his friends' houses. I loved it though, I remember rushing my homework so I could get to spend time at the piano with her."

"You know how to play the piano?" I asked, a smile forming on my lips as I pictured a dark haired boy sitting at a piano, smiling as his fingers tinkled the keys.

He looked up at me with a soft grin and replied, "I'm good with my fingers."

"For a minute I thought that you were going to last the whole conversation without any innuendos and dirty talk."

"It takes the edge off the crappy stuff." He shrugged and picked up my left hand, inspecting it as he continued. "The last memory I have of her, and him, is of them arguing over a party. She was seven and a bit months pregnant with Eleanor and she was tired all the time, she didn't want to go. But he refused to cancel and she didn't want to let him go on his own. She looked so pretty that night."

My heart broke at his words.

She looked so pretty.

So pretty.

Pretty.

They echoed in my head and rattled around in my chest, and then all I could hear was the way he called me *pretty girl*.

"I still remember her bright red dress. It was so long that it puddled at her feet a little. She never wore bright colours, and Ruth likes to tell me about how she would tease her about her red lipstick. She tells me the same story every time she wears it." He laughed, but even his laughter was tinged with sadness. "That night, she had her hair up. I remember thinking it looked darker than it normally did. She had these big earrings on, the way they dangled made her neck look really long. He didn't like them, so she took them off and left them on the kitchen side. He'd moaned about the dress too, but when she went to change he said they didn't have time."

His breaths trembled, his swallows audible. The tops of his cheeks reddened as he took a moment to himself. I knew what was coming from the way he kept sucking his bottom lip into his mouth and dragging it back out between his teeth.

It was heart-breaking, and it was taking every ounce of strength in me not to burst into the tears he fought with himself to hold back.

"She practically begged him not to drink, but the moment her back was turned he was at his mini bar with a drink in his hand. I watched as he poured himself one and then another, and another. I didn't know any better, I didn't understand the danger. His parents got to the house to look after us and he carried on drinking with his father. The two of them sat and talked and drank until they were ready to leave."

He gasped for breath as he squeezed my hand in his. His body was so tense, so still over mine. Unnaturally so.

"The last thing my mother ever said to me was that she would be back in time to tell me about the party. She said she'd bring me back a treat and a story. She was about to kiss me, but he dragged her away. He took my mother away from me and he killed her. If the doctors hadn't decided to deliver Eleanor when they did, he probably would've killed her too. He should never have gotten behind the wheel of his BMW. He loved that Beemer more than I think he ever loved us, I wish he'd known he was going to wreck it, maybe he wouldn't have been so intent on going to that party. I wish I'd understood why my mother had begged him not to drink, I wish I'd told her he'd been chugging back his expensive scotch like he owned the distillery."

"You were a child, Jacob, and she probably knew."

"I know, but maybe if I'd told her I wouldn't feel like I had a hand in killing her too." He breathed out the words like they were something he'd said so many times before.

"You didn't," I told him softly as I squeezed his hand with the one he was still holding onto tightly and stroked his face with the other. It was the only thing I could think of to comfort him. The only thing that didn't involve moving us. "He made a bad decision, not you."

"I know that too. I also know that she should've stopped him. I know that she let him get away with being a shit father and a crappy husband. I know a lot of things, but none of them make any of it better."

He made to get up, the water was starting to get on the tepid side, but I had this feeling that if I let him go the conversation would be over. I wasn't ready for it to end. I wanted to know every little detail.

I wrapped my legs and arms around him, holding him to me. "How did you end up with Ruth and Levi?"

"My mother's parents couldn't cope; they were devastated when she died. My grandmother locked herself away and refused to talk to anyone. Isobel was her only child. She was everything to my grandmother. My grandfather couldn't handle a teenager, a child and a premature baby."

"What about your other grandparents?"

"My grandmother wasn't a nurturer. She handed David and Levi to a nanny the moment they could get on without her. My grandfather was like my father. He cared about money and things. If it made him wealthier, he loved it. That's why he loved David so much, because he put the money first too. It was a paid for love, nothing like Ruth's or Levi's. They took us all in without a quibble."

"They're good people."

"They are, and they're even better parents." He sighed and for the first time since we started this conversation he smiled. "Ruth didn't have to take us on. I'm sure she wanted kids of her own, but instead she raised another woman's children. Another man's. A man who was quick to call her all manner of things. He took advantage of her father's German roots to insult her, to make her feel like an outsider, and the worst part is that my grandparents let him do it."

"Why didn't Levi stop him?"

"I think it was a losing battle, so they distanced themselves. They got on with their lives away from them. Ruth would visit my mother when David wasn't around, that's how they became such good friends. She was our saving grace. She picked us up from the hospital after the accident, our grandparents weren't in any state to look after us. Ruth took us home with her and Levi and then she went back every day and sat with Eleanor like she was her own baby. She did that for weeks until she brought her home too." He sighed and his body relaxed into mine.

His arms wrapped around mine on his chest and we both sat there. Quiet. Listening to each other's breathing.

He chuckled softly after a while and looked up at me. "She's the one that started me on the Magic Stars. When they took us in I was scared that they'd grow tired of us and that they'd regret their decision. I didn't talk unless I had to. I never asked for anything, not even when it was something I really needed. But one day she sat me down and put a packet of them in front of me." His smile grew brighter as he recalled his memory, and I could feel his joy over it seeping into me, making me smile.

"She used to sing the star song from Pinocchio to Eleanor all the time and when she gave me those stars she said I could make as many wishes as I wanted, and they would all come true because those stars were magic."

"What did you wish for?"

"The first wish I ever made was that she would never leave us, and every day she would give me a small packet after school, and I would wish the same thing. My wish never changed, I still wish it every single day. I owe her and Levi everything, they're my parents by choice. They chose to love me, Eleanor…Ryan. They didn't have to, but they did and they did it better than the parents that birthed us, at least better than David ever did."

He turned the hot water on and moved to the other end of the bath before he grasped my waist and pulled me on top of him. He held me so tight to his chest that I could feel his heart beating.

It felt so right being with him like that. Letting him hold me and enjoying being held by him.

As I listened to his heart beating and his calm breaths I couldn't stop thinking of his words—*they chose to love me.*

All I could think in return was how could they not?

Not loving him is an impossible thing to do.

It was such a sobering thought, and although a part of me told me to get up and leave, it told me to protect myself. For that one moment I let myself be okay with it.

I held onto him tighter as the urge to run clawed at me. It reminded me that I'd allowed myself to feel those things before, and it had almost destroyed me.

CHAPTER 26

Jake

I could feel her staring at me, even with my eyes closed, her gaze warmed me. It soothed my racing thoughts of last night. It filled me with relief that she was still here with me, after the last two times that we'd fallen asleep in my bed and she'd left before I'd awakened.

I opened my eyes to find her sat on the other side of the bed, looking at me with wide eyes. Her arms were wrapped around her legs as she held them to her chest. There was something in the way she was looking at me that tightened my chest. I didn't know what it was, but it wasn't right.

She didn't move as I sat up and shuffled up the bed to lean on the headboard. She looked like she had the weight of the world on her shoulders, and it made me feel like shit because I couldn't help but feel like I'd done that to her. I'd laden her with all my shit. Something I swore I would never do to her.

"About last night…" I murmured, my heart aching with the pained look she gave me. "I didn't…I shouldn't…"

I froze as her features pinched at my words. Her look made me swallow down the apology I was about to give her, and I sat there in silence watching her watch me. Her eyes dropped from my face to my chest. She bit the inside of her lip like she was trying not to say something she needed to.

The absence of her words made my insides twist and knot with dread.

This is it, she's going to tell me we're done. She doesn't want to do this anymore. She doesn't want me anymore.

My lungs burned at the thought. My body stiffened with the cold that assaulted me.

She took a deep breath as she tightened her hold on her naked body. "I've sat here for hours trying to understand why you feel like what happened is your fault. You did nothing wrong. Nothing."

I wanted to reach out and stroke her sad face. Her eyes glistened as she looked at me, she looked a little pale and there were dark circles under her red rimmed eyes. I wanted to argue with her and explain to her that maybe it wasn't entirely my fault, but I should've said something to my mother.

"Maybe if I'd told her…"

"It wouldn't have made a difference, when you love someone, things are complicated. Doing the right thing is complicated." She breathed. "Sometimes you think you're doing the right thing but it makes it all worse."

Her eyes focused on the ring on her hand and as eyes

followed, my heart skipped a little at the notion that she'd taken it off her ring finger. It was such a silly thing to bring a little light to the heaviness between us.

"I thought I was doing the right thing for all of us. Me, him, our unborn child. I said some pretty hard things to him the last time we spoke. I regretted them. I loathed myself for saying them the way I did. For saying them at all. It's not that they weren't true, I think contrary to most women, my pregnancy hormones actually made me see things clearer." Her sigh was melancholy and full of hurt.

"I missed him. I loved him. I hated him. I felt all those things at the same time, but the worst thing I felt was resentment towards his ability to leave me when I was pregnant with our little boy."

"He should never have left you." I had never understood how Phillip was able to leave her the way he did. Thinking about it made my blood boil with anger, he should've been there for her.

"I used to think that too, but I've had a long time to think about everything I did, everything I didn't do—he may have left me, but I let him go too." Her body shuddered as her breaths started becoming shaky and fast. "I was always so scared that he would leave me, like he did when he found out that I knew about Quincy and Richard. He was so disappointed in me, and he made sure I knew it. When he left me that time, I shouldn't have gone back to him. That's when I should've let him go."

"But you wouldn't have Daniel."

"No, I wouldn't and that thought pains me. He's my life, everything I've done since I found out I was pregnant, has been for him." She wiped the tears from her cheeks. "It's why it kills me to resent Phillip. He gave me my little boy. A part of me hates him, but then I remind myself of all the things I said to him. I told him that there wasn't a place for him with me, and I think it was true. I know it was, but I wish I'd waited to tell him after he got home. If I had, maybe things would have been different. Maybe he would've still been alive."

"Maybe, but he deserved to hear them, and so much more."

She smiled forcibly through her strained, quickening breaths. "Oh, Jacob…" Her words were mangled. Her voice sounding strangled as she gasped for air.

Her tears sluiced down her cheeks heavily and it wasn't until she started clawing at her throat that I realised she was in trouble.

"Hey," I cooed softly at her as I dragged her onto my lap and rubbed her back. "It's okay, pretty girl. It's okay, baby. Just breathe, please." I held her tightly to me as I tried to calm my breathing enough to get her to focus on it.

It felt like forever until she'd settled back down. Her tears thinned out and her body went lax on mine.

It took me a moment to understand why she'd decided to share that with me. I thought I'd known all there was to know, but I hadn't. It killed me that she felt responsible for what had happened to Phillip.

"I know what you're trying to prove, but it's different, Dor. I knew that what David was doing was wrong, I just didn't want to see my mother sad. You wanted him back. You were fighting for you and Daniel. It's not the same thing."

She turned her face into my chest and whispered, "I wasn't fighting, I was protecting myself. But I ended up causing more damage."

It wasn't true, no matter what she said, she didn't have a selfish bone in her body. She was so much like Isobel, she'd put her love above herself. Even when he didn't deserve it.

God, I was so jealous of him right then. How wrong was it to feel that way? To envy a dead man for the love he'd taken for granted?

He might've been a good guy, but he was stupid. Blind. He was looking for something that he already had in her. How had he not seen that?

She'd given him everything that I wanted, so freely, and he'd thrown it all away.

I shuffled back down and laid her next to me. She felt so tired…so limp as I pulled her back to my front and held her tight until her hoarse breaths settled into sleepy ones. And the whole time all I could think was that I wanted her so badly.

But how could I ever compete with a dead man?

* * *

She must've been knackered, because she slept for a good few hours. I'd put the television on, practically muted as she laid huddled to my chest. It felt so good having her there. Even with everything that had been said last night and this morning.

My mind was still fixated on how easy it had been to tell her about David and Isobel. Maybe not *easy* easy, but it was like once I'd started, I couldn't stop. The hardest part, the one thing that I had been afraid to tell her about was that I'd known my father hadn't been alright that night.

Even as a child I'd felt the wrongness of the state he was in. That was the hardest part to live with. That was what made me feel like an accomplice to his wrong doing. I was nine, I was old enough to know it wasn't right, but not old enough to understand how bad it was. And yet, knowing that, the guilt that ate at me never subsided.

It wasn't merely the guilt, it was that I was still scared of what would happen if Mum and Dad weren't here. If they hadn't taken us under their care, I had no idea what would've happened to us.

It made me sick imagining what life with my grandparents would've been like. No love, no affection...no care.

When Levi told them they weren't fit to look after us, they'd been relieved. They didn't care that the only child they had left was taking their grandchildren away from them.

Well, that wasn't entirely true, they didn't want to give Ryan up. They wanted to keep him because he was the eldest and he showed promise. That was the sort of people they were, and when he enlisted and decided he didn't want anything to do with the family business they shunned him like they'd done me and Eleanor.

They tried to worm their way back into our lives when they heard I'd finished my Aesthetics and Onco-Plastic fellowships—I just wasn't interested. They never cared before. They tried again once I made Consultant and went into private healthcare. I certainly didn't give two shits about them then. They were strangers to me, to Ruth and Levi, they were nothing.

The loud ringing from Dorian's phone pulled me out of my reverie. She stirred next to me as I glanced at the screen.

Shit, you need to get her up!

I woke her as gently and quickly as I could, her eyes were a little bloodshot from where she'd struggled to catch her breath earlier. I'd never seen her like that, *never*. I never wanted to see her like that again.

"Hey, pretty girl," I murmured as she rubbed her temples. "Gwen was calling you. You should call her back."

"My head is pounding." She moaned as she closed her eyes again.

"I'll get you some painkillers and water," I dropped a chaste kiss to the tip of her nose. I felt her smile as she brushed my hair from her face.

I walked over to my wardrobe and got the medicine box I kept hidden right at the back. Eleanor didn't visit often, she'd only spent a couple of nights here and there, but I still kept anything that might tempt her hidden away. I grabbed a couple of paracetamol and some ibuprofen before I filled a glass with tap water.

Dorian was already sitting up, one of my white t-shirts engulfing her slender frame.

"Call Gwen back, make sure Danny is okay." I told her as I gave her the tablets and the water. "I'm going to have a quick shower, and then we can do something about brunch?"

She smiled as she threw the caplets in her mouth and washed them down with the water. "Thank you."

"It shouldn't take long for them to kick in." I took the glass from her and dropped another kiss to her forehead only pulling away from her when her phone started ringing again. "Answer it."

I left her to it as I headed for the shower. I wasn't in there for long, or at least I thought I'd been quick. The only reason I had taken as long as I had was to give her space to talk to Gwen. I figured the last thing she'd want was the man she was fucking in the same room as she spoke to the mother of her dead fiancé.

I knew she was gone before I even stepped back in the

bedroom. I could feel the absence of her presence. The loss of her company.

I wanted to be okay with it. I wanted to feel alright about it. But I didn't. I didn't know what I felt. I was disappointed. I was angry. But worst of all, I felt that roiling uncertainty inside me, the same one that had prevented me from telling her about all my crap.

CHAPTER 27

Jake

Dorian and Quincy arrived at Jamie's whilst we were busy wrapping gifts. Seeing her, being in the same room as her and not being able to touch her was torture. It was only made worse by the way she was looking at me, like she knew I was pissed, because, truth be told, I was. I hadn't replied to her message telling me why she'd needed to leave. Apparently, Gwen had showed up at her house to drop Daniel off earlier than expected.

I should have responded, but then shit got messy with Eleanor and my head wasn't in the right place. I didn't want to say something that would hurt whatever it was we were.

I'd been ready to go at it as soon as we had those few moments alone in the kitchen, but the way she'd looked at me with those fucking bright eyes of hers…I couldn't. Somehow, I think I managed to get through to my pretty girl how I felt about her repeat disappearing act.

Still, the minute that Jamie and Quincy had walked in, she'd pulled away so fast that it hurt. I couldn't understand why she was acting like we were doing something wrong. Despite what I'd told her about it being fine that we were sneaking around, it was beginning to weigh on me.

I didn't want to hide from our friends and family. I didn't want to lie or pretend like we were the same old Jake and Dorian. We weren't. I wasn't.

I wanted to sit next to her and hold her hand rather than being sat on the sofa next to Willow. My cheeks were still stinging a bit from how hard she'd whacked me after calling her a weirdo Vegan earlier. I could tell she was trying really hard to wind me up. I knew full well she was vegetarian, I just liked to tease her. She was so easy to get to, and quite frankly, I knew that once she got her frustration out she was dandy.

That's what I liked about her, she might be forward and cutting but once she vented, she didn't hold a grudge. Well, not unless it was something serious.

I chuckled as she kicked my feet off the edge of the table. Her ridiculously flared jeans almost catching on my toes. As I looked up my heart stuttered at the look Dorian was giving us both. She looked positively fucked off.

Her twisted pout and glower focused solely on me. I knew that I shouldn't want to laugh, but I did, and it took everything in me to compose myself and school my face into a nonchalant smile.

I watched as she took a long sip of her wine and looked to

Willow again.

"Why are you screwing your eyes at me?" Willow gave her one of her own playful scowls. "I'm not the one doing God knows what in there!" Her indignant sigh was accompanied by an accusatory point of her finger toward the kitchen.

"They're not...they wouldn't..."

"They would and they very clearly are." I replied as I took a drink from my beer. It was so warm it tasted awful. I didn't often drink it, and this was exactly why.

"You could've said they weren't, you know. Now, she's going to get all awkward about—*oh, God!*"

"What are you oh, God-ing about?"

Willow's face pinched into a disgusted grimace as her finger raised and pointed towards the kitchen again. "Someone needs to go get them before I can't stomach my food. It's dawned on me that it's Jamie and Quincy and it's totally weird even thinking they could be up to something in there."

"Don't be melodramatic, you can't hear or see anything... ignore it."

"Really? You wouldn't be able to ignore it if it was your sister and her boyfriend." Dorian gave me her *I dare you to contradict me* stare.

She had a point, but with their very big and very final bust up last night, that wasn't going to be a problem I needed to worry about.

What I was worried about, was how Eleanor was doing. She'd refused to talk, she'd locked herself in her room and ignored my every attempt at trying to pry her out of it.

"Not a very nice thought, is it?" Willow snarked as she poked my shoulder her eyes narrowed on Dorian like she was fishing for a reaction.

"No," I sighed as I got to my feet and started for the kitchen. I paused for a beat as Dorian called out my name and I spun slowly on my heels, trying to plaster a smile on my face. "Yeah?" Her eyes rounded in concern as she searched my face and before it got awkward between the three of us she said, "I think we need more wine. Please."

"Sure." I replied trying not to let my voice waver.

"Thank you." I heard her murmur from behind me as I disappeared down the hall to the kitchen.

I had to take a moment to compose myself. But it was so hard when my chest felt so tight with all the thoughts running through my head about all the ways that Eleanor could fall apart.

I needed to stop thinking about it for a couple of hours. I needed to keep my shit together. I needed to stop overthinking the women in my life.

My head was all over the shop with how confused I was about all the pushing and pulling from Dorian. Together with all the shit with Eleanor, I could feel my composure fraying. I could feel my emotions bubbling to the surface of my equanimity.

I took a deep breath before I made it closer to the kitchen. Quincy's faint, breathy murmurs had me stopping in my tracks. Before I ventured in I called, "I'm coming in!"

I held back the teasing comment that popped into my head and instead decided to give them a less intrusive countdown. "In five…four…"

"Fuck off, Jake!" Jamie gritted.

His frustration strangled voice had me chuckling. "Three, I'm coming in whether you like it or not." I teased as their whispers filtered into the hallway. "We need more drinks if we're going to have to listen to you two go at it some more!"

"I fucking hate him sometimes." Jamie's almost inaudible growl had my mind buzzing with all sorts of innuendos and smart remarks, but again, I didn't have it in me to spill any of them.

I was so relieved and happy that he was enjoying himself again. It felt like he was finally getting back to the old Jamie, and as silly as it was, it filled me with admiration for him. The last few years had been so hard on him.

"Two!"

It also made me wonder what it would feel like to be so open with Dorian. It made me question whether she would ever want or ever be ready to have that sort of relationship where people knew about us.

The realisation of how much I wanted that drew the breath out of me.

"One!" I called trying to set my thoughts at the back of my mind. "Ready or not, here I come!"

I walked in with loud footsteps, as much as it didn't bother me, I didn't want to walk into something private and intimate. Quincy's heavy breaths had me averting my eyes from where she was sat on the counter.

Jamie had never been one for PDAs, but the way he held onto her tightly…it was like he couldn't bear to let her go. I knew how that felt, not wanting to let someone go so badly that you had to physically hold onto them. What I wasn't so sure of, was how it felt to be held with the same need and want.

"You could at least stop whilst I'm here." I chuckled, I hoped it didn't come out as contentious as it had sounded in my head. And as Jamie pulled away from her and gave me the finger, I knew that all they'd heard was a half-witted, teasing jab.

* * *

I could tell Jamie was ready to kick us out. He had that look on his face that said he was physically present and he was being polite, but his head was somewhere else altogether.

Quincy was just as bad as they sat on the couch opposite the one Dorian and I occupied. Her on one end and I on the other. Willow had left not long after dinner and I was ready to go.

"I'm going to make a move." I got up and stretched, my body was aching from spending most of last night sat outside Eleanor's room. "Eleanor's staying and I don't want to leave her alone."

Jamie's eyes shot to mine like he was giving me his full attention. "Is everything okay?"

"Yeah, I think," I sighed my response. My eyes glanced to where Dorian had stood from the sofa too.

"I should get going as well, I think we've imposed enough on your lovey dovey time."

"You're not driving!" Jamie said, firmly and without leaving any room for arguments.

"Of course not! I was going to call an Uber."

"No, you're not. I'll take you." I told her, a bit snappily, before I could think better of it.

"It's okay." She replied at the same time as Jamie said, "Thanks."

Little did he know he had no reason to thank me. I wasn't doing it for him, or because she was his sister. I was doing it because I wanted to make sure she got home safe. I was doing it for the purely selfish reason that I wanted to spend some alone time with her.

After our little tête-a-tête earlier, things felt odd between us. It was like we had no idea how to act around one another. Like we had so much to say, but the words were jammed. It was driving me insane.

I needed to smooth it over and get us back to…

To what?

I had no idea, except that I wanted our ease back. I wanted to touch her. I wanted to kiss her. I just wanted her. Full stop.

I needed the comfort and peace she brought me with her presence alone. My mind and my heart were a fucking quarrelling mess.

Dorian and Quincy said their goodbyes. Their soft whispers lending themselves to girlish giggles and I couldn't help but smile at their exchange.

Whatever it was it had me curious as the blush on both their faces deepened.

"Thanks for the help," Jamie said as he bumped my fist and then slapped my shoulder with his hand, coming close enough to say in a hushed tone, "If you need anything, I'm here."

"Thanks," I said in return with a playful, light punch to his shoulder.

"Let me know when you get in, mush." He turned to Dorian and gave her a hard hug.

"Will do." She smiled as we left and called the lift.

The moment Jamie closed the door behind us she looked up at me and reached for my hand. It should've made me happy. It should've filled me with relief, but instead it taunted me.

It made me wonder why it was so easy for her to reach out when no one else was looking. The possibility that she might in some way be ashamed of us had my breaths cutting my lungs.

"You don't have to take me home. I'll be fine in a cab," she said as she let my hand fall from hers.

It was the wrong thing to say. The wrong thing to do.

My mind was whirling with loud and clashing thoughts of her, us and Eleanor. She tucked herself into one of the corners of the lift. I stood in the opposite corner and pressed the button for the garage.

My thoughts raged in my head mercilessly, and then she looked at me with a broken and jaded intensity that had my insides knotting.

I wanted to reach for her and kiss her. I wanted to suck and bite on her flesh and mark her as mine.

But she wasn't ready, she might never be, and I'd waited a long time already.

From the moment I'd met her. Even when she was heartbroken. When the only thing keeping her going was the baby inside of her. I'd waited for her. I had no idea it was what I'd been doing as I'd watched her slowly rebuild herself. I'd watched her raise the smartest and sweetest boy whilst building a successful career.

I'd waited for her. I'd wanted her. I'd craved her.

I couldn't wait any more.

"I haven't pushed, Dor, and fuck knows I've wanted to. I've waited for you to come to me," I murmured as I took in her wide, overwhelmed eyes. "Dorian, I've waited for so fucking long. I can't wait forever."

She took a deep breath. Her breasts stretched her tight blouse making the buttoned gaps gape slightly. Her eyes closed as she exhaled a long shaky sigh. "I know."

"I don't even know whether you realise how much I want

you, and maybe it's my fault for making light of everything... maybe—"

"Jake..." She shook her head as she uttered my name in a hoarse whisper.

My lips burned for hers. I wanted to grab her face and kiss every fucking inch of it. I wanted to lick her lips and I wanted to suck and bite my way down her neck to her perfect breasts.

"I've seen you in your darkest moments, and I want to bathe you in light...give you nothing but light always. But I need you to want me just a fraction of how I want you."

"I do, Jake. *I do.* I do want you."

"Do you, Dor? Do you really?" My hands ached to reach out and soothe her, like my tongue ached to tell her exactly how I felt.

"I just need time, Jacob, please?" Her eyes searched mine, "I thought you were enjoyin—"

"I've given you time. I've given you years. Nine years and seven months to be precise."

She flinched.

"Time means nothing. It does nothing, unless you make use of it. Unless you make a move." That's what I'd come to realise from all that had happened between us.

Her hands clasped together at her waist as she scraped the light purple-ish pink polish on one thumbnail with the other.

"Are you going to?"

The lift felt so small. It felt like we were crammed into a box and any minute it was going to fall apart.

"What do you want from me?" her voice cracked with her strangled yell, and even as she looked at me with hurt and anger blazing in her hazel eyes, she took a couple of steps closer to me.

"I want *you*! I'm standing right here, Dorian. What are you going to do?" Her eyes went to the lit up control panel and then wandered slowly back towards me, falling to her hands before she met eyes again.

Come on, make your move, baby.

Her sorrowful gaze met mine, and I knew that her move was never going to come.

My chest ached like it had been ripped open. My aching body felt like it was one second away from collapsing in on itself.

"I'm not waiting anymore. I'm sorry, but I can't." I turned away from her before I'd even finished saying the words.

I took a step towards the opening doors as her teary sob sliced through me, her hand lightly grasping my shoulder.

"Why are you being like this?" she cried as her hand fisted and pushed at my shoulder, my body turning to hers with the force of it.

"You want to push me, Dor?" My voice came a little louder and harsher than I intended it to, bouncing off the concrete walls of the garage and echoing around us. "Huh?" I barked at her, my ability to hold myself together completely frayed.

I hated the way she flinched at my harsh words. Her body stumbled and hit the wall next to the now closed lift doors. As I came closer to her she pushed at my shoulder again, with one hand as the other clutched at her chest.

"Stop it," she gritted and glared at where her hand had dropped to my chest and fisted my t-shirt.

She pushed again, but the fact was that as much as she was pushing, she wasn't letting go.

She couldn't. I could see it in her eyes, but I needed her to realise it because I didn't want to have to let her go. She was in my head like a raging storm, all my thoughts spun around her. She'd worked herself into my heart and branded herself into my being.

Fuck, if she forced me to let go, it would break me. However, the reality was that I couldn't live in the hope that one day she'd see us for what we were…for everything we could be. I saw it now, and there were times I thought she saw it too, but then she'd run away.

"You pull me in and then you run, you push me out." I stopped as my throat tightened around the words, my fists balling at my sides as I tried to expel my frustrations by digging my nails into my palms. "You want to keep pushing?"

I took another step toward her and like she was answering my question she pushed again, and again when I didn't move.

"Good, keep pushing, because I'll push back. Harder. And I'll keep pushing and pushing. I'll push all your buttons. Every bit of you, you want to know why?"

She shook her head vehemently and tears sluiced down her cheeks.

I wanted to grab her and hold her to my chest so, so tight. I wanted to feel her tears seep into my skin as I dried them for her.

I felt like a bastard, pushing her and hurting her like this. My heart felt like it was about to disintegrate in my chest. But I needed to make her see what she was doing to me.

"I'll push every bit of you because I can." I whispered as I reached up and cupped her cheek. "Because you want it. You need it."

She gasped for air as her tears continued running down her

pretty face.

"You need to feel like you have control. It drives you, it makes you almost forget all the shit he did to you." Her eyes cut to mine on the last part. Anger, sorrow and hurt glistening in them as her jaw clenched. "Am I right? Does fighting me…us… does it make you feel like what he put you through was okay? Does it make you feel like you're in control?"

Her hands fell, pressing flat to the wall like she was trying to hold herself up. "Please. Please, stop."

"*You* pushed *me*, so no, I won't stop. You want to know why?"

Her head leaned back on the cold concrete wall like she was praying for mercy. And regardless of whether there was a God or not, I was going to be the one to give it to her. I wanted to. I needed to. It was me who was going to give her what she wanted, because whether she admitted it to herself or not—she needed me as much as I needed her.

"It's not because of him. It's not because of them. The dead have no place between us, Dorian. They're gone. Their mistakes. Their failures. Their misgivings. They're gone with them." She slipped down the wall a little and instinctively my hand hoisted her up as I stepped almost flush to her, my other hand stroking the tears from her face. "It's only you and me, pretty girl. You're all I have room for."

Her eyes closed as she breathed out. Her hair a static mess as it stuck to the wall. Her tear reddened nose twitched as she hiccupped her silent sobs.

God, she was so fucking pretty. She was so fucking perfect, and she didn't even know it. She didn't understand.

Make her understand!

That was all I could tell myself as I kissed the tip of her nose and rested my forehead to hers.

"I just want you. Only you," I breathed into her open mouth. "I love everything about you, Dorian."

Her eyes lifted to mine, they were so wide and they looked so green with the tears still glistening on the rims.

"I love your brilliant mind," I told her as I took in her flushed face, "and your beautiful body. I love your tenacity and your unwavering strength."

"Jake…" She whispered hoarsely, her eyes never leaving mine.

"I love the great mother that you are. I love your amazing boy…and you."

"Jacob." She sobbed, her hands grasping my wrists as I cupped her face with both of my hands.

"I love *you*." I took a deep, clear breath as I let the words settle between us. The minute they were out a massive weight felt like it was lifted off my chest. Even if her quiet searching eyes had me shaking like a shitting dog.

Fuck it, what do you have to lose?

Her nails dug into my wrists, deeper and deeper the longer we went without saying anything. My heart raced emphatically as the urge to kiss her burned so brightly that it set me on fire.

I'd never loved anyone like this. Like my every heartbeat depended on it. Like that was the only reason I existed. And the frightening thing was, it didn't even matter whether she loved me in return.

I wanted her to. I wanted her to love me so badly, but the only thing that felt like it mattered was that she would allow me to love her.

"I want to love you so damn, fucking much that anyone who looks at you will know that you are loved by me. They won't ever wonder if you belong to anyone, because they'll know you're mine just from your smile."

She sighed breathily as her hands fell to the crook of my elbows and then to the top of my jeans.

"That's all I want. I don't need to go anywhere. I don't need to look for anything. I know what I want. I know what I need... who I need. It's just you."

She smiled softly at me, her breaths still hiccupping from her settling sobs. "It's not that easy, Jacob."

"I know, I understand that. But all I want from you is to let me love you. Please, please let me love you, pretty girl."

She sucked her bottom lip into her mouth and released it with a slight pop. Her eyes looked from mine to my lips and back up again before she said, "I'm not even your type."

I had to laugh at that. I'd never had a type. I simply went with what worked and was on offer.

"What's so funny?"

"You're way more my type than Lady Mary. Question is, who'd you prefer...me or Matthew?"

She burst out laughing at that. The leftover tears slipping down her face as she tried to wipe them, and for that moment our ease was back.

"Let's get you home, shall we?"

"After all that, you're just going to take me home?" She looked at me incredulously.

"I didn't say whose home." I said as I picked up her coat and bag that had fallen on the floor. I took her hand and walked us to my car, and before I got in I made sure her Volvo was locked.

It was a private garage with tight security, but it didn't hurt to make sure.

As soon as I got in she turned to me with a serious face. It was so serious that it gave me pause. It made everything that had just happened run through my head in a quick recap. All my words zapping through my brain and echoing in my ears.

Fuck, maybe I should've been softer. Maybe I should've reined in my frustration.

Shit, what if everything had finally sunk in for her and she didn't want any of it? What if she didn't want me?

God, what is wrong with you? Why couldn't you do things the normal way? Take her out. Woo her. Maybe give her an orgasm or two before you dropped everything on her?

I put the car into drive and started for home, hoping that she wouldn't tell me she changed her mind and wanted to go back to hers.

Not that she'd said she wanted to go back to mine.

We drove in silence for a while, and when I couldn't take it anymore I asked, "Why are you staring me out?"

Her brow hitched as she took in a deep breath and said, "Most people go for sweet words and romantic settings."

Shit.

"I think we've established I'm not most people."

"Hmmm," she mused as she turned to look at the road ahead, "so you're not, Doctor Roth."

CHAPTER 28

Dorian

I shouldn't be feeling like this. I shouldn't be feeling like everything was falling into place. Like maybe, I could let Jake love me. I could trust myself to let him take me into his heart and that even if in the end we fell apart, I would be able to keep myself together for my boy.

I shouldn't feel any of those things. I should've truly pushed him away, battened my gates, steeled my defences and walked away. But I couldn't.

Maybe I should've said no.

No, I can't let you love me.

The meshing of that sentence alone felt wrong. Thinking of it made my stomach turn. The bile rise up my throat.

The thought of shunning his affection was intolerable.

Unperceivable.

He was right, I was scared of letting go. I was scared of falling and not having anyone to catch me. Of falling alone. Of breaking. Of having to pick up all the pieces and having to put myself back together.

I was shit scared of losing another person I cared for, more than I cared to admit to myself. I was so scared of losing him, that I'd convinced myself that it was easier keeping him strategically at arm's length.

But I was so tired of being afraid that for once, I wanted someone to be scared of losing me instead.

And he was. I'd seen it in his eyes—Jacob was terrified of losing me.

The crazy thing was that in my fear, I could've lost him. The one person that understood my worry, my dread, because he knew what it felt like to feel lost in this world.

I looked over at where Eleanor was sat at the kitchen table with her phone in her hand. If for some reason I hadn't realised the importance of his words before, looking at her, made them pretty damn meaningful.

Again, she was so quiet and she had an air about her that made you feel for her. She barely said a word with the exception of answering her brother's questions and greeting us when we came in.

"You doing okay?" Jake asked as she got up and made for the stairs.

She stopped in her tracks and turned to him with a small smile. Her eyes flitted between me and him before they fell to her fluffy socked feet. "I will be."

"I'm here if you want to talk, if you need...anything.

Anything at all."

"I know," She said as she looked back up at me. "I seem to keep skewing your plans, I'm sorry."

"I have a knack for it myself." I had no idea what it was about her, but there was something that made me feel like I needed to know all there was about her. It was almost like we were different parts of the same hymn sheet. In some way, somehow her pain called out to mine.

She turned to Jake, "Mum dropped off your tux for the end of year thing earlier, and she brought doughnuts. They're in the warming drawer, she said not to leave them in there otherwise they'll go hard."

"Did you have dinner?" he asked as he took the Pyrex box from the drawer and put it on the side.

"She brought soup too, and latkes. Someone told her I was sick, so she had to come and nurse me."

"I told her you weren't feeling great, I didn't know what else to tell her, Eleanor." He murmured as he leaned on the kitchen side with his hip. The dark circles under his eyes and the concerned look on his face made him look older.

"I don't want her to worry." She looked at me again from the corner of her eyes. "I need to go get the rest of my things tomorrow."

"That's it?"

"Yeah, it's for the best." Her voice quivered and I thought I'd see hurt and sadness in her eyes, there wasn't any. There was pain, but it had an edge to it that felt angry. "Anyway, thank you for letting me stay."

"This is your home too."

"Maybe," she breathed as she looked around, turned and

made for the stairs.

He stood, quietly, staring after her. My heart breaking for him as he sucked on his bottom lip like a helpless child. All I wanted to do was make it better. I couldn't fix anything, but I could make him feel better.

He took a deep breath and then looked to me with a smile so sad that it was so much more affecting than any tear drenched frown. His steps toward me were muted and surprisingly light for someone who's shoulders bore so much weight.

I couldn't wait for him to get to me. I needed to wrap my arms around him and hold on. I needed to hold on to him, share some of that unwavering strength he said he loved so much. The strength I wasn't even quite sure I possessed, but for him I'd find it. Somehow, I'd muster it and I'd give it to him. Every bit. Every ounce. Everything.

He sighed deeply as my arms surrounded his waist. His chin rested on the top of my head as I listened to his fast beating heart. I couldn't help but wonder which one of those beats belonged to me.

I want them all.

The more of them I counted the more I wanted them all for myself. Maybe it was a selfish wish, but if they were mine I'd do my damned best to make each one happy. Whatever it took.

"So, I let you love me," I murmured into his chest before I looked up at him. "What does that mean?"

I squeezed his lower body to mine as his eyes met mine cautiously. His arms loosened around me and ever so tenderly his hands trailed up my arms to my shoulders. All the while his gaze searched my face like he was looking for an answer to some age old question.

"Dor…" His voice was a low hum that sank into my pores and warmed my blood.

"Come on, Doctor Roth, you talked a good game back there." I brushed his impossible curl away from his eyes as I kept my one arm tightly around him. He bit the side of his lip as I cupped his cheek. "You've got me intrigued. What does it mean if I let you love me, Jacob?"

"It means," he rumbled huskily as his hands travelled up my shoulders to my neck, and then cupped my face. He kissed the very tip of my nose lightly before he touched his forehead to mine. His eyes held mine fixedly and I could see his smile in the way they shone as he said, "I love you."

My heart skipped a beat like the first time he'd said those three little words. I knew that it wasn't what they meant that managed to stop a fraction of time, it was the way in which he meant them.

I could see it in his eyes. I never understood what it meant to see love burning in someone's eyes…in their soul, but looking into his warm chocolate depths I could see it all so clearly.

It was unlike anything I'd ever seen. It wasn't beautifully perfect. It wasn't all light. It wasn't even all warm. It was a reflection of our lives, I suppose. There was pain and hurt. There was darkness. There was blood and scars. But in spite of it all, he was willing to risk more…for me.

The only other love I'd known was selfish and cowardly. It cared more for itself than the person who it existed for. It may have been apparently beautiful, but appearances changed. They diminished with time.

That's the love I was scared of. A love that ebbed and flowed like mood swings. It was inconstant and inconsistent.

I didn't want that, and moreover, I didn't want to give it to this man who'd braved the cold just to offer me warmth. Who'd endured the cold to hold me when nobody else knew how.

I wanted to give him everything he was giving me, and one day I would. I would be deserving of all that he'd given me and continued to give me.

"I like that," I smiled back at him as his fingers tangled in my knotted hair and he kissed each of my cheeks.

My mouth watered as his lips drew closer to mine, my heartbeat hammering the back of my throat and making my breaths quiver. Before I could level them out his tongue was sweeping into my mouth and drawing out deep and desperate moans from the base of my tummy. Moans that tangled with his own.

His warm hands twisted in my hair as he cradled my head, his elbows rested on my shoulders as my hands trailed to his and splayed on his collarbone. My thumbs pressed perfectly into the hollow of his throat.

I could taste his peppery heat, his citrusy bite and his leathery strength. I could taste everything that made him, and I wanted it all.

I wanted him, full stop.

I wanted him for who he'd been.

I wanted him for who he was.

I wanted him for who he would become.

I wanted his heartbeats, his breaths, his touch, and his taste.

Because I loved him too.

Maybe I couldn't form the words and say them aloud. Not yet, but one day maybe I could be brave. One day I could say them.

His teeth sunk into my lip and he drank my breathy gasp with a growly rumble. My skin pimpled as he kissed the edges of my mouth and peppered kisses on my face. Each kiss felt like a prayer and a promise.

"What does it mean, Jake?" I asked as his hands drifted down my body to my bum and hoisted me up his body until my legs were wound tight around his waist and my arms wrapped around his shoulders.

"Tell me," I smiled as his bright brown eyes collided with my hazel ones. They prickled with fresh, warm tears. Tears that burned and stung and yet were filled with so much happiness.

His eyes flitted down to my stretched lips and he gave me the Jake smile I adored. The one that made the butterflies in my tummy flutter to the point that it felt like I could breathe them out.

He touched the tip of his nose to mine and without a tremor, with absolute certainty he said, "I love you, pretty girl."

Bliss. Beautiful, perfect bliss.

Who needed summer suns and thick winter blankets, when they could have this?

No one. Not even me.

He pressed a soft, chaste kiss to my lips and started for the stairs. His hands splayed on the curve of my bum as he carried me so effortlessly. So steadily.

I couldn't help but wonder if that was how it would feel to have him love me every day. Effortless and steady. To have a beat of his heart all to myself.

No, I want them all.

"Wait!" I blurted before he made it another step up the stairs.

"What's wrong?" he asked, panicked.

"Where are your stars?" He looked at me like I'd lost my mind. Maybe I had. "I need one."

"What?"

"I need to make a wish, you said they have to come true, right?"

"I did," he replied with a hitch of his brow.

"I need one now. Please. Please?"

"Okay," he smiled at me dubiously as he continued up the stairs. "I have some in my bag."

"Good. Come on, faster!"

"Jesus, you're a bit demanding." He chuckled as he picked up his pace. "What're you wishing for?"

I tapped the end of his nose before I pressed a kiss to it.

He took me straight to his bed and put me down gently before he went to search his bag. He came back with a victorious smile on his face. "Becca likes to sneak them into the small pockets."

"I like her thinking."

"She likes you," he grinned as he handed me the small packet of chocolate stars. I stood on the mattress so that I was looking down at him. "What are you wishing for, Dor?"

"If I tell you it might not come true." I needed it to come true too badly to risk telling him. "How about I share it with you?"

I ripped the packet open and popped a star on my tongue and as it melted, I looked into his eyes and wished for one more of his heartbeats.

One more of his heartbeats every day...until I had them all.

I cupped his still confused face and licked into his mouth quickly before the chocolate was all gone.

He hummed, his hands holding my waist tight. It felt so

good. His touch. His feel.

His tongue tangled with mine as my hair fell around us. He chuckled when I pulled away and brushed it back, the chocolate all gone, just the sweet aftertaste mingled with Jake's.

"That wish tasted so good, pretty girl." He smiled and I couldn't help but smile too as my hands slipped to his chest, knowing that at least one more of his heartbeats was mine.

CHAPTER 29

I was smiling. Like fucking, goofy smiling. My chest was vibrating with how happy I was. Ever since Dorian and I had started this thing between us, the morning after the night before was always tense. She was either gone or I could feel the distance she slowly put between us.

This morning however, things were different. It was a completely different kind of morning after. I don't know what it was that happened, apart from my little outburst in the garage, but again things had shifted. It wasn't a subtle shift either. There was major change.

Even with our talk last night when we'd gotten into bed and simply cuddled, things were different. All we'd done was laid in bed with Downton in the background, because we were so close to the end and I think we both needed the closeness of being with one another, but the space and time to think without letting sex be the driving force of what we were feeling.

I could sense her mulling it over in her head. Her thoughts were so loud as they tumbled about that I was surprised I couldn't make out exactly what they were.

The smallest contact from Dorian felt so deep. With her it was so easy to go off on a tangent of touch and limbs and the feel of her. The problem was that although that was definitely something I more than enjoyed, it was also something we used to try and excuse the feelings. To turn a blind eye to what was happening between us.

At first I thought it was just me feeling this way, but then she listened and she understood. She went out of her way to be there and comfort me, and things got real. The feelings got so fucking real that they were pushing and pulling, clawing and begging me to let them out.

I didn't quite understand how badly I'd wanted and needed her, not until she'd walked out the last time. The anger and the disappointment at her absence. The fear that I was setting myself up for a major loss. All those things and still I fucking wanted her so fucking badly. I would've done anything to bring her back.

Anything.

But at the same time the hurt part of me wanted to give her a taste of her own medicine. The other part, the maybe not so rational but nonetheless thinking part was having a field day analysing all my thoughts and feelings.

You love her.

That's all it said, all fucking night when I'd sat outside

Eleanor's room and hoped that she'd be okay. That her tears and her silence weren't the precipice of another relapse. Even when I was tired, that voice was so fucking loud, no matter how hard I tried to shush it or push it out of my head.

I knew it though. I'd known for a very long time. But I chose to ignore it. I thought if I ignored it that even if she didn't feel the same, I could still keep her close.

How fucked up is that?

I couldn't help but chuckle dryly at the thought. It was so stupid to think that I could do it, that I could stand by and watch her forever, without ever having a taste.

But then I had the taste. Fuck, I didn't just have a taste, I ate the whole damn platter and it felt like it was never enough. I kept needing and wanting more, and yet she found it so easy to pull away…to push me away. It was frustrating, and frustration was something that I could never tamp down. So the verbal explosion happened.

Her tears. The fear in her eyes. The sorrow. I thought I was going to lose her for good, and if that was the case then I might as well lay it all out there. Love and all.

Typical Dorian, she found a way of surprising me. Just like her arm sliding under me and wrapping around my chest. Like her body pressing to mine. Her warm soft front pushing into my back as her other arm crossed over mine and pulled me tightly to her.

"Morning, Doctor Roth," she cooed huskily into my ear as her hand slipped down my chest to my hip. Her hips softly thrusting to my arse as her hand splayed on my groin.

Her voice was so fucking beautiful first thing. It was raspy and soft. It was so warm as it brushed my skin and tickled my ear. It was heavenly and sinfully promising all at once. And fuck, her moan as her fingers brushed the morning wood jerking in my boxers zapped through me like a sparking fuse.

I felt her smile as her hand stroked up and then her thumb hooked into my underwear. Her lips puckered light kisses over my shoulder as she pulled the stretchy cotton down over my erection, and holy fuck her warm hand grasped my throbbing dick. Her thumb massaged over and around my tip, making me gasp.

"Do you like that, Jacob?" she murmured teasingly into my ear, her hand tightening and stroking.

My fucking lungs felt like they were about to explode in my chest with how fast I was breathing. Her long breaths sharpened and deepened as I reached behind her and stroked my fingers between her cheeks, pulling her thong to the side before continuing through her wet folds.

"Do *you* like that, pretty girl?" I asked as I teased her pussy with the tip of my finger.

Her moan was breathy and hot on my skin. Her hand squeezed as her pulls on my cock became firmer. The edge of her thumbnail lightly dragging as she swirled her thumb over my crown. Her other hand tightened around my chest pulling me impossibly closer to her as her body undulated behind mine.

I could picture her rosy blushed cheeks as her breathing shallowed with the stroke of my fingers through her pussy. My mouth watered as her slick arousal coated my fingertips, my mouth watered with the yearning to taste her. I needed to.

She yelped as I turned quickly to face her. Her eyes wide as they caught on mine and her lips parted on a silent sigh as I pulled my t-shirt she was wearing up, rolling her onto her back as I tugged it off her. Her arms stretched over her head to the headboard.

"That feels so good," she blew softly as my lips caressed down to her rosy tipped nipples.

God, her tits were so perfect. So fucking round and soft, and they fit perfectly into my palms as I kneaded them.

Who needs stress balls when I have these?

Her whimpers dragged out as I licked and sucked the sides of her breasts. Her body squirmed beneath me and her hands pushed at the solid wood above her head as I made my way down her body. Pinching and rolling her nipples between my fingers.

Her body was so fucking beautiful as it opened up for me. Her legs fell to the sides as I settled between them. She was so fucking soft and slender, and blushed beneath my wandering hands. Her barely there, lace thong pressed to my face, teasing me with how wet she was.

Her whole body tensed as I curled my arms under her and my hands gripped the top of her thighs. Even her breaths quietened like they were waiting for me to taste her. Her half-lidded gaze flitted down her body to find mine.

It was so fucking bright, even in the early morning light that seeped through the cracks in the curtains.

"Jake…" Her whisper was so raspy that it vibrated through her body. I could feel it rumbling under her skin and permeating into mine. Her pelvis pushed off the bed and her scent filled my senses.

"Do you want me to eat your pussy, baby?"

Her desperate nod as she begged, "*Please*," had my hands twisting at the sides of her underwear. With a firm tug the lace tore at the seams. The sound had me grinding my pulsing cock into the sheets.

I pulled the torn underwear from her with my teeth, eliciting a drawn out, desperate breath from her. Before she could get it back I swiped my tongue along her slit. Her legs quivered along with the strangled hum that caught in her throat and I swear she got wetter. Her arousal slicked over my lips and chin, spreading to her thighs as I licked and sucked at her pussy.

My hands pushed down onto the base of her stomach, holding her gyrating hips in place. Her tight cunt clenched around my tongue as I greedily pushed in. Her whimpers muted as her hand slapped loudly over her mouth. Her other hand twisted in my hair, pushing my face into her.

Sweet fucking suffocation.

My lungs ached as I gasped for breath between licks and nips. Her hoarse cries getting louder behind her hand. She was right on the edge; I could feel her shaking. Every part of her clenching. Pussy. Arsehole. Thighs. Stomach. Every bit of her begging for that last little push.

Her humming sigh as I pushed my middle finger inside her had my bollocks tightening. I swear I could come from finger fucking her alone. From her whimpers and groans. From the feel of her walls clamping around my finger.

Shit, with the way my cock was becoming harder I could've been buried inside her pussy.

"More," she husked as her hands slapped onto her tits. Her fingers sinking into her supple flesh as she squeezed her breasts in her hands roughly, like I liked to do.

She growled as I pulled my finger out and whimpered as I added another and shoved them back into her slick pussy.

"No, give me more." She huffed with frustration colouring her words. "I need more, Jacob. I need you to fu—"

I pulled my fingers out and pushed her leg to her chest as I shuffled up the bed. She looked so fucking pretty with her mouth gaping and her eyes focused right where our bodies met. I braced myself over her and as I slammed into her, her breath pushed out in a high-pitched cry.

Her cheeks were blushed a deep pink, her lips gnawed to a glistening red and god, her tits were decorated with half-moons from her nails.

So fucking sexy.

My lips brushed her forehead again and again as she moaned into my chest. Her leg hooked over my forearm as I thrust into her in hard, fast and unrelenting strokes. Her hands grasped at my sides, her nails raking over my ribs at the same time as our skin slapped together.

My cock was so stonking hard inside her that it ached every time I bottomed out in her pussy.

"Oh god, Jake, right there," she whined as I shifted the angle of my thrust. Her whole body quivered and her eyes glassed over with pleasure.

"Are you going to come for me, baby?" I ran the tip of my nose over the bridge of hers as I drank her desperate breaths into my lungs.

She nodded frantically as she cupped my face with her hands. The slapping of our bodies so loud it echoed around us, and fuck if it wasn't the most beautiful sound I'd ever heard.

Her thumbs pulled at my lips as the sweat made it impossible for her hands to keep a hold of my jaw.

"Come on, pretty girl, give me your pleasure." I breathed

before I licked into her mouth.

Her tongue tangled with mine desperately. Before I could pull away to tell her to come on my cock her body shook beneath mine. Her nails dug into the nape of my neck and her loud moan vibrated down my throat to my balls. Her pussy greedily clenching and sucking at my dick.

I sat back on my calves, the feel of her cunt fighting with me to keep my dick inside her made my muscles tense and my bollocks pulse.

"No," she gasped as I pulled out. Her protest halted as I pushed three fingers into her pussy and gripped my cock over her stomach, stroking roughly with the unrelenting need to come. Her hands grasped my thighs tightly.

"Fuck. Fuck, fuck, *fuck*." She repeated as her body curved off the bed, her eyes never leaving my cock as I finished myself off above her quivering body.

I'd be lying if I said that her lust coloured obscenities didn't urge me on. I'd be lying if I said that her laying there, watching as I yanked myself off over her still shaking body, with my fingers buried deep in her pussy and her ragged breaths wobbling her fucking perfect tits didn't make me want to mark her as mine.

This woman that I craved, loved and, quite frankly, adored.

I'd happily worship at her feet for as long as she'd let me, and beyond.

Her eyes widened as I fisted my cock faster and harder, and with every spurt of my hot cum over her body her teeth bit down harder on her lip.

With every milky rope of my cum that painted her beautiful peachy skin, my heart thudded while every part of me yelled— *mine*.

It yelled and yelled until it was a constant, deafening roar.

Mine. Mine, mine, mine.

My fingers slipped out of her pussy and trailed up to her stomach. Dorian's gasp as they worked my cum into her skin had my slowing pulse picking up again.

Her brow quirked, her teeth still gnawing on her lip, her nipples hardening and blushing as I rubbed every drop of my release into her goose pimpled skin.

She sighed as my fingers trailed up between her breasts and as I cupped her chin, my thumb pulling her lip from her teeth, she leaned up on her elbows and smashed her mouth to mine. Her kiss was hard and clumsy at first, but as our lips worked over one another, it became soft and deep, her tongue licked at the seam of my mouth and as I opened up to let her in she hummed as her tongue twisted with mine.

She pulled me down with her, our bodies sticking together as her hands worked into my hair. I couldn't help but smile as the feel of her heart beating into my chest had my own thundering away.

"What are you smiling about?" she asked as she opened her eyes to look up at me.

My smile stretched to a grin as I rolled onto my back and took her with me. Our skin stuck together and pinched as it pulled at each other.

She crossed her arms over my chest and rested her chin so that she was looking down on my face. A sigh escaped her lips as she narrowed her eyes at me.

Fuck, how can someone be that fucking pretty even when they look just fucked dishevelled?

"You have that lopsided grin on your face," she husked. A

knowing smirk split her face before she asked, "What does it mean?"

It means you're mine, and I love you...so fucking much it doesn't even make sense.

My hands cupped her arse as she shimmied over me, making my dick twitch. Her eyes closed as it slid between her cheeks and a long breathy sigh blew past her lips.

"Does that feel good?" I murmured into her slightly gaping mouth.

One corner of her mouth hitched up into a soft, sultry smile and she nodded. "You always feel good."

"Snap!" I chuckled, one hand lifting from her arse and smacking down with a loud *slap*. My dick jolted to full attention at the feel of her arse cheeks clenching around it.

Her eyes widened on mine, her pupils dilating to the point there was just the thinnest golden green ring around it.

"Stop it," she gasped in a cracked whisper. "We need to talk before round two."

"Round two, talk and then round three?" I thrust my stiff cock between her arse cheeks and ground my body into hers.

"Nah-ah," she shook her head with a puckered, teasing smile plastered on her mouth. "Talk now, fuck after."

I loved the way she sounded so proper even when cursing. She made crass classy and it made me hard. Every. Single. Time. It didn't matter how she used the profanities, it was the way they smoked out at the back of her throat before they left her lips.

Jesus, even thinking about it. Hearing them in my head had me more than ready to go again.

CHAPTER 30

Dorian

fter last night and the start to this morning, I was feeling blissful. Something I hadn't quite felt in a long time. Not like this.

Daniel had been the fountain of all my happiness for so long, and now, with Jake, that fountain seemed to be overflowing.

"Are you going to talk?" Jake asked as he pulled me closer to him. His hand grasped my thigh and hooked my leg over his. "If you've changed your mind we can always go for round two now…"

"Nice try, Doctor Roth." I smiled as I combed his ruffled hair back.

He was so bloody handsome that just looking at him like

this was enough to make the heat between us scorch.

The brown of his eyes swirled like the most delicious molten chocolate and for a fraction of a moment I wanted to say fuck it and leave the talking for later.

I couldn't though. He deserved to know where I was at, I couldn't lead him on. I couldn't let him think that a declaration of feelings was going to slot everything else around us into place. I wish it would. That it could, but that was all it was—a wish.

Somehow, I didn't think that any of his Magic Stars could help this one. This one was going to need time.

My heart stuttered at that and his words came back to taunt me.

"I've given you time. I've given you years."

All of a sudden it wasn't so warm anymore. The realisation of how this conversation would go down had my insides freezing over.

I cupped his face a little too tightly between my hands and before I said the words that could well break him. Break me. Break us. I kissed him.

I took my time to taste him, enjoying the way he still had me on his tongue. Enjoying the way he hummed and his arms wrapped tighter around me, the way his hands splayed on my back.

Maybe he knew what was coming. Maybe he could feel the chill inside me through my skin.

He yanked the duvet over us and as I opened my mouth to speak, he kissed me with the same slow urgency I had kissed him. He tangled our legs together and his hands wrapped around my shoulders like he was holding me hostage.

I hoped he wouldn't let go when I spoke the words that I needed to. I would utter a hundred and one prayers if it meant he would understand. That he wouldn't push me away and leave me with the ice in my veins permanently.

I kissed the hollow of his throat lightly as I breathed him in and before I chickened out I cleared my throat. "About last night…"

I felt him still, his breathing pausing even as I felt his heart battering my chest. When I looked up at him his eyes closed and when he opened them again they were completely shuttered. I couldn't see anything in them except for deeply rusted, corroding steel.

"I heard everything you said, and I believe every word," I murmured as I looked down to his body. I took in the way his Adam's apple bobbed whilst my fingers traced the throbbing vein along his neck. They ached and burned as they caressed down to his chest and smoothed over his light smattering of hair.

"But?" he gritted so softly that it was impossible for me to pretend I didn't hear the hurt muffling his question.

"But I have Daniel to think of here, and I can't just put this on him. I can't put this on everyone else either, there's so much going on already and this time of year is so hard for them."

I felt his hands ball at my shoulders as his arms tightened like a vice around me. "I don't care about everyone else," his voice cracked and with it my heart ached a little more, if that was even possible.

"You care about Jamie, which means you care about Quincy. I care about her and then there's Gwen and Liam. They've been like second parents to me all my life." I kissed the pec his heart was probably bruising from the inside out.

"What does that even mean, Dorian?" His hand rounded my chin and tilted my face to his.

The hurt mingled with a spark of hope in his eyes. The rust morphing into a slightly shiny dark copper.

Christ, the way they bore into mine, it felt like he was pulling my sinking heart from the depths of my belly and the ache up to my swelling throat.

"It means we have to be discreet." I breathed out, my eyes closing so I didn't have to see the disappointment I was sure would glass his eyes.

"By discreet, I'm assuming you mean you want to keep us a secret?" I knew it was a question, but the way he said it, it sounded more like a resigned statement. "Look at me."

My eyes opened and I cringed at the sting I could feel from his piercing gaze.

"Are you ashamed of me?" he asked so quietly that in that moment what I was ashamed of was myself for making him doubt my affection toward him. "Of us? Are you ashamed of your feelings? Of mine?"

God, I wish I hadn't said anything. *Why did you have to talk? To ruin a perfectly great moment?*

"I'm not ashamed of you, Jacob." I tried to smile, but I couldn't. I couldn't smile when I knew that I had taken his away. "I'm not ashamed of wanting you, or of being with you. I used to be, and not because of you. You're more than I deserve. I felt guilty because of the way you can make me feel just by saying my name."

I brought my hand up to his jaw and cupped it as I smoothed my thumb over his lips, hoping to caress a smile onto them.

"Dor…" He sighed, closing his eyes as my thumb continued

stroking his lips.

"I love the way you say my name. I like the way you whisper it. I like the way you murmur it. Even the way you grit it out when I annoy you." I pressed a light kiss to the underside of his jaw. "I love the way you grunt it when you're coming inside me, it does things to me. Makes me feel things. No one has ever said it like you do. Like you're a saint and it's your prayer to your God."

"I'm not a saint, pretty girl." He breathed as his eyes searched mine.

"Fine, you say it like it's a spell for everlasting life." I parted his lips with my thumb and craned my neck to kiss him. His full cupids bow cushioned my lips. "I need that. I needed someone to say it like that so badly. It scares the crap out of me, because if you ever stop saying it that way…"

His eyes looked between mine with so much brimming in them. So much love pouring out of them that it was overwhelming.

"Don't break me, Jacob. I can't let that happen, I have a son who needs his mother. He's everything to me, and if he's going to share my affection with another, it's only fair that he receives their unwavering affection in return."

"Have I ever given you reason to doubt my affection for him?"

"No, it's part of the reason I fought this and it's also part of the reason I gave in. You chose to love us, it takes a special person to do that."

He smiled at that. He smiled with fucking glistening tears in his eyes. His breaths hiccupped in his chest and it was enough to make my eyes sting and blur.

"We need to ease Daniel into this. I know he'll be more than happy, but he's a child and he doesn't understand what it means."

"Okay," he murmured. "I respect that. I understand it...but everyone else?"

"We can be discreet, can't we? I don't want to hide, I just don't want to rub it in their faces and open us up to their judgement."

His face fell serious as his eyes narrowed on mine, "Anyone that judges us, isn't worth our time. You got that?"

"It's not that simple, Jake. Jamie is your friend. Quincy is mine..."

"And they want you to be happy, Dorian."

My insides melted with how he put intense emphasis on my name. His hands grasped my face tightly as he pressed a hard and burning kiss to my forehead and then wrapped his arms tightly around me. So tight I could feel his muscles rippling between us and under my hands as I held on just as tightly to him.

I hoped that it would be as easy as everyone wanting me to be happy. I hoped that it would be easy for me to let myself be happy.

* * *

By the time we got up and made it downstairs it was almost early afternoon. Eleanor had left a note on the kitchen side saying she'd gone to pick up the rest of her things whilst Miles was out.

The house was so quiet and still that I couldn't help but take in all the little things that made it feel so homey.

For the most part it was actually quite bare, the furniture

was cosy, but minimal. There weren't many knick knacks, and unlike his parents' house there weren't many photos. There were one or two, but they were mostly of other people, not of him. In fact, there was only one photo of him. It was a little grainy and the frame didn't fit in with any of the others.

I felt him pause in the doorway as I studied it. He looked really young, the only reason I knew it was Jake was from the way his fringe curled into his eye. He looked a little older than Daniel was now. His eyes were furrowed and a sad pout gave his face a lonely downturn. He didn't look at all happy as he stood next to an older boy holding the smallest baby I'd ever seen.

"Ruth took that photo when they brought Eleanor home." He said as he took the photo from me and placed it back on the sideboard, behind a couple of other photos of the kids, his parents and Eleanor. "They wouldn't let me hold her standing up, so Ryan got to. I wasn't impressed."

"I can tell."

"He didn't even want to hold her, he just got to because he was older." He scowled at the photo before he turned to me and smiled lightly. "Ready to go get your car?"

"Yeah, Jamie and Quincy aren't in, but the doorman knows me so he'll let me in."

"Where are your keys?"

"I gave them to Quincy a while back, and when she tried to give them back I thought she should keep them. I don't want to be walking into anything, and well, I don't need them."

"Fair enough," he said sounding a little confused and surprised at the same time.

"What's the look for?"

"What look?" He pulled his phone out of his pocket as it

beeped. "Taxi's here. You ready to go?"

"Yes, once you tell me what that look was about?"

"I was surprised, Jamie didn't say anything about her already having keys."

Something about his answer and the way he shuffled me along to the door didn't sit right. He was acting odd. Jake didn't do odd. Ever.

"Why would he tell you? It's his home." I watched as he picked up my small bag from the sideboard by the front door along with his keys and wallet.

He eyed me as he held my coat up for me and once it was on, handed me my handbag. He put his own coat on quickly as he ushered me out of the door and locked it behind him. He turned toward me and started for the Uber waiting for us.

"Mr. Roth?" The driver glanced back at me.

"That's him." I replied as I pointed at Jake.

He got in next to me after I shimmied along to the other side. "Jamie and I had a conversation a few weeks back. Given the nature of the conversation, I thought he would've told me Quincy already had a key, that's all."

That wasn't all. I could tell from the way his hands rested on his thighs and squeezed.

"That's not all." I looked up at him as he took my hand and threaded our fingers together.

He took a deep breath and then said, "It's not, you're right. But, I swore I wouldn't say anything and I'm going to keep my word to your brother. Now, will you stop acting like a miserable cow and relax?"

Keep his word to Jamie? What the hell are they up to?

"I'm not a miserable cow."

"I didn't say you are, I said you're acting like one." He chuckled at the glare I gave him.

"Twat."

"I love you, too," he laughed and pressed a kiss to my still damp hair. My insides squirmed at his words and a smile forced its way onto my face. "I should've given you a hat. You're going to catch a head cold."

"It's fine."

"You're going to argue with the doctor?"

We both looked up at the rear-view mirror as the driver laughed. He looked at me in the mirror and said, "It's cold, I'd listen to the doctor, Miss."

"Yes, Dorian, listen to the doctor." Jake teased, his chuckles turning to a pained moan as I elbowed his side. "Vicious."

We rode in companionable silence the whole way to Jamie's building. I was just a little bit excited to spend the rest of the day together. We'd decided to take Daniel to the Winter Wonderland, he'd loved it last year, and after our conversation it seemed like the right thing to do. Spend time together.

CHAPTER 31

Jake

D orian had always been a quiet person, she observed. However, today she was the sort of quiet that was buzzing. She couldn't buzz anymore even if I stuck one of those magic rabbits inside her pussy on the highest setting.

Her thumbs were drumming on the steering wheel to her random mash-up of eighties and nineties music. If it wasn't for the cute little head bop she had going on to Daryl Hall and John Oates, and the happy little pout that lit up her face, I'd be cringing for her. The playlist was worse than the DJs I'd been subjected to at some of the Jewish weddings I'd been to over the years.

Well, at least there's no Babs, Bette, Billy or Bob.

I smiled at the way she wiggled in her seat. It felt so fucking good to see her like that. Happy suited her. Giddy looked so good on her that I wanted to tell her to pull over and fuck her even with the shitty music in the background.

"What are you sniggering at?" she asked as we stopped at the traffic lights, her cheeks blushing as she realised just how into the music she'd been.

"I'm not sniggering."

"You're doing that silent laughing thing you do when you're taking the piss out of something in your head." She tapped my temple with her index finger.

"I am not!" I chuckled as I playfully smacked her hand away from my face. "I was appreciating your mummy dancing to the shit music."

She gasped in mock shock horror, "I do not mummy dance!"

"I'm sorry to break it to you, pretty girl, but you dance like a female that's popped a tiny human out of her hoo-hah."

"Prove it." She quirked her brows at me with a twisted smile lighting up her face. "Oh, and my music is not shit, they're classics."

"You know that the reason they're called classics is because they should be retired and never heard again, right?"

"Well, since you're such a music connoisseur, why don't you show me what you consider good music?"

"Oh no, I'm enjoying your dancing far too much." She gave me her fuck you look and carried on driving to her parents'.

We'd just left her flat. She'd needed to change into fresh clothes and apparently she couldn't show up at her mum's without make-up and her hair sorted out.

With the exception of the underwear, the clothes she'd left

at mine that first night weren't warm enough or suitable for a day out with Daniel.

That night seemed like a lifetime ago and like yesterday at the same time.

Whilst I watched her doing her adorable dance, I couldn't help but wish for more of these moments with her.

Happy moments, where she was even fucking prettier and chirpier than the girl I first met. The girl with the kind eyes and shy smile.

It pained me to think of all the shit she'd endured, but fuck me, if I wasn't grateful that somehow she saw me through it. Somehow she wanted me, even with all the shit that came with me.

I didn't believe in luck or fate. I'd worked my arse off for everything I had. I'd never been too good to get my hands dirty or too important to do the hard graft. I'd always done what it took to get to where I wanted to be. However, if there was something in my life I'd put down to luck, it would be Ruth and Levi. And now, her and Daniel.

She parked the car on her parents in and out drive. We both sat there for a moment.

Me wondering what was going to happen, if she wanted me to go in with her. It wasn't the first time I'd been to their house with her, although normally I came with Jamie and with forewarning. She was probably wondering the same thing and after our conversation this morning, I was more than happy to sit in her car and wait.

"Are you going in?" I asked as she chewed on her lip, looking at the Christmas light decorated porch.

Susan had decorated the little conifers on either side of the door and her wreath was a monstrosity that was very clearly orchestrated by the kids.

"Are you coming in with me?" She turned to me with wide eyes.

Was that an invite or an ask for an assurance that I wouldn't be offended if she asked me not to?

She must've seen the confusion on my face because she repeated, "Would you like to come in with me?"

Yes, I did, but I didn't want to push her. Shit, this discreet thing was harder than I thought it would be. I knew it wasn't going to be easy, but we weren't even a day in and it was already baffling the shit out of me.

"Do you want me to?"

"Yes, it's not like you've never been before." She gave me her shy lip biting smile. "Mum might string me up if I don't take you in, never mind Daniel."

"Let's go then." I risked a kiss to her forehead and as I pulled away she pulled my lips down on hers, her hands holding me in place as she almost fell over the centre console onto my lap. Her sweet, full lips pressed hard to mine. "What happened to discreet?"

"Blacked out windows." She giggled like an excited school girl, pointing at the car door beside us. Somehow in the moment, that little nugget had slipped my mind.

"Mmm…" I hummed as I gave her another peck on the lips and a light one on the tip of her nose.

She pulled back and combed her hair back with her fingers and tapped her lips like she was cleaning up and spreading the leftover gloss. "Ready?"

"Yup," I replied as I opened the door and got out.

It was so fucking cold my ears hurt. She made quick work of opening the door with her keys, and the minute we got in we were greeted with the smell of Christmas.

Daniel came bounding down the long hall from the kitchen with icing all over his hands. He paused when he saw me, and for a moment my heart stuttered.

For a moment all I could think was what might be going through his head at seeing me here with his mum.

"Hi, Jake!" He gave me his usual toothy grin, but it was a little stilted like he was trying to work something out in his head. "Mum, you didn't say Jake was coming with you."

"It was a last minute plan." She kissed the top of his head, avoiding his sticky fingers.

"Cool," he shrugged, his usual bright smile making an appearance as Susan paused in the kitchen doorway looking between the three of us.

"Oh, hi, Jacob." She greeted as she tried to look behind us. "Is Jamie here?"

I felt Dorian look to me and as I looked at her, her cheeks were so bright, they were glowing. Her hands were combing at the tendrils of hair framing her face. It was one of her giveaways when she was flustered.

"Actually, we sort of made plans to go to the Winter Wonderland…like last year." I managed to croak out. "With Jamie and Quincy doing their own thing…"

"Oh, that's nice." She smiled with her brow hitched knowingly.

Rumbled.

"We thought it'd be a nice thing to do." Dorian brushed her fingers through her hair again as she took her knee high boots off and left them on the rack behind the door. "I have a couple of bits I still need to get in town and Willow's been quiet lately, so…"

Susan nodded as she listened to Dorian, and once she was finished she shook her head on a quiet laugh and said, "You might want to work on your story before she gets here."

"Wh-what?"

"I'm getting older, not blind, sweetheart." She said before she turned back to the kitchen. "Don't forget your shoes, Jacob."

"Why's Nanny being funny?" Daniel murmured to us.

"She's not being funny, sweetie, she's being nosey." Dorian glared toward the kitchen and he ran off in the direction Susan had disappeared. "So much for being discreet, I swear she has fucking mind reading powers or radars or something."

"Language!"

"F.M.L." She shook her head as she laughed at her mother's admonishment of her cursing. She started for the kitchen, but then turned back around and grabbed my hand taking me with her. "Mum knows anyway…might as well make ourselves at home now."

Alrighty then, and now I was completely flummoxed as to what the fuck I was meant to be doing.

This shit is not easy.

* * *

Turned out it hadn't been as hard as I thought it would be to keep things discreet. Mostly because we left before Willow got there. I was relieved we did too, because she was like her mum. She would've spotted something and she would've latched on.

As always, Winter Wonderland was packed, we spent more time queuing to get in than actually going around the funfair.

Daniel wasn't a fan of the big rides and the smaller, kid friendly ones weren't as busy. Given that Christmas Eve was tomorrow, it was mostly tourists. Everyone else was crowding into the shops for last minute bits and bobs, like we were now.

"Why don't you guys go to the tea room upstairs?" Dorian asked as we headed to the lifts in Harrods. "I need to go grab a couple more presents."

"Can I get a hot chocolate?" Daniel asked as he pulled his bobble hat off and shook his flattened hair until it was back to its puffy curled mess.

"Yeah, can you get me one, too?" She smiled down at him and brushed his hair back from his face before she looked up at me. "Do you mind?"

"Of course not, will you be alright on your own?"

"It's only a couple of bags." She brushed back her hair and then took her scarf off. "It shouldn't take me long. I had to order their presents in."

"Okay." I took her scarf and put it into one of the bags with the trinkets we'd bought at the fair. "And you want a hot chocolate, not a coffee?"

"Yup, and cake!" Her wide happy grin had my heart squeezing in my chest. It was the most incredible and rewarding thing to behold. I wanted to take a photo and look at it every chance I got.

"Hot chocolate and cake. Got it!" Daniel sang as he grabbed my hand and jerked me toward the lifts. "Come on, it's always busy up there."

"I reserved a table earlier. It's under my name, we're a little early but they're usually good with that." She said as she walked with us. "I know he says he wants the hot chocolate with every single thing in it and on it, but—"

"But he likes it all on the side apart from the cream and the chocolate sauce on top."

"Yeah," she sighed, her smile faltered for a fraction of a second as she blinked and then she murmured, "thank you."

I had absolutely no idea what she was thanking me for, but her eyes were glassing over and she was sucking her lip into her mouth like she did when she was a little emotional or overwhelmed.

She shook her head almost unnoticeably and said, "I won't be long. Don't forget my cake."

"Any in particular." I already knew that she wouldn't want chocolate cake with her hot chocolate, but sometimes she liked to surprise me.

"Not chocolate." She replied as she made for the escalators. It was so busy that it didn't take long for her to get lost in the sea of heads.

"Should I hold your hand so I don't get lost?" Daniel held his still green gloved hand up to mine. "It's really busy."

I took his glove off and held onto his hand. I'd never realised how small his hands still were. They weren't much bigger than Molly's, somehow I'd assumed they were given their two-year age gap.

I held him close as we let people off the lift, the heat from all the bodies making me wish we'd taken the escalator route.

Fuck it, the last thing we needed was for him to get overwhelmed with the heat and stuffiness and have a full-blown asthma attack. I wasn't even sure whether he had his pump on him or whether Dorian had taken it in her bag.

"You want to take the escalators?"

"I don't mind."

"Come on then, it's way too packed for me."

We had to go around all the lift crowd to make it somewhere I could get my bearings. By the time we'd made it out of the crowd we were on the opposite side of where we should've been, but like my mother always said—*"Everything happens for a reason."*

I walked us toward the patisserie, his chatter leading to a squeal when he saw all the macaroons in the displays.

"This is my mum's heaven."

"I'm surprised she didn't want to come in here instead of the tea rooms."

"She always takes me to the tea rooms, their hot chocolate is the best." He looked at me a little funny as I let go of his hand. "Maybe we should get her a cake from here?"

"How about we get her some treats from here and we can hide them for tomorrow? That way she can have a treat as you get ready for Santa."

"That's a good idea, but I know that Santa isn't real anymore."

Of course you do.

"But it's okay, I make believe that I don't know so that Molly and Pippa can still believe in magic."

I didn't know any kids that had his outlook on things. He was just so good. Every last bit of him. He was exactly like his mother. Good, kind and extraordinary to the core.

I let him pick a few flavours and colours he thought Dorian might like, and added a few I knew she'd appreciate into the mix. It was meant to be a treat, but by the time we were done, there was enough to make our own display.

Daniel grasped my hand as soon as we were out of the patisserie and we managed to find a less populated route towards the escalators. It took almost as long to get to the fourth floor as it had taken us to pick and pay for the macaroons.

I think we were both so happy to finally get to where we were meant to be, that neither of us noticed a very amused Dorian standing by the desk outside the tea rooms until we got close.

"I think we've been busted, Jake." Daniel murmured as he pulled on my hand, his eyes falling to the bag of treats in the other.

"We'll just have to tell your mum we went on a detour."

"But don't tell her about her surprise, okay?" He gave me a look I wasn't quite sure whether it was meant to intimidate me or make me laugh.

"Okay."

"Are you coming to our house tomorrow?" he asked at the same time as we approached Dorian. "And where have you two been?"

"We went on a detour." He replied very matter of factly as he looked at the bags she had by her feet. "What did you get?"

"I'll only tell you if you promise not to tell Nanny or Aunt Willow." She smiled at him before she turned to me and asked, "Was he alright? I got a bit worried that he might start feeling sick in the lifts. He gets a bit funny with the heat and his asthma."

"We took the escalators, the lift was mad, and then we got side-tracked looking at things."

"We figured." She replied with a teasing chuckle.

"We?"

"Who's we?" Daniel looked up at her, distracted from his

bag rummaging.

"I bumped into Eleanor at one of the concessions in ladies' wear. I had to go and pick up my dress for New Year's and there she was. So, I invited her to come have tea and cake." She directed the last part mostly at Daniel before she looked up at me and asked, "Is that okay? I didn't want to be rude, but I also didn't want to assume…"

"Dor, she's my sister. Why would it ever not be okay?" I looked around, now noticing the other bags behind her. "Where is she?"

"She left a bag at the Chanel concession and she went to get it. She messaged me saying she's on the way back."

"She messaged you?"

"Well, I was waiting for a bigger table since there's an extra person and in case we were seated and she couldn't see us…she took my number?" She looked at me questioningly. Like she thought she'd done something wrong.

"You gave her your number?" I felt my chest tighten with panic. It wasn't that I didn't want Eleanor to have Dorian's number. It was that I didn't want Dorian to ever be pulled into the drama. I didn't want to be a burden.

"Yes?"

Well, eat a dick!

"I wasn't expecting that. But okay."

"You're not mad?" she winced as she asked.

"No, of course not. I…look, with everything, I just want you to be careful. I don't want you to get dragged into anything. I know how chaotic she can be…"

"Jake?" she smiled softly up at me, her hand pressing to my chest and then sliding up to cup my jaw. "Relax. She's okay."

"At the moment." I added.

"That's what matters, right?" She caressed my cheek and the way she looked at me, it soothed my panic. "One day at a time, baby."

And shit a brick, my heart's stopped.

Now, being a doctor and all, I knew that if my heart had actually stopped that I'd not be standing there unable to breathe let alone say anything. But fuuuuuck, that was the first endearment she'd ever used that didn't have a lilt of humour to it. She always used my name, or since Becca, *Doctor Roth.* Which was growing on me. Especially when she said it with lust husking her voice.

The way she'd said baby, there was no humour behind it. Just pure unadulterated affection. I don't think I'd ever felt my chest so full. I'd never had the breath wooed out of me. I'd never had my vocabulary rendered useless.

"You alright, Jake?" I looked down to find Daniel looking at me with worry in his eyes.

"Yeah," I managed to smile at him before I turned to his mum to find her holding her laughter in. "Something funny?"

"Nope." She shrugged. "I thought you might pass out for a minute there."

"So did I, pretty girl."

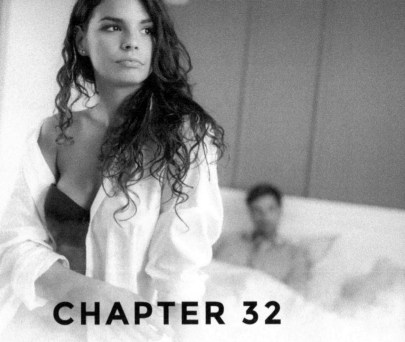

CHAPTER 32

Dorian

I was about to have a full-on panic attack. The kitchen was a mess, the lounge was a fright and the TV was so loud that my ears were ringing. I don't know what possessed me to think that Daniel's impromptu invite for Eleanor to come over for Christmas Eve was a good idea.

I was covered in all sorts of meat juices, my hair that I'd spent ages on was knotted on top of my head in a greasy, sticky wreck and my make-up was melting off my face. All because I'd left the heating on at the same time as the oven. It was too cold to open the windows, and too hot not to.

I didn't even know why I was making such an effort to cook a full dinner. Daniel had been right—we should've ordered a Chinese and watched a marathon of the Home Alone films whilst we wrapped what was left of our presents.

Instead, we were both running around like headless chickens trying to tidy the flat whilst I tried not to burn the dinner.

Bravo!

I drank what was left of my wine and made a start on unloading the dishwasher, if I could clear the sides then everything would look so much better. It'd look like I had everything in control.

I could imagine the look on Jake's face. The way he'd try not to laugh his head off, but fail, because we both knew that aside from peeling vegetables and cleaning up, I wasn't exactly a Masterchef.

Maybe I should've listened to him and let him cook dinner at his house. But I wanted Jake to see that it was okay that his sister was around me and Daniel. I wanted to show him that he could relax on that protective front. I wanted to prove that I'd meant what I said—I wanted us and I didn't want to hide it. I really did just need to ease everyone else into it.

I was crapping myself over what Gwen and Quincy would think. How they'd react. Not to mention Jamie. I already had a child by one of his best-friends. To tell him that Jake and I were a thing? He'd probably tell me not to scare this one off too... or worse.

Shit, what are you doing, Dorian?

I knew that it wasn't my fault, the whole Phillip dying thing. Not entirely. It was sod's law that he'd planned to go off to Africa before we found out I was pregnant. Plans that he didn't put off. Wills and whims that got him killed.

My eyes stung at my thoughts. This time nine years ago I'd still been hoping it was all just a nightmare. One I would wake up from and everything would be rosy. Whilst everyone around me was pulling together to arrange a memorial, I'd been trying to keep going for one more day.

One more day.

Isn't it funny how in swings and roundabouts you go from being the one living that way. Taking one day at a time. Hoping that today isn't the day you'll fall apart. To witnessing another person's fight.

I think that's what drew me to Eleanor. Her fight, as battered and tired as it was, it was still going. Like mine had been all those years ago. Except my fight had been for my son. I'd had him to pull me through. I'd had Jake. She had Jake, and now, she had me too. Because letting him love me meant that I had to let myself love him too. And loving him meant that I would fight to protect what was his.

She might not know it, but she was his. He loved her in a way that only a parent knows to love. It was awing, but at the same time it made me sad for him. Sad that somewhere along the way he'd felt responsible for her mistakes. It pained me to think that somehow he saw her as his atonement for not speaking up when he thought he should have. For not being able to save his mother, when it wasn't his responsibility. When he was just a child.

I looked over at Daniel running around putting all his things away in his elf onesie and I hoped that he never had reason to feel like that. To feel responsible for something that was out of his control.

That was another reason why I didn't like to talk to him about Phillip's death. I didn't want to have to explain all the details of why he never had a chance to meet his dad. He knew he'd died, he knew the good parts and that was enough. I never wanted to plant a seed of doubt in him as to whether he was wanted. Because I'd always wanted him.

I finished clearing up the sides and cleaning them down. The relief as I looked around and found a semblance of restored order to our home was instant. Now, I needed to get my head straight. I needed to restore calm and quiet to my thoughts.

It happened every year, everything was okay and then as Boxing Day neared it all started to fall to shit. All the walls crumbled like limestone battered by a stormy sea. I tried to ignore that feeling of impending doom for as long as I could, but eventually it would always pull me under and drown me.

Maybe things were different now. Maybe this would be the year that I wouldn't cry and relive all my regrets. I hoped that I could just hold on to all the good I had. That I could hold on and let it keep me above the waves.

I can do that. I can let myself be happy. I can let myself be loved, and I can love in return.

That was the frustrating thing, I knew I loved Jacob. The mere thought of him set fire to my heart and it made the ache in my bones and soul soothe. It wasn't a question of whether I loved him, it was a question of whether I deserved to be loved by him. To have the love of someone like him—good, strong and devoted.

"I've finished!" I looked up from the pot of over boiled potatoes in my hands. Daniel was sat at the breakfast bar with his *Star Wars* Lego ideas book. Another thing Jake had bought him so they could do their usual Christmas Lego building marathon. "Obviously I don't know what you've bought me, but you know I'm hoping it's the Millennium Falcon, right?"

"Yes, Daniel, I know exactly what you hope it is. You've reminded me every day since you got the PlayStation." I laughed as he shrugged and mouthed, "Just saying."

I drained the potatoes, cringing as they fell apart in the colander.

"I thought you were making roast potatoes, not mash."

"Well, we're going with mash now." I said feeling a little embarrassed even in front of my son. "So, have you wrapped your present for Eleanor?"

This morning he'd dragged me out of bed to go buy her a present. Not just any present either, apparently, he'd done his research, and eavesdropped enough to know that she was auditioning for a musical in the new year, and therefore needed a good luck charm.

Not any good luck charm. No. He'd researched Hebrew good luck charms. Which meant that we'd spent the best part of our morning looking for a Hamsa charm with red string. Apparently, they're both good omens.

If I wasn't a little proud of his thoughtfulness, I'd have told him to pick something else. But he was eight, and for him to think of someone like that. To want to do something that caring for someone.

Don't start with the tears!

"I put it in the little bag you bought instead with lots of tissue paper."

"But you said you wanted to wrap it." I went about turning my disastrous attempt at roast potatoes into mash.

"I did, but it looks nicer in the bag." He shrugged as he continued going through his book.

"She's going to love it either way, it's a very thoughtful

present."

"Do you think so? I hope she likes it, she's so beautiful. She doesn't look like Jake, though."

"Well they're brother and sister. Uncle Jamie and I don't look alike that much."

"I suppose," he said as he nodded his head from side to side like he was debating it in his head. He paused at the sound of the buzzer, his head perking up in the direction of the door. "I'll get it!"

I followed behind him as he ran to the door and pressed the intercom button. "Is that you, Ellie?"

Soft giggles filled the hallway followed by, "And me. Yes, I'm here too!"

"Hi, Jake!" he sang loudly, jumping on the spot with excitement. "I'm letting you in now!"

"Thanks, bud." Jake's chuckle had me laughing.

He opened our front door and paused. For a moment I thought he'd had a sudden turn. Sometimes when he got excited his breathing went all out of whack and it brought on an attack. But he was fine.

He stepped back slightly, to the side and pointed at the floor by the stairs. The lights on the small conifer he'd decorated were still off.

As I switched them on Jake and Eleanor appeared. I could feel the minute his eyes were on me. It was such a silly thing to notice, but it made my cheeks ache to smile. It filled my chest with warmth. Being so close to him...it felt right.

"You're decorating?" He stopped and gave me a questioning look.

"Just turning on my lights." Daniel answered before I got

the chance.

"Very festive."

"Yeah, we've gone all out this year." I stood and took in his handsome smile.

My insides felt like mush just looking at him. For the first time in my life, the nickname that my family had endeared me with seemed fitting. Jacob Roth, turned me into mush.

We both laughed as Daniel almost dragged Eleanor inside, talking at her like he was running out of time. I felt his arm wrap around my waist from behind me. His lips pressed onto my neck, behind my ear and my knees almost gave as the residual cold on his skin made me shudder.

"You're cold," I managed to murmur as his warm tongue licked at the patch of cooled skin.

"I don't feel cold right now," he rasped back as he stepped flush to me. He inhaled deeply and the groan that left his lips had my head lolling back onto his shoulder.

"I'm smelly and sweaty. I need to shower before we eat."

He laughed as he walked me inside, "Yeah, you do smell a bit meaty. But I still so would!"

"I don't know how I feel about a food fetish, that might be a little too far for me."

"Don't you worry, pretty girl, my only fetish is you... in those ridiculously high heels you like to wear, preferably wearing nothing else."

I turned to him as he propped a couple of bags on the hall table and took off his shoes and coat. Once he'd put them in the closet, he stood and pulled me to him. He walked me back until we were behind the open closet door, my back pressing to the wooden frame.

I couldn't wait for him to kiss me. It was physically impossible. My arms latched around his neck and before he even had a chance to draw in another breath I smashed my lips to his. The cold completely gone. It was only his pillowy warmth that met mine. God, I felt like I'd been waiting for that one little touch all day. For his taste as his tongue dipped into my mouth and tangled with mine.

Heaven.

"Mmmm…" I moaned into his mouth as our breaths caught on one another.

So, so good.

The feel of his hands tightening on my waist. Of his hard chest pressing into mine. Even the way his feet stopped mine from slipping.

How did I ever manage to resist this thing between us?

"You're right," he mumbled as he ran his lips over mine softly. My eyes darted to his, his words sounding like a breathy reply to my thought. "You need to shower. It's like you've used Le Eau de Boeuf."

A loud abrupt laugh broke from my lips as I rolled my eyes at him. "Seriously, you could've ignored it until you were done kissing me."

"Dor, you smell like you've been chilling with the cow in the oven, not cooking it."

"I feel like I have too. It's all sort of gone tits up, Delia and Nigella very clearly have no idea that the rest of us womenfolk can't keep up with their recipes."

"Do you need help?" he asked as he lowered his lips to the tip of my nose.

"Aren't you my knight in shining armour tonight?" I

giggled, his curl tickling the bridge of my nose.

"If you want me to be."

"Right now, I do. I managed to make mash...out of the would be roast potatoes, the veg need to be cooked through. I don't even want to know what the meat's saying because half of it is splattered on me."

"Come on then," he linked his fingers with mine as he walked me towards the open living space. He paused before we made it and reluctantly started to pull his hand from mine. I tightened my hold on his and smiled at him as his confused gaze met mine, and before either one of us could quibble, I tugged him with me into the kitchen.

* * *

The dinner had been nice in the end. The clearing up wasn't so bad either with Eleanor demanding I let her help me whilst Jake and Daniel finished the game they'd started when I'd been in the shower. Next to her I still felt like a bit of a hot mess considering I hadn't bothered with make-up and I'd simply tied my hair up again.

It wasn't like we were going anywhere. I'd managed to let Mum down gently on the Midnight Mass front. This year I couldn't be bothered, and I didn't want to rush Jake and Eleanor out of the door to go sit in a cold church being told of all the things I should be grateful for this Christmas. I already knew what they were and I was going to make the most of them.

I put on the kettle to make a pot of coffee as Eleanor sat at the breakfast bar. Her phone kept going off. She kept ignoring it. The annoyance on her face making it obvious who it was.

"Someone really wants to get to you, huh?" I asked as I sat next to her.

"I wish he'd stop." She huffed back.

"Have you told him to?"

That earned me an irate glare. "I shouldn't need to after—"
She shook her head as she quietened abruptly.

"Take it from someone who should've said a lot of things
but didn't, if you want him to stop, make it clear. If you think
that you're going to want to mend fences, do it before the option
is taken away from you."

She looked at me curiously as I got back up and poured the
freshly boiled water into the caffettiere. I took a few coffee cups
from the cupboard and lined them up on the counter next to her
with the milk and the brewing coffee.

"You sound like you have regrets." She rasped as I sat back
down next to her, watching Daniel and Jake. I listened to their
laughter as the go karts on the television did all manner of crazy
stunts.

"Don't you?"

"A tonne. Sometimes it feels like a lifetime's worth," she
sighed.

"Will you regret ignoring him?" She looked between my
eyes and my finger pointing at her phone.

"No. My only regret when it comes to him is the way I
treated him at times, and the way I let him treat me." The pain in
her eyes was breath-taking. It should've dimmed her spark, but
somehow it lit so fucking bright that it made my insides crawl.

"If he hurt you—"

"I hurt him first. I was selfish and too absorbed in…" Her
eyes flitted to mine for a beat of a second and I thought that she
was going to get up and walk away. Instead she sat straighter
and turned to look at me. "I don't know what my brother's

told you. It can't have been everything because if it was, you wouldn't want me here."

"You're right, he probably hasn't told me everything. Honestly? He doesn't need to. Mistakes are inevitable, I've made a few and then some. Thing is, once you've made them you can't undo them. You figure a way of living with them, of maybe forgiving yourself for making them."

"Your mistakes have nothing on mine." Her retort was dry and ladled with regret.

"Perhaps, but if you ask me, it's a subjective thing. I think we all feel our mistakes are bigger than everyone else's."

She laughed, it was such a resigned and bitter laugh that it felt wrong coming from her lips. "I told him my mistake, my biggest regret, and he used it to excuse his. He doesn't have regrets. He sees it as life levelling us out. I know I messed up, I let my stupid need overtake my life. For a while, Miles fulfilled that need and then it was like he wore off and I just…every time I closed my eyes…" She closed her eyes and buried her face in her hand.

The desolation that rolled off her made my heart truly bleed for this girl, who was so fragile and broken. I couldn't even pretend to understand how she felt as she looked around with tears brimming in her eyes.

I wanted to reach out and hold her, to give her the comfort she so very clearly craved.

Her deep, pained sigh was another slash to my heart, and for a moment I wasn't quite sure she was talking to me—it felt like she was reminding herself. "I understand why what I did is unforgivable now. I get why he cheated on me and why he put me in the middle of everything I needed to stay away from."

Her eyes caught on mine and it was as though I could feel her pain. My chest physically ached for her even as anger unfurled in the pit of my stomach.

"He taunted me like a wild dog with a hunk of bloody meat. He put my weakness right in front of me and watched as my body turned on me. I think people believe it's an itch…" I watched as her hands shook, her thumbnails scraped viciously down the insides of her delicately manicured fingers. I didn't know what was worse, what hurt more, her words or the way she clawed at the insides of her hands. "It's an ache. It's an ache you can't quite place. It's everywhere. It's on my skin, inside my bones, ripping through my veins and tearing up my insides. It fills up every little space except for that one hole. That void that nothing quite seems to touch, it's a black hole that sucks everything in."

I had no idea when my tears broke loose, but it felt like I had a waterfall behind my eyes and it was never ending. The sobering part of it all was that not a single one escaped her. Her eyes were swimming with them, it looked like there were oceans in her eyes. Not one single drop fell.

"I'm sorry," she murmured before she cleared her throat. "So sorry. I don't know why I—"

"Can I ask you something?" She looked at me with expectation on her face. "Why stay with him? Why not get help?"

"He filled the hole for a while, and I never understood why it didn't last. Why it had to end. I thought that if I held on to him, that maybe that feeling he'd given me before would come back." My eyes lifted to where Jake and Daniel were still engrossed in their game and I had to wonder if he knew anything she had told me. "If I told Jake about Miles, if he knew that he took me to his parties and made me watch as he and his friends did the one thing I was fighting with myself not to...he'd kill him."

"I think he'd be warranted." I bit out, my voice filled with equal parts repugnance and disdain.

"Maybe, but Jake's the only person I've hurt more than myself. I dragged him into every one of my mistakes. They could've cost him his life, his career...everything. You, your brother..."

"Jamie?"

"He and Jake, they—" A parallel string of tears ran down her face as she sagged on her stool. Her chin rested on her hands as she looked up at me. It was like she'd reserved all her tears for her brother. Like in everything that she'd shared with me, he was the only one worthy of them. "I would've died if they hadn't found me, amongst other things. All I remember is waking up in the back of Jake's car, your brother holding me, begging me not to destroy his friend. That's the sort of person I am. That's why Jake didn't really want me around you, he gave me the talk on the way over."

"The talk?"

"Yeah, he does this broody thing where he warns you not to fuck up without actually saying the words. You know? The *'I love you and I'll always be here for you. But don't make me regret this, Eleanor. I'm trusting you with them.'*" She rolled her eyes and a smile quirked her lips. It was so soft and filled with love that it made me smile too. "So this conversation isn't Jacob approved. I think he might have a heart attack if he knew I've told you more than I have him."

"Why don't you tell him? He's your biggest ally."

"Because of exactly that. He almost killed for me before, that's what your brother told me when he gave me *his* talk. He told me that if I love Jake, I'll either stay clean or I'll cut the cord and release him. I love my brother, Dorian. I think I love him more than I love myself. I know I do. So, I'm trying to stay clean. I'm trying to keep going just…"

"One more day?"

She chuckled lightly, shaking her head as she glanced over at Jacob. "Yeah. That's what he tells me. Keep trying. One more day."

I turned my attention back to the coffee and poured us both a cup of the now bitterly strong brew. I added a good measure of milk to mine, rendering it more of a summer drink than a winter caffeine fix and watched as Eleanor cringed as she took a straight up black mouthful of it. Her instant heaves had me reaching for the tissues as she almost sputtered it back into her cup.

"Shit, I think we might have let that stew for too long." She burst out laughing as she wiped her tongue off with her fingers. "Ohmigod, it's burning my tongue in completely the wrong way!"

I couldn't help the laugh that erupted out of me as Jake looked between us. His eyes rounding on our faces. I could make out the worried creases around his eyes as he made towards us.

We both looked at him but before either of us could get the words out through our fit of silly laughter, he'd already poured himself a cup and taken an over generous gulp.

Eleanor grabbed the wad of napkins between us and pressed it to his mouth before he sprayed us both with the contents of it.

"What the fuck was that?"

"Bad coffee." I managed to say as I wiped the tears from my face at the same time as Eleanor dabbed at her eyes.

"That wasn't bad, Dor, that was horrendous."

"We might have forgotten about it." She laughed and it started off my own again.

"It's cold and thick and...nasty!"

"I should step out of the kitchen, today is not my day."

"Understatement of the year." Jake chuckled as he stood behind me and wrapped his arms across my shoulders. "You want to do the Christmas special?"

"Christmas special?" Eleanor looked between us like we were talking a foreign language.

"Yes, I do!" I tilted my face up to his, catching his jaw with my puckered lips.

"Daniel and I have something for you to have with some non-killer coffee."

"What's this Christmas special?"

"Downton," Jake answered before he dropped a kiss to the top of my head and went about making fresh coffee.

"Downton?" Eleanor asked in a hushed voice. When I nodded at her she started laughing again. "Oh boy, it just gets better. Mum is going to love this."

She got up and went to sit on the lounge rug with Daniel. He'd gotten his Lego book back out and was sorting through the blocks to build one of the projects in it. He had a thing for separating the blocks he needed into bags before he started building. Apparently, it meant that if he didn't finish in one sitting he didn't lose the pieces again. It made perfect sense, and it was another thing that Jake had taught him.

"Your coffee, ma'am," he whispered in my ear. His hot

breath had goose bumps breaking out all over my skin. "This time it's drinkable."

"Thank you."

"I have something for you…" He said as he sat on the seat Eleanor had vacated.

"If it's in your trousers, I'm already well acquainted with it." I butted my shoulder into his side with a low laugh. His eyes narrowed on mine with a pursed grin.

"My dick is yours anytime you want it." He kissed his knuckles and smirked before he ran them down the side of my face.

How did he manage to do the sweetest things even when he was smirking like that and teasing me?

"You know, there's a lot more to you than just your cock." I kissed the heel of his hand as he cupped my jaw.

"Well," he stood and stretched across the counter to drag one of the small bags he'd brought with him towards us. "Daniel and I thought you might like these."

The way the muscles on his back rippled under his shirt had me unable to look away. The dimples that peeked just above the top of his jeans as his long sleeved t-shirt rode up his back had my smile spreading across my face.

He handed me a beautiful white and silver gilded box that was bigger than my hands.

"You spoil me." I put the box down on the kitchen top and stroked my fingertips across his brow and down his face.

"Hardly, they're macaroons."

"You don't need to tell me what they are." I chuckled as I wrapped my arms around his shoulders. "I don't need you to spoil me all the time."

"What *do* you need?"

I kissed each of his cheeks and then the tip of his nose, like he always did to me. "Right now, I need nothing more than this."

"Good answer," he murmured into the crook of my neck before he pressed a kiss just under my jaw. "But so you know, I'm going to spoil you every chance I get. Get used to it, pretty girl."

CHAPTER 33

Jake

It was chaos. Everyone was flustered as they debated whether or not to continue cooking Christmas dinner or wait until they heard back from Jamie and Quincy. They'd both rushed Jenna and Richard to the hospital—something about the baby, nobody seemed to know the details. But according to Willow, I'd missed enough awkward to last me a lifetime.

We left the kids to finish off their game and went to the kitchen where Dorian, Susan and Gwen were gathered around a bottle of champagne.

The three of them looked to us and then continued discussing what to do about the dinner. Dorian looked about ready to hit her head on the kitchen island top, instead she took a long sip of her fizzing wine.

"It's still Christmas. We'll all have to muck in and carry on. They're going to be hungry when they get back and it'll be nice if they don't have to worry about feeding us all." Susan said as she looked around the kitchen.

Dorian took a deep breath and smiled. She wasn't herself, she looked exhausted like she hadn't gotten enough sleep.

Her eyes met mine briefly and all I wanted to do was reach out, wrap her in my arms and tell her to take a breath. Of course, I couldn't because that would make things not so discreet and I wasn't about to add to her soured state.

"Why don't you ladies sit back for a moment and gather your wits about you?" I sat on the stool next to Dorian's and topped up their glasses. I might not be able to soothe her how I wanted to, but I could take another responsibility off her shoulders. As inconsequential as dinner might be, it was one less thing she had to worry about. "I'll make a start on the dinner."

Willow burst out laughing, "I know you can cook, but this is *Christmas* dinner."

"Oh, is that you volunteering to do something other than bitch and whine?"

"It's fine, I'll give you a hand." Dorian smiled up at me a little too weakly as she got up and brushed the full skirt of her navy dress down her slender thighs.

She looked a beautiful picture with her long hair curled down her back and two braids wrapping around the top of her head with only a few loose tendrils framing her face. The deep V that accentuated her breasts making her neck look elegantly long and giving her that ballerina princess look that made me want to do nothing more than drink her in.

"Don't be silly," Gwen sighed. Her eyes narrowed on me and then flitted to Dorian and back. "Have you ever cooked Christmas dinner?"

She had a point, I hadn't. But how hard could it be, right? Essentially it was a roast dinner. I'm sure Google could help me. "No, but there's a first for everything."

"He can actually cook," Willow shrugged.

"And you know that how?" Dorian gave her that same scowl from the other night.

"Because I've eaten his food." She looked between us like all of a sudden she'd stepped into an alternate universe and she was unsure of how to act. "Jamie and I took the kids over to his one time and we had to eat." She smiled at her almost knowingly.

"Oh."

"Yeah, oh."

"Okay then, well, we'll leave you kids to it." Susan tapped my shoulder lightly like she was wishing me luck and wandered out, taking Gwen with her. Her head was shaking as she laughed, but I was all too aware of the assessing look her friend was giving me and before she disappeared from sight she called, "Don't ruin the dinner."

"Tell you what," Willow sighed as she looked between us, "I'm going to go and see if the kids want another round of Pig Goes Pop. I wouldn't want to get in the way of things, I can't cook for shit anyway…" She filled an empty flute with champagne and gave us both a look, I wasn't quite sure what it meant.

"You realise there's pork in almost everything, don't you?" Dorian asked me as she brushed her hair over her shoulders and tucked the loose tendrils behind her ears.

"It'll be fine. We'll Google it."

"*Google it?* That's your plan?" She marked me with a glare that wasn't half as playful as the one she usually gave me.

"That's the plan, pretty girl, once you've told me what's wrong." I sat her back down on one of the stools and pushed the flute of wine away. "Before you try to tell me it's nothing, I can tell something's up."

"I'm tired and grouchy." She sighed gruffly as she reached for her drink, her jaw clenching as I took it from her and put it far enough away that she couldn't get to it.

"You need to take a break, baby. You're running yourself into the ground."

"I'm fine, I'm just trying to get this case done. But there's something that I'm not seeing and it's bugging the crap out of me."

"What do you mean?"

"My brother is a neurosurgeon, my best friend is a cardiothoracic surgeon, you're a plastic surgeon...do you know what you all have in common?"

"We're fucking amazing?"

"Apart from that." She rolled her eyes as I sat down on the stool next to her and reached for her glass. I took a small sip before I handed it to her. "None of you have a clean slate. All of you have had something go wrong."

She looked at me apologetically, like she was picking at a healing scab.

"It's impossible to have a clean record when it comes to surgery."

"Exactly, that's why I was up at crazy o'clock this morning going through my paperwork, trying to figure out what I'm missing."

"You need to rest, Dorian."

"I can't, it's not that easy…my brain won't switch off.

"I get that, but you can't run on empty."

"I won't lose this case, it's my record. My career. It's a permanent mark…"

I got that she was driven. I got that she had ambitions. I did. But, my worry wasn't about her career, I knew that she would manage to wipe the floor with whoever came at her. My worry was for her wellbeing. Her health was far more important than another notch on her wins tally.

"What am I missing, Jake?" she gritted as she finished her drink.

"I don't know, Dorian, but at some point, you're going to have to decide if it's worth risking your sanity and wellbeing... Daniel needs you." I cringed inside, I knew that was below the belt.

"That's not fair." She pushed up from her seat and wandered over to the sink. She washed her hands like they were covered in sticky, invisible dirt. Scrubbing until her skin was red and raw. "Everything I do is for my son. *Everything*."

"I get that you've worked hard to get to where you are. I admire how dedicated you are to getting to the top. I love that about you. I love that you push and keep pushing until things go your way and you get to where you need to be."

"But?" She spun towards me, her hands tightening around the edge of the sink on either side of her. Her knuckles so white that they were a stark contrast to the dark granite.

"But there are times when we need to pull back, so we can press on another day." I stood from the stool I was sat on and ambled to her. Her body strained flush to mine as she looked up at me with resignation in her eyes. I fucking hated having to be the one to push for her to slow down, but on this particular occasion, it was the best thing for her.

"I'm so close to getting where I want to be, Jake. So close I swear my fingertips can graze my goal." She sighed, her breath pushing out of her raggedly as I anchored my hands on either side of hers. Her heaving chest pressed into mine.

"Pretty girl, you are an incredible force to be reckoned with, and anyone who thinks otherwise…they just have no idea. This is one wave, there's a whole sea of them you can ride. Don't let this be the one that drowns you. It's not worth it, nothing is worth more than you are."

Her eyes flitted from mine to my lips, the corner of her mouth quirked up as her tongue swept over her pout.

"Take a break, look after yourself. Please." Her eyes rounded as I cupped her face.

"You're not playing fair."

"I will never play fair when it comes to you and Daniel. There is no line I won't cross when it comes to keeping what's mine safe."

"We're not your property."

"Property?" I laughed at the way she thought I saw her and Daniel as belongings. She was fucking clueless even with the way her eyes drew on mine and her pout pinched. "It's fucking biology, Dorian. You and Daniel are a part of my biology, my anatomy. I'll do whatever it takes to keep my heart intact."

Her eyes widened, the green so vibrant that the golden flecks didn't blend and bleed with it.

"Alright. Fine. God, you're impossible, you know that?"

She cupped my face lightly, her nails affectionately grazing the stubble on the underside of my jaw.

"I love you, Dorian, but fuck me, you don't make things easy."

"Do you want easy?" she whispered into the hollow of my throat.

"I want you." That was as simple and easy as it got. I wanted her and Daniel. That was all, and I would never let them go.

* * *

We managed to get on with dinner successfully. Jamie and Quincy had made it back just as we were finishing up and despite the situation with Richard and Jenna we were all sat at the dinner table. The kids were excited to get to the presents they'd been eyeing all day.

It felt like a real family affair. We'd never celebrated Christmas in our house, but I had to admit that this made me wish we had.

Dorian sat quietly next to me, her knife and fork busy with the food she was pushing around her plate. I almost felt bad for giving her shit over the whole work thing, but I couldn't help it. When it came to her and Daniel, despite what she said, things were black and white. I could only be happy if she was. It was like her joy was mine and I couldn't feel it unless she felt it too.

She looked up at me and smiled softly, but it was clouded over. It wasn't her smile, hers were easy and warm. This one was troubled. She was in her own head and I wasn't the only one that noticed it.

I righted the yellow paper crown that Pippa had swapped with the pink one she'd got in her cracker.

"What are you doing?" she whispered breathily between us.

"I'm fixing your crown." I winked at her and a faint flush rose high in her cheeks. "Real queens don't go around with wonky crowns."

"What about yours?" Her eyes went to the purple tissue paper still folded by my glass.

"I don't need a crown. I'm a rebellious bad-arse."

"Could've fooled me."

I shuffled a little closer to her and lowered my voice so that I was certain only she could hear below all the other chatter. "The only crown I'm interested in is the one your hands make when they twist into my hair, pulling my tongue deeper inside your—"

"Don't even go there," she gritted lightly between her hitching breaths. "Now is definitely not a good time to..." She swallowed her words as my hand landed on her knee and travelled up her thighs. My pinkie skimming her knickers. "Stop it!" Her gruff, lust hazed words had me chuckling and as she readjusted herself on her seat, her thighs tightly pressing together, my dick jolted behind my now too tight fly.

"I can't wait to get you home." I rumbled almost too low for even me to hear as I took my hand off her warm skin and proceeded to finish my dinner. "Eat, baby, I have plans and you're going to need all the energy you can get."

"Is that so?"

"You bet, counsel." She giggled at that and turned back to her dinner.

My heart thrummed wildly as she made a show of eating every dainty forkful she took to her mouth. Her clear smile making mine cut my face in two for how wide it was.

My eyes met Willow's as I looked around the table and the

curious look she gave me had my smile faltering slightly. She'd been giving me curious looks and studious glances whenever we'd been in the same room. Often flitting from me to Dorian.

"I have to hand it to you," she started, her eyes narrowing on mine before they swept to her sister. She held up her fork with a bit of her nut roast and chuckled, "Your nuts aren't half as bad as I thought they'd be."

She grinned as Dorian looked up at her, scowling.

Oh, man.

I should've seen this coming. Willow was like a sniffer dog. She somehow managed to clue into everything. Unlike Jamie who was more of a *I only want to know what you want to tell me* sort of guy. He was so easy to get along with. He never pushed. Never pried.

"Yeah, thanks for helping out with dinner." He smiled as he wrapped his arm around Quincy's shoulders.

"It's delicious. I didn't realise how absolutely famished I was until now." She chuckled, her head resting on his shoulder like it just fit. Like it was the sole purpose of it.

"Except for when we got in the car and you told me you were starving."

"Except for then," her giggle was light and infectious as she tilted her head back and kissed the side of his jaw.

"I had help from your mums."

"Limited," Susan grinned at me and then looked over at Dorian, "I could get used to this."

"Couldn't we all?" Gwen laughed, following her friends gaze. A contented smile forming on her mouth as she and Dorian exchanged a look.

I wasn't quite sure what happened in that exchange but

Dorian's expression fell and all of a sudden this searing look glazed her eyes. It was so serious that it took my smile with it.

She stood slowly, her throat constricting with every swallow. "I'll start cleaning up so we can do the presents!" I could tell she was trying hard to sound overly happy and excited, but her tone fell flat in the pit of my stomach.

"I'll help. I should do something considering we're meant to be hosting." Quincy rose from her seat and started piling the plates on their side of the table together. Dorian did the same on our side.

The kids who'd been quietly wolfing down their food to get to the presents started herding the rest of us towards the Christmas tree.

I sat on the floor with Molly as she picked out her presents. Creating her own pile next to us. She looked up at me with a curious look on her face as she held up the envelope with the riding lessons voucher. "What is it, Uncle Jake?"

"The whole point is that you open it and find out, isn't it?" I straightened my legs in front of me as she plopped herself unceremoniously on my lap. "Let's try and be a little more graceful when we sit on laps. What did they teach you at ballet all this time?"

"I told you it was a waste," she whispered into my ear. "I'm not the best ballerina, that's what Mrs. Frost says."

"She has no idea, you're the best at everything." I took in her pretty smile, letting it fill me with warmth even though I was still thinking over the look on Dorian's face. The way she seemed off.

"I wish that was true." She shrugged as she went back to analysing all her presents. "But she used to be a prima ballerina.

She danced for the Queen that was on the telly today. Pippa's better than I am, and that's okay. I'm better than her at running and the violin. She's better at the piano."

Fuck me, I'd forgotten how competitive being a kid was. There'd always been a big enough age gap between my siblings and I that we didn't feel like we were competing with one another. At least I never had, I sort of did my own thing.

I paused as she turned in my lap and sighed. She looked around and then tucked herself into my chest like she needed a moment.

"What's up, Molls?" I gave her a tight hug and she tucked herself into me even more, if that were possible. Her little arms wound tightly around my chest, her hands grasping the back of my Henley.

"Ummm," she looked up at me with tears rimming her eyes. "Is my mummy going to die?"

Oh shit on a schnitzel!

"Come on, Robin," I brushed her dark hair back from her face, her blue eyes wide and swimming. "We always try and think good things, because what happens when we think of only good things?"

"Good things happen," she murmured wetly at me.

"So what do you want to happen?"

"I want my mummy to get better and the baby too." She smiled with a shrug.

"Well then, how about we only think about your mum and the baby getting better?"

"Can we wish for it?" She tapped my pockets and then looked at me quizzically.

"Of course we can, I've got the goods in my coat pocket.

Tell you what, I'll go get the stars and you carry on making piles with Danny and Pippa. That'll make it quick when we open the presents." I got up, my tear blurred eyes catching on Susan's and then Willow's. Shit, they even managed to catch on Gwen's.

Fuck my fucking life.

I took a deep breath and grabbed the half full bottle of champagne from the coffee table, offering to top up their glasses before I went to search my coat pockets.

"I think we're way past the wine." Susan said as she searched my face for something I wasn't quite sure she was looking for. "Give me the good stuff."

"She means the home potion," Gwen added.

"Jesus," Willow rolled her eyes as she got up and started for the wet bar in the corner. "Top me up and I'll do their Bailey's. You want something too?"

"The usual."

"Gotcha," she sang as she opened the bar. "You want lime? They seemed to have raided a whole farm for you."

"Please."

I took the bottle of champagne with me, I could use a top up as an excuse to check on Dorian. Something about the way she'd wilted in front of me had me unable to ignore the ache in my chest.

I took a deep breath to steady myself as I rounded into the kitchen. Quincy was giving Dorian a look that said something was passing between them. It bordered on pity, and for a fraction of a second I wanted to turn on my heels and walk right back out of there, but her eyes met mine and all I could think of was the bottle in my hand.

Drinks. Offer them another drink.

"Would you ladies like a top up?" I managed to say with a forced smile as I took Dorian in.

Her eyes met mine for a quick tick of a second before she continued rinsing the plate in her hands. They were so muddied with sadness and frustration that I was ready to put the bottle down and fuck off her discreetness. I wanted to wrap her in my arms and take the brunt of her feelings from her.

"Your mum and Gwen are on the Baileys, so if you would prefer—"

She looked back at me with a pleading look in her eyes. Like she was asking me to give them space and when she rasped out my name, my heart winced. My ribs felt too tight. My insides claustrophobic.

I couldn't help my acquiescence. As reticent as it was. I questioned my decision to walk away and give her what she wanted every step that I took towards the coat rack.

I found what I was looking for and wandered back to the living room. Molly was huddled into Jamie, and as I gave her the small packet of Magic Stars she'd asked for she murmured a small, "Thank you."

I didn't even give my friend time to question my actions. I didn't have it in me to tell him about the conversation Molly and I had just had.

I went and sat at the dinner table. Trying to gather myself before Willow came and sat next to me. She put my drink down in front of me and before I could take a sip she asked far too quietly for her, "You and Dorian, huh?"

I didn't know what to say. I didn't want to straight up lie like I was ashamed of how I felt. I didn't want to disrespect Dorian's wishes either. So I took a sip of the tequila and hoped that she would drop the line of conversation.

"You want to know what gave you two away?" Her grin was positively glowing. "That night we went out and you two disappeared, she was breathless when she answered her phone. Not just any breathless either, it was the sort of breathless she used to get when she was sneaking around with Phillip."

Oh great, thank you for the insight.

"She was also smiling like she hasn't in a very long time." Her grin softened to a smile that she didn't often give. "Of course, she's also been a right moody bitch whenever we banter…"

"Your point is?"

"Fuck my sister over and I'll fuck you up." Her tone was sickly sweet in contrast with her words. "Hurt my nephew and I'll hurt you. Also, wrap it up," she glanced down at my lap and then back up at me, "and tell Jamie. There's enough drama going on."

"She doesn't want to." I wanted to pinch the words right out of the air and swallow them down again.

"God, you're so fucking whiney, like a puppy dog with hearts and stars in its little sorry eyes." She took a leisurely sip of her drink, whilst I remained a little lost for words at the picture she painted of me. "Since when do you do as you're told? You're almost forty, break the rules, redesign them…I don't know. Just don't make this another drama, it's been bad enough watching you moping around her the last God knows how many years. Don't get me wrong, you're still a manwhore and she deserves better, but she's done a lot worse. I liked Phillip, but he was a dick to her."

"Don't hold back. Say it how it is, even about the dead."

"Listen, she's my sister. My loyalty will always lie with her.

Plus, it's not like you've never thought that of him. Dead or not."

"You helped him propose to her. You were all about pushing them together." A part of me got riled up at that thought.

"I'd do the same for you," she breathed, her voice softer. "I'd do the same for anyone that wanted to make her happy. At that moment in time, he was it."

"You would do it for anyone, would you?"

"Yes, because whether I like you or not. Whether I believe that you are the best for her or not. At the end of the day, what I think and feel is unimportant. She's the important part of the equation. If she's happy that's all that matters to me, to Jamie... Quincy. To everyone. Her and Daniel have been through enough, do not put them through more. I will Liam Neeson your arse... and not the *Love Actually* Neeson."

"You're such a pain even when you're trying to be nice." I sighed with a chuckle as she shrugged at me.

"Yeah well, I'm not the one sat here when she's probably having another heart to heart with Quincy about all the ways she failed. About all the ways she doesn't deserve to move on." Her eyes rolled like it was a conversation she'd been privy to many a time. "It's a pointless conversation, it never changes, the outcome is always. The. Fucking. Same. She fails to see that even if she did let him go, he made the first move. He put his tail between his legs and planned to leave her. He was selfish and because he was nice about it, because he did it under the guise of something good, everyone treats him like a fucking martyr. He may have been my friend, but he was also a coward. He hurt my sister. She is the saint in all this because she carried on. She's done nothing but her best for their boy, right down to honouring

Pip's memory."

She shook her head and looked over at where Daniel was sat with Pippa. The pair of them laughing as they tried to guess what was in each other's boxes.

"That's his memory right there, that boy. Everyone always goes on about how Phillip did this and Phillip did that. He was this and he was that. He had no idea what he wanted, who he was or what he should do with himself. He was a child. We all were."

"Why are you still talking about him to me? You realise it's awkward as fuck, right?"

"Fucking Jesus, Mary and Joseph...even I do it. Sorry." She gave me a sheepish grin that was entirely new to her. "My point in all that rant was that you should probably go in there," she pointed toward the kitchen, "and rescue the fuck out of Dorian."

"She doesn't need rescuing."

"God, what is it with you men? You want to be the hero and Mr. Big Bollocks but when push comes to shove you're all like, she's fine. She doesn't need protecting. She doesn't need rescuing." She groaned with irritation, frustration colouring her cheeks. "It's not about whether we need it, dickhead, sometimes it's nice for someone to shut you up and take control of the freaking situation."

"I'm going to go out on a limb here and say that that particular part to your rant isn't about me. If it is, you should know that I have taken control of the situation. Everything is in hand. But I'm not going to be the guy that changes her by telling her how she should feel or deal with her feelings."

Willow looked at me all wide-eyed, a soft smile lighting her face.

"I'm not going to be the guy that pushes her to be the ideal version of herself, that's not the person I'm in love with."

"Holy freaking angels on earth, halle-fucking-lujah! You, my friend, are as whipped as the cream going on the Christmas pudding."

"Whatever guy that rant was aimed at…good fucking luck to him!"

"Fuck you!" she bit out, her middle finger right in my face as I got up and picked up the drink she'd made me.

I wandered back towards the kitchen, my heart hammering the back of my throat like it knew what was coming. I didn't know what I was going to walk into, but I knew it wouldn't be pretty. It was like my heart was so tied to hers that it felt every tear I heard in her voice as I stood in the doorway.

"I let him go. I watched him pack his bag and I drove him to the airport. He didn't even let me go into the terminal with him. He gave me some blasé kiss and waltzed off." Her pained exhale was a sucker punch to my gut, and although Quincy had her arms wrapped around her so tight that they were glued to one another, I wanted to be the one to hold her. I wanted to be the one to listen to every one of her words.

I fucking wanted to take her in my arms and kiss her. I wanted to kiss her until that hurt dissipated and there was nothing left but *my* pretty girl.

My heart felt like it was battering and ramming its way out of my chest to try and get to her.

"I could take his resentment if it meant that he was still alive. I could live without him if he was still here to be a father to his son." She hiccupped woefully into her friend's chest.

Every one of my cells burned with envy as I watched

Quincy comfort her. Her hands combing through her hair. Her arms holding her up. It was killing me standing there, and yet I couldn't bring myself to turn around and leave them.

I needed to make sure she was okay, or that she would be.

I put the drink down on the side closest to the door trying to be as silent as possible. I had to ball my hands at my sides to stop myself from launching at her. I had to bite my lip to stop myself from telling her that I was there when she needed me.

I was an idiot, I stood there taking every fucking hit that she didn't even know she was delivering.

Walk away, dickhead. Just walk away.

Was all I could think as my gaze met Quincy's. Her light blue eyes shining with pity. I think even she knew that I could never compete with her dead brother.

I was fucked.

I was in love with someone who might never be completely mine. The frustrating part of it all was that I'd be happy with whatever she gave. I would take it as the biggest honour. The greatest gift.

I would cherish what a dead man had been so quick to let go off.

My eyes flitted down to Dorian as another sob ripped out of her, I couldn't stand there anymore and watch. I had to leave them before I disintegrated.

I smiled softly at Quincy as I mouthed, "Look after her." If I couldn't be the person to do it, then I was glad that she was able to.

She pulled Dorian impossibly closer to her and before I lost the last vestiges of my cool I left them.

I left my heart in the hands of my friend's girlfriend, and I hoped that it would find its way back to me.

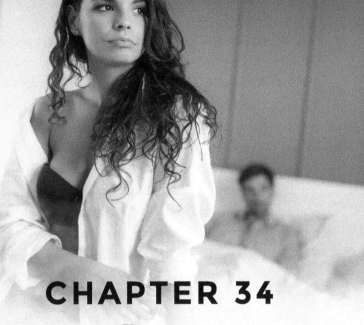

CHAPTER 34

Dorian

I t was a fucking stupid notion. I knew it was. But the truth of the matter was that I felt him. I felt the minute he stepped into that kitchen and I felt it the second he left. His hurt sliced through me. His quiet roared in my ears, and more the fool me for being too concerned about what Quincy would think to reach out to him.

I could tell in the way that she was still holding me that she thought I was crying for her brother. In a way I was. I was so angry with myself for letting his ghost constantly get in the way. Constantly fill me with doubt over whether I could sit back and let the chips fall as they may. I was always so damn worried about hurting other people, of having to live with myself knowing that I had ruffled feathers.

The silliest part of it all was that in every other aspect of my life I didn't care. I was used to being the bad guy to one person or another. I was used to having to contend and dispute. I'd built a solid career on it. But when it came to moving on, it was like all of a sudden I could hear every Jack, Jill and John murmuring in my ear. I could feel the eyes and the judgements. The sad thing was that it was all me. I put all that pressure on myself.

At no point since Phillip had died, had anyone said they expected me to be alone forever. I'd just assumed that I couldn't ever bring myself to love anyone else. To trust anyone else with my love. To trust myself with another person's heart. Yet, somehow, Jake had shown me I could do all those things.

"Dory?" I straightened at the sound of Willow's clipped tone. Quincy's arms dropped from around me and she took a step back.

"I'm going to go check on the kids and on your brother. Everything is probably sinking in, I think he was trying so hard to keep everything together for me…" She smiled and gave Willow their silly secret message wink as she walked past her.

"I still have no idea what that wink is between you two." I croaked out as I watched her sniff the drink I'd come to associate solely with Jake. "Why're you drinking tequila? We bought rum when we went shopping."

"I'm not drinking this shit. I'm smelling it to see what I did so wrong that Jake didn't back it before he left."

"He left?"

"He didn't *leave* leave, no, he's sat with Daniel. They're building Lego with Molly." She rolled her eyes, "Only she would ask for bloody Batman Lego."

I couldn't help but smile at that. Molly and Daniel shared

the same obsession with DC comics as Jacob did. He could sit with them for hours and read comic after comic, and with the recent Hollywood superhero buzz, the lot of them would spend entire days having Batman marathons.

They'd even quiz each other on all the actors who'd taken on the Batman role. It was scary how into it the three of them got.

"So, I'm just going to straight up say this—I love you, but you need to get your head out of your arse, mush."

"What are you on about?"

"Jake." Her eyes met mine, her brows quirked in a way that told me not to even try and deny anything. "I'm going to tell you what I told him. He's my friend, but you're my sister and my loyalty lies with you. But if you hurt him, I'll hurt you too."

"I thought you said your loyalties lay with me."

"I also said he's my friend. Dorian, he annoys the crap out of me and I annoy the shit out of him. It's what we do, but at the end of the day, he's a good guy. He's the sort of guy that won't leave. He's the sort of guy that will wait until you're ready to go home before he leaves himself. He'll make sure you're safe even when you leave with a random guy. Which is odd because he is the biggest man-slut I know, and sluts tend to be out for themselves." She put the glass down next to her and kicked her legs out like a child.

"You're instilling so much confidence in me right now." I sighed a little taken aback by the topic of the conversation.

"God, you're like a stubborn mule, please don't make me whip you into action."

"You don't whip donkeys, you dangle carrots."

"You're irritating as fuck right now." She spat at me. "He

loves you. He told me he's in love with you. He doesn't care that you're this mess," she gestured from my head to my toes, "he cares in spite of it. It kills me to say this, but if you don't jump on that, you are an absolute twatwaffle."

"And he told you all that because…?"

"Because I've known you two are at it for a while. The looks between you two when we went out. The bitchy scowls. Mum may also have told Dad and I overheard. The woman is worse than I am."

"What is wrong with the women in this family?"

"Speak for yourself and her, I'm a freaking specimen of perfection." She gave me her piss take grin and I couldn't help but burst out laughing. "I'm a little bit hurt that you didn't share even when I gave you shit the other evening. I thought we were better than that. Plus, I am dying to know what his dick is like. Tell me it's impressive for your sake, but please give me something to give him shit over."

She was a nightmare. However, I wouldn't trade her for the world. Especially not when she could make me laugh when minutes before I'd been crying.

"It's impressive."

"How impressive?" she asked as she jumped off the side at the sound of Jamie's voice getting closer.

"Impressive." I whispered both because I didn't want Jamie asking questions and because all my breath felt like it was seeping in a slow puncture.

"God, did your eyes just roll to the back of your head?" she gasped in mock surprise. "He's got you dicknotised."

"Believe me, if you saw his junk, you'd be just as taken."

"I feel like I'm missing out." She took quick steps toward

me with wide, excited eyes. She stopped dead in front of me and before I could take a step back and look away from eyes that were a little more hazel than my slightly greener ones she trapped me between her arms. Her hands slapped loudly on either side of me onto the counter behind me. I could smell her signature Dior perfume. Its tangy, citrusy and floral notes hitting the back of my throat with how generous she was with it. "Do you love him?"

"Chooch..." Damn, the way she'd asked so quietly like she was asking me to tell her my greatest secret.

The words were right on the tip of my tongue. They burned the insides of my mouth and the back of my throat as I tried to swallow them down.

Yes, I love him.

But if I couldn't say them to him yet, I had no business saying them to her. He deserved to be the first person to hear them. To be the first person to savour them.

"Don't chooch me, it's a simple question. Yes or no, mush?" Why did she have to be the one asking me? She was the only person who could see right through me. "Doesn't get much easier than that."

"Easier than what?" Jamie asked from the doorway, his arms crossed over his chest as he leaned on the frame. He looked between us like he always did when he thought we were up to no good.

Willow took a step back and gave him her puppy dog, *I'm so innocent* eyes.

What a crock of shit.

"Falling in love with your best friend." She shrugged like we were simply having an off-handed conversation. She said it like she was teasing him, like we'd been talking about him and Quincy.

His smile broadened, his arms fell to his sides before he tucked his hands into his back pockets. "No, it doesn't. Although, it would've been a lot easier if we'd cut to the chase."

"Yeah, some people need a good cast iron pan to the head."

"I don't know about that, brain damage is a serious thing." He laughed. It was such a wonderful laugh too. It seemed like forever since I'd heard it from him.

"Okay, Mr. Neurosurgeon, no need to get all professional about it. I was just saying." She rolled her eyes at him in a way that only she managed to. I'd never met anyone who could have a conversation by only using their facial expressions, and considering she had the gift of the gab...

Lord have mercy on us all.

"Anyway, good to see you happy." She lightly patted his cheek as she walked past him, her hand linking with mine as she dragged me behind her.

"What are you two up to? Why are you so quiet?" His eyes narrowed on mine and I felt my cheeks heat as I tried to give him my best nonchalant smile.

"You should get back to your *girlfriend* and leave us to our own thing." She turned and stuck her tongue out at him as she took careful steps backwards. Her emphasis on the girlfriend a clear jab at his little outburst the other night.

He chuckled behind me and the smile on her face was enough to let me know that she'd succeeded in winding him up.

* * *

It was so late by the time everyone started leaving. The kids were about ready to pass out on the sofas as they watched the ending of *The Snowman*. With the exception of the piles of presents, the place looked tidy enough that Jamie and Quincy were both laying on the floor in front of the TV too.

It was finally peaceful and quiet. The madness and excitement of the day was lulling towards a need for sleep.

"I'm heading out," Willow sighed as she walked back into the room with her coat hanging on her arm and her phone in her hand. "My Uber is almost here. Thank you guys for a fun day. Mush, I'll see you tomorrow for brunch as per our tradition. Do not let me down." She marked me with a cautionary glare. "Mum, I'll pop by for dinner."

Willow had never been great at goodbyes, so she always did this massive long speech that told everyone when she'd see them next. That way it wasn't a goodbye, it was a see you soon.

"See you tomorrow," I said as I got up to give her the few bags we'd managed to put her presents in. "Is Beth coming?"

"We're on together," Quincy said from where she was trying to push herself up but Jamie kept pulling her back down. "We got the Boxing Day shift this year."

"Well, at least you have decent company."

"Thank god for that! I couldn't spend my entire shift on Raj's sick sense of humour." She sighed as she managed to untangle herself from Jamie and make an escape. "Although, sometimes it's nice when things get a little tense in theatre. Plus, he's the best anaesthetist in the hospital."

"Don't ever tell him that, you won't hear the end of it." Jake said as he finished his lemonade. He'd moved on to soft drinks after leaving his glass in the kitchen when I was talking to Quincy.

"He's already made sure everyone knows it." Jamie laughed.

"My ride is here, I've got to go." Willow gave the kids a quick hug and a kiss before she sauntered out of the door with Mum on her heels to give her a goodbye cuddle of her own.

The pair of them were inseparable. They fought like cat and dog, but they couldn't go a day without talking to one another.

Little by little we started getting ourselves ready to make a move. Jake was helping a sleepy Daniel into his onesie as I managed to get all the smaller presents we could carry wrangled together.

"Would you like me to take the bigger ones and drop them off when I pick you up tomorrow morning?" Gwen asked from behind me.

I hadn't forgotten about our visit to the cemetery, and honestly, I couldn't bring myself to tell her that I wasn't going this year because I needed to go. I needed to make peace with myself over all the feelings inside me. Not going would be another thing that I'd end up feeling guilty about.

"I meant it when I said that you didn't have to come. Life goes on, you know that, don't you?"

"I do," I smiled at her.

"Good."

"I'll see you tomorrow, then."

"Who's looking after Daniel?"

"I am," Jake said from behind me and as I turned I couldn't help but smile at the way he had Daniel tucked into his chest. "We still have a lot of Lego to get through to get that Millennium Falcon finished. Seven and a half thousand pieces sounded like so much more fun when I was at the store."

"I did tell you it was a bad idea, but at least you bought superglue to go with it."

"Well, I'll see you both tomorrow." She put on her coat and meandered over to the lift where Liam was holding the door open for her.

Gwen was every bit the socialite she was raised as. She was glamorous even in her casual clothes and she wasn't one to be overly touchy feely in public. When Phillip died that changed a little, but essentially she was still her reserved self. She was the complete opposite to my mother. However, as I watched her cup her husband's face and kiss his cheek as he ushered her into the lift, a part of me felt for her.

She'd lost one of her great loves and she somehow managed to love harder. To hold on. I'd never thought about that aspect of her loss. I knew it'd been hard for her to come to terms with what had happened, but she'd come through it. And if she had, why couldn't I?

"Are you ready?" Jake asked as he pulled his coat snuggly around Daniel before he handed me mine. "He's wiped."

"Yeah, I can tell from the snoring." I laughed lightly as I opened up the gap where the coat was sheltering Daniel's face. "You don't have to look after him, my mum will do it."

He looked down at me with a warm smile. A smile I didn't deserve if I was totally honest. His arms tightened around Daniel as he said, "I want to."

"Okay." I pulled my coat on and checked my phone. It was echoing around us in the hall. "Willow's home already."

"That was quick," Mum walked over to us from where she'd been helping Jamie and Quincy put the girls to bed. It'd taken all of twenty minutes for the kids to pass out whilst we got our butts into gear.

Dad followed behind her with Jamie and Quincy in tow.

The pair of them looked ready to collapse into a deep sleep right where they were.

"Bless my little man, he was so good with the girls today, Dory." Mum cooed as she rose on her tiptoes to press a kiss to Daniel's forehead. "Do you need a lift?" She turned to me and asked with a coy look on her face.

"I have my car. I'll drop them off."

I watched as Mum's eyes lit up at that and her arm wrapped around Jake's waist. She looked at me with a blissful sigh broadening her smile, "That's so very nice, isn't it, James?"

Dad looked between the three of us, his pensive gaze stopping a little longer on Jake before he said, "Yes, Sue, it's very nice, darling."

"Right, well, we probably should go before Daniel starts stirring and has a miraculous new lease of life." I said quickly trying to take the focus from Jake. Mum was rubbish at keeping anything hushed, I should've known the moment she put two and two together that our discreet plan would go down the drain. But, in all fairness, it made me happy in a way. It took pressure off us.

It felt good that she and Willow knew and not one of them had made a big deal out of it. It felt good that they weren't opposed to the idea.

Mum made hard work of leaving, but eventually we were out of the door and in Jake's car. Daniel had fallen soundly asleep again the minute the car had started moving. The radio was on so low that all you could hear was the soft murmur of the music and not the lyrics of the carols.

"Do you want to stay the night?" I asked Jake as his hand landed softly on my thigh. I twined my fingers with his and then cupped the back of his hand with my other. "We could get up and have breakfast together before I go with Gwen."

"And Daniel?" his voice was soft if a little hoarse.

"Jacob," I looked up at him, his eyes were fused to the dark road as he drove, but his hand clasped mine tighter, "Daniel will be happy that you're there, and if you're serious about this... about us, then he should know."

"What're you going to tell him?"

This was it. My heart was like an elastic band, stretching tight with the one thing I'd been desperate to tell him since Willow had asked me point blank earlier.

"I'll tell him that I love him more than anything, but that I also love you more than I ever thought I could love anyone else. If that's okay with you?"

His hand loosened on mine and I could feel that elastic in my chest threatening to snap. He was so quiet. His eyes stuck on the road ahead. He didn't even blink at my statement.

Shit, maybe I should've waited. Maybe I should've said it differently.

I turned to look at the same quiet darkness that he was so glued to. My breaths painfully clogging up my lungs and throat as I fought to keep them steady.

"Fuck," his hand squeezed mine so tight that it bordered on painful. My knuckles felt like they were popping off my fingers as his hold carried on tightening around my hand. "Now? You chose to tell me this now? Why?"

I turned my head to him again, and the way his eyes were so bright even in the dark had my stomach knotting around itself and the butterflies in it. His Adam's apple bobbed as he swallowed down his heavy breaths that seemed to have his chest rising and falling frantically.

"I'm sorry." I didn't even know why I was apologising. I'd never seen him like that before. He was beside himself.

"You're sorry for what?" his voiced cracked a little as he looked back to me from the road.

"That I didn't say it better." He laughed at my words, and it made the ache rising in my chest so potent that it felt like it was seeping through my pores and burning my skin.

"God, Dor," he sighed as his hand crushed mine and his eyes closed for the briefest of seconds. When they opened again, on the road, a soft almost teary smile cracked his lips. "You have no idea how badly I needed to hear that. I don't care how you said it, it's that you said it at all when I thought you'd never—" His words cut off with a rasp and all of a sudden I felt like the biggest idiot and a freaking superhero all at once.

"I mean it, Jake, and I am sorry that I haven't shown you how much. It's not that I wasn't sure of how I felt about you, it was that I didn't know if I could trust myself to do it right."

"What do you mean?" If I was looking for a reason not to tell him again, he'd asked me the perfect question.

"Can we talk about it later?"

"Dor..."

"Please?"

"Okay," he replied as he took a deep breath. "But so you know, you could never do it wrong."

My chest warmed at his words and I had to swallow down the tears that prickled up my throat to my eyes.

"I love you." I told him again the minute his eyes touched mine even for the shortest of moments. "Very, very much."

His smile was so big as he continued navigating the almost

empty roads that his eyes were just two happy slits beaming. His grip on my hand loosened, but he never once tried to take it from me.

A sense of satisfaction unfurled through my limbs as I watched his unwavering smile in our contentedly humming silence.

I did that. That's all mine.

I'd never felt as sure of anything in my life than I did in that moment. Had I known how happy loving him, and having him know, would make me, I would've done it so much sooner. Maybe it was a purely selfish and self-indulgent reason to be happy, but he was happy too.

"We really need to work on this romance thing, you know?" he said as he managed to squeeze the car into a parking spot right outside my building. It was a miracle.

Between us we managed to cart all the bags and Daniel up to my flat. I got a very groggy Daniel into his bed and managed to get him back to sleep with a quick cuddle and a light head rub. I took a moment to watch him for a little bit, it was something I couldn't help. I used to stand in the same spot every time I put him in his cot as a baby. I'd listen to him breathe. I'd enjoy the clean scent of the laundry conditioner mixed in with his own. It was soothing.

"Do you want more?" I couldn't help my body's sigh as he wrapped his arms around me. The back of my head fit perfectly on his shoulder.

"More kids?" I tilted my head so I could see his face. His arms tightened around me and his eyes smiled softly in the direction of where Daniel was sleeping.

"Yeah."

"I would never have a child with someone I don't love, and well, until now…I never thought about it. I have him, if he's all I ever have, I think I'd be happy." I turned in his arms so I could see him better. "Do you?"

"Yes, I do." It didn't surprise me, he was great with kids. The way he cared for Eleanor and the way he doted on Daniel, Molly and Pippa…it was impossible not to see that he would make an incredible dad. "You're looking at me like I hung the moon."

I had to chuckle at that, it reminded me of a song Mum used to sing to Daniel when he was a baby. "I don't know about you hanging the moon, but I know that you'll be an amazing dad."

"Not too soon, though." His lips puckered on the tip of my nose and my knees almost gave like warm jelly. "I want more time with you, just the three of us."

"Now hold on a minute, Doctor Roth, I think you're jumping the gun a little."

"There's no ifs, pretty girl, I'm as serious as serious gets when it comes to you and me."

"That sounds like something Forrest Gump would say," I giggled unabashedly. "*Stupid is as stupid does*…serious as serious gets."

"Don't take this the wrong way, baby, but you should never, ever try and do the southern accent again. I'm embarrassed for you," he laughed lightly as he walked me towards my bedroom.

"It wasn't that bad."

He looked at me with unfeigned humour colouring his face as he led me to my bathroom. "There's a reason Willow is the one with the acting career."

He had a point. "Touché."

He turned me around to face the mirror and pulled the zip of my dress all the way down, past the top of my bum. His eyes shifted from mine in the mirror to the base of my back and as his fingers traced the thong all the way to where it disappeared between my butt cheeks, he licked his lips.

"I ran us a bath, hopefully the water is still nice." He murmured into my ear whilst he pulled my dress down my body letting it fall to my feet as he kissed my shoulder softly.

"You ran us a bath?"

"You said later, well, it is later and last time it was nice when we talked in the bath." My eyes flashed up to meet his in the mirror from where they'd been enjoying the way his hands had looked on my hips. "Relax, Dor."

I was trying to do as he told me. I was trying to calm my overreacting head and heart, but I had this feeling that was making it impossible for me to even breathe properly. "What do you want to talk about?"

I eyed him anxiously as he stripped out of his black clothes. He dropped them in a pile next to us and added my dress to it.

"Phillip." He said without a single quiver to his voice as he straightened behind me with his eyes on mine. His arms wrapped around my waist as he pulled me flush to him. His warm skin so soft that it felt like molten velvet over his hard muscles.

"Why?" I asked him as he spun us toward my clawfoot tub and walked us to it.

He turned to me slowly and before he said anything else he loosened my hair and pulled the braids out. Once he'd shaken it loose around me he cupped my face. "We're going to say all there is to say about him, and then we're going to park him in the past and we're going to move past it, Dorian. I want to move forward with you, but I can't do that with him constantly there. I can't compete with the dead, no one can, and more importantly, I won't. I don't want to. That's not the life I want. You, me and Daniel, that's all there's space for, do you understand?"

CHAPTER 35

Jake

If eyes could talk, hers would've said everything without uttering a single word. But in a world where everybody appeared to have so much to say, and where for the most part I just wanted them to be quiet and listen, her words were the only ones I didn't want to miss. I didn't want to quieten them. I wanted them all as I watched her sink into the bath water opposite me.

My hands wound around her ankles as she looked at me from under her dark lashes. Her eye make-up slightly smudged from where she'd swiped her hair out of her eyes with wet hands. She had little white, minuscule bubbles sitting pretty on her lashes in contrast to her black mascara. Even so, she was the epitome of beauty to me.

We'd been sitting in the bath in silence for a while now with only her nod of understanding, and every second that went by that she didn't say anything was like a hit straight to the gut. I couldn't stand it anymore. I needed to know the depth of her feelings. I needed to know that I wasn't in this alone, despite her telling me she loved me, I couldn't stop thinking of what she'd told Quincy.

I could take his resentment if it meant that he was still alive. I could live without him if he was still here to be a father to his son.

What did that mean? That she wanted him back for her or for Daniel? Those thoughts had been kicking and screaming around in my head all evening.

"Would I stand a chance if he was here? Would you take him back and forget everything that he put you through?" It felt like I was handing her a loaded gun and helping her point it straight at my chest.

Her chest hiccupped as her eyes fell where my hands were still tightly holding on to her ankles. An almost inaudible gasp snaked between her parted lips and as she sat up I had to tell myself to let go of her limbs.

Bubbles collected around her delicate shoulders as her body waded through the water and came closer to mine, her hands gripping the edges of the roll top bath and once she'd settled with her legs crossed at her chest she gave me the softest smile. The dimples in her smile lines pinched ever so slightly as her chin rested on her knees.

She took a deep breath before she said, "People aren't set in stone, Jacob. We change. Our desires change. Our feelings. Our hearts, they get a little battered and bruised. They crack a little here and there and it changes the way we feel things. The way we allow ourselves to feel. It's like growing up, as a child we think we're invincible. We think we have endless time ahead of us, but as we grow and get older, as we learn through our mistakes and our virtues, fear finds a place in us somewhere. It makes us cautious of who we let in and of who lets us in." Her eyes roved up from my chest to my eyes and there was an odd sense of peace in the way she was focused on me.

"I don't know how things would've worked out between Phillip and I if he'd made it back. I want to say that I wouldn't have welcomed him back and carried on like nothing had been broken between us. But that would be me telling you what I think you want to hear. The reality of the matter is that I don't know what I would've done because I didn't have the option." Her hands slipped from the sides into the water and splayed lightly on my thighs. Her fingertips traced my skin in soothing circles before she said, "Jake, it's not about whether you would stand a chance or not. He's not here, you are. You've always been here."

Her hands trailed up my thighs until they found mine. She linked them together and sat them on her knees before she rested her chin back.

"It's sad and it pains me to say this because I will always love him. He gave me my boy. How could I not hold a special place in my heart for that reason alone?" My chest burned hotter than the water we were sat in. It ached with how tight it banded around my lungs and heart, like it was trying to hold them together. Keep them where they needed to be to keep me going.

"He was a good person, but he was also still just a boy trying to find his way, his place in this world. I needed a man. I needed a man to be there for me and my son, unfortunately he wasn't it. Maybe he would've changed, but it would've been too late."

"Then why can't you let him go?"

"I think you know why. The same reason you can't let go of your mother. I wished I could've been enough to save him. I wish I'd known what he needed so that he hadn't run off to his death. I feel responsible for the way things happened and sometimes when I think of how I felt back then to how I feel now, it shames me to think that we both deserved more than we gave each other. I wasn't what he needed and vice versa."

"You loved him." Saying the words…it was torture.

"I did. I loved him so much, but there are different ways you can love. Pip was so much more than a friend to me. We did a lot together even before we became an us. He was always there and he was always ready to shield me. He was all impulse and fire and I was the complete opposite. He looked at me and saw me, when everyone else was too busy looking elsewhere. I wanted love and he gave it to me, it was so easy at first and when things got harder, when the seams started pulling I refused to let him go. I was scared that no one else would ever look at me and want me like he did. I was a child and all the love stories they were about fighting for love, I thought that was what I was doing."

I pulled my hands from hers and before she could ball them up again I pulled her onto my lap so that she was straddling me. Her beautiful eyes searched my face before they focused back on mine. Her hands splayed on my chest as her arse rested just above my knees.

"How do I look at you, Dorian? How do I want you?" I asked breathlessly as all the feelings inside me sucked the air from my lungs.

Her chest rose and fell jaggedly as she bit her lip. Her eyes furrowed on mine before she whispered, "With need."

"Yeah, there's a lot of that, but that's not how I see you. Your body isn't what I want, it just so happens to encase everything I crave." Her eyes narrowed in confusion, like it was rocket science.

She shook her head slightly, like she couldn't make heads or tails of what I was asking her. "Dor, you can't see those things because you're still scared that no one will see or want you like he did. But I do, I see your heart and your soul, pretty girl, and I want them. You've become my heart and imprinted yourself in every part of my being."

"Jacob…" She murmured as her hands fell to my sides. She shook her head like what I'd said was somewhat impossible.

"You know what your problem is, baby?" I cupped her face, holding it still and waited until her eyes opened. "Somewhere along the way you convinced yourself that you don't deserve love. You've overthought everything so much that you twisted it all up here." Her eyes widened a little as I thumbed her temples. "You're wrong though, it's not up to you to decide whether you deserve to be loved, it's up to me to trust you and give it to you. I decide who's worthy of my love, and you're the only one I can part with it for."

Her long sigh and the way she sagged onto my chest with her hands rounding my back and her nails biting into my skin made my heart hurt. She might've looked strong on the outside, but on the inside she was complicated and tender. She had a world of doubt and misplaced guilt eating at her and I would be damned if I didn't show her different.

"It kills me that we have to talk about this. Listening to the things you said to Quincy fucking hurt, but I would listen to them a hundred times and more because I love you." She looked up at me with regret in her eyes and I knew that I had to tell her why we needed this conversation. It might make me look like a pansy arse motherfucker, but something had to give when it came to us. "You asked me not to break you, Dorian, don't break me either. Don't force me to share you with a ghost. I can't do it. We can't keep coming back to this, to him. He's dead, I'm not. I'm right here."

"I'm sorry," she whispered like all the wind had been pushed out of her.

"Don't be sorry, pretty girl. I know it's hard to let go, but I need you to. I need you to decide whether you want me or whether you want to keep him."

"I don't know what you heard," she swallowed down a deep breath and sat back. Her posture straightened like she was about to pour everything onto me. "I don't know what you heard, but I don't want to keep him. I want you. I love *you*, Jacob. I wish that Phillip was here for Daniel, because every child deserves to know their parents. Wanting him alive doesn't mean I want him with me."

"Good, because he had his chance and he fucked it up. He. Left. You. Regardless of whether you let him go, he made a bad choice when he walked away from you and Daniel. It angers me that he was stupid enough to think he needed more than what he already had because to me, *you*. Are. Everything. His loss is my gain, and I know that it probably hurts you to hear that, but it's the truth."

Her face tilted to the side as she brought her hand up to my face and caressed my cheek before she combed my hair back with her fingers.

"I'm sorry I'm hurting you. I don't want to, but the truth always stings. Good or bad it always comes with a little pain. It's not you that doesn't deserve love, it was him that didn't deserve you. Fuck, maybe I don't either, but I won't walk away from what's mine. I never have, and when it comes to you and Daniel, I never will."

"I know, baby." My heart stammered in its fast erratic thrum. My throat closed up as her hand tightened on my jaw and her other traced up my torso to my chest. We'd managed to make it this far into the conversation without any tears, but the minute her eyes roved up from where her hand openly traced the left side of my chest they sparkled with them. "Would you like to know what my conversation with Quincy was about?"

"I don't know," I breathed out as her thumb ran from side to side on my lips. My hands banded around her small waist as she shuffled up my thighs, trapping my dick between us.

"Gwen and I don't ever really talk about Phillip. We skirt around him, even when we go to the memorial together we sort of just keep quiet like we don't want to wake the dead or something. But last year she brought up Daniel going with us tomorrow, and I let her say what she wanted and forgot about it because it's not something I'm ready for. I want to save him from the realisation that he doesn't have a dad. I know everyone assumes that it's something he understands, but I know my boy and I know that somewhere inside he doesn't quite grasp that Phillip isn't ever going to be here. He doesn't understand the finality of death." She brushed her damp hair back and her hand splayed on her chest much like her other was on mine. Like she did when she slept.

The thought of opening Daniel up to that kind of hurt had my hands balling at her back. I knew what it felt like all too well, to realise that your parents were gone. But at least he had his mother. Dorian was a lioness when it came to him. "He's a baby, he doesn't need to understand that."

"Exactly, anyway, we got into a bit of a heated discussion a few days ago and I felt things shift. I didn't feel like I belonged there anymore, in her house and you want to know why?" She smiled at me and something told me I wasn't ready to hear what she was going to say. "I looked around and there were so many memories, but the one memory that stood out above the rest, was you. You giving me your jacket and sitting with me. You grounded me with that one thought."

"I don't get why that's relevant to your conversation with Quincy." I sighed.

"I'm getting to it, Jesus!" She rolled her eyes as a soft giggle escaped her lips. She held up her right hand between us, the engagement ring on her finger made all the ache in my chest return. "That's when I knew I had to let go of one of you. I knew I was in trouble, all the feelings inside me were for you and I couldn't let you go. She knew that something changed and it was the first time that she insinuated it was okay for me to move on. Not that she'd ever told me not to or made me feel like I couldn't, but I didn't want to hurt her."

"You said you wanted to be discreet because of her and Quincy…"

"Her telling me it's okay to move on doesn't mean it'll be easy for her to watch it happen. She'll have to watch another man influence her grandson like her son would've done. I can't imagine how that must feel for her, like she can't imagine what it's like for me to want to let go of her son, but keep enough of him to make sure that her grandson knows his father."

Fuck, now I felt like the biggest dickwad on the planet for pushing her. For not understanding the source of her fear and reluctance towards us. "And you couldn't explain this to me before because…?"

"Because I'm inherently bad at discussing feelings and of making sense of them for myself."

"You're an intelligent woman, Dorian."

"I don't think intelligence comes into the whole feelings business, if anything logic seems to go out of the window." She shook her head like she was berating herself. "Anyway at the table I could see she was studying you and me…us and then she gave me that same look she gave me when she told me I was still young. It crushed me, for so many reasons, but mostly because I felt like I cheated everyone I care about. I was so fucking angry with myself that just for a little while I wanted to stop existing, to be invisible so I could get my shit together. It was why I wanted to do the clearing up alone. I needed space to clear my head and make peace with myself."

"Why not say that?"

"Because I thought that maybe Quincy needed the break too. Everything was so full on today for her that my feelings felt unimportant compared to hers." Her shrug was laden with self-deprecation. "She mistook my feelings about how I'd handled our…relationship?"

"I don't know why you're saying it like a question, Dorian. Remember, you're intelligent, put two and two together, baby."

"She mistook my feelings for the way I handled our *relationship* for feelings over tomorrow. It's hard going every year, but it's gotten easier and I think that because she wasn't in a great place herself, she assumed the wrong thing and I went with it because I'm an idiot and she gave me the perfect moment to air my frustration over what her brother did to me. We'd never spoken about it, she had no idea how he really felt because of the whole situation with Richard. That put a strain on their relationship and he wasn't exactly open with her after it."

"But what you said, the way you said it…you were crying." I fisted my hands in her hair with my own frustration because *fuck*, my mind was being fucking blown in every which way.

"What I told her was that her brother wasn't ready for me or our son. What I told her was that he ran off. I told her that I wanted him to come back for his son, if not for me. And yes, I was crying because he hurt me. He hurt our child. My son should have a dad. He deserves to have that not a fucking ghost." She gritted and ground every one of her words as she spat them between us, her voice cracking and rising as her hands balled on my chest. She was pissed.

I'd seen many sides to Dorian, but this anger was something completely new. It oozed out of her like pus from an infected wound. It was ugly and yet, it made me fall in love with her a little bit more.

"I didn't want him back for me, Jake. I don't. I wouldn't tell you I love you when I want another man. You deserve better than that, and so you know, our romance thing does not need work."

"You're a little bit sexy when you're angry." I laughed. My chest tightened only with the air I breathed into my lungs. For the first time today I felt like I could actually fill my lungs and there was no anxious burn or apprehension.

"Don't make fun of me."

"I'd never make fun of my girlfriend."

"You're dropping the G-bomb now?" She gave me an amused wide-eyed look. Her hair falling over her face as she tilted her head to the side.

"If Jamie gets to do it, I don't see why I can't." I ran my fingers through her hair, knotting them in it as I pulled it back from her face and kissed the tip of her nose.

She pulled her face back a little and cupped mine, her arms resting on the insides of mine. Her face was softly serious as she dragged in the breath I had just exhaled. "I love you, Jacob Roth, even when you make fun of me. You can hold my hand and skip down the road, I'll even let you share my Happy Meal." She sang the same jibes I'd thrown at her brother when he'd called Quincy his girlfriend in front of us. "Aww…it's so sweet and cute to call you my boyfriend." She cooed as she continued reminding me of what I'd said to Jamie.

"Don't expect me to piss up your leg and mark you."

"Well, I'm not sure, but maybe that warm liquid that I trickled down you wasn't all amniotic fluid." She gave me a wide grin.

"I hate to say this, pretty girl, but you've been around me for too long if that's what you're throwing out here."

"Not long enough."

"We're going to fix that."

CHAPTER 36

It took me a moment to realise where I'd woken up. The feeling when I did was fucking phenomenal. We'd never once fallen asleep together in her bed. We talked, watched television and we fucked. That was what we did, until last night.

We talked in her bath, I wasn't quite sure why I'd never tried the whole bath thing, but it was fucking miraculous. If I had my way, I'd draw us one every day. Even when we didn't have anything to talk about, I'd do it just to hold her and feel her relax in my arms.

We fucked in her bed, although it was more loving than fucking. Even when things escalated, it was pretty soft for us. I couldn't help but smile at the way she'd murmured again and again about how much she loved me as her pussy clenched around my dick.

The best part however, was falling asleep with her tucked into my chest, much like she was now, knowing that this morning everything would be different. Knowing that we'd wake up together, get ready together and have breakfast with Daniel. I was shitting myself a little bit. I didn't want him to feel like I was taking his mum away from him. I didn't want him to see me differently.

"Why are you so tense?" She yawned still with her eyes closed. Her hair a messy tangle on my chest and shoulder.

"I'm not, how come you're awake already?" She looked up at me, her face upside down as she stretched. Her arms were up in the air as I felt her toes graze the top of my feet as she pointed them and her back curved off the bed.

"I'm excited," she smiled. "You're here and it feels good."

"Do you think Daniel's going to be okay with this?" I asked as she rolled onto her tummy and rested her chin on my chest. "I can always go and come back."

"Is that what you want to do?" Her eyes shone up at me from under her long lashes and there was a hint of sadness to the way they blinked.

"I'm more scared of telling your son than I am of telling your brother about us."

"You shouldn't be scared of either. Jamie won't blink an eye and Daniel, he'll just be Daniel and talk tech to you."

She had a valid point.

"Let's establish something, I'm not scared of your brother. I have a few solid inches on him not to mention muscle mass."

"You have feet on my child."

"Yeah, but I care about what he thinks and feels. I don't want to make things awkward between us."

"Okay, well, invite Eleanor over after breakfast and I can guarantee that all will be right in *Janiel* land." She laughed and pressed a kiss to my stomach. "Now, muscles…what were you saying about mass?"

Her hand trailed up my thigh and under the leg of my boxers and I couldn't control the gasp that pushed out of me as her cool fingertips traced up my bollocks whilst her tongue trailed down from my belly button. My dick was barely contained in my underwear as she licked across the top of my V lines. Her hair tickling my already sensitive skin.

My whole body shivered as she bit lightly into the top of my hip. She leaned up, her hand snaking out of my boxers as she kneeled between my legs. Her eyes feasted over my body before they settled on my hard cock.

"This muscle clearly has good memory." She said as she swiped the tip of her index finger across the exposed tip. Air rushed out of my mouth, whistling slightly between my teeth.

She giggled at that reaction. Her hands deftly yanked on my boxers till the elastic sat below my balls. Her eyes skittering up my body as she continued to tease me.

Her light brown tresses caught the light the minute I switched the bedside lamp on. The deep chestnut and dark copper shining like a beacon to my hands.

"You are so fucking pretty," was all I could say as her gaze held mine whilst her lips pressed kisses over my stomach.

She groaned as my dick bobbed between her tits at the same time as she moved down my body. Her nails raking down my torso as she traced each muscle like she was committing every single one to her memory.

God, the feel of her touch is...

"Mummy," we both froze as her bottom lip touched the rim of my crown. Her half-lidded eyes widened as I pulled her next to me in a clumsy fluster of limbs. "Mummy, your door's locked."

His voice was raspy and high-pitched like he was panicking.

"Shit," she spat as she got up quick smart and ran to the bathroom.

I adjusted my underwear and started to get up when she raced back through the room with a light, creamy grey silk and lace robe tied over short pyjamas she hadn't been wearing before.

"I'm so sorry," she whispered as she unlocked the door and opened it a crack. "Hey, baby, are you alright?"

I watched her slip through it as I pulled on the shorts I had in the gym bag I'd brought up with me last night. I took the toiletries bag into the bathroom and brushed my teeth, washed my face and wet my hair enough that it stayed out of my eyes when I brushed it back.

And then it hit me, Daniel could've walked in. He could've walked in to find his mother with her mouth wrapped around my dick.

Fuck, try explaining that to an eight-year-old.

I hadn't ever thought of locking the door. She clearly had though. It was a good thing one of us had their head screwed on properly.

I was about to put my t-shirt on when Dorian came bounding into the room with Daniel wrapped around her. Her hair was stuck to her pale grey robe, dripping with sick. Her face was pale as she tried to keep his face off her shoulder.

"I need to put him in the bath." She said calmly as her eyes met mine.

"I'll take care of the bath," I followed her into her bathroom and started the water as she sat him on the vanity and stripped him out of his PJs. I picked him up off the counter and let him down gently into the bath. "I'll take care of him, you go get yourself cleaned up, okay?"

"It's just mucus and bile, he's done worse." She sat on the floor next to the tub. "He had a coughing fit, which means he's about to have an attack."

How she was so calm I had no idea. But it was keeping me cool and my guess was that it was what was keeping Daniel soothed too. This wasn't the first time I was around when his asthma was playing up, but it was the first time it was so bad he'd vomited.

"Mummy, my chest hurts." I held his hand as he tried to sit up in the shallow water. His closed lip smile opening to a toothy grin. "Mu-mu—"

"Buddy, you need to stop talking and take deep, long breaths, okay?" I pressed my fingers to his neck as I watched the skin sucking in at the hollow of his throat with his every breath. "That's it, bud, nice, long and slow." I smiled as he leaned his head on the arm I was bracing myself with on the edge of the bath.

"Is he okay?" Dorian looked up at me with a deep set worry rounding her eyes.

"Yeah, the steam will help relax him and loosen the mucus."

"I think I'm wearing the worst of it." She chuckled lightly as she went up on her knees and leaned over the edge. "You did good coming to get me this time."

He gave her the same grin he'd given me and nodded with pride. The way he was holding on and keeping his spirits high had me in awe of him.

"Now that your breathing is a little better, we need to get the inhaler and give that a go, okay?"

"Okay." He murmured quietly and for a fraction of a second I saw the confusion in his eyes. His little face scrunched up as he looked between me and Dorian, and then a smallish dubious, closed lip smile took its place.

"Do the blue now, six nice big puffs, alright?" She handed me the inhaler with the tube spacer as she smiled at him. "I'm going to shower, no funny business until you're all better."

She watched as he took his first couple of puffs and then disappeared into the bedroom. I finished giving him the rest and sat with him, watching as his breathing levelled out and some of his colour came back.

Watching the way she'd handled the whole situation filled me with a whole new brand of respect for her. It also made me realise how much she'd had to handle on her own. It didn't matter how many people she had around her that were ready to jump in and help whenever she needed it, she still had to go through situations like this alone. It made me understand why he was at the forefront of her mind with every decision she made.

By the time she'd finished cleaning herself up and finished taking care of him it was mid-morning. Luckily she'd had the brilliant idea of washing my clothes from the day before and I was able to get dressed properly.

The three of us sat at the breakfast bar with a bowl of Frosties each. Daniel was still a little quiet and his eyes were so dark that it was obvious how tired he was.

"I need to call Gwen and tell her I can't make it today." Dorian sighed as she looked through her phone.

"You should go." After everything we'd spoken about last night it didn't seem right for her to cancel. "We've got this, and if we think that it's getting worse we'll let you know. Right, Danny?"

He smiled and nodded at us both before he got down from his stool and went straight to the sofa, his bowl of his favourite cereal barely touched. He laid down with his back propped up on the mound of cushions Dorian had brought in from his room.

"He'll be fine, the Salbutamol is working and I'd say it's safe to give him the Beclomethasone now." I watched as she finished her cereal and took our bowls to the sink. "How often does he have those episodes? I've never seen him like that."

She turned from the sink to look at me. "Not too often. They tend to happen when he has too much dairy or he's run down. Yesterday was a bit of a biggie for him, and his grandmothers were feeding him chocolate till it was coming out of his ears. It's gotten a lot better over the years where he's old enough to know the onset of an attack. It was a lot worse when he wasn't able to communicate properly with me. He'd get worked up trying to tell me what was wrong, that there was something wrong and I'd get flustered because I had no idea what he was trying to tell me so I had to guess what he needed."

"I didn't know it got that bad," I said as I watched her put the dishes in the dishwasher after rinsing them. "I've never seen him…"

The way he'd been and looked reminded me of all the times I'd had to help Eleanor. Different situations, but the panic was the same and for a moment I felt a little foolish for having taken a little longer than I normally would to react.

"It's scary the first time it happens or you see it happen, but after that first shock, every other time gets easier and you're quicker to react."

"Easier?" Was she kidding? How could seeing him like that ever get easier?

"Maybe it's the wrong word, but you become desensitised to the shock and action comes a lot quicker. It's an experience thing, I don't know. My dad was always slower to react when I had an allergic reaction, my mum though? She was in there with the Epipen and sometimes by the time my dad came out of his stupor I was pretty much back to normal."

I had to chuckle at that, if not for her grin that was almost identical to Daniel's, then for the way I pictured Susan and James in my head. "Your mother is nuts."

"I think she kind of had to be with her being a child psychologist." She wandered back to the breakfast bar and leaned close to me. "She's probably seen and heard a lot of things we would never even imagine."

I bet. I thought as I straightened on the stool and pushed back enough to make room for her. I pulled her between my legs and perched her on my thigh. "You should go with Gwen today, I've text Eleanor, like you said, and she's coming to cheer him up. She's bringing his present. She also said that no one has ever given her such a thoughtful gift. It had her and my mother all teary last night."

"No way," she laughed, leaning her head on my shoulder. "Daniel will appreciate that. He did all the research himself and he picked it out. He made me go around the shops until he found what he was looking for."

"I've never seen Eleanor so content and herself like she is with him. I've missed that." I had to swallow back the tears prickling up my throat.

She looked up at me and smiled softly, "It's not Daniel, Jacob, it's you. She loves you and she can see how much you love him. We all can. I think that she's trying for you." Her hand stroked the side of my face lightly, her nails dragged along the overnight scruff and her lips slowly meshed onto mine. The kiss was so gentle and slow. No tongue. No teeth. Just our lips puckering and moving with one another.

"I knew it!" Daniel's low giggle had her pressing one last kiss to my lips with a smiling sigh.

"You knew what?" she asked him with her eyes playfully narrowed as she stood from my lap and meandered to the sofa he was now sat up on with his chin rested on his folded arms on the back. She crouched down, her hands holding onto the back of the sofa on either side of him as she kissed the top of his head.

He brushed one side of her hair back and whispered in her ear as his eyes smiled at me. I knew she was laughing from the way her whole body was shaking with mirth, and it was one of the most beautiful sights I'd ever seen. Especially after this morning.

"What makes you think that?" she asked him in a semi-hushed teasing tone.

"He looks after you like Uncle Jamie looked after Aunt Quincy." His small hands brushed her long messy curls back before he wrapped his arms around her neck. A very serious look fell on his face as he pulled back and quietly said, "I'm sorry I was sick this morning and that I peed the bed. I got scared and it just happened."

Man, this kid was killing me. He genuinely looked remorseful, like he'd committed a crime and not had a pretty terrifying breathing episode.

"You don't ever apologise for feeling poorly, we all feel that way sometimes, buddy. All that matters is that you're feeling better now."

My phone rang and as I looked down at it Eleanor's sulky face shone up at me. I had to get a better photo, especially since she was smiling a lot more lately than I'd ever seen her smile.

"Hey, chipmunk."

"I'm outside, I didn't want to ring the bell in case Daniel was still asleep." She replied with a softness to her voice that was also very new to her.

"I'll come let you in."

"Thanks," she chirped before she hung up.

I got up off the stool and went to where Daniel was still holding onto Dorian.

"So, you have a visitor, Danny. Want to come let them in?" I asked as he looked up from his mother's shoulder and asked, "Who is it?"

"Come and find out." I teased him as I picked him up from the sofa and started for the front door. His legs wound around my waist as he laid his head into the crook of my neck. "Don't get too excited, we don't want to give your mummy another fright."

"Okay," He replied so low that it was almost impossible to hear the slight wheeze of his breath right next to my ear.

"Once we've opened the door, we need to get some puffs from the other inhaler."

"My chest doesn't feel so sore anymore." I could tell from the way he was beginning to talk. His sentences were getting longer and he was trying to have a conversation rather than just giving short answers.

"That's good, but we don't want it to get sore again, right?"

"No."

"Do you want to answer the intercom?" I had barely finished asking and his head was up and his face bright with excitement as he nodded.

I pressed the button and he lightly asked, "Who is it?"

"Hey, handsome, are you going to let me in?"

"Ellie?" he gasped with surprise and proceeded to press the button to let her up. "She came to see me?"

"Yup, she came to help us build the rest of the Millennium Falcon. How does that sound?"

"Don't tell her I peed my bed though." He grimaced with embarrassment tinting his cheeks. It was so good to see the colour on his face, it felt like a weight had been lifted off my shoulders and the vice loosened in my chest. "Okay?"

"Of course not," I replied as I opened the door. His arms tightened around my neck, his hands tapping excitedly between my shoulder blades.

"Good, because now that my mummy is your girlfriend, I have to like you. If you tell Ellie, I won't like you anymore."

Fuck me he's already got it all figured out.

"Well I better stay in your good books then."

* * *

Dorian had been gone for almost two hours. It had taken a while for her and Gwen to leave. They both went through exactly what to do if Daniel got worse. Gwen insisted on giving me her number in case I couldn't get through to Dorian.

It was a little bit disconcerting that she didn't bat an eyelid at Eleanor being here or when Daniel told her how I knew what to do because I'd helped Dorian this morning.

She simply took a deep breath and smiled. All the while my heart was pounding in my chest and I could feel the heat tinging my face. If she was struggling with the obvious situation between Dorian and I, she was not letting on. I had to admire her for that, especially after what Dorian had said last night about how hard it must be for her to watch me fawning over her son's boy.

We'd just managed to finish putting together another part to the Lego when I started noticing his face pale a little and his breaths dragging. The hollow of his throat was sucking in slightly more than it should as he drew in his breaths.

"Are you feeling okay, mate?"

He sat up straight against the sofa. His legs stretching in front of him on the floor as he looked up at me, his face pinched like he wasn't all too sure. He shook his head as his hands splayed either side of him on the floor.

"Eleanor, I need you to grab the blue inhaler from the kitchen." I managed to croak out. The panic in my chest flaring as his pupils dilated with his gasping breaths and I watched her run to the kitchen and back.

She crouched next to him and handed me the inhaler at the same time as she cracked open a tin of Dorian's instant coffee right next to his face.

She glanced at me warily as I popped the chamber on the end of the inhaler. "It always worked for me when…it helps."

My chest winced as a slice of pain cut right through the

middle of it. My hands became clammy as I put the mouthpiece to Daniel's lips and pressed down on the tube to release the medication.

I repeated it another nine times, watching as each breath became longer and deeper. His cheeks started pinking a smidgen. I put the inhaler down on the coffee table and sat on the edge of the sofa. I pulled Daniel onto my lap and lifted his top to check how much he was working for his breaths.

"I'm okay," he murmured as he gripped my wrist and tightened his hold to the point that I could feel it pinch a tad.

I knew what he was doing, Dorian had him do it every time he'd had a minor episode. She said that when he was struggling he couldn't squeeze properly, so she got him to squeeze her wrist to make sure that he was recovering.

"I'll call Dorian. You focus on our boy." Eleanor sounded so much like Mum right then that it made me smile.

"No." Daniel whined, his face scrunching in protest.

"We have to, mate, otherwise we'll be in big trouble. Your grandmother would tell us all off." He seemed to settle at the mention of Gwen. She was soft as can be with the kids, but somehow she was the one person none of them wanted to upset.

"Fine."

Eleanor sat next to us as she explained to Dorian what had happened and that Daniel was okay, but half way through the call she handed the phone over to me.

"Is he okay?" she asked even before I'd managed to let her know it was me on the phone.

"He's fine, he's settling back down. We just thought you'd want to know."

"I'm on my way back, I'm sorry I've been so long. Gwen

and I needed to talk and I didn't want to rush her."

"It's alright, Dor, he's doing fine. No need to panic." I could feel her alarm as she breathed heavily. "Take a deep breath, we're good."

Daniel nodded as he took the phone from my hand and said, "Jake and Ellie have sorted me out."

His face pinched at something she'd obviously told him and his eyes started glassing over with tears before his breath hitched and he told her sternly, "I don't want to."

My arm tightened around him as a tear rolled down his cheek. Eleanor got the pump from the table and held it up to me. She was surprisingly good with the whole situation. I'd imagined she'd be scatty and that she'd flail, but no, she was calm. A lot calmer than I was as I watched his breaths pick up pace.

"No hospital," he sobbed as he handed me the phone.

Eleanor sat back on the sofa and tapped the cushion next to her. He didn't waste any time clambering to her side and as she cooed over him holding the coffee tin under his nose he settled back down.

"What's going on?" I asked as I stood and went to the kitchen, the last thing I wanted was for him to get worse listening to our conversation.

"I need to take him to the hospital, he's had two attacks in the last six hours, Jake." She sighed wearily.

"He's alright now, and this one was minor. I gave him six puffs just to make sure it didn't escalate, but to be honest, he probably only needed three or four. The inhaler's working, baby, I don't think there's any use causing him distress by taking him to the hospital."

"Maybe I should call Jamie." That hurt. That hurt a lot, considering her brother was as much an expert on asthma as I was. The funny thing was, I'd had to spend a lot more time dealing with acute referrals and trauma during my training. Technically when it came to emergency medicine like this, I was a lot better trained.

"You realise I'm a doctor, right?" Considering she liked to call me Doctor Roth so much, I hoped she did.

"Shit, I'm sorry. It's just..." She took a deep breath before she continued, "My mind is boggled at this point. I'll make a decision when I see how he is for myself."

"Okay." Again a little disconcerting that my judgement didn't count, no one ever questioned my judgement when it came to medicine.

"You're probably right, Jacob, but he's my baby and I need to see that he's okay for myself before I can rest easy." Her voice was soft and placating. "I'm almost home, Willow called me earlier to say that she had brunch with Mum instead and that she was heading over. She'll likely get there before I do."

It was like her words had summoned her, because she came waltzing in with a shit eating grin on her face until she looked at me and then at where Daniel was sat with Eleanor. Her face dropped and she was marching herself to where they were sat.

"Yeah, she's let herself in. I need to go before she gets Daniel all worked up."

"Good idea." I sensed the light smile in her voice. "Jake?"

"Yeah?"

"Thank you." She breathed.

"Don't, that's what this is about, right? Me and you?"

"I love you, Doctor Roth." She chuckled lightly like she'd

heard my thoughts across the line.

"I love you, too, pretty girl." I waited for her to end the call and it was only then I noticed how friendly Willow and Eleanor were being toward one another.

The pair of them were chatting like they were more than acquaintances. Daniel was sat on Willow's lap with his legs up on Eleanor's. She was even rubbing his feet as she and Willow laughed.

Alternative. Universe.

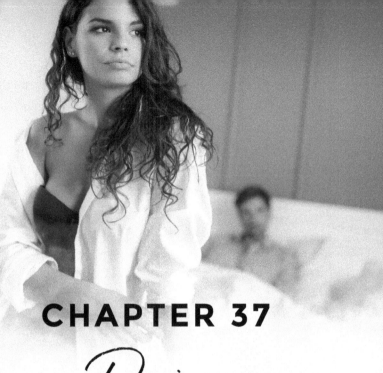

CHAPTER 37

Dorian

Jake had been right, of course, I was an idiot for ever doubting that he could've been wrong. Especially when it came to Daniel. Instead of spending hours at A&E like I'd done so many times before with my son, we'd had a pretty chilled out evening.

Eleanor, Willow and Daniel had commandeered the television and put all the Pixar hits on back-to-back. It'd taken me by surprise how well Willow and Eleanor were getting along. There was no bitchy ribbing on my sister's part, which was a miracle in and of itself.

Throughout dinner Willow had somehow managed to wrangle Eleanor into the last bits of planning for the New Year's gala we'd spent months toiling over. It was a nice gesture on her part considering that she'd done it to get Eleanor's name out there a little. She'd even gone as far as to tell her what the producers and directors Eleanor would be auditioning in front of in the new year were like. Of course, they'd been extended an invite, so no doubt having Eleanor's name as an organiser would bring them a little familiarity.

For once, Willow was on good form verbally and mood wise. It was a pity that I had to turn down a dress shopping trip with them the next day to sit with Sophia and go through Heather's case.

The reality was that there was no way that any doctor had a clean streak as long as Arthur Fletcher did. Something that I already knew, but when I'd sat in bed that night with Jake he'd pointed it out again. He'd been able to give me the initials of most if not all the patients he'd had serious complications with or worse.

"The procedures that go well always seem to fall to the back of my mind, it's the ones that don't that I can't forget. I need to know where I went wrong or where the procedure failed. It's also hard to forget the families you have to give bad news to, it always leaves a mark. A scar of sorts. Telling someone that the person they love has perished on your table, it's gutting and not ego or pride wise. You sort of feel like you failed them in some way, even when you know you haven't."

That's what he'd told me with a seriousness that was gutting for me because I could tell just how thinking about it made him bleed.

So, as Sophia and I sat in my office going through record after record, it astounded me that there weren't any of his failings. Except for his wife, who he'd already started to look into divorcing. Maybe I was looking at this all wrong and trying to find something where there was nothing to find, but that didn't strike me as coincidence.

"The US offices are all shut till the new year, so there is no way we can expect anything from them before the second week of January. That's if they're not snowed under when they get back, which they always seem to be, but I contacted Andrew Peters' office earlier." She stood at the side of my desk hopping from one foot to the other like she always did when she got excited. Especially when her snooping paid off. "His assistant said that he'd asked her to look into their accounts because there were random amounts going missing. There wasn't any pattern to them either, but he thought that maybe he'd been syphoning off funds into an offshore account so that when it came to the divorce he had a nice plush mattress squirreled away somewhere."

"Okay."

"But they gave up on that idea when they realised that he'd been doing it for years and the accounts weren't hidden." She squealed as she drummed her hands on the top of my antique mahogany desk.

"They're payments."

"Yes!" She punched the air and I half expected her to do a Laurel and Hardy stooge dance about my desk. "This is so good that I'm literally begging my bladder not to let me down right now!"

"Do you know what they're payments for?" I had to give it to her on the job dedication front, I'd heard her talk about a lot of things on that phone call that quite frankly didn't sound interesting. But she'd stuck at it to get this information. Still, she could be getting ahead of herself and it was my job to get the facts on the suppositions.

"Well, that's the thing, they weren't payments to companies which leads me to think that he's been paying people off." She stopped for a moment as she gave me her thoughts and then carried on her power walking stance dance.

"We can't build a case around payments from his personal account. We're speculating, we can't beat his dodgy arse with a case built on looks like and leads me to think."

"Oh, I've never heard you talk dirty before. It suits you."

"Don't get used to it." I told her trying not to sound amused by her surprise. "If you could get Peters' assistant to send you the documents so we can go over them and look a little more into the recipients, we might be able to link the payments to something tangible. We'd need to match the receiving accounts to patients and prove they're silent compensation. If we can prove that he's had other surgeries go wrong like hers, it puts him in a spot of bother."

"We win, right?"

"Potentially, but it might also get him to give her enough to settle outside court. I can't imagine that he'd want to chance people finding out that he isn't such a scalpel whizz. It also might help the divorce, it definitely casts a shadow on his character and that might be enough for him to drop the custody of the kids. But as it stands, it's all hearsay and we can't take it to court."

I checked the time on my phone as she started for the door. It was ridiculously late already, and I had a few texts from Jamie and Quincy. Before I checked them, I sent Jake a text telling him I was calling it a day.

He'd dropped me off earlier this afternoon before he and Daniel spent the rest of the day doing whatever they did on their man days.

Normally it was football, however given the severity of Daniel's asthma attack a few days ago, they were probably going to go to the cinema. The new Star Wars spin-off was out and with the gala tomorrow, the safest bet was not to push him.

JAKE

We'll come pick you up now. Be there in 15. x

I was about to check the other messages when my phone started ringing. Jamie's name flashed up at me as I picked it up and answered getting to my feet.

"Sophia?" I called to her as I put my phone to my ear. "It's getting late, send Peters' office the email requesting the documents and then you can go, alright?"

"Yes, boss." She chirped at me from her desk outside my door.

"Jamie?"

"Hey, mush," his voice was strained and worried, something that always put me on edge.

"What's happened? Is everything alright with Jenna?" I had to ask after everything that had happened over Christmas.

"She's fine, it's actually Quincy I'm worried about."

"Is she okay?" I asked as I gathered my things ready to leave.

"Something's happened at work and she's been suspended... it's all a fucking mess." He sighed and I could imagine the way his fingers were probably worrying his forehead.

"What did she do?" I asked as I slung my handbag over my

forearm and did the same with my coat. I managed to put my scarf around my neck as I listened to him tell me what happened.

I was walking out of my office door when Sophia handed me a manila envelope mouthing, "The documents."

"Jamie, if they want a formal apology she needs to give it to them." I stopped on the other side of her desk.

"Seriously? After *everything*, she needs to apologise?"

"Look, as much as I want to high-five her for finally standing up for herself, I can't tell you anything different. In this situation she's in the wrong, she either goes somewhere else or she gives them what they want. I'm sorry, I wish I could tell you something different." I watched as Sophia packed up her desk leaving her computer to last. "Listen, I have to go, but I'll come over in the morning and go through it with her. Don't panic, it doesn't sound like they're after her job. It sounds more like they have to be seen to do something."

He breathed wearily. "We're heading to Mum's tomorrow morning to drop off the kids before the gala."

"I'll see you both there. In the meantime, please don't lose sleep over this, okay?"

"Alright, mush, see you tomorrow."

He hung up as I got the text from Jake letting me know he was outside. I replied letting him know I was heading out before I opened the envelope and peered inside. "That was quick."

"I gave her a call and she forwarded the documents over from her phone!" Her shocked expression made me laugh. "By the way, I'd never do that because it's grossly unprofessional and it's asking for trouble."

"I'm glad you have more sense than Peters' PA," I smiled as I motioned for her to walk with me once she'd shut down her computer.

I took a good look at the information on the papers she'd handed me and my heart pounded in my chest with excitement. "We might have something here, I need you to contact Carter and get him to do some sleuthing for us."

"Yes, boss."

We stepped out onto the street and before I even had a chance to respond to her, Daniel was at my side, his arms wrapped around me. The bobble of his hat going every which way as he swayed me from side to side. "Hi, Mummy."

"Hey, buddy."

"Oh. My. Word." My gaze followed Sophia's and a brash laugh ripped out of me as I realised she was pretty much drooling over Jake.

"I know." I sighed with a satisfaction that had me smiling to the point my cheeks ached.

"Who is he?" she asked before he rounded the car and came over to us.

"That's Jake, my mum's boyfriend." Metaphorical hands to the face, my son had managed to outdo his uncle on the G-bomb front. Or was it the B-bomb? Jake was going to laugh his butt off when I told him about this later.

"Hey, pretty girl." Jake smiled at me as he kissed my cheek. His hands rested on my hips as he looked at a still very giddy Sophia and said, "Hi."

"This is my assistant, Sophia. Sophia, this is Jacob who, as Daniel very eloquently put it, is my boyfriend."

"High-five, mate!" He and Daniel slapped palms as he gave my hip a squeeze.

"Well, now introductions are done, back to business." I

managed to get her attention back. "Make sure Carter gets on this as soon as, we need to get this case wrapped up. It's taking up too much time and too many resources, Stuart will start nipping my heels if it drags on much longer."

"Ready to go?" Jake asked.

"Yeah," I replied before telling Sophia, "I'm sorry you couldn't work from home today. No more work on our part until we're back in on the fourth."

"I meant to thank you for the tickets to the Gala. Hugo and I are really looking forward to it."

"You're most welcome." I chuckled at her excited grin and shift of her feet. "I'll see you tomorrow then."

"See you," she chirped as she touched fists with Daniel before looking up at Jake and saying, "nice to meet you."

I could tell even in the evening light that her cheeks were flushed a bright red.

I know how she feels.

I chuckled as I let Jake walk me to his car. I let him buckle my seatbelt as I took the time to do nothing more than admire him. The incredible man who somehow could not get enough of me.

CHAPTER 38

Jake

Everything was hectic today. From the moment we woke up Dorian was running around like a headless chicken, packing Daniel's things to take him over to her parents' and making sure everything was A-Okay for tonight. Her phone was going off like there was a big crisis. As it turned out the crisis was Willow telling her how to dress tonight.

Honestly, I didn't think she needed to take advice from her sister. She always looked stunning regardless of how much make-up she wore or what outfit she'd picked. But apparently tonight she was marching to the beat of Willow's drum, as was Eleanor from the sound of the conversation they were having on loudspeaker around me.

I'd been given specific instructions to drop Eleanor at Dorian's by one in the afternoon and only to return at five to pick them up. I checked my watch as I looked at the almost standstill traffic. I was almost fifteen minutes late. The only reason I wasn't losing my mind was that neither one of them had called or text me to ask me where I was. Which meant they were probably running late themselves.

Twenty minutes later and almost forty minutes late the driver was sat outside her flat. I'd called them to let them know I was waiting, and was assured that they were on their way down. Short of half an hour later the door to the building opened.

Willow as ever had her own thing going on with some insane bra/top thing that left very little to the imagination. It was lacy and frilly and that's all I'd managed to make out before I averted my eyes. Her long skirt was decent and flowery though, so looking down was definitely acceptable.

I felt for the small box in my pocket, I'd been meaning to give Dorian these since Christmas eve, but there was so much happening, that I'd decided to wait till tonight. Plus, Eleanor had assured me that they would finish her outfit perfectly. Whatever that meant. All I knew was that she was wearing a pretty dress according to Eleanor.

I opened the door of the black cab, I swear the driver sighed when he realised it was them we were waiting for.

As I stepped out though, I faltered. My heart must've stopped for a moment because all of a sudden the cold felt a lot stronger and my eyes were playing tricks on me.

Eleanor smiled at me as she reached up and straightened my bowtie. Her eyes sparkled as she kissed my cheek with the side of her mouth, like she always did when she didn't want to ruin her lipstick. "I'm glad you listened and wore the bowtie."

Fuck, even her voice all of a sudden sounded identical to what my mother's had that night. Everything was fucking surreal as I took in the way her hair was neatly pinned up on her head, the red lipstick, the red dress…her muddy green eyes that shone with kindness and love.

Shit, I could feel the tears prickling behind my eyes as my chest tightened and all of a sudden breathing didn't feel like first nature anymore.

Get your shit together, Jake. It's Eleanor. Just Eleanor. Breathe in, breathe out and relax. Breathe in, breathe out and relax.

I kept telling myself as I helped her into the taxi. Willow had sat herself on one of the flip down seats and she'd sat opposite her on the bench seat. The pair of them smiling at one another like they were in on something. What? I had no idea, but fuck I don't think I could've taken any more surprises. Seeing my mother's ghost was enough to unsettle me, especially with the party ahead.

"Stop staring at me and turn around." She laughed as she shooed me with her hand. Had her voice always sounded like that? So light and trilly.

I shook my head as I did what she asked and then it didn't matter. Nothing else really mattered because there she was. Dorian.

So. Fucking. Pretty.

My breath came rushing back, filling my lungs so quickly that the air rushed to my head and made it feel like I was standing somewhere outside my own body. She looked like a dark Cinderella with her black dress flaring out somewhere between her waist and hips. The deep V of her tight bodice showing enough cleavage to be sexy but at the same time demure and elegant. The longer back just missed the ground.

She took a few steps toward me and I had to ask myself if she was wearing glass slippers because the light from the streetlamp reflected off her shoes and I swear they were clear like black glass adorned with clusters of tiny, shiny black stones and the red soles I'd come to associate only with her.

Even when I'd seen other women wear them, they never looked as good as they did on her.

"You alright there, Doctor Roth?" her voice was husky as she looked up at me from between her lashes. Her deep reddish pink lipstick made her already soft, plump lips look fuller. They made my own lips sting with the need to feel them. To kiss her.

"Yup," was all I could muster as she tucked her small bag between her upper arm and chest. Her breasts pushing together slightly as her hands splayed on the lapels of my tux jacket.

My hands banded around her waist and when she tipped her face up to touch her lips softly to mine, the ends of her hair tickled my skin.

"You trimmed my scruff." She murmured sounding a little disappointed as her fingers trailed up to my jaw and her nails scratched lightly at the short stubble.

"I had to make an effort, right?" I smiled down at her and the way her hair was rolled back and pinned away from her face had the little bejewelled earring at the top of her ear sparkling. Reminding me of the small box in my pocket. "I have something for you."

"So do I," she smiled as she took her clutch and opened it. She took out a small box a little bigger than mine and held it out to me. Her hands shook and it was only then that it occurred to me that she must be freezing with her shoulders completely bare the way they were.

I took the box from her, as I handed her the one from my pocket. "Let's get you inside the car and then we can open them. It's too cold for you to be standing out here."

"No," she said quickly as I began to usher her in. "If I had it my way I would've given it to you upstairs in private, but they made a massive deal of making you wait. Anticipation or something…"

"Okay." I said as I turned my back to the taxi, turning her with me and bringing her closer with my hand on her shoulder. Her skin felt warm in spite of the cold surrounding us.

"Open it." Her voice was breathy and excited at the same time and I couldn't help but notice the way her hands closed tightly around the small black velvet box I'd given her and she drew it to her chest.

"Open yours first."

She gave me a smiling glare before she said, "Fine, we'll open them at the same time. Deal?"

"Alright." I chuckled as we held each of our boxes next to one another.

She took a deep breath and said, "Now!"

I opened mine as I watched her open hers. Her eyes rounded as she drew in a soft gasp. She held the box open in the palm of her slightly shaky hand whilst the other teased the soft curls behind her shoulder.

"Do you like them?"

She nodded as she sucked her bottom lip into her mouth. Her eyes were glistening. Her hand falling from her hair and her fingers pressing to the red stones adorning the centre of the small flower earrings.

"I was going to go for plain studs, but I kept thinking of that tattoo on your finger when I was talking to the jeweller and when I asked him if we could maybe do something with it, he suggested this." I picked one of the dainty studs from the box and held it out to her. "I know you love sunflowers, but I also know that they remind you of your past. Maybe we can change that?"

"They're so beautiful, Jacob." Her voice was wet and slightly cracked. Her eyes were brimming, shining with tears.

"You know, I held onto my mother's earrings for all these years. I would look at them and all I would feel is pain and regret, but looking at this part of them now, all I feel is love for you and hope. That's what you've brought me, pretty girl, a love that I never thought I could feel and a lot of hope. So much hope, baby, that I don't even know what to do with it."

"Oh, boy." She rasped as she gathered her tears on her fingertips and then reached out and swiped mine with her thumb. "Jacob Roth, I wish I'd never let go of you on that bench. I wish I'd known then what I know now—how much I love you. How much you love me."

"I don't think either of us let go, we just took our time."

"No, I took my time and you waited for me." She smiled as she took the earring from my hand and placed it back in the box. She closed it and held it tightly in her hand, pressing it to her chest again. "I'm sorry that I made you wait so long. I'm sorry that I made myself wait all this time to let you in where you belong. Right here," she clenched her hand even tighter around the box and gently tapped her chest with it.

She took a deep breath as she blinked the tears from her eyes. Her hand fell to mine, the one that was still holding the box she'd given me. I hadn't even looked. I'd been too mesmerised by her to even remember that it was in my hand until she'd grasped it.

"Man, my gift doesn't seem anywhere near as great, now." She chuckled as she took the box from my hand and took out a cufflink. She held it to me and I couldn't help the smile that stretched my face.

"I can't eat these."

"No, but they're my wish." Her grin was knowing and tinged with so much want that my heart rammed into my ribcage, like it was desperate to get to hers.

I studied the platinum star with the smallest heart etched into its centre. "Your wish?"

"I wished that every day I could own one more of your heartbeats. I wished them all for myself. I'm hoping that every time you look at them, you'll think of me and that in that moment it doesn't matter how long or short it is, your heart will beat only for me."

"Only for you." I croaked out, my voice breaking with every syllable.

"That's what mine does all the time, Jake. Every freaking beat is yours, you gave me my heart back when I didn't realise it was missing." Her voice cracked as two heavy tears rolled down each of her cheeks. "I didn't realise that I was missing you."

Her arms wrapped around my waist tightly, her clutch falling between us in her rush. Her chest wracked with her heavy sobs.

"Why are you crying, baby?" I took her bag from where it was tightly pressed between us and wrapped my arms around her.

"I needed you and…" Her sobs muffled her words, making them incoherent.

"You had me, pretty girl. You will always have me, Dor."

She looked up at me, her darkly made-up eyes beginning to get red and puffy.

Shit, Willow was going to kill me.

"You deserved to have me too. You deserved everything I could give you." She sobbed, a tear stopping breath pushing out of her mouth.

"Everything you can give changes over time, Dorian. Everything you can give me today won't be the same as what you can give me tomorrow. Some days you'll be able to give me the world and others it'll be just your smile. But it's okay because ultimately I have the most important thing—you. Smiles, tears, moans, laughs…the world, I don't care what it is, as long as it's yours."

She gave me a chuckling smile as she stroked my face with the back of the hand she was still clutching the earring box in.

"We should probably get going. I can feel Willow's glare right between the shoulder blades." I murmured into her ear, her laugh vibrating between us. "She's probably thinking of what she can do to me for ruining your make-up."

"You're all good. Everything is waterproof. Even the lipstick."

"Good thinking, Batgirl!"

"I bet you've been biding your time to call me that," she giggled as she took a step back and handed me the box with the other cufflink in. "Now I get why Eleanor kept telling me not to bother with earrings. She turned her nose up at everything in my jewellery box."

"Yeah, I also get why she was adamant I wear this bloody velvet bowtie." I stroked my hand over the soft bodice of her dress. "I don't feel like such a twat anymore."

I ushered her into the waiting cab, I'd have to give the guy an extra generous tip. Even if the fare counter was still ticking, he could've made a lot more with short fares.

"Ready to go, son?" he called back the minute we were both sat in our seats.

"Ready to go." I called back behind me, adjusting myself in the flip down seat opposite where Dorian sat next to Eleanor.

The pair of them fussing over Dorian's make-up before she put the earrings on. The rubies catching the light reflecting off the diamond looked so radiant with the shining green swirling through her hazel eyes.

My eyes caught on her deep red nails as she brushed her hair over her shoulders, and it was only then that I realised, she wasn't wearing her ring at all. She hadn't just moved it from one hand to the other. She'd taken it off altogether.

A simple slim black stone band adorned the base of her middle finger with another smaller identical band sitting above the middle knuckle and another even smaller sitting below her cuticle. That was all she had on either of her hands.

I couldn't help the smile that rose from my chest to my lips. The realisation that we were moving forward filling me with a happiness and satisfaction I didn't think was possible for anyone to feel.

In that moment, I knew what being the happiest man in the world was like because it was me.

CHAPTER 39

Dorian

I took another sip of my champagne and smiled as one of my clients continued to chew my ear off about their case. I think sometimes people forgot that they could talk to me about anything other than what they were paying me for inside office hours. It was one of the things I'd come to accept along my career.

However, tonight my head wasn't in the right headspace to talk about work. Nope, my head was very much on the man sat at our table talking to Willow. She had been funny all day, she claimed she wasn't feeling great, but knowing her that normally meant that she was stewing over something. It also meant that I was going to have to wait until she was good and ready to talk about it, because she was like a stone when it came to her feelings and prying them out of her was like trying to draw blood from said stone—impossible.

I took another step to the side as the client I was talking to made a point of stepping right in front of me to gain my attention. When I looked over at his wife, who looked positively bored out of her wits, she gave me an apologetic look.

"I'm sorry, Mr. Matthews—"

"Colin," He corrected me abruptly.

"Colin." I gave him a terse smile as I drew in a nice long steadying breath. "I'm really sorry, but I have to check on something. Being one of the organisers means I'm a little short on time to stop and talk."

"We understand," his wife sighed with a knowing smile. "Sometimes he forgets that he isn't the only one who needs to step away from the nine-to-five every once in a while. This is a very lovely evening, though, and it would be a shame to spend it caught up in work. Right, darling?"

"Right, sorry." He gave me a very sheepish look and took my free hand in a very tight and strong shake before we parted ways.

I took a look around, my eyes catching on Eleanor's red dress as she spoke to an older couple. The man had salt and pepper hair that was a little wild whilst the woman had beautifully long, blonde hair. She was draped in what looked like expensive jewellery and a deep green dress that made her look tall and waifish. I watched the way he pinched Eleanor's chin and laughed at something the woman said with so much affection. It was obvious they knew each other well.

"Am I going to get my dance yet?" I smiled as Jake spun me to face him. "You look incredible, and so far all I've managed to do tonight is sit beside you at dinner."

"I know," I sighed, draping my arms over his shoulders. "This hostess gig isn't nearly as fun as I thought it would be, especially when all Willow seems to be doing is chugging back the rum."

"She's being funny. I tried to tease her but she wasn't biting, I thought it'd be best if I left her to it." He kissed my cheek lightly as he swayed us to the soft, lyrical music.

"Probably for the best. Who's Eleanor talking to? I asked as I let him sway us closer and closer to the dance floor.

"My mum's brother and his wife. You want to meet them?" He looked down at me with amusement. "No? I don't blame you, the Herschels are very tactile and once they start talking to you, you have no hope of escaping. It's probably why my parents made quick work of leaving their table once the dancing started."

I laughed as he spun me on the spot, completely out of sync with the music. "We are definitely not meeting them tonight then. I've had enough people talking at me to last me the rest of the year. I'm perfectly happy swaying right here with you, even if you make some very questionable tuneless moves."

"Pretty girl, I'm a god in bed, my moves are perfectly in tune." He chuckled as his eyes went down to my chest. "I only wanted to catch a glimpse of those babies, they've been teasing me all night. Every time you move it looks as though they're about to slip out, but they never do."

"No nip slips here. I made sure of that, you dirty perv." I chuckled as he pulled me impossibly close and kissed the tip of my nose.

My fingers locked at the nape of his neck as we rocked to

the music. I don't know how long we danced like that for. Just the two of us in the smallest, cramped space on the dance floor, but it didn't feel anywhere near long enough when we were interrupted.

He kissed my cheek before he turned to the older woman who'd tapped his shoulder lightly.

"I'm sorry to interrupt," she said with a smoky rasp to her voice. Her smile was broad and friendly. "I've been looking for you all evening, Jacob."

"Hi, Shohreh," he grinned at her and dipped to kiss her cheeks like they were long-time friends greeting one another. "I saw you earlier, but Sam had you tucked away and I figured you probably didn't want me moseying over."

"Well, I wanted to talk to you about Miss Cavendish. Since our call last night I've been going over things. I made some calls."

Okay, she had my ears perked at Quincy's surname. But I couldn't remember Jake being on his phone last night with the exception of talking to Jamie.

"Oh, great," he smiled at her with a victorious gleam in his eyes. I watched as she looked between him and me. Her eyes widening in expectance. "I'm sorry, this is Dorian Anson. Dorian, this is Mrs. Miller. She's head of Paeds Cardio at the clinic."

"Hello," she chuckled as she reached for my hand and came a little closer until she was close enough to press a kiss to my cheeks. "Lovely to meet you."

The slight twang to her accent was warm and sultry.

"Lovely to meet you, too." I smiled a little taken aback by her very familiar greeting. "Should I leave you to talk?" I asked

Jake as he started toward our table with her following behind us.

"No, you can listen to this. Quincy will probably talk to you about it anyway."

"Oh?"

"After you told me what happened and I spoke to Jamie, I thought that maybe if she had other options, Quincy wouldn't feel like she has to do something she doesn't want to."

My heart picked up a little at the way he spoke so mindfully of my friend and my brother. But that was him through and through, always looking out for the people he cared about.

It astounded me that someone that good could sit around and wait for me. That he even saw me in the first place when there were so many other women, worthier women, who would've jumped at the chance to love him.

I listened as we sat at our table and they discussed their conversation and the outcome of it. The more I listened the more I wanted to make sure that he never, not even for one second, doubted what he meant to me. Not because he was trying to help my friend or my brother, but because he deserved to be loved as selflessly and be cared for in the same way he did others.

My eyes flitted up from where my hands cradled the stem of my champagne. The DJ was already announcing the upcoming countdown to the new year and the lights were dimmed to a deep purple glow. Even in that light I could see Jamie's disgruntled expression as he marched over to our table with his hands deep in his pockets. His jaw was set firmly into a scowling grimace.

I didn't even hear when Jake introduced Shohreh to him or what they said. My body rose on auto-pilot as Jake and Shohreh stood. My attention firmly glued to the set of my brother's shoulders, it was only when they started chatting that I began to relax once Jamie did.

"I think we'll be seeing a lot of each other, Mr. Anson, I hope we will anyway." She extended her hand to Jamie and shook it before she turned to me and gave me a light hug and another of her continental kisses. "I'll hopefully see you too, Dorian." She murmured.

She gave Jake a pat on the shoulder and wide smile before she wandered a few tables down and sat on her husband's knee.

She was such a curious person, something about her exuded confidence and sheer will power. She had a kindness and softness about her, but she also had a presence that made it clear she wasn't to be messed with.

"Have either of you seen Quincy and Willow? They were right here when I went for a smoke." Jamie asked as he looked around the room, searching.

"They went in the direction of the loos at the back." I shrugged as I topped up my champagne glass. I'd seen them wander off when Jake and I were dancing. "You want some?" I offered them both a drink.

My eyes paused as I looked around the room. Eleanor was stood at the far side of the room. Her hands were balled at her sides as she shook her head angrily at a young looking man. He was taller than her and as she tried to walk around him he lifted his arms out to the sides like he was penning her in.

I'd never met her ex, and football wasn't exactly my thing so I wouldn't recognise him. But the way she was interacting with him…I knew who he was, and immediately my heart started racing as Jake searched the room.

"I need to go find my parents and say hi before I get the worst son award." The contents of my stomach settled as he brought his gaze back to me. A questioning look furrowing his brows as he searched my face and followed my line of sight. My heart sighed as Eleanor disappeared through one of the doors that led to the lobby.

Shit, that was close.

The last thing I wanted was Jake losing his shit big time at the stroke of midnight. I didn't think Eleanor could've taken it, not in front of so many people.

He looked back at me and smiled.

"You're both going to ditch me, aren't you?" I gave them both a belligerent look, even though I was hoping they would so I could go after Eleanor.

"You can come with, if you want. Mum, would love to see you."

"And leave this amazing champagne?" I teased trying to find all the doors within my line of sight.

"You can bring it with you." He took my glass with a wry grin and moved it about, the bubbles sloshing around the rim of the shallow coupe. "See? It goes wherever you take it," he laughed.

Jamie shook his head as he looked between us and said, "I'm going to go find the strays."

He said nothing else before he sauntered off in a hurry.

"Come on, if she doesn't see you tonight, I'm never going to hear the end of it. I'll be the biggest disappointment to her. She might never forgive me." He pouted at me, giving me his puppy dog eyes.

"Okay, okay…" I said as I took my drink from him and had a sip. My eyes landed on his sister's ex at one of the tables at the front. "I wonder where Eleanor is."

His face pinched as he looked around. "I don't know, I'm guessing she's still with my uncle and aunt. They're pretty clingy."

"Maybe we should save her or something." I tried for a nonchalant chuckle.

"If you're that against seeing my mum, I can leave you here." He laughed but it was a little too dry and tinged with hurt.

"You are such a mummy's boy, it's cute." I pressed a kiss to his lips. "Lead the way, Doctor."

I threaded my arm through his and as we started walking towards his parents' table he pressed his lips to the shell of my ear and whispered, "You're going to need a fucking doctor when I'm done with you later."

"Is that a threat, Jacob?" I murmured back, my voice catching at the back of my throat as flames licked up my body.

"Nope," he grinned. "It's a fucking guarantee, baby."

"Incorrigible." I laughed as we stopped right where his parents were sitting.

Ruth stood the moment we stopped. Her smile was so wide that it was impossible not to return it. Her blonde hair was neatly tucked into a low chignon showing off the high turtleneck of her champagne satin gown. The colour a little darker than her fair skin. She was beautiful. The full-length sleeves emphasised the elegance of her limbs as she reached towards me and wrapped me in a warm hug that only a mother knew how to give.

"You look absolutely stunning," she cooed as she took a step back and took a long look down my body. "That dress, those shoes…and the earrings." Her voice cracked a little, one of her hands dropping mine to clutch her chest.

Jake laughed and the look they exchanged was enough to

make the burning in my nose and stinging in my eyes far too strong to ignore.

"Isobel always loved big earrings, but I have to say that they make even prettier smaller ones." Her German twang licked at her words. "They're so beautiful, you're beautiful."

"Let's give the poor girl room to breathe, Ruthie." Levi chuckled as he gave my arm a soft squeeze.

"Yes, Mother, let's not start the waterworks. There's been enough already." Jake wrapped his arm around her shoulders and kissed the top of her head.

"Will you stay with us for the new year toast?" she asked with a beseeching look in her bright blue eyes.

"Well...I..." Jake wrapped his arm around my waist as he gave her shoulder a soft pat.

"We'd love to," I replied for him. His hand squeezed my side as he peered down at me with happiness brimming in his eyes.

She and Levi smiled at one another as he pulled her close and tugged her down onto his lap when he sat in his seat.

"Come on, take a seat. It's almost time." Levi urged as he looked down at his watch. "Two minutes."

Jake sat in his mum's chair and after carefully arranging my skirt, I perched myself on his lap too as his dad poured another two coupes of champagne.

"Oh, there's my girl!" his mum beamed as Eleanor appeared seemingly from nowhere.

She looked alright. There was a bit of a slip to her smile, but she was keeping her chin up.

"Uncle Rudi was so very happy to see you, Eleanor, as was Bette. They kept telling us how wonderful you look and they said you told them you're going for dinner soon?"

Eleanor rolled her eyes on a drawn out chuckle, "I had to make my escape somehow. They were in true Herschel form tonight." She sighed as she took in the rest of the table and then said, "I need a drink."

"Here." Levi extended her a tall glass of water.

"Thank you," she smiled.

The DJ gave the thirty second countdown announcement and there was a flurry of scraping chairs and merry hoots. Jake helped me up before he stood with his champagne in hand.

Everything got so loud all of a sudden with people counting down, and even with all the noise the fast beating of my heart and the rush of my blood in my ears drowned it all out.

Before I even registered that this was it, old year gone and new year begun, Jake spun me to face him. My body flush to his as he whispered, "Happy new year, my pretty girl."

Warmth flooded every one of my cells as I took in his smile and replied, "Happy new year, my Doctor Roth."

My breathing hitched as he cupped my cheek, the cheers, loud music and fireworks close by all melded together as I rolled onto the balls of my feet and he leaned down to meet my lips halfway. It was the softest kiss he had ever given me. The most reverent. The most delicate. And yet, it felt like the fiercest touch I'd ever had. There was so much love, hope and happiness in that one kiss that it was enough to burn itself on my soul.

I felt his smile broaden on mine as he took my drink and put it down on the table next to his. His arms wrapped around me as he breathed into my ear, "This is definitely the best new year I've ever had."

"Me too." I kissed his jaw. "Next year will be even better."

"And the year after that." He pulled back and looked at me with earnest affection.

"Yeah," I laughed expecting him to laugh with me, but instead his eyes left mine and stuck behind me.

The way his arms stiffened and his back straightened had alarm bells going off in my head. My instant fear was that he'd spotted Miles and that he was about to lose his shit.

As I tried to turn he held me tighter to him, tucking me into his chest at the same time as a hand that wasn't his squeezed my shoulder.

"Umm…" Quincy's soft voice rasped from behind me, making me spin on my heels.

Her eyes were wide as she looked between me and Jake and it was like a vice was squeezing my chest, until she quirked an amused brow at me. "We wanted to say goodbye."

I looked up to find Jamie staring me out, his eyes narrowed on me and his jaw set.

"Mate…Jamie…" Jake sighed to a halt as my brother lifted his finger in the air in a silencing gesture.

"We're going to head home," he looked down at me. "Walk with me, Dory."

I looked to Quincy trying to gauge his reaction from her, but she just shrugged. I stepped away from Jake, taking a deep breath as he squeezed my waist.

"You okay?" he asked quietly as he kissed my hair.

I nodded and followed Jamie's retreating back through the crowd. It took me several long strides to catch up to him.

"I can explain." I told him as I slotted my arm around his. "Jamie…"

"Dorian…Jake…" He took a deep breath and looked down

at me. "You're my sister, he's my friend…"

"And?"

"And I love you both. Jake's like a brother. He's loyal and I don't want you to hate me for saying this, but his life…it's complicated."

I stopped in my tracks in the middle of the hotel lobby, holding him in place as I stood in front of him. "I know that, Jamie, but he makes me feel like I'm not drowning anymore. Shit, he just makes me feel and I need that. I need him."

He looked at me in thought for a moment and then he wrapped his arms around me in a warm hug. "He's a good guy, Dorian. Don't lead him along because you feel you need him. He's had enough disappointment in his life."

"Wait," I took a step back and looked up at him. This wasn't about me at all. This was about him protecting his friend…from me. "You don't trust me with him? I'm your sister."

"I don't want either of you to get hurt, Dory."

"I won't hurt him, I promise. I only want to love him, Jamie." He sighed as he nodded. His bright blue eyes piercing mine. "I know he's your friend, and you know what?"

"What, Dorian?"

"He's my friend too. He's more than just my friend, actually. It took me a while to realise it and to allow myself to accept it, but I won't let him go because you think we might hurt each other. I'm sorry. You're my brother, but Jake is my heart. I love him, so you can either like it or lump it."

He rolled his lips together like he was trying to rein in a smile. His eyes glanced behind me and without saying a word he walked around me. I turned and followed him to where Jacob was standing with Quincy.

The way she wagged her brows at me whilst she traipsed over had me giggling.

"So Jake, huh?" She stood next to me and turned to look at them. "We already knew, your mum and Willow let it slip at breakfast."

"Why didn't you tell me?"

"Because I knew you would eventually...or something like this would happen." She shrugged.

We both watched the exchange between Jake and Jamie quietly. Jake's eyes met mine. They were so bright and soft that I couldn't help but smile at him.

Jamie looked over and shook his head before they both started towards us. Jake wrapped his arm around me tightly and the smile that split my brother's face had relief flooding through me.

"Fuck my sister over, and I'll fuck you up." He pointed at Jake with a warning grin.

"Now I know where Daniel got that gem from." I laughed.

"Come on then, babe." Quincy rolled her eyes at him as she pulled him towards the exit before she said to me, "We're definitely doing brunch tomorrow."

CHAPTER 40

Jake

The new year kicked off nicely. Dorian and I were in a great place, and whilst we hadn't gone out of our way to tell people we were together, everyone knew. Everyone was chipper about it too. Everything was going swimmingly well.

I thought that maybe once the holidays were over things would slow down between us, but almost a month in and I was surprised at how easy it was to hammer out time for us. Even when we were both busy. We'd gotten into our own little routine of sorts. Some nights I'd stay the night at hers, once or twice at the weekends she'd stay at mine and Daniel loved it when they did. He and Eleanor had this wonderful friendship that filled me with warmth and hope for her.

She was so happy. The audition she'd attended had gone well and they'd called her back in for the next stage where they wanted to interview her one on one. She said that it was the hardest part because that's where they would sound out what she'd bring to the role. I knew she was apprehensive about it given that the other people that had been called back had overflowing resumes. They were also a little older than she was, which meant that automatically they were seen to bring a lot more experience to the role.

Honestly, considering everything she'd gone through. Everything she'd put herself through. She had a lot to offer. But maybe I was biased.

"Have you tried to talk to Eleanor about what happened between her and her ex?" Dorian asked as she sat at the kitchen table doing the last bits of work for the week.

She'd asked me the same thing several times the last few weeks. I wasn't quite sure why she kept trying to push me gently into having that conversation with Eleanor. But I'd watched the pair of them talk quite a bit, they'd sit in front of the TV and chat away. It always seemed a little too private for me to pry, however, every time she brought up me talking to Eleanor, I wondered if that's what they talked about.

"Not really, I don't want to dredge things up for her. She hasn't mentioned Miles once since their break up and I don't want to be the one that pushes her too hard. She's doing so well. She's been clean almost a year and I don't want to ruin it." I told her as I finished clearing up the dishes from dinner.

"She's stronger than you give her credit for, you know." She smiled up at me from where she was sat.

I still got a little overwhelmed having her in my home. The

way she seemed to fit in it so naturally. I don't know, it reminded me of what it had felt like as a child. Living here with my mother and my brother. When it was a real family home.

"Does she talk to you about it?"

She pushed away from the table and wandered over to me with a pensive look on her face. "I wondered when you were going to ask me. I know you think you're stealthy and all, but I've seen the way you try and figure out what we're talking about." She murmured as she backed me up to the counter. Her hand reaching between us and trailing up my chest to my jaw.

"I take it that's a yes, she does or has spoken to you about it." I kissed her thumb softly as she stroked my bottom lip with it.

"She has, and I would tell you what she's told me, but I think it would be better coming from her. She's scared of how you'll react, so when you talk to her, make sure you think of how she's chosen to handle it and not how you want to."

"You have a very subtle way of pressing this, you know that?"

She chuckled a little nervously as she took a step closer, flush to me. Her teeth gnawing on her bottom lip as she tightened her hold on my jaw. Her other hand pressing firmly to my chest as my hands gripped the counter on either side of me.

"She needs closure, I don't think she'll get it until she tells you what happened and why this time it's so important for her to stay on track. I don't think she realises it, but she is desperate to show you that this is it for her. She wants your seal of approval, so to speak, but she doesn't want to put you in a situation that could potentially blow up in your face."

"Blow up in my face or make me blow a gasket?" From the

way she was being so soft about this and cryptic, I had a feeling it was the latter.

She was sounding me out, I could tell from the way she was thinking about how she said things. The way her hand would lift from my chest and brush through her hair in that way she always did when something was bothering her or she was trying to conceal something. Even the way she chewed the corner of her lip like she was having to think about what she was saying.

"Dorian, if he did something to her…"

"They broke up. Do you think that the way it happened means that their relationship fizzled out?" She gave me a look that told me to put two and two together, at the same time the way her fingers caressed my face and the way her hand pressed to my chest, it was like she was trying to tether me down to her.

"What did he do?" I gritted trying to focus on the feel of her hands and the affection in her eyes.

"Talk to Eleanor about it. You'd be surprised at how incredibly she's held her head above water. But also, don't be the thing that pulls her under. You can't change what happened, you can't fix it for her, but you can be proud of her for how she's dealt with it. Like I said, she's a lot stronger than what people give her credit for."

"She's my sister, Dor, it's my duty to protect her. To fix things for her." My hands slipped from the counter and like she could tell that I was thinking of all the times I'd had to step in and take control, where my sister was concerned, she dropped her hands into mine and twined them together. "I am proud of her. I really am, but it doesn't mean that I'm not shit scared that…"

"I know, and I'd be worried if you weren't concerned about

keeping her on track. But all I'm saying is that she's done good dealing with the break-up and the reasons for it on her own so far."

"Did she ask you to temper me?" I had to ask because of the way that she'd approached it and was handling the whole conversation.

"We're together, Jacob, and she's your sister. I know what she means to you and that if you ever found out about the situation, and that I had known and didn't tell you…you'd be hurt and angry. I don't want that. I don't want to hurt you, but at the same time I don't want to break her trust by breaking her confidence. I'm trying to do the right thing for everyone."

"How do I even approach the subject? I asked her before and she didn't want to talk to me about it. I don't want to push her."

"You pushed me," she grinned up at me as she squeezed my hands.

"That was different."

"Was it? The way I see it, it's not so different. You love her, you care about her and you want her to keep moving forward, right?"

"Are you lawyering me right now?" I should've seen this coming a mile off. Of course she was arguing her case, even if it was gently and in a roundabout way.

"I'm a barrister."

"Same thing, pretty girl." I couldn't help but chuckle at the pouty scowl she gave me. "I guess you're sort of right."

"You know I'm absolutely, bang on the money, right." Her laugh was gentle and teasing as she rolled onto the tips of her toes and planted a smiling kiss on my lips.

"You don't play fair." I murmured before I kissed her back a little harder than she'd kissed me.

"What was it you said to me before?" She pulled back slightly with a winning grin on her face. *"I'll never play fair when it comes to you and Daniel. I'll do whatever it takes to keep my heart intact. There is no line I won't cross to keep what's mine safe,"* she pretty much repeated what I'd told her verbatim in a deep voice that I was guessing was meant to sound like me?

"I don't sound like that." I let go of her hands and poked either side of her waist, her body squirmed as I tickled her. "And yes, I did say those things, I meant them, too. But they were under completely different circumstances."

"Well, it doesn't matter the circumstances, I won't ever play fair when it comes to you, Jacob. Eleanor is an extension of you. I don't want to see either of you hurting, and despite the happiness she's found, she's still hurting over this." Her face grew serious as her eyes paused over my shoulder and after a moment she smiled so very softly as she took a step back from me. "The pair of you need to talk whilst I go and sort Daniel out for bed."

She wandered to the kitchen cupboard where I kept the alcohol and took out the bottle of Don Julio, she was going straight for the good stuff. A part of me warmed as I realised that she was very much at home here, and another filled with apprehension that she thought I needed something to wash the conversation with Eleanor down with.

"You two, sit," she pointed at the kitchen table as she reached for a tumbler from another cupboard and then a mug. She poured out a generous measure of Tequila over the couple cubes of ice she'd dropped into the glass and then went about making one of the soothing herbal teas she sometimes liked to drink before bed.

She looked over at Eleanor who was still stood by the doorway, her mouth hanging open slightly like she was still processing what was happening. "I haven't said anything, that's up to you, but I think you should."

"I only came to tell you that Daniel was already asleep on the sofa."

"We don't have to do this, to talk…if you don't want to." I told Eleanor even as I sat down at the dinner table. "But I'm here if you do."

She narrowed her eyes at Dorian. "You said that you wouldn't tell him."

"I haven't." Dorian replied very matter of fact as she finished making her tea and then brought both drinks over with her to the table. "For you." She put the tequila down in front of me and then closed her laptop and put the tea down where she'd been sat before. "And you," she gestured to Eleanor. "The only way you're going to stop feeling like everything is going to catch up to you is if you put it out there. No matter what happens after that, at least you know that you have everyone you need in your corner."

At that point I had no idea what was going on, but the look they shared, it told me that something was about to go down. I might not know what it was, but I was already steeling myself for it.

"Are you going to stay?" Eleanor asked as she trudged over to the table and sat a little too stiffly.

"I don't need to. Tell him what you told me. All of it, he deserves to know especially after the conversation we had earlier."

"You said you were going to help me fix it." She murmured.

"I am. This is part of how we're going to do it because tomorrow's going to be a lot harder than you think."

I took a sip of my drink as I let the words sink into my brain. "What the fuck is happening tomorrow? What's going on?"

"Please stay, I can't…I…" Eleanor pulled out a chair for Dorian and it was only then I noticed the fearful set of her face. Her eyes were so dark and wide. Her hands were shaking as she wrapped them around her drink.

"Okay," Dorian sat down next to her, and the way that the pair of them were sat so upright in front of me had my heart racing. The burning alcohol was doing nothing to tame the chill that was coursing through my body. "Do you want me to show him what you showed me?"

Eleanor nodded and she opened up her laptop. The clicking of the keys was making the dread build up inside me. Dorian pushed her laptop in front of me with a look that was pleading with me not to lose my shit. But as the headline registered, every ounce of anger that was inside me bit and scratched at my insides.

Miles Thompson caught in
flagrant affair with teammate's wife.

The alcohol that had burned down scorched its way back up.

"I'm going to kill him!" Those were the only words that came close to pushing the contents of my stomach back down where they should be. "Why didn't you tell me?"

"Because I didn't think it'd end up like this. I thought it was done, that whatever happened afterwards wouldn't involve me." She sighed. "The newspapers have other ideas though, and they've been calling me all day."

"Ignore them. Don't get involved."

She looked between me and Dorian with a defeated look on her face. "They know about me."

"You broke up."

Her panicked gaze widened on Dorian like she was conveying something to her.

"His PR have prepared some sob story statement to paint him as some sort of emotional victim. He must have told them about Eleanor's history and they're going to use it as a means to excuse his actions."

"Excuse his actions?" I murmured as the severity of the situation hit me. "Why didn't you tell me before all this?" All the pent up anger that I was trying so hard to dampen down burst out of me and it was completely directed at Dorian.

She knew better than to let these things slide. She was intelligent enough to know that something should've been done about this shit before it got out of control.

"This only happened today," Eleanor bit out at me. "I only told Dorian because she knew why we broke up and I thought that she might be able to help me do something about it before the newspaper's print it tomorrow."

"One of you should've told me. All this tip toeing around..." I couldn't bear to sit for another second. My legs were burning with the need to walk out of this house, find the arsehole and tear him apart limb from limb. "I'm going to find the bastard and I'm going to rip his precious legs off. I'm going to crush every bone...I'm going to kill him."

"Sit. Down!" Dorian gritted loudly from where she was sat

next to Eleanor. "I have a plan."

"You do?" Eleanor and I turned to her at the same time, my words tinged with anger in contrast to her hopeful ones.

"I was going over what you told me that first time we spoke about your break up? The drugs and partying?" Dorian twisted towards Eleanor. Her words aimed directly at her. "Willow always goes on about how these celebrity scandals break out and then each party goes on the attack and tries to one up the other. Now, you don't have PR management yet, and it makes this a bit difficult because it means we're going to have to go straight to your ex."

"No. I don't want to talk to him or see him. He's ruining every chance I have of—"

"Listen to me," Dorian reached out and took her hand cupping it between hers in a calming affectionate way, "there might be a way around it." She looked up at me with her own anger burning in her eyes. "Sit."

I wanted to bite back at her and stomp my feet in protest. However, the way she was handling Eleanor, trying so hard to keep her grounded when her eyes were wide with fear and her breathing was so erratic that I could hear it whistling in and out from where I was stood, I had no choice but to listen to her.

"If I was in your position," she carried on talking to Eleanor, "I would reach out to him with a potential story of my own. It's petty and normally I would go against this, but that article hasn't got anything on you that you need to worry about. It simply states that you were his girlfriend and it suggests that the reason for your break up is that you knew. It's not a lie, if anything it'll make the readers empathise with you. So that's not our worry, our worry is the statement from his PR. I have an idea of how to fix it, but it includes talking to Willow and using her contacts."

"That's your plan?" I asked her, disbelief and confusion colouring my words. "You want to tell your sister?"

"Do you have a better plan? She's with an agency, she's also good friends with her agent, so she might be able to get him to help us out. I also happen to know the person that heads up the drug testing for FIFA. I handled a case for the department and that ended on good terms, so if I was to approach him and give him pause to think that a player who's already looking shady might have partaken in recreational fun…well, I just know he'd get on that like a dog with a bone. Especially with all the criticism their department gets for not doing enough when it comes to doping."

"I don't understand how that would help me."

"Willow's agent would meet with Miles' and he would negotiate your name off their statement in exchange for not bringing his drug use to the football association. I'm not a football person, but I'm guessing that his contract although worth a lot more, when it comes to the use of drugs, it is like any other employment contract. One strike and you're out or at least severely sanctioned."

"You're going to blackmail them into changing their statement?" I spat.

She looked at me with disgust and then said, "It's a negotiation. We both have something we don't want getting out, so we silence one another. It's not blackmail, they're not losing anything whilst we're gaining something. It's a stalemate between both parties. Apart from a beating down of his character, he gets to keep his contract and you get to keep your career."

"That's all I want. I want to move on from this, the only

thing I want from this is for him to stay away from me. I want him out of my life."

I had to say that it made sense, and having heard it all, I felt fucking awful for blowing up the way I did. I knew how brilliant she was, but in the moment I panicked. All I could see was everything falling apart and Eleanor going back down the dark rabbit hole she'd managed to pull herself out of.

"And you're sure this will work?" I asked.

"Nothing is ever one hundred percent certain, and this is me using my knowledge of contract law. It's not my area of expertise, but at this point, you don't need to get wrapped up in litigation. The best way to stop this from looking less like an attack and more as an exchange of needs, is to go down the negotiation route." She looked at me with a straight face. A face that I imagined her to wear when she spoke to her clients. Or even the opposition. "If his agent is worth his paycheque, and I know how big it is because I looked into him, he'll know that this is the only way for his client to keep a clean track record. One thing I do know, is that when it comes to doping the rules are changing and getting stricter and stricter."

"What if Willow doesn't want to help me again?" Eleanor asked, her voice a soft wavering murmur.

"I know my sister, and there's nothing she loves more than to stick it to arseholes."

"That's Willow through and through." I chuckled and it earned me a scowl.

Fuck, she's pissed.

That's all that kept running through my head as I watched her call Willow. I listened to her give her the whole story. And then I felt even more like a complete bellend.

I listened as she went through the reasons Eleanor and Miles had broken up; her cheating, his punishments; the cheating, and putting her in tempting situations. Everything. I felt like the biggest motherfucking arsehole in the world. She'd known all that and she'd never once treated Eleanor differently. She knew I'd lose it and so she'd kept my sister's confidence, she'd helped and supported her when I couldn't. Until the time was right.

I'm such a dick.

I was so quick to snap. And I'd been more than fucking warranted to do it because, shit, it was my sister and I should've been able to wring the bastard's neck for what he'd done to her. For what he was considering doing to her. But, not my girl, she had a plan…one that wouldn't land me in jail.

"Willow's going to call Frank and then he'll call me back. She thinks that he won't have a problem sorting this out before Miles' PR have time to get their statement out."

"We're just going to wait?"

"Yes, Jacob, we are." She sighed like she was fed up of answering my questions, and the weariness on her face had my heart falling to the pit of my stomach.

I felt like a complete and utter arsehole. "I'm sorry I jumped down your throats. It caught me by surprise and I…"

"You turned into a condescending twat." Eleanor turned to me and for the first time since I'd lost it, I caught sight of the hurt in her eyes.

"I did. I jumped the gun, like you warned me not to. I'm sorry."

"So am I, because you're better than that," Dorian said as she closed her laptop, stuffed it into her bag and headed for the doorway.

CHAPTER 41

Dorian

I knew he was going to lash out. I knew he was going to lose his shit. That was the whole point of the conversation I'd had with him beforehand. I thought that if I somehow pre-warned him that he'd suck it up and think about Eleanor. He hadn't and his reaction had all sorts of alarm bells going off in my head because I'd been there before with Phillip.

As much as I understood why he was so angry. I knew the circumstances were different, but still, it brought back a lot of feelings from my past that I never thought I'd have to deal with again. The worst part was that I knew he was sorry, Phillip had been sorry too. It hadn't stopped him from carrying on like he was the victim somehow.

I couldn't deal with that. I thought Jacob was better than

that. I was trying to help him, to help his sister, but he'd turned on me like I was the one at fault.

I picked Daniel up from the sofa, he was getting so heavy that it was becoming impossible for me to do it. It seemed like only yesterday I could perch him on my hip and carry him anywhere. I missed my little baby that always smelled like a mixture of baby oil and baby powder. I missed bundling him in my arms and getting lost in his warmth as he burrowed into me.

I hitched him higher up my body and like always, he wrapped his arms around my neck. His hands tangling in my hair with every jostle from my steps.

"Here, let me take him," Jake murmured as he came into the lounge. The sorry look in his eyes playing tug-of-war with my anger and disappointment.

He gently took my son from me and cradled him like he was that newborn I missed so much. I'd like to say he knew what he was doing. That he knew that the fastest way to get me to forgive him was to remind me of the kindness and love he had for us. The reality was that it wasn't something he did to manipulate my feelings. It was a natural instinct to him.

"I know you're upset with me, I am too," he said swiftly as he held Daniel tightly to his chest with one arm and wrapped the other around me. "For what it's worth, I am so sorry for the way that I spoke to you and how I reacted."

"Eleanor's right, you were a condescending twat. She needed support not a self-indulgent strop. This is not about you. I get that it's hard for you to keep yourself in check when she's being hurt. Believe me, I would like nothing more than to let you loose on the scumbag. But it wouldn't achieve anything. It wouldn't nip this whole situation in the bud."

"I know that, but I trusted him with her. I trusted him to keep her safe when no one else was there. My parents trusted him. They welcomed him into our family, they treated him like he was one of their own." He gritted, his arm tightening around me. "He could've ruined her, Dor."

"He didn't."

"What if he had? She might not be here at all."

"Oh ye of little faith, Jacob. You're focusing on the what ifs when what you should be focusing on is that she didn't let herself get sucked back in. She fought. She's still fighting and you're making it harder for her with your petulance."

"What if it was Daniel? How would you feel?"

"Eleanor is not your child. She's your sister. She is a grown up and you need to have faith in her ability to fight her own battles. She can stand on her own two feet and give as good as she gets. That's the way to make sure that she can carry on trying. This babying you do of her, needs to stop. You need to let go and realise that she's made it this far even with all the crap going on that you had no idea about. You know she'll come to you for help when she needs it."

He nodded and a sadness tinged his handsome face. "I think that maybe she's found someone else to go to."

"Jake, we both know that she would've come to you if she hadn't thought that you would've lost it on her. Which you did. The only reason she came to me is because of you." I wrapped my arm around his waist, and the heavy feelings that had been tightening my chest lightened. "No one is replacing you."

He chuckled lightly before he said, "It's not about me being replaced, Dorian, it's that if I know what's going on, I know how to look out for her. I don't want to have to walk into a rotting building to find her out of it, as some guy…"

"She doesn't want that either, but keeping her wrapped up in cotton wool is only going to make it harder for her to thicken her skin and push back. You don't want her vulnerable, Jacob, you want her strong and armoured."

"I do."

"Well then, let's get this boy to bed and wait for Frank to call. I think she might gain something out of all this. He might want to take her on as a client, he's good at launching careers, or so Willow tells me."

"I'm sorry, pretty girl," he murmured as he kissed my forehead.

"Apology accepted. But if you ever turn on me like that or talk to me the way you did in there again, the remorse you're feeling right now will be nothing compared to how sorry you'll be in every sense of the word. I've been down that road of sorrys and regrets that mean nothing and I am not doing it again. I deserve more than that and you're better than it too. Got it, doctor?"

"Loud and clear, counsel."

* * *

It was D-day, dick crushing day as Willow put it. Frank was all ready to go, turns out that Miles' agent and he weren't exactly professional buddies. According to him the guy was ruthless and a leech that liked to suck careers dry. Which made the whole situation a little more satisfying for everyone involved.

"You put the bubbles in the fridge, right?" Willow asked again as we all sat around Jake's kitchen table.

He was an anxious mess. His legs were bouncing all over the place as we waited for the call from Frank. He'd managed to get the other party to meet him early this morning. Apparently in PR there was no such thing as the weekend, and clearly the same went for the tabloids because Eleanor's phone hadn't stopped going off so far this morning.

Willow had brought a selection of newspapers with her and the headlines on the front were all pretty much the same. Not surprising, but infuriating all the same. There were so many other happenings that were so much more important and that should be the focus of the news, yet, they were all more preoccupied with the ins and outs of some sleazy affair between a footballer and a married woman.

"Why's it taking so long?" Eleanor looked between Willow and I with trepidation and anxiety marring her pretty face.

"I'm guessing that there'll be quite a bit of chest beating and ego stroking. But they'll also be drawing up some sort of confidentiality agreement for you both to agree to. The paperwork will need to be carefully worded so that if either of your pasts come out, the agreement still stands."

"Will I get into trouble if it comes out that I knew and didn't say anything?"

"No, it doesn't work like that. If it were a criminal act, then yes, because you'd be hindering the law from doing what it's set out to. But this is completely different."

"Will the agreement still stand if it comes out?"

"I spoke to Frank and made sure that he puts a clause in the agreement that states that if Miles' doping comes out, there won't be any mention of your knowledge of it. Just to cover all the bases. The last thing you want is to have your name embroiled in that. Hopefully this will serve as enough of a scare that will make him think twice when it comes to taking recreational substances."

"Yeah, maybe he'll have enough brain cells to work that one out for himself. Although, his agent will probably be keeping a very close eye on him from now on. That's what Frank would do." Willow smiled at her. "Have you given much thought about his offer to take you on? He's a bit of a hardball and his fees aren't exactly small, but he's great at keeping you busy and relevant. He also takes care of his people in every way."

"It's worth thinking about, you can never have too many people in your corner."

"He's the Eddie Hearn of theatrical management."

"Eddie Hearn is a promoter." Jake told her.

"I know, my point is that Frank is as big and great as he is in his field." She rolled her eyes at him like he was an idiot.

"How do you even know who he is?" Jake looked at Willow like she'd sprouted another yappy head. "Are you into boxing now?"

"No. I saw him on the TV the other night and the way that the commentators were going on about him…"

"If you're not into the sport why were you watching it?" He tipped his head to the side in the way he always did when he was trying to suss something out. It beat me what he was trying to figure out, but good luck to him.

Maybe there was something there with the way that she got up and made for the doorway as she grumbled, "I didn't realise that you had to be a die-hard in order to watch a fucking program."

"She's up to something." He looked at me with a mischievous grin on his face. It was so good to see him with something other than a worried frown.

"She's always up to something, leave her to it. Don't be an arsehole, we've got enough going on without one of her tantrums."

"Oh come on, be serious, since when does she like boxing? Scrap that, since when does she watch any sport? She throws a huff when we turn the channel to check the results when she's around."

"Maybe she enjoys the...ummm...whatever people enjoy about watching two guys beat the crap out of one another."

"It's a gentleman's sport, Dor. The adrenaline burst you get from watching is fucking phenomenal."

"Well, maybe she likes the rush too."

"It's all a little bit too gruesome if you ask me, and I've seen a lot of gruesome." Eleanor mused with a sad lull to her voice. "Still, if she likes it, why do you need to get on her case about it?"

"I'm not getting on her case, it's just that I never thought she'd be into something like contact sports. Honestly, I'd hate to sit next to her and watch a match, you'd probably have to hold her back when she got into it."

"Why are you still going on about it?" Willow marched over and shook her wet hands inches from his face. "You don't have a hand towel in your toilet." She said as she wiped her hands on his t-shirt.

"You better have washed your hands thoroughly with plenty of soap." He gritted as he looked down at the wet marks on the black cotton.

"No, I fancied getting them wet, just. For. You." She teased him as she sat back down across from me. The smile on her face antagonistic, maybe I should've let him at her.

"How do you live with them?" Eleanor sighed as she checked her phone.

"Don't get me star—" My phone started ringing and all of a sudden it was so quiet that a feather landing on the tiled floor would've been heard.

"Answer it!" Willow and Jake both burst out at the same time.

"Calm down," I told them as I answered the phone and put it on loudspeaker. "Frank?"

"Dorian, hi, we're done. They've taken the deal we set up, however, they want to add a clause of their own."

"Right?" Three pairs of eyes widened on me and even though I was used to it, it felt like I had been put on the spot.

"They want a compensation clause in case the agreement is broken."

"Okay, how much?"

"It's ludicrous. I tried to lower it, but they won't budge, so it comes down to Miss Roth."

"How much, Frank?" Given his hesitation I knew it wasn't going to be a pretty sum.

He chuckled wryly, "They'd want the remainder of his contract at the time. His current contract is twenty-six million. It's steep considering his STATS, but it's neither here nor there. His agent thinks that next season the club will renew with another ten on top, but with the headlines being what they are today I'd be surprised if he stays."

"That's fucking unreasonable," Jake bit out at the same time that Willow laughed, "I hope you told him where to shove his dick."

"If Miss Roth, Eleanor, doesn't have any plans of ever

rehashing this. That means that she will not talk, write or even breathe about it. If she agrees to that, there isn't any worries. No memoirs or biographies with his name in them. No mention of him in interviews. He basically fails to exist to her."

"Eleanor?" I looked at her as she looked across the kitchen with a resigned look on her face.

"Do it. He might as well be dead for all I care." Her voice was vapid and devoid of emotion. She sounded done.

"Alright, you heard her view on that. Anything else?" There was always something else, I'd come to learn that over the years. Normally the last item was the one that could break everything.

"Well, Mr. Thompson said he'll only sign the agreement if Miss Roth is present. He wants to do it face to face and with only them in the room."

"No." That's all Eleanor said before she got up and left with Willow going after her.

"That's not happening, Frank. He's done enough, and if he won't sign without her present then the whole thing is off and he can expect a request for all the required samples."

"Dorian, I'm with you on this, but if we want this to go away—"

"You think I want this to go away? I don't, I want this to be seared into his brain. I want this to be the first thing he thinks of when he wakes up so he realises how fucked he is. I want regret and remorse to eat at him until he grows a conscience. So, you're going to give them the compensation clause and that's all that he'll get. He's lucky that she hasn't requested for one of her own, because I'd make sure his pockets would be a lot lighter."

I rolled my eyes at the way Jake's mouth hung open at me. His eyes wide and brows hitched like he'd seen me in a completely different light. Then it dawned on me, that this wasn't a side of me he was used to seeing at all. And for some reason the glint in his eyes as a grin stretched across his face made me feel incredibly powerful.

"I've amended the agreement accordingly and I'll send it over to your email now for you to read through it with Miss Roth. I'll get Mr. Thompson to sign and then have it couriered to you to get this over and done with today."

"Great," I managed to smile. "Thanks for your help, Frank."

"No problem. Speak soon."

I'd be lying if I said I didn't expect another call within the next few hours in regards to the agreement, but it didn't stop me from hoping that it would all go our way. Just this one time. It'd be so nice not to spend the rest of the day worrying and working around demands that were only being made to boost egos and have the last word.

"Maybe I should visit your office, that might've been the sexiest thing I've ever seen." Jake chuckled with a heated edge to his voice. "On a serious note, though, that compensation clause is hefty, I mean what if it comes out and they think it's Eleanor?"

"They would have to have substantial proof that she was the source of the information. It's not as easy as pointing fingers and speculating, especially not with that sum of money. It was more of a power play because they wanted to add something to the terms that we'd already stipulated. In affect it's just another part of the confidentiality agreement."

"So she's good?" he asked before he drew in a deep breath.

"She will be once it's signed. I'm guessing they'll want to get it done so they can focus on another angle to approach their press statement."

He nudged my chair towards him with his feet and pulled me across onto his lap. He released the breath he'd been holding as he buried his face in the crook of my neck. "I'm so sorry about yesterday, Dor. So. Fucking. Sorry."

"I know."

"I was an idiot and the truth is that I have no idea what we would've done without you. My mother would've had a heart attack if Eleanor's drug problem came out like that."

"You asked me to let you love me, Jacob, and I did…I am. In every way you want to, whichever way you can, however you choose to. So, I need you to let me love you, too. In every and which way you need me to. Even if it's letting me take the weight off your shoulders for a little bit, I can do it. I'm strong enough to do it if it means you can breathe easy for a moment."

"I'm so fucking tired of all of this, it's never-ending." His voice was so low and filled with hurt that it pained every fibre of my being.

His hands wrapped tighter around me as he breathed me in like I was the air he needed. "I know you're tired, baby, I know. That's why I'm here."

CHAPTER 42

Dorian

The whole saga with Eleanor was dying down. The agreement was done and even though Miles had pushed to see her, in the end his manager took matters into his own hands and put an end to that particular problem.

With the shit storm avoided, one good thing came out of it—Frank was more than keen to take Eleanor on. So keen that it'd only taken him a few days to get her to sign with him. It was a good move for her and for Jake. Having Frank in the picture meant that he would be keeping an eye on her wellbeing too. Which maybe would give Jake some reprieve from his constant worry over her.

At least I hoped it did. I couldn't bear to watch him stress over something that quite frankly was out of his control. Even when he tried to cover it up with his jokes and his smiles, I could see it in his eyes. The turmoil and anxiety. The waiting for something else to happen. The past week he'd been unusually quiet, like he was taking stock of everything. Trying to work through it all in his head.

"I've already got all the documents ready for you." Sophia popped her head into my office to let me know that Heather was waiting for me in one of the meeting rooms.

"Thank you." I gathered the papers I'd been going through and grabbed my laptop.

"I've ordered lunch from that deli you suggested. Their menu was crazy. I've told Hugo he needs to take me there on a date. I mean burgers, bagels, champagne and caviar on the same menu? Yeah, I'm up for that." She laughed and then said, "I've also arranged for lunch to be sent over to the clinic."

I was hoping to cheer Jake up with one of his favourite dishes—schnitzel and buttery pasta. I hoped that it would keep his mood on the up after the fiasco during the weekend.

"Thank you. Did you send over a soup for his assistant?" I asked, I knew Becca would probably appreciate not having to go out in the heavy, late January rain.

"All done." She sighed triumphantly with a salute as I stopped in front of her to hand her a couple of papers I needed photocopied.

"Great, I'm going to head out after this meeting. It's been a long week." I adjusted my blouse and trousers before I headed off.

The Chambers were quiet for a Friday. Normally there was a rushing buzz everywhere you went. But for some reason, today it was almost eerily still. The half dark wood panelled walls with their jewelled coloured tops felt like they were narrowed in more than usual and even the old paintings seemed to have an air about them that made it feel like their subjects were looking down. Watching. Observing in quiet judgement.

I couldn't wait to be done and get out of here. I couldn't wait to spend my Friday night doing nothing but spending time with Jake and Daniel. It seemed like that's all I could think about lately. Spending all my time with them, and the amazing thing was that nothing made me happier. Not even the prospect of getting promoted and making Silk.

My happiness was all about them.

CHAPTER 43

Jake

I couldn't help the smile that cut my face in half as I pulled up to my house and parked my car behind Dorian's. I had no idea she was going to be here when I got home. The text she'd sent me in reply to mine thanking her for lunch, had only said she'd see me later. I'd assumed that would've been back at hers.

The house was warm and smelled of butter and sugar as I opened the door and let myself in. I could hear Eleanor and Daniel singing along to the radio. Some catchy, girlie song blaring along with their loud voices. It was fucking divine, and as I walked into the kitchen the two of them and Dorian were crowded over a small plate on the counter.

The place was a mess of floured surfaces, bowls and trays.

It looked very similar to what my mother's kitchen had looked like when we used to bake together. It made my chest fill with nothing but warmth as a longing to walk into this everyday spread through me.

I could do nothing but stand and watch as the three of them laughed. Daniel wiggled to the beat of the music as he sat on the counter pushing something into the rolled out dough on the baking tray with satisfaction before stuffing what was left in his hands into his mouth.

"Hey, you're meant to be putting those into the shortbread, silly." Dorian admonished him playfully before she looked up and her eyes met mine. "Hi."

"Hi to you, too. What're you making?"

Eleanor looked up at me with a big smile that matched Daniel's chocolate coated one. "It's a surprise!" she giggled, as Dorian came over and pressed a kiss to my lips.

"Why do you taste like my stars?" I murmured into her ear as she wrapped her arms tightly around me.

"It's a surprise." Her husky voice melted smoothly into the crook of my neck. "We're having a movie night with pizza and lots of sugar."

"Why're you so chipper, pretty girl?" I asked as she squeezed her arms tighter around me and rocked us on the spot.

"Life is good," she all but squealed with happiness. Her cheeks were flushed and her eyes were shining. So fucking bright that the green in them was luminous. "I'm going to finish up here, you should go and get changed."

There was something in the way she said the last part that had me ready to bolt up the stairs if her arms still weren't tightly wound around me.

"What are you up to, Dorian?" I asked as she pressed another kiss to my jaw.

"Nothing." I could feel her happiness buzzing between us. "I love you, that's all, Doctor Roth." She gave me a wink and took a step back, her hands smacked onto my chest as she said, "Go!"

There was definitely something going on. I didn't know what it was, but it felt like something good. And for some reason it put a pep in my step as I took the stairs up to my room two at a time. My heart thudding with excitement even though I had no clue what I was supposed to be excited about except for them being here.

The curtains were already drawn and the bedside lights were on. With the winter days being shorter it didn't surprise me that she'd done that.

I stripped out of my clothes, pacing up and down the length of the room slowly.

"Are you alright?" I turned towards the bedroom door at the sound of Dorian's voice.

She looked so pretty and glowing as she stood in the doorway in her bright, mustard yellow jumper. Her hands were behind her back as she leaned on the doorframe with a mischievous glint in her eyes.

"You're acting funny." I said as I slowly made my way to her.

Her smile grew the closer I got, I didn't even realise that it was possible for her to smile that big.

"Want to share a shower?"

"Is that a proposition to get busy in the shower or are you telling me I smell?" I took a sniff of myself, to be sure. I definitely didn't smell, and it seemed my dick agreed with me as it jerked toward her.

"You most certainly do not smell." She sighed and just as I stopped in front of her she pulled a small posy of sunflowers out and held them to me. "You know, since you like ogling them in the flower shop, I thought I'd get you some to ogle at here."

My feet paused as my whole body froze clumsily in shock. "Wha...how?"

"Well, I had a meeting with Heather Fletcher today, you remember my client that we ran into outside my building?"

"I do." I'd actually met her a few times before then. I didn't think she'd remembered or recognised me. "How did it go?"

"Good. Actually, it went great. I think with us discovering the compensation payments to the patients who'd had something go wrong, her husband will be more than happy to settle out of court. I think that he'll also be more than happy to keep shared custody of their kids in the divorce too." Her grin was so big that it brought out my own.

"Couldn't have happened to a nicer person, the guy sounds like a prick."

Dorian nodded, her brow quirked. "She was so happy that she let something slip."

Uh-oh.

"Yeah?"

"Yeah, she told me some very curious things." She sauntered past me to the chest of drawers and put the flowers down before she went and sat herself on the futon at the end of the bed. She tapped her hand on the seat as if urging me to sit next to her.

"She did?" I chuckled as I wandered over to her and sat down.

"Yup. Have you visited any flower shops lately? If so I hope you've bought something, because she said that you survey her sunflowers and leave without buying."

"I've been rumbled."

"You have." She shrugged as she leaned back on the bed and placed her feet on my lap. "Why don't you buy them?"

"Because…" I pulled her fluffy socks off her feet and smiled at her yellow painted toe nails.

"That's not an answer."

"I don't want to hurt you," I told her as I looked at the small bunch on the dresser. The thought that she'd gone and bought them because I hadn't made me cringe.

"I love sunflowers." She slipped her feet off my lap and scooted to me. She pushed herself onto me as her legs straddled my thighs. "I love you, too. I'm never going to stop loving either you or my flowers."

"Me more than the flowers, right?" I chuckled as her hands smoothed down my chest. Her eyes following their way down to the top of my boxers as she sucked her bottom lip into her mouth.

"Abso-freaking-lutely," she sighed, her eyes meeting mine with lust and something akin to adoration swirling in them.

"I did get you sunflowers," I tucked her hair behind her ears and smiled at the small ruby and diamond earrings as I thumbed them.

"So you did," she chuckled, shaking her head before she reached for the hem of her jumper and pulled it over her head.

"You know, one of these days I'm going to make you walk around braless just for the fact that you have the best fucking tits I've ever seen."

"Right, because Daniel and Eleanor aren't always around." Her laugh morphed into a moan as I sucked a pebbled nipple into my mouth. Her nails clawed into the muscles at the base of my torso as she brought her body flush to mine. Her crotch pressing to my hardening cock. "You know we have to be quick, right?"

I released her nipple with a pop. The wet sound making my bollocks tighten with the need to get inside her. "I can do quick, but later, I'm taking my sweet, sweet time."

My hands grabbed her rounded arse cheeks as I pushed off the seat. Her legs wrapped around my waist as her warm legging covered pussy rubbed up my erection. Her breasts pressed to my chest as her mouth met mine with desperate hunger and need. Her arms draped over my shoulders and her fingers wound into my hair.

"Yes, please," she gasped as I walked us to the bathroom, my hands working her leggings and underwear over her arse until the fabric protested with the stretch.

One of these days, we were going to do nothing more than spend a whole weekend stark-bollock naked, doing nothing but fucking. Maybe we'd need to eat…energy and all that. But we were definitely going to have a fuck-a-thon until we either couldn't go anymore or we had to get back to life.

* * *

Movie night was a good call. Even with the musical that had Daniel crooning along to the catchy songs. The kid was happy as Larry as he sat sprawled across Dorian and I on the sofa. Eleanor was snuggled up in the loveseat with a manuscript Frank had sent over earlier. A content smile on her face as she went between the papers in her hand and the screen.

By the time the film was over Daniel was asleep and Eleanor and Dorian were both humming along to the credits music.

"I freaking love Hugh Jackman." Dorian sighed as she scooted herself carefully off the sofa so as not to wake Daniel.

"Yeah, but my appreciation for Zac Efron just got a little crush worthy." Eleanor replied with a girlish giggle that had my heart melting in my chest.

"Personally, I think the bearded lady would make for an interesting date."

"Eww, you always have to take it there," she groaned as Dorian smacked the back of my head with laughter bubbling out of her.

"I forgot about the cookies." She said as she made for the kitchen.

"It's shortbread, Dory!" Eleanor called after her and the use of her family's pet name had me pausing to look at her.

"What?"

"Dory?"

She shrugged as she hid behind her script.

"Someone's getting comfortable, huh, chipmunk?" I teased her.

"I like her. She's good for you…to you, even." She put the papers down on her lap and looked at me with a smile so warm that it made me smile. "I'm glad you found someone like her, she's the sort of person that'll take your shit but won't suffer your twatishness."

"That's not a word."

"It is now."

"Are you doing okay?" I asked as her smile softened and faltered a bit.

"Last weekend, I wasn't and it's taken me a lot to settle the last few days. There were times that were a lot harder than I thought it could be. But being here helps. It's like a living breathing reminder that I need to keep trying to keep going. It's a reminder of all the reasons I don't want to do the easy thing."

"You should've said something."

She smiled as she looked down at my lap, where Daniel's head was laid on my thigh. I hadn't even realised that I was combing through his hair.

"I know that you're there, but this is my life. It's my daily fight, some days it's harder than others, but I have a lot to look forward to and I won't fuck it up. I just have to keep reminding myself that every fight is worth something great, and that it's okay that for me those things aren't as easy as they are for other people."

"Nothing worth having comes without a fight, Eleanor. I've loved Dorian for longer than I remember. She's been that constant thing that I always looked to, even when we were friends. I mean I have other friends, but she's the first person I think about for a lot of things. Good and bad. She gives me perspective when I need it, and with her it's always easy to feel like everything is going to be okay."

"I can see that. I've never seen you smile the way you do for her, and him." She looked down at Daniel again and a tear fell down her cheek.

I realised then that she didn't know that at one point in my life, she'd been the reason I smiled. She didn't know that she had been a light at a very dark time.

"You made me smile like that. I used to sit and watch you sleep when Mum brought you home and I used to smile. I used to wish that you'd never feel lost or scared like I did."

"I'm sorry I disappointed you," she murmured, her hands swiping at her cheeks.

"You didn't disappoint me. You're not a bad person. I think you sometimes fail to see that even good people do not so good things. Everyone makes mistakes. Everyone gets a little lost sometimes. That's all that happened to you. You got lost in ways I didn't really know about."

"Am I still lost, Jake?" Her question threw me through a loop.

It took me a moment to think it through and realise that, "We're all a little lost. I think that's the point of life, to find our way to the things that matter. Even when you do, you're still a little lost trying to navigate through life with them. Those things they're like buoys in deep water, they keep us afloat when things get rough."

"I'm glad you found something that matters in her, that she keeps you afloat." She smiled widely at me, her big open mouthed, perfect teeth smile.

"No, Eleanor. That's not what Dorian is to me."

Her smile fell as she looked at me confused. "But you said you love her and that she makes you feel like everything is okay."

"She does more than that, but all those moments, they're the things that matter, they keep me afloat. Dorian, however, is my life. I get a little lost in her all the time, it's sort of a constant thing actually. Just when I think I have her figured out she takes me by surprise. It's a great way to be, lost in her, the funny thing is I always thought that love was all about finding yourself. But it's about losing yourself to someone and yet, feeling like you are more than you ever thought you'd be."

I'd never thought of my life in that way. Not until that moment, talking to Eleanor, did I make sense of everything. I often found myself thinking about what Dorian meant to me. I liked to think of her as my heart, but she was so much more.

I ran my fingers through Daniel's hair one more time as I looked up at her. Her eyes were so wide as she wiped her hands over her tear streaked cheeks.

"Wow," she half gasped and half laughed.

"What?"

"That's probably the most beautiful thing I've heard anyone say. I'm caught between wondering where my stooge brother's gone, feeling a little jealous and hoping that one day, maybe, I can get a little lost that way." She paused for a moment and then a giggle erupted from her, tears trickling down her cheeks. "You'll have to marry her, you know? Maybe you could make some babies, too. With twins running in her family…"

Fuck. My. Life. That's what she got from *the most beautiful thing* she'd ever heard.

"I'd love a couple of little nieces to fuss over. Willow could have one to spoil and I could have the other. Isn't that an idea?"

"No." I deadpanned just as Dorian waltzed in with a tray of drinks and whatever they'd baked earlier, a smile on her face as she asked, "What's an idea?"

"You don't want to know." I replied while she set the tray on the table and handed me a small plate piled with the makings of a very happy tummy. "Chocolate chip shortbread?"

"Eleanor said it was your favourite, and Gwen's recipe for shortbread is not only amazingly tasty, but it's fool proof too. Even for me." She said as she sat on the floor between my legs with her coffee. "They're not chocolate chips, they're Magic Stars. Eleanor also said that's what you like in them."

"I know, I'm the best sister ever." Eleanor jumped from her seat, grabbed a shortbread bit and sat back in the loveseat, dunking it in her coffee with a satisfied groan.

"Make that comment again and you won't be." I scowled at her before I took a bite of the treat.

Dorian looked up at me with a grin on her face like she'd just won star baker on the baking show she loved to watch. I held out my hand to her and she laughed, "Really? Are you trying to give me the Jacob Roth handshake? It's not the same, you know."

"I know, it's better."

"How so?"

"Because it's me, and you love me."

"I do."

CHAPTER 44

Jake

Six months later...

My body was aching more than it did after a workout, yet the happiness and excitement that simmered inside me. Even after the long day of moving Eleanor into Dorian's flat and Dorian and Daniel into the house, I felt like I had more energy than a Duracell Bunny.

"Today was crazy," Dorian murmured as she closed the door to Daniel's room, leaving it open a crack.

We took the stairs up to our room. Her hands rested on mine at her hips as we navigated each step.

"It was," I agreed as we traipsed to the bed.

She paused halfway there and turned to face me. Her arms wrapped tightly around my shoulders as she went up on her tip toes and brushed the tip of her nose on mine. "In a wonderful kind of way." She whispered with a soft smile.

She tilted her face to the side a little and then touched her lips to mine.

"I love you, pretty girl."

"I love you, Doctor Roth." Her voice was warm and rusty as her eyes bore into mine. Her hands already pulling at the hem of my t-shirt as she worked it up my body and yanked it off. She dropped it on the floor beside us, taking a step back before she took her own top off. "You know, I don't think I got sweaty enough today."

"You didn't?" I took a step toward her and she shuffled back just enough to leave the smallest, excruciating gap between us.

"Nah-ah," she shook her head as she replied and unbuttoned her baggy jeans. They slipped down to her knees, sticking as they tapered down her long legs. "Think you could take care of the bra?"

I watched as she turned around, her hand pulling her hair loose from the knot on her head. She shook her curls free, the floral scent of her shampoo filling my lungs whilst I unclasped her bra. The translucent, black gauzy lace falling to the floor as she straightened her arms.

She curled forward slowly, her arse so close to my hardening dick that I could feel the heat radiating from her skin. The matching barely-there lace knickers leaving nothing to memory as she pulled her jeans off. She straightened and turned to me with a teasing glint in her eyes.

"Why, Doctor Roth, you're looking a little flustered there."

She chuckled huskily as her fingers ran down my chest, her tongue dipping out of her mouth in sync with her fingers as they dipped between my muscles.

She unbuckled my belt and popped the button of my jeans, her teeth biting into her bottom lip as she watched the zipper whir open with the pressure from my erection. Her hands grasped my sides as she walked backwards toward the bed, spun as the back of her legs touched it and pushed me onto it.

Her eyes widened as they roved over my body, her mouth pinching like she was trying to figure out where to start. What to do next.

"We need to figure out a way of having this naked day you keep mentioning." She breathed as she slowly went to her knees on the floor between my legs. "I could look at you all. Freaking. Day." She worked my jeans and underwear down my thighs and off my legs.

Her eyes ran the length of my hardened cock as her hands worked up my thighs and then set on my eyes. A deep scarlet flush coloured her cheeks as she leaned forward and moaned with a warm sweep of her tongue from the root to the tip of my dick.

Holy shit!

A breathy gasp pushed out of my lips as hers puckered around my cock, slowly tightening as she took me deeper. She sucked, licked and rubbed. With every stroke of her hand and plunge of her mouth that had me swelling and aching as she took me so deep that the back of her throat squeezed around my crown with her soft gags, all I could think was—

Fuck me, she's graceful, even with my dick in her mouth and tears rimming her eyes.

Her hooded eyes narrowed and her brow furrowed as I pulled her up my body. Her fingers swept across her reddened lips as she wiped away her spit and my pre-cum.

"You're far too good at that, pretty girl."

"I always liked a gobstopper." She replied quickly as her legs straddled my hips, her soaked through underwear rubbing along my shaft, her hot, covered pussy grinding gently as she nipped and licked at my lips.

"I love it when you're so wet you coat my cock even with your knickers still on."

"Hmmm…I love it when you fuck me, Jacob." Her lips popped around the last letter of my name, the tip of her tongue licking at the tip of her cupid's bow as she said it.

"Yeah?" I groaned as I flipped us over, my cock pressing harder to her pussy. "What do you want, Dorian, my fingers or my cock?"

"Everything," she replied in a breathy whisper as I pushed off her and quickly slipped her knickers off.

"That can be arranged." I watched her half-lidded eyes widen as I flipped her onto her front. Her arms stretching over her head as her hands grasped tightly around the duvet. "On your knees, pretty girl."

She didn't hesitate a beat as she tucked her knees under her and pushed her arse up in the air. Her arms pulling tight as she kept them stretched. Her groan as I pressed my cock to her pussy, inching in slowly had my bollocks tightening, my stomach muscles clenching as my thighs tensed with how good she felt squeezing around my crown.

"Spread those cheeks, baby." I ordered as I watched my dick inch out of her tight cunt.

She turned her head to the side, resting her body weight on her shoulders as her mauve manicured fingers dug into her arse cheeks and pried them apart. My cock throbbed at the sight of her tight arsehole.

"Jesus, Dorian, you're so fucking gorgeous...your mouth...your cunt...your arse, I want to fuck them all. I can feel you dripping down your legs. I can smell your delicious pink pussy begging me to make you come on my cock."

I was about ready to bolt my load into her, all over her, at this point I wasn't fucking fussy as long as she came too—I was winning.

"Fucking hell, *Jesus*, I love your mouth and your filthy tongue." She rasped, her voice sounding strangled from the way she was kneeling with her shoulders anchoring her. "But I need you to fuck me."

"What do you want, Dor?" I asked as I stroked the head of my cock down to her clit and back up through her blushed, glistening lips to her clenching arsehole.

Her hands dropped down the back of her thighs before they braced by her shoulders. "God, give me your cock."

"How do you want it?" I teased my dick back down to her pussy.

"I don't care. Just fucking fuck me already," she gritted with impatient need before she added softly, "please."

It was a carte blanche to fuck her however I wanted, and I wanted to fuck her in every which way.

"One of these days, pretty girl, I'm going to fuck you right here," I groaned as I pressed my thumb to her arsehole and slammed my cock deep into her wet cunt. "But right now, I'm too fucking hungry to do it right."